SCANDALOUS
Games

ARRANGED GAMES
BOOK II

SIMRAN

Copyright © 2023 by Simran.
Scandalous Games (Arranged Games #1)

All rights reserved.

No part of this book may be used or reproduced in any manner whatsoever without written permission except in the case of brief quotations embodied in critical articles or reviews.

This book is a work of fiction. Names, characters, businesses, organizations, places, events and incidents either are the product of the author's imagination or are used fictitiously. Any resemblance to actual persons, living or dead, events, or locales is entirely coincidental. All songs, song titles and lyrics contained in this book are the property of the respective songwriters and copyright holders.

Cover design: Mary at Books n Moods
Formatting: Charly at Designs By Charlyy
Editor: Rumi Khan
Proof reader: L.L Lily
ASIN: B0BTXFZL6X
First Edition: June 2023

To all the girls,
The ones who secretly crave a morally grey man to treat them like his queen in public and his little whore in the bedroom.

DICTIONARY

Beta – Son/daughter
Jiju – Brother in law
Lehenga – Indian traditional wear
Biryani – Indian food recipe

Author's Note

Hi my lovely readers,

I can't tell you how excited I am to finally share Bianca and Dash's story with you all. I took my time because I wanted to give you the best version of their love and the journey to their happily ever after. It's everything I wanted it to be.

This is the first time I've dipped my toes into contemporary romance with angst, suspense, drama, laugh out loud moments and sizzling romance. Of course, it comes with my brand of spice which I always serve extra hot and loads of dirty talk. Dash Stern is no different and will have you panting like he had his woman, Bianca Chopra.

Please note the book doesn't have dark themes but it does have a morally grey mmc who is extremely possessive and will stop at nothing to make her his. At last, I hope you enjoy the book as much as I did writing it. Please make sure to leave a review on Amazon and goodreads and anywhere else you can share as it helps others readers to find my books.

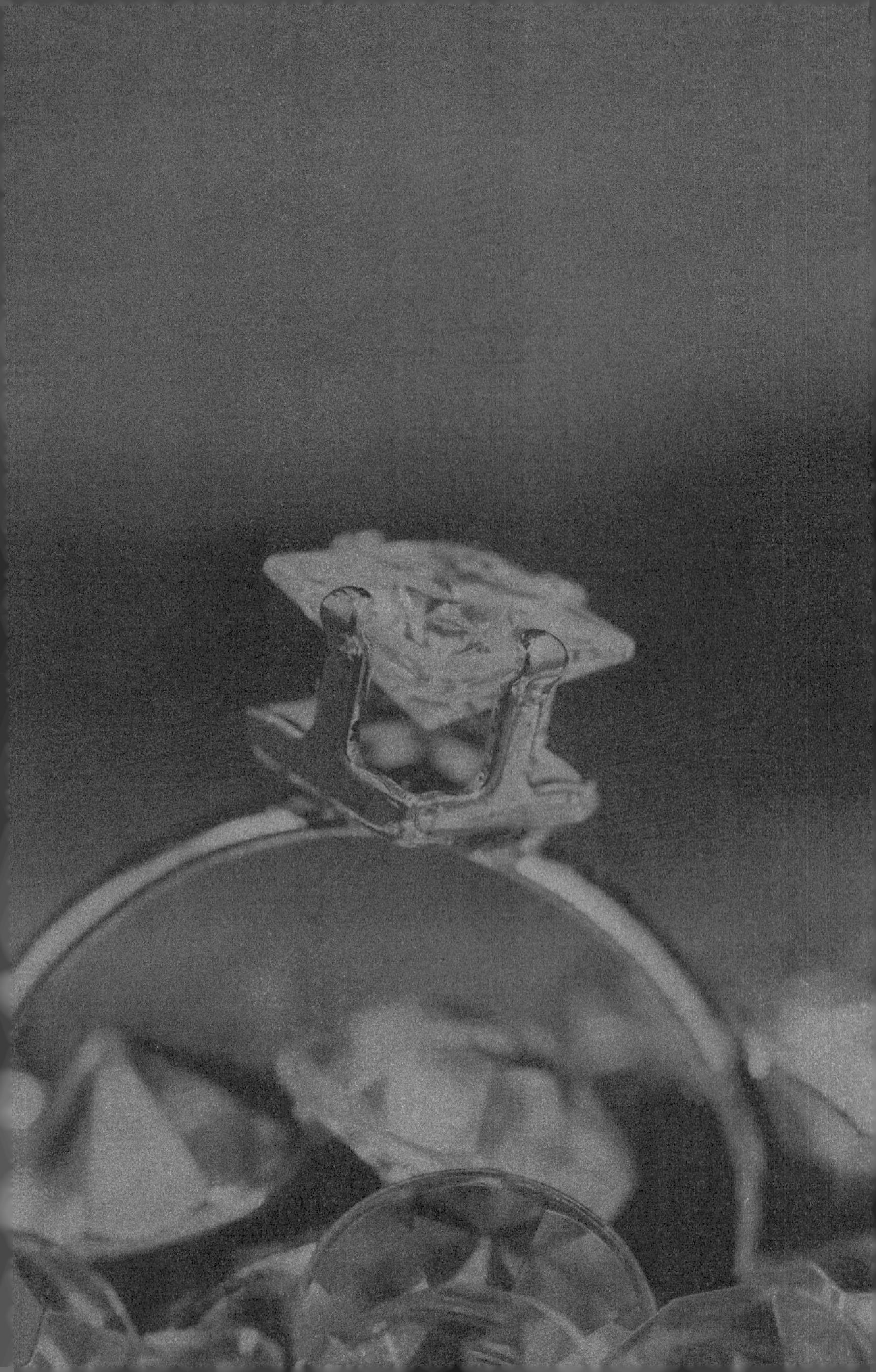

Playlist

Reflections – The Neighbourhood
HEAVEN AND BACK – Chase Atlantic
3:15 (Breathe) – Russ
Te Amo – SAYAN
Mi Amor – Sharn, 4k, The Paul
Hurts So Good – Astrid S
Low – SZA
Love you like me – William Singe
Black Sea – Natasha Blume
Closer – Monoir, Loredvn, Geanina
Creepin' – Metro Boomin, The Weeknd, 21 Savage
Back to you – Lost Frequencies, Elley Duhe, X Ambassdor
Virtual Diva – Don Omar
Who do you want – Ex Habit
I'm yours – Isabel LaRosa
STAR WALKIN' – Lil Nas X

Br

Chapter One

BIANCA

"You need to get married, Bee."

My head reels back from the shock of hearing those words from my little sister's mouth. Younger than me by two years, yet Arya is the bossy one out of the two of us. Pampered and spoiled her whole life, she's the baby of our family.

Though now, I'm questioning if it's gone to her head. There's no other explanation for why she's haughtily demanding I get married.

A laugh bubbles up in my throat as I wonder if she's joking. When her expression remains serious and her lips set in a firm line, I swallow the sound and straighten to my full height.

"No," I firmly answer and turn around.

Arya's footsteps follow me as I walk farther into the living room of my penthouse. The stomping sound of her feet is similar to that of a stubborn child.

When she called me earlier in the evening asking to come by my home, I assumed she wanted to hang out like old times before the chaos of our lives drifts us apart. The memories bring a pang to my chest at how close we used to be. Sure, we still love each other, but over the last two years, I've felt her slowly pulling away, almost as if she resents me.

For what, I've no clue.

SCANDALOUS GAMES

Unlike me, Arya has a loving boyfriend, tons of friends, and now a job at a huge media and entertainment firm. She has her life put together in every aspect, while mine is slowly spiraling. Or so it feels.

I'm twenty-five, single, and living alone. The only two good things in my life are my two best friends and my career.

Apparently, those two aren't enough to lead a happy and satisfied life. Or so says my parents every time I have lunch with them on the weekends. Something I've managed to avoid the past two weeks.

I wouldn't say that my parents are strict and domineering, but they do hold traditional values like most Indian families. It's ingrained into their very being. According to them, I should be looking for a man to soon settle down with since I'm of age.

My dad believes it's high time that I at least start searching for the one. He's even gone as far as to look for potential suitors for me to meet. In other words, men I would never foresee myself falling in love with, let alone spend the rest of my life. Someone old-fashioned, boring, and looking for a dutiful wife to parade around.

Aren't girls supposed to want a man like their father? Apparently, not me.

Even my mom is in his corner, when she of all people should understand my sentiment after getting herself married at just eighteen years of age. It's even more barbaric that she didn't even see my dad until the day of their wedding, a fact she reminds me of every time so I know how lucky I am to at least have a say in choosing my groom. Fucking insanity!

I hate that none of my other achievements matter to my parents until I'm married.

When it's all you've ever heard your entire life, it takes the magic out of the whole occasion. Most girls dream of their wedding day while I dread it.

Not to mention, my sister isn't helping matters by coming here.

"Bianca!" screeches Arya. At least, that's the way I hear her voice in my head.

With a sigh, I whirl around to face her and raise one eyebrow. "Like I've said a billion times, I'm not marrying anytime soon, Arya. If Mom or Dad bribed you into convincing me, don't even bother. For fuck's sake, it's not something you guys can make happen at the click of your fingers. Or stomp your foot, in your case."

"I did not stomp," she retorts.

"You're doing it now." I point at her right foot. With the rate she's going, she'll dig a hole in my floor with her four-inch heels.

Why she's even wearing them for a casual meetup in the first place is beyond me. How she manages to stay prim and proper all the time is also a mystery. She's everything my parents desperately yearn for me to be. They've molded her into their perfect daughter.

Obedient and dutiful. Polite and sophisticated. Most importantly, someone willing to settle down and have a family. Maybe that's why they cater to her every whim.

I didn't know I had to tick the necessary boxes to earn my parents' affection. The realization saddens me despite being used to it.

"You're not even giving it a thought," she accuses sharply.

SIMRAN

"Stop throwing a tantrum, Ari," I scold, raising my voice slightly, and her lips flatten into a thin line. "They won't work on me. Seriously, what kind of demand is this anyway? Marriage is not a joke."

"Believe me, I know."

"Do you? Because it appears as though you don't."

"I understand it's a big deal and a life-altering decision," she replies seriously.

"Could've fooled me."

Her eyes narrow while she retorts, "But you can't keep avoiding it, Bianca."

"Forcing me into one isn't the solution."

There was a time when I longed for the same things. You know, meeting a man and falling in love, marriage—the whole nine yards. Then reality crashed into me like a tidal wave and shattered all my dreams.

Love isn't real and neither are happily ever afters.

"Why are you so against it, Bee?" questions Arya, pulling me out of my thoughts.

"I never said that." I sigh, frustration lacing every word. The topic has become a trigger for me in the last year. Calming down, I softly explain, "I'm just not ready, okay? And I certainly won't get into an arranged marriage."

Arya frowns while processing my words in the tensed silence. I take in her shoulder-length hair which she curled into waves. It complements her round face with full cheekbones and small lips. My sister is stunning and has people wrapped around her fingers with her witty personality, while I'm reserved and don't trust people easily and like to keep my group small.

We're as different as day and night.

Her looks and features are soft, whereas mine are slightly edgy. Black hair, brown eyes and full lips with sharp cheekbones. My body has curves for days with double *D*'s, which I have both a love and hate relationship with. Arya, on the other hand, is lean and fit due to being athletic her whole life.

When my sister stays quiet for too long, I plump down on the sofa while pondering why she's being so insistent in convincing me. There's obviously more she isn't telling. The old her wouldn't have hesitated in sharing her secrets.

"You're seriously fucking up with my plans." Her words confirm my suspicions.

"What plans?"

Ignoring my question, she guesses, "Do you not know how to date? Having problems meeting a guy? I could always set you up with Aryan's friends."

"Are you fucking kidding me?"

I'm actually offended that she believes that could be the reason. Is the idea of a woman being happily single and not running toward marriage so foreign? I've been on dates, but none that turned into something more.

Because you never really tried.

I shake the taunting voice out of my head.

"Oh, come on. It's nothing to be embarrassed about," Ari consoles.

"Oh my god!" I shake my head.

"Arranged marriages aren't that bad either."

"Are you seriously that desperate to marry me off, Arya?" I lose my cool. "What has gotten into you?"

SCANDALOUS GAMES

"Jeez. You're so stubborn." She huffs.

"And you're acting spoiled."

A mocking laugh spills from her throat and I recoil at the sound. When worry twists her features mixed with frustration, I pause and softly demand, "Talk to me, Ari. Why are you really asking me for this?"

She looks away before meeting my gaze while her fists clench and unclench. The action makes me push aside my annoyance and really observe her. I notice the bags underneath her eyes and the stress lines bracketing her forehead. It's a telltale sign of distress, and I become concerned.

"What's going on?" I probe softly.

Soft brown eyes—the exact replica of mine and our mother's—meet mine, and her head tilts sideways as she explains, "I need you to marry first so I can marry Aryan, Bee. I want to start a family with him, and I can't unless you do. Papa will never agree to my marriage until the eldest daughter of the family does. Don't even think of cajoling me, because we both know it's the harsh truth."

I'm stunned into silence. I didn't see that coming from a mile away.

Unfortunately, she's also right. Our father would be absolutely against it. If he allows her, we'll be the center of hot gossip among our extended family. It's a sure fire way to make him go ballistic.

"Why so soon, though, Ari? You're still young," I can't help but argue weakly.

"Aryan isn't," she confesses in a torn voice. "His parents are pressuring him and I can't lose him, especially when I want the same. He can only hold them off for so long before he has to make a choice."

My heart hurts at her dilemma and my hands sweat as I desperately think of a solution. I more than anyone understand the pressure, but still, I can't just agree.

Because firstly, it's insane. And secondly, who the hell am I going to marry?

It certainly won't be the man my parents pick. They wouldn't know the first thing about what I'm looking for in my partner. Though, they might say otherwise.

At the same time, I also can't stand in the way of my sister's happily ever after. Is that why she's been distancing herself from me all this time?

"Ari."

Closing the distance, she sits down beside me and takes my hand in hers. Squeezing it desperately with tears shining in her eyes, she pleads, "I know I'm being completely selfish for asking a lot from you, Bee, but please think about it. I'm not saying you have to do it right away. Just don't be so closed off to the idea because, who knows, maybe you'll meet the man of your dreams. I still believe the part of you that always yearned for love is still inside of you, no matter how hard you try to bury it."

It's my turn to look away, because her words hit too close. Was I that obvious? I want to deny that it isn't true. I want to say she's wrong and that I don't have my heart closed off. But it'll be a big fat lie.

The truth—*my past*—is an even harder pill to swallow.

Because no matter how hard we try, we could never let go of our past. It always has a hold on us, whether happy or painful, big or small. It shapes you into who you are, and so has mine.

SIMRAN

I gave my heart to someone with my whole being, only for it to be carelessly thrown aside. Ever since then, I've been guarding the broken pieces. It took me months to finally let go, enough to cherish the other good things in my life. I learned my lesson and it was ugly.

Love is a curse and heartbreak is its penance.

Until today, my decision never bit me in the ass and had me wishing differently. I'm not okay knowing it's affecting Arya, whom I can't bear to hurt. I can't be the cause of her heartbreak. It's the one thing I despise the most.

So even though I have no clue on how to help her, I still nod and smile encouragingly. "I'll give it a thought. I promise you'll get your wedding like you've always dreamt, Ari."

Jumping in excitement, she stands and wraps her arms around me while chanting, "Thank you, Bee. I love you."

"I love you too."

She pulls back and the blinding smile on her face has me in a chokehold. It's the one I haven't seen in years pointed at me. She always brought out my elder sister's instincts to protect and love her unconditionally. Now, I must find a way to not break my promise.

Even if I have to sacrifice my own future.

Chapter Two

BIANCA

> ROSA: We're going out.

> ROSA: Wear something sexy.

My best friend's texts came just at the right moment. I desperately needed the biggest distraction I could find after the bomb my sister dropped. So without any questions asked, I said yes and went into my closet to pick my most daring dress.

I want to forget that I have a big decision to make ahead of me. A decision that will change my entire world. Something I'm far from prepared for.

I want to forget I have responsibilities. A future that's uncertain and murky.

Tonight will be all about bad decisions and regrets. Letting loose and enjoying my freedom before it's captured.

Standing at my vanity, I stare at myself in the mirror as I tie my long wavy hair into a messy bun atop my head. I free a few curls so they frame my face, giving it a sexy yet girly look. My purple lace dress leaves little to the imagination as it molds to my curves with a sweetheart neckline and ends right below my ass.

My breasts sit high and perky and I love how the dress complements them. I paint my lips in pink with matching blush on my cheekbones. Bending down, I put on my favorite pair of Versace pink high heels.

Iris—the third of our trio—always says that sometimes all a girl needs is a hot little dress to make them feel at the top of the world. She may have been right, even though I won't ever admit it to her.

My outfit fills me with confidence and power, making me feel there's nothing I can't handle.

I text Rosa on my way out after grabbing my car keys, purse, and phone and take the elevator. Another perk of having a penthouse is my private elevator which saves me time. One of my biggest pet peeves is being late, and I hate it even more when I'm on the receiving end of it.

The only exception is Iris, who for the life of her can never be punctual. God knows I've tried. But apparently, all of the mundane shit happens to her.

Once the elevator stops at the parking lot of my building, I walk toward my BMW parked in my spot and press on the key fob until I hear the familiar beep. My heels clap on the cement with each step, which echoes loudly in the empty space. Unlocking the door, I slide behind the wheel, connect my phone to Bluetooth, and drive into the starry night.

The low music playing in the background distracts me from drowning in my unwanted thoughts. I breathe easy once I finally reach my destination. It happens to be a tall building in one of the most expensive areas in the city.

The valet opens my door and I slide out while he waits.

"Good evening, miss."

"Hello," I softly greet while handing him my keys so he can park my precious car. It was the first thing I bought with my own money.

My job as an interior designer pays me well and when I got hired by one of the top firms in the country, it was the happiest day of my life. It had always been my goal ever since I could remember. I love turning a place beautiful and filling it with life. One day, I'm going to start my own company and live my dream.

"Bee."

The sound of my nickname being called pulls me out of my reverie. My head jerks to my right and my gaze collides with Rosa's. Her flaming red hair sparkles under the lights, making her stand out among the crowd. It matches her red lips while the rest of her is as dark as a beautiful night. Most girls are obsessed with pink but Rosa isn't.

She's quiet and moody and has no filter.

And has a weird obsession with everything black.

We've been best friends since kindergarten with our families being in the same circle, and I've never seen her wear any other color. It fits her dark personality perfectly. She may come off as cold and a bit scary, but she has a heart of gold and is the most loyal friend anyone can have.

"You finally wore the dress," murmurs Rosa while running her gaze over me appreciatively. A knowing look crosses her eyes before they narrow and she demands, "Something happened. Spill."

Sometimes I hate how she can read me so easily. Still, I act nonchalant and retort, "It's just a dress, Ro."

SCANDALOUS GAMES

"You're a terrible liar."

"Shut up."

Her lips tilt into a smirk and she warns, "I'll let it go for now, but you're not off the hook."

Wow! That was too easy. Instead of relaxing, it rattles me because she's a hound until she gets to the bottom of the truth. It's my turn to narrow my eyes and observe her closely.

She's dressed similarly to me in a short corset dress, except hers is, you guessed it, black. It accentuates the shape of her waist and hips in an enticing way. Rosa is lean and has curves in all the right places, which she doesn't even have to work for despite being a foodie.

I'm one of those girls who will drink water and somehow gain weight. It's so unfair.

My attention goes to the drink in Rosa's hand, and I ask, "Were you here already when you texted me?"

"Yep."

I dart my gaze around and notice we are the only two women here. I'm taken aback when I realize it's an elegant gentlemen's club. The way every man watches us as they pass by, makes me feel like an expensive hooker.

While I begin to feel shy, Rosa is all confidence and indifferent to the leering.

Then again, she's used to being the center of attention with her family being the richest in the country. My father is wealthy and a well-established jeweler, but nothing compared to Rosa's. Hers is can-buy-my-own-state kinda rich.

"Care to share why we're at a gentlemen's club?" I ask while she casually takes a sip from her drink.

"I have someone's night to ruin."

Fuck. Looks like I'm not the only one looking for trouble tonight.

I don't need to ask to know who she's talking about. Only one person exists who's capable of causing a crack in Rosa's calm façade. Her sworn enemy and bully, Nova D'Cruz.

Oh, and her soon-to-be husband.

If my future is gloomy, hers is pitch black. Much like her favorite color. I swear, irony can be cruel.

"What the hell did he do now?" I sigh.

I don't want to spend my night keeping her from tearing his limbs off. Nova is more than capable of handling himself but like an unhinged psychopath, he enjoys toying with her. Sometimes I feel like he does it because he actually likes her but there's no telling when it comes to him. He keeps his cards close to his chest.

Rosa and Nova were betrothed to each other when they were kids by their parents. Their engagement is more of a business arrangement to tie the knot between the two powerful rival families. No wonder their relationship was doomed from the start.

Rosa links our arms together and pulls me in the direction of the bar, while answering in a pissed voice, "He crashed my date tonight."

"And?" Knowing Nova, that wouldn't be all.

"Brought two girls with him until he and my guy left with one on each of their arms."

"You're kidding."

"Nope." She ends the word with a pop before smiling darkly. "Well, if I'm not getting laid tonight, neither is he."

"So what's the plan?"

"Cutting his dick off."

"Rosa!" I gasp at the seriousness in her tone and the excitement in her gaze.

"My dress is too pretty to ruin with his blood, though," she murmurs. Like it's the only thing insane about the plan.

I steal the glass from her hand and put it out of her reach while signaling the bartender not to serve her any more alcohol. Ignoring her glare, I suggest, "How about an option where we don't end up in jail?"

"Way to kill my buzz, Bee."

I roll my eyes at the disappointing pout on her face. "How did he even know you were out tonight? It's not like you two have the same set of friends."

"He has people keeping eyes on me," comes her reply through gritted teeth. "He'll do anything to remind me that I'm his property."

"Please tell me he hasn't actually called you that."

"Like I would let him." She huffs.

"How do you know he's here?" I question curiously.

"He's not the only one with people loyal to him."

"I don't think women are allowed inside, Ro. How are you going to find him?"

"Find him?" Rosa says this like I'm being silly. "His goons must have already tattled that I'm here. He'll be by my side soon enough. As for us going further inside, who will be stupid enough to stop his fiancée?"

I can't help but smile because she's right. Nobody will dare stop her since everyone is too scared of her family. Despite having grown up beside her my whole life, I'm still not used to the power behind her last name.

"I still don't understand why I had to dress up for this…"

"You'll know soon enough," says Rosa before smiling. "Come on."

She guides me past the subtly elegant lobby, down a well-lit hallway toward a black door. Our heels clap on the tiled floor and we pause as Rosa opens the door like she's done it many times before. I expect to see a private elevator or stairs leading upstairs, but instead another lobby greets my sight.

It's completely opposite to the one we just walked through and is painted a deep shade of red while the floor is covered with a plush brown carpet. I feel like I've stepped into another era as chandeliers hang from the ceilings while a wooden door waits for us at the end.

"What is this place, Rosa?"

"Rich and bored men's playroom, apparently." Her voice comes out flat, unimpressed.

Meanwhile, I can't help but admire the way it resembles the eighteenth century's era with a touch of modern. The decoration and architecture is subtly inspired by it and the interior designer in me can't help but appreciate its beauty.

SCANDALOUS GAMES

"Stop drooling, Bee. I can't have you losing it when we go farther."

"Hey! I can't control it."

She tugs me forward when my feet stay rooted to the spot. Even the door has intricate designs woven into it as we prowl closer and I shove it slightly. I'm surprised yet again when I notice steps leading underground.

"Don't tell me the playroom is a dungeon," I deadpan. "I feel like I'm walking into a lion's den."

"Jeez. Relax. It's just an underground club to make men feel like kings," says Rosa from behind me. "Don't worry. We won't be staying for long."

Our quiet breathing fills the space as we carefully take the stairs and as we go lower, I hear soft music playing. Soon, we reach the landing in front of a double door. It's like a freaking maze with too many unnecessary doors. Though this one is locked and heavy.

Rosa knocks twice and a second later, it pulls open and a heavy bodyguard takes us in before hardening his gaze.

"Who allowed you two in here?" he demands in a cold voice.

I shift to the side as Rosa steps forward and commands in a steel voice, "Move."

He stills at being spoken back to but before he can say anything, a beautifully dressed tall woman rounds from behind him. I'm guessing she's the hostess.

"Good evening, Miss Kapoor," she politely greets my friend before meeting my gaze, "Miss Chopra. I'm Tasha. Come this way, please."

The guard blinks in recognition at hearing our last names and swallows thickly. I bite my lip to hide my smile. He backs away as we walk past him and follow the hostess.

"I'm sorry about the guard, Miss Kapoor," says Tasha.

Rosa nods once before speaking smoothly, "We can find our way, Tasha."

The woman hesitates like she's conflicted and offers, "I can arrange a private—"

"That won't be necessary," Rosa cuts her off and the poor woman becomes nervous. "You can let Mr. D'Cruz know I wanted to be left alone."

Tasha appears shocked at first, then it twists into fear and guilt at having been caught. Her position at being stuck between their war has me feeling pity for her. Knowing Rosa won't budge, she finally relents and leaves us alone.

"I think it's safe to say you've ruined Nova's night just by being here."

The dark victory shining in her eyes is unmistakable as she shrugs and says, "Not yet. My date was a pussy but the men here aren't. He can't scare or manipulate them so easily."

"You're playing with fire, Ro."

"Just because I'm forced into a marriage with him doesn't mean I'll make it easy for him. Either he lets me go or I make his life a living hell."

"I wish I could help," I softly murmur, and her anger ebbs away.

"I'm afraid there's no solution to my predicament," she replies before quirking her eyebrow at me. "So how about we fix yours? Tell me what happened."

My mood deflates at the reminder. I almost forgot about my dilemma. Knowing Rosa won't let me off the hook again, I decide to confess. Although, I'm afraid I only have one option.

SIMRAN

"I'm going to need a drink first," I finally say.
"Pretty sure there's plenty here." She winks and it makes me smile.

Chapter Three

BIANCA

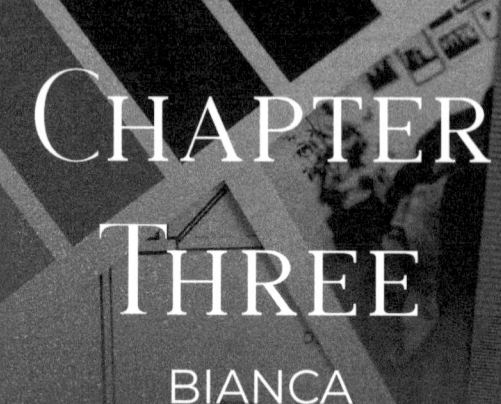

"Arya is being a self-centered bitch, Bee."

"Rosa!" I scold, but she peers back unflinchingly.

We're sitting at the bar that we found easily by following the low hum of chatter and music. I'm drinking a gin martini while she's sipping red wine. If I expected high-class hookers and strippers dancing on men's lap, I was dead wrong.

The place is all elegance and silent wealth.

I was drooling, just like Rosa warned, except I acted cool outwardly. The minute we had taken a step inside, all the men halted and stared but as soon as they recognized Rosa, the conversation eased.

The inside is so much more stunning than I imagined. The walls are painted in a navy blue that almost appears black under the lighting while the bar sits in the middle. Just past it is a casino where I could see men sitting in circles around tables, laughing and betting. Everything they could desire is waiting to appear at their command.

Power is a heady drug and all of us are its slaves.

Men all laugh and joke like old pals and yet most wouldn't hesitate in stabbing the other in the back just to succeed. It's the one thing I hate the most about our world.

SIMRAN

No one is trustworthy.

"You know I'm right?" Rosa says, arching one perfect eyebrow.

"How would you feel if the situation was reversed and Jasmine told you to fend for yourself?" I ask hypothetically by mentioning her older sister, who is already married.

"God I hope so. She doesn't possess a cheating bone in her body," huffs Rosa, not taking me seriously.

"You know what I mean."

She sighs and settles her free hand on mine.

"You're too young to settle down," she states. "Especially with a stranger you'll probably meet twice before the wedding day."

"I know," I murmur.

"Hell, I've known Nova my entire life, yet I want to run away."

"I would like to see you try," taunts an arrogant voice, interrupting us.

My head whips toward Nova's who has his dark eyes fixed on Rosa with part hate and part possessiveness. They trail down to the drink in her hand before slowly rising back to her glaring face.

Nova is a few years older than us and runs in a completely different circle. Though his circle of friends is big, it's mostly superficial. He only has one close friend, Nathan Singhania, who also happens to be dating our friend, Iris. He must be around here somewhere.

I wonder if Iris knows.

"You'll never catch me if I choose to," Rosa taunts back before turning to ignore him.

I watch as he inches closer and crowds her against the bar with his hands on each side. Rosa isn't intimidated as she meets his gaze head-on. I might as well not exist to them both as he leans down to whisper in her ear. Whatever he says has a shutter going down Rosa's eyes and her hand tightening around her glass.

Their marriage won't be dull, that I'm certain of.

Mine, if I choose to, the same can't be said.

I'm about to intersect them, when my attention is caught by someone else. My heart stutters as I blink rapidly, thinking my eyes are playing a cruel joke.

It can't be him.

The pounding of my pulse says otherwise as I stare at that familiar broad back. I would recognize that smooth and cocky gait anywhere. Long-forgotten memories assault me like a freight train.

Soft lips kissing my tears away.

Rough hands eagerly pulling each article of my clothes off.

Mouth licking and sucking my skin while fingers caress the inside of my thigh as they inch closer to my heat. The burn of his hard length, which is piercing my walls.

A deep voice whispering, "Call out my name, Bianca."

I swallow thickly and shiver, feeling those invisible hands on my body, and search for him. Rosa and Nova are still bickering like an old married couple and don't notice when I slip away. My feet carry me in the same direction as *him*—the man I swore to never run into.

SCANDALOUS GAMES

The one I tried harder to forget than the one who broke my heart.

The one who shouldn't even belong in my world, least of all this place.

The hallway he walked into is narrow and deserted with only dim lights to guide. My heartbeat thuds in my ears as I glance behind, expecting him to sneak up on me. I tell myself he hasn't seen me and even if he did, he will never approach me.

He only ever liked to watch me from afar.

Just like I did with him, despite promising myself not to each time.

Maybe I deserved what happened to me...

No. I shut down the doubtful and accusing voice inside my head and keep moving ahead. I have to take a left until I stand before a door marked as *The Mirage* and below it—*private*. My curiosity is piqued as I wonder what lies beyond because no noise comes from the other side.

Maybe there is a sex dungeon, after all.

There's a horizontal brass door handle, so I grab and give it a shove, but it doesn't budge. I'm disappointed to find it locked and search for another way inside. Do I need a code or a card to enter? I saw him go in this direction, so he obviously didn't just disappear.

"Ma'am."

I jump at the voice from behind me and twist to look back. A different guard, this one dressed in black, watches me with a suspicious gaze.

"Women aren't allowed back in here alone," he informs me.

"I'm with someone," I lie, and he notices the subtle hitch in my voice and takes a step forward. "I only came out to get a drink from the bar."

"May I know their name?"

Fuck! I'm about to tell Nova's name when I'm whipped backward as the door opens behind me. My grip slips from the brass knuckle while strong and steady hands grab my shoulders.

"Careful, beautiful," a silky smooth voice says in my ear.

I look up into the brightest blue eyes I've ever seen and push away from him. He feels familiar but I can't place from where. He's handsome and tall but I can't find it in me to admire him as I hear the guard's footsteps come closer.

"Ma'am. I need you to come with me," he orders like I'm trespassing.

I look between the two men as they keep me trapped. Suddenly, an impulsive idea that will put me in trouble forms at the tip of my tongue. I need to know if it was him I saw. So, just as the guard makes a grab for me, I run past the other man into the still open door.

I hear one of them curse but I don't dare slow down, and I feel like I've stepped into a whole other world. My feet halt as I land in a room filled with men and women. Seductive acoustic music is playing in the background as bodies writhe at every corner of the freaking dungeon.

It isn't as crowded as I expected it to be, though.

Unlike earlier, no one pauses to stare at me and it's a relief. I've never liked unwanted attention. It always makes me nervous and shy. The girls are all dressed elegantly in lace and silk as some sit on men's laps while a few roam around the space.

SIMRAN

I look around to see if the guard followed me in here and breathe in relief when I don't see him. It would've been embarrassing if someone saw me being escorted out. If my dad finds out, he would certainly reprimand me. Though I can't seem to worry about it now as I lose myself in my surroundings.

The middle of the room has a table decorated with a fountain of champagne pouring into the pyramid of glasses. Several private booths line the corner of the rooms and you can only tell people are inside upon looking closely.

How the hell am I supposed to find him in this maze? *Maybe it was just my mind playing tricks on me*, I can't help but wonder, and as a waiter passes me by, I grab a drink from him. I'm so desperate for a distraction that I'm making one up.

But why did I conjure him up, of all people?

My mind tells me that I should just leave, but I stay rooted to the spot. Rosa is already busy with Nova, so I might as well take advantage of my surroundings. It's not often that I come to a lavish private party held in a gentlemen's club. Because that's what this is.

Cloaked and hidden below the world outside.

Taking a sip of the hard whiskey I just took a second ago, I circle around the room until I'm walking down another dark hallway. The crowd lessens the deeper I venture, and I gasp when I hear a low moan. My skin heats and goosebumps rake along my arms as they get louder, followed by the sound of bodies slapping.

Light spills into my path from a widely arched doorway a few feet from me. Silhouettes of a trio form on the wall as I stare at them move erotically. It looks like a man and two women and instead of turning away, I prowl closer like a stalker.

A sick thrill courses through my body, twisting into heat when it enters my lower belly.

I swallow when I see the shadow of the man yank one of the women's hair roughly until she whimpers in pleasure. There are other rooms with sex taking place in them yet I'm drawn to the last one. My heels don't make a peep on the plush carpet and I'm glad because I don't want to be caught.

But is it getting caught if the invitation is obvious?

My heart is in my throat when I finish the last two steps and peek inside. My head spins at the erotic sight before me, and an involuntary gasp spills past my lips.

The earth tilts as I stare at the man.

The guy who stole my virginity.

My ex's older stepbrother.

Dash Stern.

Chapter Four

Bianca

Tangled limbs. Greedy hands. Rough thrusts. That's all my mind screams while my eyes are ensnared by Dash. I forget all rational thoughts about him being in my city. Including the fact that he is now rich enough to be able to come to an elite men's club. All I feel is the strongest urge to watch and never look away as I stare at the threesome in the mirror in front of them.

He looks the same, yet nothing like the last time I saw him.

Those piercing green eyes are the same but they hold an edge and hardness in them.

I'm hit with the flashbacks of our one and only night together like it happened only yesterday. It hits me with a force that even as he takes the woman, his gaze doesn't hold the desire they once held for me. The hunger I saw in them is missing.

Even more disturbing is how easily I'm able to tell.

His rich brown hair curls against the collar of his shirt that he always wore in a military buzz cut. It drew attention to the cuts and sharp angles of his face. Though his hair is longer now, it doesn't soften his lethally handsome face. I can't decide which look is more attractive.

Then my brain taunts me that I shouldn't find either appealing.

The hands that once held me delicately are now digging hard into the woman's waist as he mercilessly fucks her from behind. None of them notice my presence.

The girls and I are lost in him but only they are lucky to have his attention. Lucky to feel the pleasure he's bringing them.

Why wasn't he rough with me?

What we shared was intimate, soft… like making love. The exact opposite of the ruthless fucking before me.

Unexpected jealousy and longing stabs me in my core at the unwanted voice inside my head. Maybe it's the shock of running into him. Maybe it's witnessing this primal side of his that I never knew existed and the truth that I haven't been with a man in months.

Or just maybe… it's the inexplicable draw of Dash.

The man I traded secret glances with while being in the arms of my boyfriend. I never wanted or desired him back then. Yet he was the one I ran to when shit fell apart.

Tonight of all nights, fate has me landing into his lap once again.

Could it be a sign? Even if it was, the meaning is lost on me.

I'm drawn back to the filthy threesome when he grunts, "Get on the couch and suck on your friend's clit."

His domineering voice raises goosebumps on my heated skin. The command seeps into my bones even though it's not meant for me.

I lurk in the shadows like a creep, unable to stop staring.

Dash only has his pants unbuttoned and sleeves rolled like he couldn't be bothered except for fucking. Both of the beautiful women are naked with one sprawled on the couch facing me, while her head is tilted toward him. The one he commanded seductively moves to lie underneath the other and tastes her friend's pussy.

They're so uninhibited and unashamed.

I wonder in envy how addictive it must feel to be so lost in your own lust that you forget about the world around you. To be so hungrily spellbound by another human.

Will I ever know this feeling before I inevitably sacrifice myself?

Love isn't in the cards for me, but will I be deprived of lust too?

The longer I watch them, the more the haze of desire vanishes until it's almost replaced by emptiness. I'm being cruelly taunted by a life I'll never live. Pleasure I'll never feel.

Even unintentionally, Dash Stern has managed to make me despise myself once again.

So before I'm caught, I decide to leave. Silently, I take a step backward, only for my heel to twist awkwardly in the carpet and the glass to fall from my grip. It shatters to the floor with a loud bang.

Time suspends as hooded dark eyes clash with mine.

I desperately wish for the ground to swallow me up or my body to vanish into thin air. Nothing happens except for the haunting recognition sparking on his face. His eyes melt into molten heat, making my pulse speed up. They darken with potent lust and I just know he's thinking about the same fateful night.

SCANDALOUS GAMES

I hate the warmth that spreads through me that he hasn't forgotten.

I hate that he's evoking such strong reactions from me.

The girls glare at me for the interruption while I capture his undivided attention. He stills inside the woman he was fucking and runs his gaze down the length of me. His stare lingering on my heaving breasts before they lock on my face.

My instincts tell me to run but it's as impossible as moving a mountain.

No one utters a word or moves an inch except for him. His grip eases on the girl as he pulls out, but I don't dare drop my eyes lower. I don't want to know if his cock is as thick and long as I remember.

My toes curl in my heels when he tucks his dick away and arrogantly walks to where I'm standing. My resolve crumbles and falls to the floor as I helplessly take in his sculpted physique. His shoulders are so broad and packed with muscles that he easily dwarfs my small frame.

I have to crane my neck just to hold his unwavering stare. Even with my four-inch heels, I only reach just below his shoulders. His height is intimidating like he could crush me any second.

There were times when he watched me with wild madness.

When he forgot to be cold and detached.

I suck in a sharp breath when he lifts a finger to my blushing cheek before dropping it at the last second. I sway closer, his musky and unique scent teasing my senses.

His chiseled and clean-shaven jaw clenches at the small gesture.

Why is he mad?

"Dash," I whisper, unable to handle the thick silence.

The heat of his body.

The familiar rush of forbidden feelings.

"You haven't changed, *kitten*," he taunts, like it hasn't been seven years since we last saw each other. When I sneaked away like a thief in the night.

His lips tug to the side when I visibly shiver at the insulting nickname. He knows how much I hate the sound of it. It used to be his favorite pastime to tease me with it and the more I reacted, the more often he did it.

"What?"

"You still stick your nose where it doesn't belong," he growls low. "Like a curious kitten."

"And you've become worse," I hiss.

"Is that why you haven't run away?"

His voice becomes deeper and he edges closer until we're only a lingering breath away. It takes all my willpower to remain still and control my beating heart. *Am I really feeling attracted to him?* No, I can't be.

I'm freaking confused with my body's reaction to his presence.

Shouldn't seven years be enough to get rid of his pull?

Or maybe it's because he was my first.

"Why did you fuck me differently that night?" I blurt out like a fool.

I wait for him to kick me out for interrupting his sex marathon or ignore me completely in his unnerving way. Like he did in the past by closing off his expressions, treating me like I was a nuisance.

He does neither and somehow, it's scarier. Because now, I have no clue on how to deal with the man he's become. Only that I can't be unguarded around him.

His head tilts to the side, making his hair spill into his eyes which flare in seduction. He's not even shocked at my unexpected question. Instead, a predatory grin crosses his lips and he asks, "Differently how?"

"Yo-you already know."

"No I don't," he denies before pushing, "tell me. How did I fuck you?"

Shit. The word *fuck,* eliciting a sudden throb in my core. Him going from never saying more than two words to me to suddenly demanding me unabashedly is giving me whiplash.

It's like falling off a cliff without knowing what lies below.

His bold stare challenges me to say the words even though my devious thoughts are as obvious as the bulge in his pants. And one thing I could never do when it came to Dash... was back down.

"Softly... like I was made of glass and you were afraid to break me."

"You were already broken, sweetheart," he viciously growls. "Or did you forget?"

I shudder but don't cower like he wants.

"I'm not the same girl, Dash," I growl back. "I don't get hurt so easily now, especially by a man who means nothing to me."

My need to find a distraction to forget the shittiness of everything going sideways tonight was a wrong decision. I'm seriously regretting ever coming out of my house. I should've just gotten drunk until I passed out like a normal adult.

Instead, I'm in a battle with a ghost from my past.

The man is still as infuriating as ever. With the same arrogance I loathed.

Having had enough, I glare at him and the two naked girls behind who are still throwing daggers at me for ruining their orgasmic night.

"Goodbye, asshole," I curse before whirling around.

I've not even taken a step when I collide into a wall of muscle. What is it with people running into me at every turn?

Strong hands steady me before I can fall and the same amused voice from earlier in the hallway teases, "You're not slipping away again, beautiful."

"You really love sneaking, don't you, kitten?" muses Dash from behind me. Then orders, "Bring her back, Justin."

The name rings a bell and my eyes widen in recognition. He's Dash's childhood best friend and if I could remember correctly, they were inseparable when I was dating Dash's stepbrother. That's why he felt so familiar. He obviously recognizes me from the satisfied grin on his face.

"My name is Bianca. Not beautiful or kitten," I hiss in annoyance.

Justin picks me up around the waist to carry inside like I weigh nothing. I jerk and twist in his hold but it's a silly attempt at best. He's built powerfully like his friend.

"Let me go," I yell.

The sheer audacity of them as they treat me however they please has me shocked and fuming. They're not even scared of the consequences and are completely

SCANDALOUS GAMES

unbothered by my resistance. My feeble fight is amusing to them.

Just who has Dash Stern become? My mind wonders.

Justin twists me around until I face Dash and shoves me against his hard chest. I back away, only for him to pull me flush and capture my arms. He holds them so tight that it's impossible to tug myself free.

"Let go of my hands, Dash," I demand.

"No."

My muscles pull taut when he takes my wrist in one hand and roams the other between my breasts up to my throat. The possessive move leaves me no choice but to feel him everywhere. I inhale his scent like it's my only air.

His rock-hard abs press against my soft ones. The top of my nipples are close to being exposed for his forest eyes because I'm breathing so fast. I helplessly shift to put space between us but it only rubs my lower belly against his hard length.

And fuck! It's as thick as it was in my memory.

"Stay still," he barks when I rub again involuntarily.

"No," I taunt and push harder, hoping he'll let go. It only makes him jerk between my thighs.

"Jesus!" curses Justin, who I almost forgot was here. "Was she always this feisty, Stern?"

Dash doesn't lift his gaze from mine and watches so intensely that it takes my breath away. His eyes roam over every crevice of my face and I look away.

He's grown even more intense. His beauty is the kind that becomes dangerous the older he gets. His aura and looks are deadly at thirty-five years old. I can't even begin to imagine the power he'll possess years later.

"Feisty, yes. But a brat, no," Dash confesses to his friend, and Justin chuckles low.

"I'm not a fucking brat," I growl, and struggle harder to free myself from his hold. "You have me here against my will, Dash."

"Didn't you sneak in here and watch me fuck like a voyeur?"

Heat rises on my cheeks and he grins savagely at the truth shining on my face. He's smug knowing he has the upper hand.

"Maybe fuck behind closed doors next time."

His smirk widens. "I never said I minded it."

"It still doesn't change the fact that you're holding me captive."

"You had your chance to run, kitten."

"Don't think I won't complain about you and your friend."

His fingers dig into my throat as he leans forward to threaten, "Then we better earn our punishment."

Something is clearly wrong in the air tonight because my instincts have suddenly malfunctioned. Instead of fear, a raging curiosity and *arousal* spikes inside me at his threat.

I watch Justin in my peripheral vision as he takes a seat on one of the couches in the room with his arms spread like a king. He pats his thigh until one of the girls crawls and straddles him. And when I mean crawl, she actually fucking crawls like a pet, and I watch as he whispers something in her ear. I blush when she begins to dry hump him.

My lips part on a whimper when Dash's grip slides from my throat into my hair. He tugs until I'm staring at him with no option to look away.

He's so close that I can make out the faint scar underneath his left eye and the dark flecks in his pupil. The dark flecks give them the most unique shade of green I've ever seen. They see everything while hiding his secrets in their depths.

My gaze falls to his lips, the bottom thicker than the top as he confesses, "I did fuck you differently, sweetheart."

"Why?"

His hand frees my wrist but he places the other on my waist in a silent command to not move. The thin lace of my dress does nothing to ward off the warmth of his palm. Somehow, he makes me feel naked.

"Because you were too innocent to handle all of me."

I wasn't, though. I chased him, after all, when I could've chosen any other man.

"And those women are not?" I ask, jealousy dripping on every syllable.

A sadistic spark lights up his chiseled face while he traces a path up my spine with his finger. Every nerve ending in my body stands to attention. I'm lulled into a trance when he turns me around toward his friend.

His arm circles my waist and he slides my hair over my left shoulder. Goosebumps rise on my neck when I sense him lean down. My eyelids close to falling both from the vision in front of me and the infuriating man behind my back.

"What do you see when you look at her, kitten?" he rasps in my ear. "Do you see innocence?"

The girl has now moved between Justin's legs on the floor. She looks up at him coyly while biting her lip. At first glance, she appears shy and innocent as her fingers inch to his cock. But when I stare closely, there's a shark-like glint as well as cockiness in her gaze.

"No," I whisper just as she pulls out his cock and deepthroats him easily. "She's acting like one."

I feel my blush go deeper when my pussy drips at Justin's pleasurable moan. My body sweats at the harsh face fucking once he takes control. I'm shocked that I don't want to look away. It's not because of Justin. Though he's attractive as hell, it's the raw act that has me spellbound and turned on.

And the presence of Dash.

"You see how she takes his dick so well?" he murmurs, letting me watch for a few more seconds before harshly growling, "It's because she's a paid whore."

I'm twisted around to face him and his eyes darken at my hooded ones. He grips my jaw and raises his eyebrow while coaxing, "Is that what you desire, kitten? Would you have wanted me to claim your virginity like a whore?"

"N-no," I murmur, my tone unsure.

I don't want to be treated like a whore... Or do I?

"I think she just likes to watch," chuckles Justin from behind.

"Does she now?" Dash hums without breaking our stare.

My heart races uncontrollably. An ache builds in my core, making my clit pulse.

God! What is happening to me?

SCANDALOUS GAMES

"You wanna watch us fuck those girls?" Dash asks. He enjoys the torment like he can read my dirty thoughts, and whispers like the devil he's become, "Or do you want to be my whore, Bianca?"

Chapter Five

DASH

Bianca Chopra has a timeless beauty.

I knew it the moment I first saw her. She was just eighteen with a sweet smile playing on her lips and slender hands hanging on my stepbrother Niall's arm.

Another thing that I knew, like a premonition? She was going to be my ruination.

Now seven years later, she stands in my arms while conflicting emotions swirl in her pretty brown eyes.

Young Bianca had an air of innocence about her, but the one staring at me is sassy and utterly breathtaking. A stunning spitfire. Even a little guarded like she's holding mysteries close to her heart.

If only I cared enough to find out.

Our paths may have crossed tonight but I have no intention of repeating it. It's for her own good that she stays as far away from me as possible. Because when close, I always have this need to orbit around her. She always manages to steal my focus.

It nearly cost me everything last time.

I had half a mind to pretend I didn't recognize her, but that's as hard as not breathing. She's the kind of woman no man is capable of ignoring when she steps into their path. Her aura is so bright that you don't care if it burns when you get near. Or dare to touch.

How did she even sneak past the heavy security here? Her father is powerful and influential but he certainly wouldn't let his daughter roam freely around greedy men. I'm guessing she knows someone else.

Either way, I'm going to talk to the manager, because I didn't pay a hefty membership fee just so anybody could walk in. I hate when my reputation is threatened, especially when I've built it with a lot of hard work.

I can't seem to care about any of it right now, though, as I look at my little kitten. A smile threatens to tug at my lips when I remember this isn't the first time she's sneaked around.

She's always been too curious.

"Answer me, kitten," I softly demand, our mouths almost touching.

When I caught her watching me fuck raptly, I thought my mind was playing a trick on me.

The woman I never wished to see.

One I'd forgotten existed except in my drunken memories.

My breath had lodged in my throat when I took in her purple dress, because it should be fucking illegal. It barely hides every delectable inch of her. Beautiful tanned skin, tits spilling out of the top of her dress, and her long legs on display.

All I have to do is bend her over the nearest surface to get a glimpse of her wet cunt.

"Dash," she whispers.

"Yes or no, kitten?"

When she opens her mouth to answer, I hear a commotion in the hallway. A lithe figure, dressed similarly as Bianca, rounds the corner and stops in her tracks.

Nova D'Cruz, sole heir to the Cruz Empire, casually strolls behind the strange woman and leans on the far wall. Dark amusement glimmers in his gaze which he keeps pinned solely on her. I know he's betrothed, so she must be his fiancée, Rosalie Kapoor.

The tabloid showed them as a happy couple, which clearly is another lie.

Mutual hatred wafts between them, especially from her.

"Bee, are you okay?" Rosalie asks her friend.

Bianca, who seemed to be in a trance, finally rips herself away from me. I don't grab her again this time. Instead, I let my fists clench by my sides at the sudden emptiness.

Damn it! She's already fucking with my head.

I steel my expression into boredom when I notice Nova observing me intently from his perch. The man is a bloodhound and as sharp as a bull behind his charming smiles. Anyone who's at the top of the world wears a mask. He happens to wear more than one.

Men like us have no room to allow our weaknesses to be exploited.

A lesson I learned the painful way soon after I made my first billion.

"I'm fine, Rosa," Bianca assures.

"He didn't touch you, did he?" Rosalie sneers in my direction and I arch a brow.

While my kitten is all light and graceful, her best friend is all bite and claws.

Justin has abandoned the girl and righted his clothes, watching the rest of us like we're in a play. He came to visit me two days ago, and as it's his last night here, I brought him to this club for a good time. Only for nothing to go as I planned. At least he's entertained by the chaos.

"Nothing I can't handle," says Bianca confidently.

"You sure, kitten?" I taunt as I stare pointedly at her hard nipples.

I smirk when she crosses her arms and goes to stand next to her friend, who stares between the two of us curiously.

"You know him?" Rosalie questions.

"I'm hurt you didn't tell your friend about me," I tease. "Don't women tell each other about their firsts?"

Bianca's jaw drops while Rosalie's eyes widen in surprise before she quickly masks it. She grabs Bianca's hand when she steps forward and pulls her back.

"Don't, Bee."

"If only you were memorable enough." Bianca scoffs at me.

Dirty little liar. Now that the haze of lust has vanished from her body, she's back to hating me. Every time we spoke in the past, which was rare, we got into a heated battle. It fueled my fire to do it often and I did while enjoying each second.

I don't know if I did it because she always gave back as good as she got. Or because I loved the flush that covered her skin whenever she was in my close vicinity.

Nova, who was quiet until now, straightens and announces, "You found your friend, Rosalie. Let's go."

Both the women glare at me and Justin, who shrugs in a gesture that says "what did I do?" before turning around. Nova waits until his fiancée walks ahead of him before following closely behind. Bianca stays a few steps behind and I catch up before she rounds the corner.

She gasps when I grab her elbow and shove her against the wall. Her nipples harden into tight peaks when I trail a single finger over the curve of her tits.

"Dash!" she hisses when I twist her nipple.

"That's for lying that I didn't make you see stars when I broke your virgin cunt."

"It was a mistake choosing you to be my first, you asshole."

I froze as rage thrums in my veins at the regret in her voice. Even though I have no right to feel this way, it fucking stabs me in the gut that she thinks our night was a mistake.

While she was my ruin, I was hers too.

Only she doesn't know it.

I should pull away and let her go, yet there's no stopping me as I put my mouth against her ear and sneer viciously, "You sure begged like mine was the only cock you wanted."

"Whatever helps you to sleep better at night."

"Is what you'll tell yourself tonight when you lay in bed, kitten." I step back and stare down, smirking, making her nose twitch adorably. "If your friend hadn't showed up, you'd be riding my dick right now."

SCANDALOUS GAMES

"Go fuck your whores, Dash."

"I'd rather you be mine."

"Never," she vows despite the slight breathlessness in her voice.

"Then don't let me catch you again, Bianca."

"I never make the same mistake twice," she sneers with a perfectly arched brow. Her eyes were breathing fire. "You, Dash Stern, will always be my one and only regret."

My eyes are glued to the sway of her luscious hips as she walks out.

Even hours after she's gone, her last words still ring in my ears. I fooled myself into believing I got rid of the effect she had over me, only to be hit with the tumultuous reality in my face.

My little stepbrother's ex is still as hypnotic as ever, now with more fire burning in her veins.

If I'm not careful, she'll scorch me again.

Chapter Six

BIANCA

Dash Stern has become a billionaire and listed as the rising businessman in our country. His company, Stern Defense Securities, raised him to the big leagues once he signed a contract with the government. The fact that he did it in just the span of four years has made his success noteworthy. Upon his accomplishments, I wasn't surprised when the top magazines named him the most eligible bachelor in their lists.

I found all this last night when I couldn't sleep—like he taunted—and spent hours searching everything I could about him. Meanwhile, screaming at myself the whole time for failing to resist and lowering myself to cyberstalking him.

If only the media saw the asshole that lies underneath.

They obviously don't know about his deviant sexcapades.

It will leave women drooling if it ever got out but will also tarnish his reputation. The government certainly wouldn't ignore it. As long as it's private, they'll look the other way.

A small part of me isn't surprised because the ambition was always apparent in his eyes. I remember his father having served in the army, which must have helped in his career path. The only thing boggling my mind is him being in my city when his headquarters is in Mumbai. I hate when my stomach dips at the thought of him leaving.

SCANDALOUS GAMES

No. I don't care.

In fact, I'll throw a party if he's gone.

"You lost your virginity to that man?" judges Rosa, yanking me out of my thoughts.

"Who are we talking about?" asks a confused Iris. "Wasn't Niall your first?"

Iris, who finally took a break from studying for her upcoming finals, is hanging out with us tonight. The girls and I decided to have an impromptu lunch at our favorite restaurant. I knew the second I stepped inside that an interrogation was waiting for me. It was in the narrowed and inquisitive gaze of Rosa the moment I sat down.

Iris looks between the two of us with her brows drawn together. Rosa's question throws her for a loop. She didn't spill the beans about last night.

"Yes," I reply to them. "Dash was my first and it was a mistake."

Both speak at the same time.

"What else aren't you telling us?"

"Wait... why does that name sound familiar?"

The second question comes from Iris and I'm taken aback as I ask, "You know Dash Stern?"

Recognition lights up her face, which slowly turns into appreciation like she approves. I'm about to probe her when Rosa tsks, "Uh-uh, Bee." She quirks an eyebrow. "Spill it."

They both lean forward when my cheeks heat as I confess, "He's Niall's stepbrother."

"Damn!" curses Iris while Rosa settles back, smug and staring proudly.

She knows how everything fell apart between Niall and me, and how devastated I was afterward. I confessed everything that happened to her when I broke down in my apartment a few nights later. She was fuming and ready to kill but I told her I already got my revenge.

Not that it made me feel better.

Iris doesn't know the whole truth except the fact that Niall cheated on me because it was only years later when Rosa and I met her. Unlike us, Iris comes from a middle-class family and became our best friend after we ran into her at a party. She was with her boyfriend, Nathan, and looked like a fish out of water.

We ended up talking to her and the rest is history.

"How do you know him, Iris?" I probe curiously.

"Not as well as you do obviously," she teases, and I roll my eyes. "His company is discussing a merger with Kian's to set up a manufacturing plant here."

It explains why Dash is here.

Fuck! There goes my plan of never running into him again.

Kian, Nathan's older brother, was in the army before he left after his first tour to focus on building his own empire. The rumor is his father forced him to leave and join the family business. In true Kian fashion, he met his father's demand but only to start his own company. He's always been the black sheep of the Singhania family and is the oldest amongst us.

"How did you find out? It's not made public, otherwise I would've known."

"I might have overheard Kian discussing it over a call." A sheepish look crosses Iris's face before she waves her hand, saying, "Don't change the subject. Why are we talking about Dash?"

"Bee ran into him last night," says a grinning Rosa. "While he was fucking two girls."

"What?" gasps Iris.

"Oh, and she watched from the shadows."

"Rosa!" I shush her. I knew it was a mistake sharing that with her while we were driving home. "Which, by the way, wouldn't have happened if you hadn't dragged me with you to ruin Nova's night."

The mischievous look vanishes from her eyes and I smirk in satisfaction.

"Now I wish I had seen your text earlier, Ro," Iris laments with a pout. "Why am I always left out of the fun?"

"Only if your idea of fun is assholes and bossy men," I scoff. "Don't you have exams coming anyways?"

Iris is twenty and younger than us, still in college finishing her bachelor's in journalism. I was surprised to learn that because her shy and kind personality clashes with the path she has chosen.

I know from experience with the media that one must have thick skin and be ruthless to succeed in the field. I'm not saying I doubt her skills, but I can't help but worry sometimes.

"I do, and I could've used a night to relax."

"It's Nathan's job and not your best friends', Iris," Rosa mutters. "Did his dick stop working or something?"

I watch amusedly as Iris steals a fry out of Rosa's plate for the taunt. She stuffs it in her mouth while Rosa fumes. It's an unspoken rule to never touch her food because she doesn't like to share.

"Bitch."

Iris simply shrugs and my belly shakes with laughter at their antics. Rosa stares at me from across the booth we're sitting in and points with her fork. "Tell Iris about Arya."

My shoulders deflate and so does the cheerful mood. I had completely forgotten that I had another problem to tackle. My morning peace was stolen by vivid memories of Dash from the previous night. I shiver when his harsh yet seductive eyes flicker inside my head.

His warning, reverberating in my mind.

Don't let me catch you again, Bianca.

I shake it off and meet Iris's concerned and quizzical gaze. "Arya came to my apartment last night and said I should say yes to marriage so she can marry Aryan. My dad would never agree unless I do it first. So, I'm torn about what to do."

"You tell her to go fuck herself."

"She's my little sister, Rosa." I sigh. "I'd hate to be the person for her unhappiness."

"So the alternative is you sacrificing yours?"

"You can't say yes if you're not ready, Bee," advises Iris softly. "Talk to your dad. Surely, he can't be that stringent."

SCANDALOUS GAMES

"He lives and breathes his values, Iris," I rant. "Besides, I'm sure he and my mom will try to use this to their advantage."

"I'll never understand parents pressuring their kids." Her voice rises slightly with anger. "It's the only reason I'm dreading turning twenty-five just to avoid this whole mess."

"You, at least, have a loving boyfriend."

"Doesn't mean I want to settle down so early." She snorts.

"I'm conflicted because even if I miraculously stall them for a year or two, it won't change the fact that I have to marry first. My sister's resentment will grow into hate and my parents will still be holding on to their precious old traditions."

The sadness in my heart matches the expression on my best friend's face. Life would be so much easier if I wasn't the elder sister. I wouldn't be sitting here in pity while contemplating my dicey future.

The thought of marrying a stranger for real gives me hives.

"God! What am I going to do, guys?" I hiss in frustration.

"If I had an inkling of a clue on how to get out of marriage, I wouldn't be stuck with Nova," Rosa mumbles, while still chewing on her fries.

The three of us fall silent, thinking about the fucked-up situation we're stuck in and by the people who should love us unconditionally.

"What would you two do if you were in my place?" I break the silence.

"Find a fake husband."

The insane suggestion spills from Iris's lips, leaving Rosa and I stunned. She's supposed to be the innocent and practical one. I look for signs of joking but find none.

Does she really expect me to consider that?

"That actually sounds good," hums Rosa. "Just don't be a fool and fall in love with the man like those girls in books and movies."

"So in order to get out of marriage, I should have one," I repeat slowly to iterate how insane that sounds. When they stare expectantly, I throw up my hands. "Have you both lost it?"

"It's your only option," replies Rosa.

"How will it work, exactly? And where am I supposed to look for this man, hmm?" I point out. "It's not like there's an app for a fake boyfriend or a husband."

Iris sits up straight, steeples her hands, and she leans forward. As if she's about to impart great wisdom like a Yoda. "It's a foolproof plan to give Arya what she wants without you becoming the sacrificial lamb. Have a fake wedding and tell your parents it was a secret whirlwind romance. Stay married for at least a year or until Arya has hers and then divorce."

"As for the man, I know someone who'd be perfect," adds Rosa.

The piercing glint in her eyes raises my hackles and awareness settles because I know the name she's about to suggest. I hate the racing of my heart when she does.

"Dash Stern."

"Hell no!" I deadpan and shake my head vehemently.

"Yes," nods Iris. "It will be easier to convince your dad if he thinks you two knew each other in the past. You can say you reconnected and sparks flew."

SIMRAN

"Think about it, Bee. It's this or being stuck forever with a husband you despise," Rosa remarks. "With Dash, you walk away unscathed and happy."

It's what I'm afraid of.

I don't think I'll be as lucky as last time.

The Dash I knew had boundaries, and this one has none.

Chapter Seven

BIANCA

The seed my friends planted inside my head, they've made sure to water and grow it religiously.

It's been four days and every morning, I receive texts in our group chat or a video call convincing me that the plan will work. Somehow their conversation always ends like it's a done deed. Hell, Rosa tried to manipulate me by taunting that I'm scared of falling for him. Hence, I'm reluctant. However, I have to commend her dedication.

If he was the last man on the planet, I still wouldn't fall for him.

I said as much to Rosa and somehow she made it work in her favor. Nothing fazes her and her relentlessness. She and Iris usually stop bothering me after a while, but not today.

The fact that I'm at work has no impact on their mission to hound me until I give in to the absurd plan. I feel like a rabbit being experimented on in a lab by my crazy best friends. I've even gotten a side-eye from my colleague because of the constant buzzing of my phone. With a resigned sigh, I read the latest messages.

> ROSA: He's a manwhore. You wouldn't be tempted to fuck him.

IRIS: He probably won't be in the city half the time.

ROSA: A nonexistent husband. That's the dream.

ROSA: Just use him to scratch your back like last time.

ME: Did you forget the part where he was a jerk?

ROSA: Even better. He'll stand up to your dad when he loses his shit.

IRIS: That'll teach the old man a lesson.

ROSA: Amen.

ME: It's official. You're both insane.

ME: And STUPID.

IRIS: What? *round eyes emoji*

ROSA: I'll let that slide. The plan is genius. You should be thanking me.

IRIS: Hey!!! It was my idea.

ROSA: Which wouldn't have existed if I hadn't led Bee to Dash.

ME: Shut up. Both of you.

ROSA: Ouch.

ME: The plan will not work. Wanna know why?

SCANDALOUS GAMES

> IRIS: It will.

> ROSA: *Drum roll*

> ME: Because Dash will never agree.

> ROSA: Hmm...

> IRIS: You won't know unless you ask.

I put my phone away once they quieten down and focus on my notes for today's afternoon meeting. But I fail in concentrating because of my friends' words replaying inside my head. My sixth sense screaming their main goal is to make me talk to Dash, who hasn't stopped plaguing my thoughts.

Every night, memories of him slither their way into my psyche.

Especially the ones I tried helplessly to forget.

So when Iris inadvertently spilled how Rosa told her that she saw a fire in my eyes for the first time in years, I didn't like it. When I confronted her about the same, in typical Rosa fashion, she said, "Your eyes were glued to him, Bee."

I denied it, not that she believed me.

You're a terrible liar.

Worse, I haven't discarded the plan altogether. I'm intrigued and leaning toward it—and with Dash, no less.

Thankfully, my sister hasn't tried to contact me since that night but the weight of our conversation is still heavy. I'm in no frame of mind to hold a serious talk with her. The dread combined with my friends' pestering, made the risky idea more enticing.

My only hope.

The last resort.

A fake marriage will solve all my problems and I'd be free of the lectures from my parents. The constant tension. The matching disappointment on their faces. Most of all, Arya will get her happily ever after without me standing in the way.

I also can't shake off the guilt that sneaks in that I'd be lying to my family. Having a sham marriage and fooling my whole family. It'll be a white lie but still a lie. Even if it ends with something amazing.

In theory, it sounds like an easy and smooth plan but in reality, so many things could go terribly wrong. That might put me in a scarier mess.

Because best-laid plans always go awry, don't they?

If the truth about my sham marriage ever goes out, it will twist into a huge scandal. My father prides on his reputation and if his own daughter tarnishes it, he'll never forgive me.

The other option… to marry for real. *No*, a shudder passes through me. I would never be an option.

A fake relationship is my best bet.

I'll stay in it for a year until Arya is settled. Surely, I can survive a few months resisting and without killing Dash. It's not like we'll have to live together. Even if his merger is finalized, he'll soon return to his headquarters. Who's to say he would even want to marry me, even if in name only?

Hope flares inside me. It could actually work.

Shit. I need to stop. I'm getting carried away like my friends. I'm forgetting about the biggest hurdle. The toughest step. The one everything depends on.

Convincing Dash to marry me and become my fake husband.

Am I willing to take such a huge risk? I ask myself. *To lean on the one man whom I vehemently told he's my biggest regret? To willingly let him back into my life?*

"Bianca."

I'm dragged back to the present by my boss and mentor Mrs. Zara Cross's voice. The queen of the interior designing world.

"Good morning, Zara," I greet her with a polite smile.

The woman is one of the most influential and sought-after names in the designing industry. She made a name for herself at the age of thirty with her iconic style and charisma. I've been looking up to her my whole life and when she took me under her wing, I almost cried because it felt like a dream.

Her career took off to an even bigger height after she designed the home of a well-known celebrity. Since then, there's been a waiting list to become her client. I must admit, I was intimidated when I began working for her closely. But she has the patience of a saint. Even when stressful situations arise, she's as calm as a sea.

"I have a new client for you, Bianca," declares Zara. "Your first solo project."

My jaw goes slack when she tells me this. I stare at her, wide-eyed, before pushing myself into action and jumping from my seat in my shared office. My boss tends to announce big news out of nowhere. I have a feeling she secretly enjoys surprising her employees just to see their reactions. A surprise test of sorts.

"They're looking for a designer for their new offices, and I believe you'd be a perfect fit for them." Her gaze is sharp while she observes me. "Do you think you can manage the workload with your other clients?"

"Of course. I could never say no," I answer with a big smile. "I'll set up a meeting with the client right away."

"No need. He'll be here in ten minutes."

"Okay." I should've known since she never wastes time. I'll have to prepare in the short amount that I have. Luckily, this isn't my first rodeo. Most of the time, I've been called into meetings at the last minute.

"My assistant has already sent you the files you'll need."

"Who is the client?" I question. "Have we worked with them before?"

"Dash Stern. The CEO of Stern Defense Securities." I freeze at the sound of his name while my boss is oblivious as she continues, "He's recently opened a new branch in the city. I've already had a preliminary discussion with him and told him

SCANDALOUS GAMES

I'd have my best designer working with him. So, give your best, Bianca, and don't hesitate if you need guidance at any step."

Although my mind is frayed with nerves knowing he's close, I still manage to mumble, "Thank you, Zara."

She nods before walking out of my office and I plump down on my chair. I stare numbly at my screen while holding my head between my hands. It seems as though destiny is throwing us together at every turn.

Could it be a sign that I should take a chance on him?

If I'm being truly honest with myself, my mind was already made up. Maybe it's a fantastic thing he's here, so I wouldn't have had to seek him out on my own. I realize I was hesitant because I'm scared he'll say no and laugh before kicking me out.

Or he'll make me eat my own words, which is still a possibility.

However, desperate times call for desperate measures. And I'm stooped as low as they come. Though one thing I won't do is beg him like he taunted I did the last time.

I check my watch and realize I've wasted minutes, and now I'm running late. I'll just wing the meeting and I already know whatever there is to know about his company.

I briskly walk toward the conference room with my notebook, pen, and tablet. He's already waiting, as informed by the receptionist. Just outside the door, I pause as my heart thunders behind my ribs.

Why does he make me so nervous now?

He won't be naked this time and I won't be distracted by his dick pressing against me. My nipples, on the other hand, can still feel the arousing sting of his rough hand.

Do you want to be my whore, Bianca?

Damn him.

Focus. I count to three before stepping inside.

My mouth goes dry and my spine tingles when I'm met with the vision of him. His back is encased in an impeccable navy blue suit while he faces away from me. He stands alone in the wide room while gazing out the floor-to-ceiling window.

A cloak of authority in his posture.

An air of untouchability.

Utterly captivating.

His quiet presence is so thick, like the room belongs to him and I've stepped inside his den. Most clients usually admire our conference room as it has been designed with the intent to represent our style. Yet Dash couldn't appear more bored or simply indifferent judging from his stance alone.

His vibe screaming he doesn't care about the stunning view of the high-rise buildings visible through the three glass walls, or the long mahogany table sitting in the middle with chairs to seat ten people and a big screen on the opposite wall for presentations and pieces of art.

My hungry eyes take in all of the six feet and three inches of masculine beauty standing with his legs shoulder width apart and right hand in his pocket. His hair, which looks sexy when disarrayed, is styled sexily. Tight muscles bunch and flex as he shifts at the sound of my footsteps.

"Da—Mr. Stern." I hate the shakiness in my voice.

Stop stuttering, Bianca, I scold myself and maintain the professional smile I practice for my potential clients. He's just like any other client and I won't treat him differently just because I've slept with him. Or the fact that I have a hidden agenda.

A noticeable tension stiffens his broad shoulders for a short breath before he decides to face me. His icy gaze roams over my legs encased in silk black pants to the red top I'm wearing underneath my loose black blazer. I'm entranced as I let him take his precious time perusing me, leaving no inch of me untouched by those sharp eyes of his.

His gaze penetrating without betraying his thoughts.

I brace myself for his vicious taunts or threats. As if he can sense it, his lips twitch and I suck in a sharp breath. He's changed and become dangerous for my sanity, I swear. I will myself to move but I'm rooted to the spot. My body, attuned to his fine one.

"Miss Bianca," he drawls. "Should I be concerned by the fact that you're stalking me?"

I'm almost disappointed when he doesn't call me kitten.

"You wish."

His eyes gleam in satisfaction when he breaks my professional calm. Without breaking our eye contact, he closes the distance between us until I'm looking up at him. My skin flushes red when his gaze drops to the deep V-neck of my blouse.

"I guess I shouldn't be surprised to see you here."

"What?" I blink at the sudden switch in topic.

"You always wanted to be an interior designer and work for Zara Cross."

"I never told you that."

"You wouldn't shut up about it whenever someone asked you." He smirks before his gaze softens as he says, "I'm even more confident you'll achieve your dream too."

"You're the last person I'd expect to know my dream."

"Yet I do."

"Oh yeah? Tell me."

"Running your own designing company," he answers confidently without missing a beat. "Turning it international."

Why am I pleased he guessed it right? I'm irritated at the butterflies taking flight in my belly that he believes I can turn it into a reality. The only person I ever told about my lifelong dream was Niall, who couldn't be less interested. He even had the nerve to tell me that I shouldn't dream so big. His excuse was that he didn't want me to be disappointed in the future if it didn't happen.

I was such a lovesick fool that I actually let it slide. Or I was too young and desperate for love. I search for signs of mocking on Dash's face but he stares back softly, no traces of a single lie.

"How did you know?" I breathlessly ask.

"You aren't the only one who likes sneaking around, kitten."

His stormy eyes lock on my blushing cheeks before slowly hardening into

SCANDALOUS GAMES

impenetrable steel. The moment ends as his softness vanishes and is replaced by the ruthless man known to the world.

Dash was always hot and cold but now he has many layers he hides behind.

I shouldn't desire to peel them back and yet I want to.

"Let's start the meeting, Miss Bianca," he sharply orders.

I open my mouth to say one thing, but my lips utter another like they have a mind of their own. Once the words are out, there's no taking them back.

"Marry me."

Chapter Eight

DASH

"Marry me."

Bianca's mouth opens and closes while her eyes widen like saucers. Her delicate hand flies to her lips as she blinks in shock at her own words. It gives me time to hide my own surprise because not even in a million years I would've expected them. Especially not from her.

The woman who, only a few nights ago, called me her biggest regret.

The one who has my emotions tied in a knot.

Whom I warned to stay away from me.

Memories of her have been distracting me ever since she stumbled into my life again, day and night. I'm haunted by her scent that reminds me of the ocean. Mysterious, addictive, and peaceful.

The vixen that is aching for a man to draw her out. To introduce her to her hidden desires ever since I glimpsed them in her doe-eyes. Her lithe curvy body is made to be worshiped for endless hours.

If I don't keep my distance, I will end up devouring her.

Neither of us wants that.

Because it will unleash deadly secrets that are better left buried. If that wasn't standing in my way, then my deeper urges should make her run in the opposite direction. I kept them leashed and hidden when I fucked her the first time because

SCANDALOUS GAMES

of her innocence and knowing she was heartbroken over my stepbrother. I let her use me to purge herself of her demons while holding mine at bay.

None of it's standing in my way now, except the truth she's unaware of. A truth that will end with her hating me and not looking at me like I'm a mystery she can't solve.

Or like right now... Like I'm the answer to her problems.

No. Bianca cannot be in my life.

She never belonged in it seven years ago and neither does she belong in it today.

Her last words awkwardly hang in the air between us, making me intrigued about her intentions. It certainly isn't because she secretly loves me. I can bet all my billions that she probably dreams of killing me in her sleep every night and then wakes up with a smile on her face.

Why the vision is amusing, I have no idea.

"Are you proposing, kitten?" I drawl, tilting my head.

The nickname for her has made its home on my tongue. It spills before I can stop it and causes her enticing tits to shake as she breathes deeply. Her body, exposing the fact that she wants me every time we're close.

Did she desire me back then too? Or maybe she simply fucked me to piss off Niall? I can't help but ask myself.

Her silky hair escapes from her ponytail as she nervously pulls on it. I trace the movement of her tongue as she licks her lip. My dick twitches, wishing she was licking it instead. I could teach her how to take me deep down her throat without choking. Well... Maybe a little.

Fuck. Thoughts like that are dangerous.

"It's not a real proposal, Dash," Bianca answers, slowly regaining her composure.

"So no marriage, then?"

"I was kinda hoping for a fake one."

"Are you serious?"

"Yes," she replies earnestly.

I chuckle while crossing my arms and peer down at her. "Care to elaborate, kitten?"

"Can we sit, please?" She huffs, pointing toward the conference table. "My neck will go stiff if I have to keep staring up at you."

"There goes my fantasy of seeing you kneel naked at my feet," I tease seductively.

"Pervert."

"Any man would be after taking one look at you."

She looks away when a blush darkens her cheeks pink. Something the old her would never have done. Maybe it's what drives me to tease her every time I'm near. It must be driving her insane too.

"Just take a seat, Dash," she rushes to say and walks toward the chair next to her. When she sidesteps me, I wind my arm around her tiny waist, pick her up, and drop her on the desk in front of me. Before she has a chance to protest, I pull her knees apart and settle between them.

Her jaw drops and she gazes at the closed door behind her before pushing at me. I take her hands and rest them on her sides with mine on top. Again, her tits heave underneath her soft blazer, making me want to pull down the neckline of her shirt and bite the hard tips.

"This is better."

"Put me down!" she growls.

"I forgot how small you are," I tease, unable to help myself.

"Or maybe you're just too damn big."

"I distinctly remember you drooling over my muscles when you left scratch marks on my back."

The night I claimed her virgin pussy lives in the dark corners of my mind rent-free. The silky feel of her walls as I shoved inside and her cry of pain and pleasure, it all came rushing back like a powerful wave. It was the only good memory about that night.

Bianca's lips part on a gasp and I rub the bottom one until she bites down on my finger.

"I'm not afraid of some teeth, kitten." My gaze darkens with heat as I lock them with her defiant ones. "Just know, I bite back harder. Now tell me about your *fake* proposal?"

"You weren't always this bossy." She sounds annoyed.

"How would you know?" I retort. "You never talked to me. Maybe I was always bossy and you're just realizing it now."

"Or maybe becoming a billionaire has gone to your head."

"So you are stalking me."

"What? No!" She scoffs, offended, yet flushing bright red. "I knew this was a terrible idea."

"Fake marriages always are."

My words make her bristle but a slight desperation crosses her eyes as she mulls them over. It makes my protective instincts, which always seem to surface around her, roar but I shove it down. As intrigued as I am, I'm not getting involved in her mess.

As if she's come to the same realization, she tries tugging her hands that I'm still holding captive. Annoyed at myself that I can't seem to resist touching and trapping her, I pull my hands back.

"Let's just continue with our meeting," she grumbles while pushing at my chest.

"No."

"Okay, now you're just doing it on purpose."

I lean over her small frame, her hard nipples brushing against my chest, and grip her chin. "You can't just ask me to marry you and then pretend like you didn't. Unless you want me to walk out of here and take my business with me, you'll explain everything."

My no-nonsense tone that I use with my employees when I demand an answer has the same effect on Bianca. The only difference is that I don't usually issue it with a threat.

Her fiery gaze doesn't stray from mine as she reluctantly nods. Her lips twitch like she wants to hurl threats back at me but the fear of disappointing her boss is holding her back. I rest my fists on either side of her body and wait for her to speak.

SCANDALOUS GAMES

Tension laces her shoulders while a sliver of sadness flickers across her gorgeous face. It tugs at parts of me that I no longer want to acknowledge. She looks away to stare out the window for a second as if aching for a semblance of confidence before she begins confessing.

"My father is a conservative and strict man who lives by old traditions and values. He expects the same from his daughters and now that I've turned twenty-five, he wants me to settle down and start my own family. He doesn't care that I'm not ready and I'm happy with the things I've accomplished in my life. All he wants is for me to find a husband, preferably one of his choosing."

"Is he forcing you?" I demand, my voice tinged with anger.

I lie to myself that it's her situation I'm mad at and not because of the woman herself. I tell myself that I don't care if she's married to another man, making her forbidden and off-limits once more. Only for forever this time.

She pulls me back to the present when a broken laugh spills from her lips. She shrugs and I listen as she answers softly.

"Just in subtle ways every time I meet them. Everyone says peer pressure is bad, they obviously haven't met my parents."

I'm keenly aware of the fact that she's trying to make it sound like a joke, but nothing about it is funny.

"How will a fake relationship fix the problem, Bianca? Why go to such lengths?"

"Because if I don't marry this year, my little sister, Arya, will never get to." She sighs, her tone sad. "My father will never agree and then Arya will hate me forever. I love her too much to ruin her future. So when my best friends suggested having a fake marriage in front of my family until Arya has hers, it felt like a perfect plan. I'll end mine shortly after and this way, nobody gets hurt."

"I don't know whether to be impressed or laugh at the insane plan you and your friends concocted. You think it'll be that easy to convince your father?" My voice is incredulous.

"Oh, trust me. He'll be all too happy when it's all he's ever wanted."

"Your father is a smart man, Bianca. Your plan is very risky," I point out. "What if he catches you in your lie?"

"He won't," says Bianca confidently. Then again, she knows her father better than I do.

"If you say so."

"So will you be my fake husband?" she nervously asks. The hopefulness in her voice as she stares up at me almost has me saying yes to her.

Perhaps her craziness is rubbing off on me.

"I still don't understand why you're propositioning me."

"Rosa actually suggested your name."

The expression on her face is so innocent and breezy that I might as well have imagined the sass and fire from before. It's amusing and adorable that she pretends Rosa is the only reason she proposed to me. I ignore the slight jealousy at the absurd thought she might have another man in mind.

It still clouds my head as I demand in a low voice, "Who did you think of, kitten?"

"What?" She nervously swallows, taken aback.

I slide her to the edge of the table by grabbing her around the waist when she attempts to put space between us. The move presses her soft curves deliciously against my abs. A shiver dances down her spine when I inch my hand underneath her jacket above her thin top.

When her scent hits my nose, my fingers dig into her skin involuntarily.

Does her cunt smell the same? I ache to find out.

"If not me, then who were you going to ask?"

I notice her hands grasp the edge of the table on her sides, betraying her nerves. Or is she aroused at my closeness and trying to hide it? It has to be if the way her nipples have turned to stone through the thin material of her blazer is any proof.

"Why does it matter? I asked you," she croaks out.

"I want to know."

When she realizes I won't budge, she huffs, "Fine. No one."

"Admit I'm the only man you wanted."

"No."

Her defiant tone angers and turns me on at the same time. Smirking, I tell her, "Then I won't give you my answer unless you do, kitten. Remember, you need me; I don't need you."

The fire returns with a vengeance but she stays quiet knowing that I have her at my mercy. I watch the play of emotions as she decides if it's worth putting aside her pride or not. Ultimately, she has no choice except to give me what I want.

Something I know is the truth.

"You are the only one I want," she utters.

"Good girl," I praise with a smile before locking my expression. "What if it becomes something real?"

"It'll never happen. We don't like each other and it'll only be in name."

"What if I want more?" I muse in a low voice. She blinks back in shock while trying to gauge my feelings. Her pulse races and I trace it with my thumb before cupping her cheeks.

"You were never a relationship type of guy, Dash," she huffs sardonically. "Please don't tell me you're looking for one now. Just last week, you were fucking two girls at the same time."

"Maybe I was waiting for the right woman."

"Then this won't work."

"Why?"

"Because my heart is incapable of loving anyone." Her words come out broken while sadness flashes in her eyes before she hides it. "And even if it was, you're the one man I'll never fall in love with."

The certainty and vehemence in her voice floors me and the words linger between us. They challenge me to prove her wrong while awakening the competitive side of me.

If only love was a game.

If only I didn't have a black and vindictive heart.

"So sure of yourself," I mumble to her before dropping my hand and stepping

SCANDALOUS GAMES

back.

    I smooth my suit jacket and tighten my cufflinks while she remains seated. Hesitant confusion dots her pretty face at the sudden coldness in my mood. It puts her into motion as she stands on trembling legs and tucks her hair behind her ear.

    Her teeth bite the corner of her mouth before she probes, "So… will you help me, Dash?"

    "As honored as I am that you chose me to be your fake husband," I say flatly, "I'm afraid my answer is a no."

    "But why?"

    Her voice flows to me as I leave her standing and walk away before stopping at the door. I twist one last time to face her and taunt back with her own words.

    "I'd rather be your one and only regret."

Chapter Nine

BIANCA

(SEVEN YEARS AGO)

Tonight is going to be the night.

I'm done being the only eighteen-year-old girl holding on to her virginity like a devoted nun or a lovesick fool waiting for her wedding night. I want to know the feel of a hard cock as it slides inside me and the orgasm that follows. It will hurt but I'm past the point of caring. Niall and I will have sex, and I have the perfect plan to entice him.

His house is quiet when I enter with the spare key he gave me. But not too long, though, as the heavy wooden door makes a loud thumping noise after I shut it behind me. Niall lives in a two-story home just outside our university's campus.

He and I met at my freshers' party when he was a senior. The second I laid my eyes on him, I knew he was the prettiest boy I've ever seen. It was hard not to look away from his chiseled face with brown eyes, sharp jawline, and hair that fell on his forehead, giving him a bad-boy look.

When our gazes collided and he gave a soft, flirty smile, I was done for.

My heart was racing when he approached and kept me company throughout the whole party. Our chemistry could be felt sizzling in the air. But, of course, I didn't give in to him so easily. I smile when I remember how he asked me out on a date daily for two whole weeks without losing his charm until I said yes.

SCANDALOUS GAMES

Since then, I can feel myself falling for him with each day that passes.

My friends say we are the cutest couple on campus and the thought makes me blush.

It's one of the reasons I'm not nervous to let him claim my virginity and just want him to be my first. We've already crossed all the bases and more, and each memory makes me hot. My favorite part is waking up to his mouth every morning.

Another thing I love about him is that he's never pushed me for sex. He always puts my needs first and I trust him with my heart and my body.

I'm ready, so I decided to surprise him tonight. He's out with his friends and won't be home for another half hour. I've been planning this moment for a week and I'm dead set on wearing the sexiest Victoria's Secret see-through lace bra and panty set I've purchased. I even went and bought condoms and lube.

A girl's gotta be prepared.

My body shivers as I imagine Niall finding me on his bed, waiting for him. I crave for him to be mindless with need, unable to contain his lust as he takes me. Just the feel of his hard and muscled body pressing against mine has my pussy dripping.

Fuck. I hope he comes back soon.

Holding the bags in my hand, I head upstairs to his room. I think it's the last one at the end of the hallway from when I visited last. We usually stay at my apartment that I share with my best friend Rosa so my memory is a little fuzzy.

There was no way I was risking our privacy, so I told him we'll stay here tonight. Luckily, he didn't protest or ask me any questions.

Maybe he sensed my dirty intentions.

Nah. He would've hinted or teased me for sure.

I step inside the last room on the left and switch on the lights while dumping my bags on the chair in the corner. The bed is slightly messy as if he left in a hurry while the rest of the room is neat. I decide to freshen up in the adjoining bathroom and put on my slutty lingerie since the clock is ticking.

Besides, the butterflies in my belly won't let me sit idly.

Ah... I can't believe I'm going to have sex. Rosa is going to be so jealous when I tell her. The poor girl herself is trying to pop her cherry, except her bully of a fiancÉ won't let another man near her, let alone touch.

Maybe I shouldn't tell her.

But then what are best friends for? At least, she'll live vicariously through me.

I stop my train of thought as I enter the bathroom and sigh in pleasure when I stand under the shower. I wash my hair, shave my legs once more, before standing in front of the mirror and blow dry the wet curls.

My fingers tremble in excitement as I pull out the purple lace set and carefully slide it on. The material is so soft that I'm afraid if I pull slightly the wrong way, it'll tear.

I wouldn't mind Niall ripping it off of me, though.

Gosh, I'm horny already and he isn't even here.

The purple color complements my light complexion while making my breasts look perky. My nipples are visible and harden a little at the slight coldness in the

SIMRAN

bathroom. I hold my hair in a ponytail as I twist to check out my hips in the mirror before releasing it. I finish getting ready and only put on a little blush, mascara, and lip gloss as makeup.

I smile, feeling beautiful and bold, and can't wait until Niall finally sees me.

My phone sits on the marble and when I check, there's a message from him saying he'll be home in ten minutes. He also asks if I had dinner and I answer yes, even though I want to say hurry up instead. However, it will ruin the surprise.

I snap a few mirror selfies to memorize the big night.

Something to tease my boyfriend with later.

Taking one last look, I stride outside the bathroom without paying close attention to my surroundings. I'm so lost in righting the cups of my bra that I miss the hulking frame in the room until the temperature in the room rises to hotter degrees.

"Fuck," a dark husky voice murmurs. "Aren't you a pretty thing?"

I let out an involuntary scream at the sound of a strange man's voice in my boyfriend's bedroom. My terrified gaze collides with the prettiest shade of green eyes I've ever seen.

They burn with calm intensity and carnal lust.

I didn't know this color of eyes even existed in real life. So unfair that I have the most boring shade of all... Brown.

Focus, Bianca. Stop drooling over a strange man's features.

"Hmm... That's not quite how I like to make a sexy girl scream." His lips tilt as he teases me.

"Who the fuck are you?" I yell, once I find my voice.

Oh my god. I'm not in the wrong house, am I? Or is he a burglar or something?

Since when did thieves become so hot and had green eyes like a deep dark forest? They are supposed to be scary and ugly. They most certainly don't flirt with their victims before looting them.

He does give off scary vibes, though.

I can feel the dark energy radiating from the way he stands tall with his arms crossed. Even his features are dangerously handsome, from his closed cropped hair that brings out the sharp angles of his face. His eyebrows slash over his eyes as he keeps them pinned on mine.

He's dressed nicely too in a black button-down shirt. The top buttons undone, exposing his upper abs while wearing washed-up blue denim jeans. Damn. He's built with thick muscles and I can tell he's older than me.

Jesus, Bianca. Stop checking him out.

His mouth tugs to the side like he can read my thoughts.

"Get out of the house before I call the police," I threaten while trying to remain strong and alert.

I wish I had something to defend myself against him, but I also can't look away. He'll probably use it to his advantage. God! Where the hell is Niall?

My words don't penetrate the intimidating man as he stays rooted to the same spot. His amused gaze, which I can somehow see despite the blank expression on his face, drops lower. I follow the direction of his eyes and realize embarrassingly

SCANDALOUS GAMES

that I'm still in my fucking see-through lingerie.

"Hey! Stop staring..."

I wrap my arms around my breasts and cross my legs while searching for something to cover myself with. The effort is futile because it only pushes my breasts together teasingly and I've never hated the size of them until now.

He, on the other hand, is completely unashamed as he runs his hot gaze all over my body. Like he has every right. Like I belong to him.

Don't know why I expected a burglar would have manners.

"Why should I, sneaky girl? You obviously wore it for me. You're standing in *my* bedroom. I can see you used my shower too," he arrogantly taunts. "I'll admit, it's kinda stalkerish but somehow I can't seem to mind. The scared and blushing act is a turn-on too. Who knew I'd have a thing for crazy stalker girls?"

Is he delusional or a psycho? Definitely both. And I'm fucked either way.

"Are you insane?" I reply angrily. "And I'm not blushing."

"You're naked and I can see the flush on your skin, kitten." His tone is deep, close to a growl, making goosebumps rise on my skin.

Maybe I should just run before he goes full-blown psycho.

He strides forward stealthily as I'm plotting my escape plan. He's halfway near me when I notice and take a step back, only to collide with the wall behind me. His woodsy scent envelops me as he rests his hands on either side of my frame.

Of course, he's got height on me too as if his hulking frame wasn't enough. I tilt my head to stare at him while my heart thunders both in fear and something else I don't want to name.

"Get away from me."

He arches his perfect eyebrow at my snarky tone. "Should you even be making demands, sneaky little girl?"

"You're the one trespassing on someone else's property."

"Did Justin set you up on this?"

"What? Who?" I ask, flabbergasted.

Yep. We've entered the full-blown crazy dimension.

"Tell me your name."

He wants to make introductions. Maybe he'll need it to erase my existence once he murders me. Great. Now I've gone from thinking he's a thief to a killer.

"No."

"Do you want me to call you little girl when I fuck you then?" he softly says and boldly runs a single finger along my arm that's curved around my chest protectively. "You clearly came here to get fucked."

My body betrays me by shivering at his words and touch, and it triggers me into action as I shove at his hard abs. He's taken off guard and I manage to run past, but I don't get far before he captures my elbow.

I'm lifted off the ground and pulled back against his iron chest. His large hand wraps around my throat to hold me still. My eyes close at the feel of his body touching my naked skin.

His warmth seeps into my own, making me feel hot and bothered.

I shouldn't feel turned on at his strength, yet I am. Like my body has a mind of its own.

He doesn't flinch at my nails digging into his arm when his mouth lowers to my right ear. His tone holds a dark, threatening note as he speaks, "Did nobody teach you to never turn your back to a strange man when alone?"

Fear should be coursing through my veins right now.

I shouldn't challenge or taunt him, yet it's exactly what I do.

"Just like nobody taught you to never prey on an innocent woman or touch her without her consent."

I feel his lips curve into a smile before he whips me around and backs me toward the bed. I lose my balance and land on it awkwardly. His vivid gaze locked on my bouncing breasts like a hungry wolf.

Formidable.

Dangerous.

He's alert and doesn't let me escape by leaning over me, glaring with a seductive expression. "Innocent women's nipples don't harden at the touch of said man, darling."

I cover my heaving breasts and curse, "Fuck you!"

"Beg nicely and I might."

I lose my patience and aim to kick between his legs but the strong asshole dodges. His fingers snake under my knees and he jerks me to the end of the bed. I swallow and pant nervously when he keeps leaning closer until I have no choice but to breathe in his woodsy scent.

"Get your hands off my girl, Dash." Niall's angry voice thunders just as the psycho's lips stop inches from mine.

Dash and I freeze at the sound of my fuming boyfriend and fear finally takes root inside me. I don't want him to think I was cheating on him from my undressed state and being in the arms of another man, who hasn't let me go.

His fingers flex on my knees as his whole body pulses with an undercurrent of tension. It comes off in waves and I'm shocked at the expression on his face when his gaze clashes with mine. It's like I'm staring into a completely different man.

Cold.

Intimidating.

Frightening.

I might as well have imagined the arrogant man who was teasing me only seconds ago. He doesn't even realize he's holding me so tight until I push against his grip.

Niall rushes to us and hauls me up against him.

For some bizarre reason, I feel the loss of Dash's warmth and hands. I shake off the absurd feeling and let Niall dress me in his hoodie. He holds me possessively against his side and stares at Dash with hate.

Wait... How does he know his name? And why is he in his house?

"Do you two know each other?" I ask while looking between them questioningly.

"He's my stepbrother," sneers Niall. "My mom is married to his dad."

My eyes widen in shock and everything clicks into place. Though, on the inside, I'm mad at Niall that he never told me about Dash. Shouldn't this be something I

SCANDALOUS GAMES

should be aware of? However, judging by the animosity between them, I shouldn't be surprised that he hasn't.

"Why didn't you tell me? I thought he was a stranger."

Niall peers down at me and winces as he apologizes, "Sorry, babe." Then he turns to Dash and says in a displeased voice, "I didn't know he was coming home."

"Does he live in your house?"

"This is my house and not his, sweetheart," Dash, who was quiet until now, says in a hard voice.

Oh my god. Does this mean I'll run into him often? Especially after the embarrassment of tonight? How the hell am I supposed to walk around him, knowing he's seen me practically naked?

Suddenly, the heaviness of everything hits me all at once.

My special plans got ruined and I'm still a virgin.

"Ignore him," Niall orders, glaring at his stepbrother, and tugs at my hand. "Let's go to my room, babe."

I fall into step beside him and I'm almost out the door when I look back, feeling the pull toward the enigmatic man. His green eyes darken with heat and intensity like he can see through me. I glare when he roams his eyes over me from head to toe and smirks.

I hate him already and know I won't like the coming days.

And every day, he proves me right.

Chapter Ten

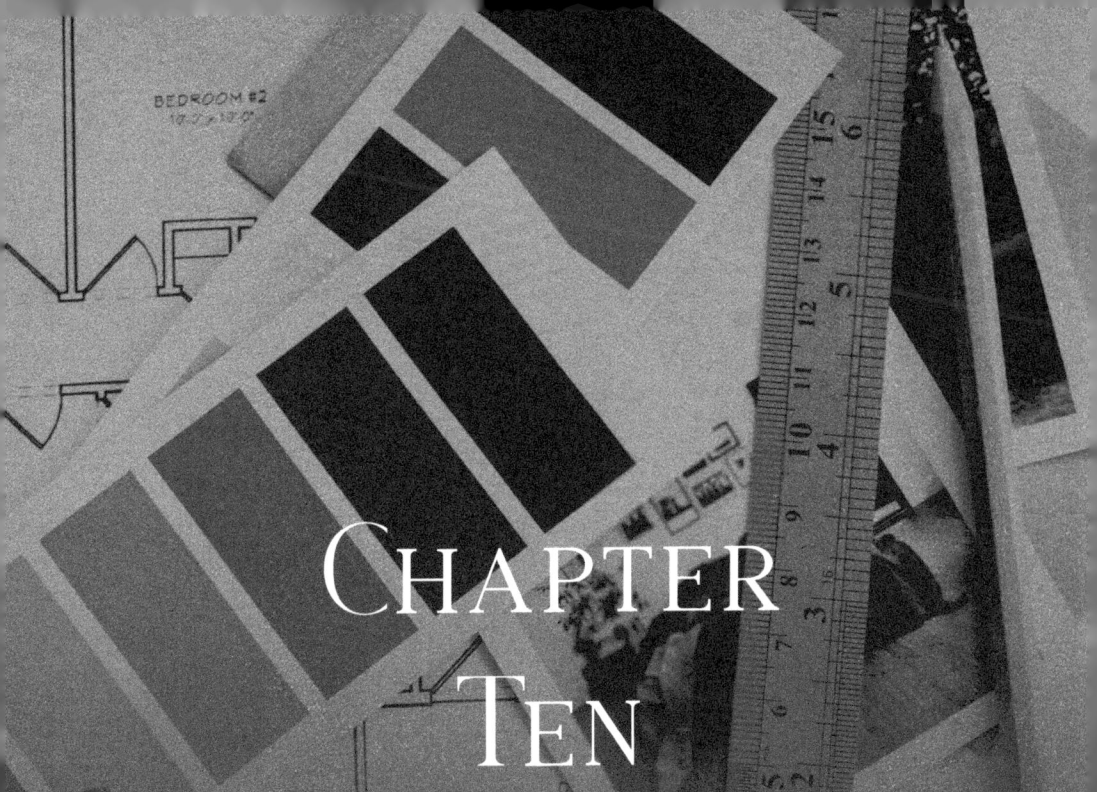

BIANCA

(PRESENT)

"Wow! He said no?" Iris says in bewilderment.

"What a dick!" curses Rosa.

All of us are sitting on the floor in my bedroom while sipping on red wine—our second bottle—and we're at different stages of drunkenness except Rosa. Our simple dinner date turned into a sleepover when I revealed I went ahead with their plan of a fake relationship and what an utter flop it was.

I had every intention of kicking them out but both of them are nosy little creatures. Instead, they went into my closet to borrow night clothes and had wine delivered. How the three of us ended up on the floor, I've no clue.

They listened intently as I relayed all about the disaster of yesterday, like how I ran into Dash at my office and as a client, no less.

Well... that's still up for debate since we never got to discuss any actual work.

Hopefully, my word vomit didn't scare him into running in the opposite direction.

I also told my friends how I accidently asked him to be my fake husband, only for him to reject me cruelly. Of course, I kept the part where he touched me and we stood inches apart while we talked all to myself.

Don't wanna give them any wrong ideas. Rosa is already suspicious.

SCANDALOUS GAMES

I'm confused about giving in to him so easily. I should've fought harder. It's like he puts me in a trance with his deep, seductive voice. I blame it on my forced celibacy and that's it.

"Seriously, Ro, it's your fault," I accuse. "You chose him."

"Well. I didn't actually think you had the balls to do it."

"So what should we do?" muses a tipsy Iris. I tug the bottle of wine out of her hand when she goes to refill her glass. Her crazy and naughty side tends to come out when she's super drunk, which happens often and fast with her being a lightweight.

"We should just blackmail him," says Rosa while Iris nods from beside her.

"Absolutely not," I say sternly. Or I try to, in my tipsy state.

They both ignore me, continuing their drunken plotting. Feels like déjà vu because it's exactly like our last lunch.

"I'm in," nods Iris eagerly. "How, though?"

"I'll get the video of his threesome and threaten to share it if he doesn't say yes to Bianca," explains Rosa without missing a beat, her thumb pointed at me. "He can't risk a scandal like that while working with the government."

"My god!" I mutter to myself.

"Won't that piss him off? He might say yes and then he'll sabotage our plan by outing Bianca to her dad," Iris replies thoughtfully before lying down on her stomach and resting her chin on her steepled hands. Looking between us, she lowers her voice and whispers, "Also... Dash is a dangerous man. Best not to make him an enemy if we want him to help our Bee."

"What do you mean he's dangerous?" Rosa demands before I can.

"There is a rumor going around."

"Tell us." This time it's me who asks curiously.

"It's regarding his contract with the government that put his company on everyone's radar. It was only him and his rival in the last round of bidding. Apparently, his rival died just a few days before the announcement and it's implied that he had a hand in the death."

"What? As in Dash killed him?" I gasp.

"Or just hired a contract killer," guesses Rosa. "I would do that."

"I mean, it's a rumor but the timing was suspicious as fuck," mutters Iris. "All I'm saying is he's ruthless and has connections which he accomplished all by himself. No one becomes a billionaire without some ugly gossip."

I don't doubt it. Dash always had this callousness and formidable air about him that screamed to keep your distance. And when I think about it, the only time he didn't have a scowl or boredom on his face was whenever we were alone.

Still, a murderer... That's impossible.

"None of it matters because he said no, remember?" I remind them both sharply before standing up to put the unfinished bottle of wine and my glass in the kitchen.

"Then who will you marry?" pries Iris.

"No one." She and Rosa frown as they peer up at me and I shrug, "It was a bad idea anyways."

"It was Iris's idea," Ro mumbles, pointing toward Iris who slaps at Rosa's hand.

"Oh, so now it was my idea."

Rosa ignores Iris without taking her gaze off me and questions softly, "Then what are you going to do about Arya, Bee?"

The one choice I avoided by giving myself false hope.

"Say yes to my parents."

Morning comes with the worst hangover of my life and I'm not just talking about the four glasses of red wine I consumed last night. It feels like a black, ominous cloud is hanging over my head, waiting to storm down on me.

I push Rosa's right leg from over my stomach to get out of the bed. My head pounds as I recall her insisting on sleeping in my room because she didn't want to leave me alone while Iris stayed in the guest room.

Actually, Rosa kicked her out when a drunk Iris began singing off-key. I believe she banged on our door before calling Nathan to complain when we didn't let her back in my room. After that, the rest of the night is blurry for me. I tiptoe to the bathroom without waking Rosa up, as she tends to get violent if anyone disturbs her while she's sleeping.

When I come out, she's still snoring lightly and I grab my phone to check the time.

"Fuck!" I curse when I realize I'm late for work. Pretty sure Rosa must have turned off my alarm before I could hear because I never sleep through the ringing.

I curse my luck twice when there's an email stating I have a meeting in an hour with none other than Dash at his office. I just know I'm not going to be there on time because the location is almost two hours away from my apartment.

He's going to think I'm tardy—something I despise—because I'm showing up late. Again. Why can't I ever have the upper hand when it comes to him?

Just the vision of his arrogant smirk is making me see red. A small part of me is still not prepared to face him after his rejection. I hate that it stings when I expect nothing else. He may have had a soft heart at one point, but now it's made of stone and ice.

Uncaring.

Frigid.

Impenetrable.

Could it be true that he had a hand in the death of his rival? The man I knew was immoral and vicious when he wanted to be, but never with violent tendencies. Although, seven years is a long time for people to change.

Dash may look the same but he's still a complete stranger to me. An enigma. A hardened version of his younger self.

If my experience has taught me anything growing up in my world, it's that everyone is capable of the worst crimes. The wealthier you become, the darker your secrets.

Yet I can't help but hope I'm wrong about Dash.

SCANDALOUS GAMES

Even more frustrating is that I don't understand why I'm hoping to be wrong. Who cares if he's morally corrupt or has a touch that sears my skin? The only kind of relationship that can exist between us is one of a professional nature.

I promise myself I'll behave like he's a potential client.

No more getting myself tangled in his mind games.

Most importantly, no touching.

Half an hour later, I'm dressed and out the door of my apartment after taking the fastest shower in history. I leave a note on my bedside table so Rosa knows I didn't get kidnapped or anything. If the traffic is light, I just might make it on time.

In the case that I don't, I pray he gets stuck in some other meeting.

My car purrs smoothly as I key in the ignition and switching to first gear, I drive out of my building. The morning light shines down on me and it lightens up my mood a little. The whole ride, my thoughts are consumed by my impending lunch with my parents.

They're going to be freaking ecstatic when I tell them I'm ready for marriage.

My mom is going to act like her prayers were finally answered.

Another half hour later, I'm nervous about another reason entirely. And yes, I'm ten minutes late as I park my car at the office of Stern Defense Securities. The building is at least forty floors tall and, as per my research, they all belong to Dash's company. The architecture is sleek and modern and eye-catching.

Since it was recently finished, I know the office is not officially opened yet. It explains the lack of cars parked in the front. I carry my bag, holding my notebook, pen, and tablet as I rush to enter, not wanting to delay the meeting any longer.

My earlier prayer is quashed when I meet the lady at the reception who impolitely tells me that Mr. Stern is waiting for me in his office on the thirtieth floor. The woman is so rude that she leaves me to find the elevator myself by pretending to be on another call.

If I wasn't late, I would give her a piece of my mind.

It takes me another full ten minutes to reach his floor and when the elevator door opens, I collide into a wall of muscle.

"We have to stop meeting like this, beautiful."

Every. Single. Time.

"Justin," I whisper before righting myself and narrowing my gaze. "I'm beginning to think you run into me on purpose."

"Can you blame me?" he flirts, and a smile tilts my lips despite wanting to stay annoyed.

Justin's blue eyes sparkle while his hands clasp my arms until I find my balance. He looks as though he came straight from a fashion magazine with his stunning model face and dressed in a crisp suit. Even his hair is styled perfectly. It's his panty-melting smile and charming personality that must have girls dropping at his feet.

Suddenly, I get a flashback of the night at the club and my cheeks heat. I can't believe I watched him fuck another girl's mouth. Ever since I met Dash again, I've done everything opposite of my very nature.

I have to be possessed. *Right?*

"I remember you, you know," I tell him once he lets me go but stands close with his hands in his pockets. "You've changed quite a bit."

"You mean I've become more handsome?"

I chuckle before replying, "I don't think your ego needs another boost."

He laughs in a deep, throaty sound and I can't help but join, missing the sound of angry footsteps in the hallway until it's too late.

"You're late again, Miss Chopra." Dash's clipped voice pierces through the air, making Justin and I halt in our banter. The temperature drops to chilling degrees as he stares between us with a strange emotion. The sudden urge to drop my gaze rises inside my chest when his eyes lock on mine, throwing daggers.

Wait... Is he mad at me? What did I do?

"It's my fault, Stern," explains Justin, but Dash doesn't look at me. "I couldn't resist talking and catching up with her."

I watch his jaw clench at his best friend's lie and his expression settles into false calmness like he knows it's utter bullshit. While he seethes silently, I'm distracted by his physique and the way his muscles flex. The black suit he's wearing with the vest and perfectly knotted tie peeking from beneath his jacket has me salivating.

His boss attire screams wealth and sophistication.

Yet only I'm aware of the savage that lies underneath.

I'm yanked back to earth when his deep voice penetrates my thoughts. "If getting easily distracted and being late is a recurring occurrence with you, Miss Chopra," he admonishes, "then I might have to go with another company."

Fucking jerk. If I knew my first solo project would be attached to his mighty ass, I would have rejected it.

Then again, I'll be damned if I let him bully or make me quit.

"Oh, come on, Dash," Justin sighs.

"It's all right, Justin," I softly whisper, touching his arm. Turning to Dash, I notice a warning flash in his eyes as he glares at where my hand is resting on his friend. It's gone as quickly as it came before I can decipher its meaning.

If I didn't know any better, I would say he's jealous or something.

I drop my hand and steel my spine as I meet his sharp gaze head-on. "Mr. Stern, I assure you it's a one-time thing—"

"Two," he cuts me off in a smug tone.

It takes all my power to maintain the fake smile on my face as I continue, "It wasn't my fault the first time because I was only made aware of the meeting a few minutes before you arrived. I do take responsibility for today, though, and it won't happen again."

"Then why are you still standing here and wasting more of my time?" he taunts before turning away and calling behind him as he walks down the hallway, "If I don't see you in my office in sixty seconds, I'm hiring someone better."

"Arrogant bastard," I mutter under my breath before realizing Justin is still here, and he laughs at my insult to his best friend.

"Don't mind him, beautiful," he advises. "He forgets the world doesn't revolve around him."

"Could've fooled me."

He smiles before reminding me, "He's a moody asshole, Bianca. Best run now."

SCANDALOUS GAMES

"Oh fuck," I grumble. "Bye, Justin."

Without waiting for his reply, I sprint in the direction Dash went and hate him even more for not telling where his office is. It takes me two tries before I find it and I'm winded by the end of my search. I don't bother knocking and immediately step inside his lair. The term feels appropriate from the energy that pulses inside the four walls because of the man himself.

It's like succumbing to his power.

He owns the room with his silent presence and commanding stare. I take him in as he sits behind his massive desk with his back ramrod straight and hands splayed on the arms of the chair. It's like seeing a dark lord sitting on his throne.

He even appears like he's about to declare a war.

And his innocent victim...

Me.

"Just in time," he taunts, and before I can sass him, he issues another command. "Lock the door, kitten."

Chapter Eleven

DASH

Everyone says your whole life flashes before your eyes when you're moments from death.

Yet my past—good and bad—seems to haunt me whenever I'm close to Bianca.

The tempting woman brings back the nightmares I want to keep buried. She's bringing back to life the ruckus that disrupted my life seven years ago: the damn rush of forbidden and twisted feelings I fought with every fiber of my being.

Yet I still fell prey to them anyway.

The worst part is that she's so beautifully unaware of the power she has over me that it makes me lose my carefully crafted control. I never once have, and yet she's made me lose it twice already, like it's a mere illusion.

It's just like it was in the past where I couldn't keep my eyes off of her whenever we were in the same room. Every time I walk away, I promise myself to stay away, only for me to pull her closer the next second. I still have no intention of being her savior and becoming her fake husband, though.

After I had left that day, I researched her father and found everything she shared were true. The man is an old misogynistic prick who firmly believes a woman's life isn't complete until she's married. I shouldn't give two fucks about whether she finds a way out of the mess she's in.

SCANDALOUS GAMES

It's a headache I don't need.

Yet the thought of her asking another man has my vision going black.

"Why? There's no one else on this floor." Her nervous voice penetrates through my fog of fury, and I remember my command.

"Because I said so." My voice is hard.

I wait for her defiance to surface but instead she disappoints me by doing as she is told. It's not as much fun when she meekly obeys. I've always been addicted to her sass and fire, even while she dated Niall.

He always treated her like she was made of porcelain, and I hated when she let him.

Her inquisitive eyes take in my semi-furnished office while I admire her curves, especially her tits that shake even at the slightest movement. It seems my rejection stung her because she's dressed like she makes me want to regret my decision.

Well, you came close, kitten.

When I saw her standing close to Justin and laughing with him, I wanted to pummel the man into the ground. At that moment, it didn't matter if he was someone who's been with me through thick and thin. She stood beside him looking like a wet dream and when she touched him, it took years of restraint to not yank her to my side.

I swear, no other woman has made me insane with petty jealousy.

Except Bianca.

My beautiful kryptonite.

My gaze locks on her silky hair spilling down her back in rivulets as she walks. The sunlight makes her tresses almost appear brown. Unlike last time, she's wearing a black pencil skirt with a silk blouse tucked inside. The material molds to her ample curves while showcasing her lean legs that look a mile long.

She's a tiny little thing with her tight waist that flares into a bite-worthy ass. My hands itch to yank her close and bend her over my desk while she begs me to fuck her. Maybe then, I wouldn't be so distracted if her scent marked my office.

Or it just might make everything worse.

"Is this the office you want me to design, Dash?"

"Mr. Stern." She blinks rapidly when I correct her in a cold voice. I need to establish boundaries and curb my instincts to hold her every time she's close. Leaning back in my chair, I explain, "I don't allow my employees to call me by my first name."

Her lips curl as she retorts, "But you can call me kitten?"

"You're not the boss here, kitten. I am, and what I say goes." I smirk as I rub my chin and quirk an eyebrow. "Besides, I didn't think you would mind."

"Well, I do."

"I don't care. Now take a seat."

She doesn't move right away in a show of defiance while I let her hold the illusion she has any control. I have learnt that this is her first solo project, so I already know she won't break so easily and I watch as she steps forward and sits down.

She takes her time—not looking up—as she pulls out a few files from her bag and lays it on my desk methodically. Her long lashes blink twice before she raises her eyes to mine and speaks, "I'm not your employee, Mr. Stern. I'll work with you, once you decide, and not for you. Better for you not to get any wrong ideas."

All she makes me think of are bad ideas. The kind that destroys lives. Like messing up her red siren lips with my teeth.

Locking her away in a tower so no man can lay their eyes on her.

To make her *mine*.

"Do you talk back to all your clients?" I ask, instead of spilling my secrets.

"Just the ones who disrespect me," she answers with an innocent smile.

I'm impressed by her confidence but that doesn't mean I'll let her get away with it. "If you want my respect, then start showing up on time and don't flirt with my friends."

Her eyes flare and she grits out, "I wasn't flirting with Justin."

"It didn't look that way to me from the smile on your face and the close proximity between you two," I growl, my calm vanishing. "Or were you asking him to be your fake husband after I said no?"

"Maybe I was, but guess what?" she sasses. "It's none of your fucking business, Mr. Stern."

"Then he better have said no, kitten," I warn darkly. "Because you're mistaken if you think I'm going to watch you parade around on his arm."

"Try and stop me."

"I'll only say this once, so listen carefully." I grunt, holding her defiant stare. "If I see you anywhere near Justin, I'll tell your father the truth."

"That's it," she grumbles, hastily standing up and stuffing her things into her bag. "No amount of money is worth this."

Her hair flies as she whips around to leave, and I bark harshly, "Take one more step and I'll call your boss. I wonder what she'll think when I tell her that you go around propositioning your wealthy clients for marriage."

She halts while a shiver races down her spine. It's obviously laced with tension. Her small fists clench by her sides as she whirls around and glares. "You're such a fucking asshole, Dash. My life is not your playground for your threatening games. Go get your kicks somewhere else."

Her chest heaves with exertion once she stops her rant and stomps her foot while anger pinches her features. My dick chooses this moment to harden at the display of her emotion like a sick fuck. My mind, on the other hand, screams she's never looked more beautiful.

Thankfully, she isn't privy to my thoughts.

It'll only piss her off more.

"Stay away from Justin and my threats go away," I order, my tone nonnegotiable. "Don't get fooled by his charm, Bianca. It's a smokescreen to hide his own baggage. Do you understand me?"

My eyes narrow when a little Cheshire cat-like smile graces her lips and she covers the distance between us, the expression on her face nothing less than smugness and mischievousness. I don't visibly react as she puts her hands on my desk and leans forward, giving me a sexy view of her cleavage.

SCANDALOUS GAMES

"Are you jealous, Dash?" she taunts sweetly.

The boldness in her tone like she knows she found my weakness—which I hate—maddens me. I may be jealous but I'll be damned if I give her the satisfaction of knowing that.

"I already fucked you, kitten." I smile when her cocky one vanishes but I'm not done. "I don't do repeats, so don't consider yourself special just because I took your virginity."

She flinches slightly and if I wasn't watching her so closely, I wouldn't have noticed. I give her a minute to gather her emotions while silently seething at me.

"Justin was right," she says. "You are a moody bastard. And just so you know, I never considered myself as special because for that, I would have to think of you, which I've never done. If I could erase that night, I would."

So would I, but not for the reasons she wants to.

"If you're done with your tantrum, Miss Chopra," I drawl, "I would like to discuss the actual topic of this meeting."

"Fine."

"You have ten minutes to impress me."

"What? The meeting was set for a whole hour," she mumbles.

"More than half of which you wasted already." I check my watch before reminding her, "Nine minutes before my next appointment arrives."

I arch my brow expectantly and she rushes to open her notebook to take down notes before questioning, "Can you tell me how many offices you want to have interior work done to and do you have a specific vision in mind?"

"I want you to design all the executive personnel offices on this floor. The basic theme and the structure should remain common while the rest you can do as per their choice. I'll set up a meeting with each of them so you can discuss the details."

"What about you? Do you have a preferred style?"

"Yes, my assistant will share the pictures of my office at my headquarters so you can design this one similarly. I like it as it is. Though I have a few custom art pieces being delivered soon which I want here."

She frowns, her pen pausing over her notebook, before she probes, "You don't want to change anything at all?"

"No. I like everything a certain way."

"Okay."

Bianca's professional side surprises me in the best way possible and I'm fascinated with the passion and enthusiasm I see and feel in her voice as she continues her consultation. She doesn't even realize the ten minutes are up and I don't stop her, too consumed in listening to her. My previous interior designer, who had more experience than her, didn't go into as much depth as she is. There's patience and eagerness in her attitude as she continues to talk.

She doesn't let our earlier conversation make things awkward and I like that she can keep business and pleasure separate.

"Do you have a budget?" she finally asks, staring up at me.

"Yes. I'll send over the details as soon as you leave."

Closing her notebook, she gathers her files as she smiles and nods. "Perfect.

I'll set up another appointment to show the renderings. If you think we're a good match and say yes, I'll send over the contract to begin our work."

"I've already decided. You're hired, Bianca."

Her whole face lights up in happiness like she didn't expect it. I've always been a good judge of character, especially when I'm hiring, and I know without a doubt she's perfect for the job.

"Really? I thought for sure you'll say no just to piss me off."

"I don't let my personal feelings get in the way of a good business deal."

"Well, thank you." Her tone holds surprise.

"Besides, I have other fun ways to make you mad."

She rolls her eyes and stands, bending down to pick up her bag. I rise from my chair and round my desk, making her look up when I come to stand beside her. My gaze is drawn to her mouth when her tongue sneaks out to lick her bottom lip.

So goddamn irresistible.

Because she doesn't even realize her teasing gestures, her unawareness is a turn-on.

I shove my hands inside my pockets before I lose the fight and grab her, "I'll walk you out."

Her addictive scent hits my nostrils, almost drowning me as she turns to stride toward the door. I don't miss her slight intake of breath and the shiver down her spine when I follow close behind.

We're at the door when I crowd her against it by grabbing the knob before she can. I don't dare to touch her soft skin at the nape of her neck when she shifts, head twisting to the side. Electricity thrums between us and I know she can feel it too.

The memory of us standing just like this years ago flits through my mind.

Our chemistry was unmistakable back then as well.

Just not this strong and naked.

"Dash," she whispers like she's remembering it too.

I lower my mouth to her ear and growl darkly, "Stay away from Justin, kitten. I mean it."

Chapter Twelve

DASH

(SEVEN YEARS AGO)

Dinner with my father is always a headache and the longest minutes of my life that I can never take back. And when I have to do it sitting across my asshole of a stepbrother, Niall, it seems never-ending. Half the time, I'm just contemplating to get up and leave without looking back, but ingrained habits are harder to kill.

My father and I have a complicated relationship. Hell, lack of a relationship is a better choice of word. The army taught him to guard and lock his emotions, so much so that he forgot his family should've been the exception. Instead, he turned me into his replica.

Like father, like son has never been truer.

My whole life, I've always felt like a burden to him and when he married the second time, it put an end to whatever little bit of a connection we had. Though we pretend one exists on the surface. He found his perfect family with a pretty wife and an obedient son. A fact Niall throws in my face every dinner while receiving endless praise from my dad. A small smile, a pat on the back, and the worst is when he says, "That's good, son."

An effort he could never make for his actual offspring in over twenty-eight years. However, it's not my father's behavior that hurts, it's the little kid inside me that burns and no matter how hard I try to kill him, he always resurrects. The only reason I even go to these awkward dinners is because of my stepmother, who tries to include me in the family.

I don't have the heart to tell her that those efforts are in vain.

The damage has been years in the making, there's no fixing it. There's no changing the man I've become now.

Days like today are when I reminisce over these unresolved emotions. Otherwise, they are kept locked away and never to be let out. After a long day at work, followed by a god-awful dinner, I just want to go home, have a glass of whiskey, and sleep in my bed.

However, as soon as I arrive and notice Niall's car parked in the driveway, the peace I used to feel at having my own place dissolves into ire. It's just my bad luck that I have to tolerate him twice in one day.

God knows I have thought so many times about kicking his spoiled ass to the curb, but my stepmom's sweet face stops me short.

Yet people claim I'm a heartless bastard.

Parking my own car beside his, I shut the door behind me after getting out while pondering why the fuck he's at home tonight. More often than not, he stays at his friends' or the last I heard, at his girlfriend's apartment.

As soon as I think of her, my annoyance shifts into burning anticipation that she might be here tonight with him. Since when was the last time I felt excited and eager to hurry inside the door? At the thought of a woman, no less? None comes to mind.

I haven't been able to forget that woman ever since I caught her half naked in my bedroom, looking like a vision from my filthy sex dreams. No other girl has ever intrigued or caught my attention for this long or so strongly in one encounter except her.

Bianca Chopra.

Too young and *forbidden*.

How Niall impressed someone like her is beyond me. Can't she see he's an arrogant prick who only cares about himself? Or maybe she's just like him.

If that plus the fact that she's my stepbrother's girlfriend doesn't lessen my attraction to her, I'm seriously fucked. Again, that boggles my mind. Women hardly ever distract me, yet I've thought about Bianca more than any other girl in my entire life. I blame it on the fact that I didn't get to fuck her out of my system that night or that she's the first girl to not fall for my charms.

Instead, she insulted me, followed by threatening to call the cops for being in my own house. I didn't know whether to laugh or admire her unafraid attitude, considering her vulnerable state. Not that I minded.

What hot-blooded man would? Those tits and them lean legs I wanted wrapped round my waist live in my head rent-free. Purple has officially become my favorite color.

If she wasn't off-limits...

I let the thought drop.

Even if she were single, one night is all I can give her. I've no intention of tying myself down to anyone for the rest of my life. It has disaster written all over it, especially for a man like me with demons that would send any woman running.

Unlocking the front door, I'm welcomed with darkness and silence as I make my way to the kitchen to find some alcohol. Sliding my suit jacket off, I throw it on the back of the couch and loosen my tie. The past week has been super hectic, more so than usual when you're starting your own company.

Soon after graduation and working for a firm, I had realized it wasn't for me and that I wanted my own business. I had grown up seeing my father build his own defense equipment company after retiring from the army and I knew I wanted to work in the same industry, except I didn't want to continue his legacy but build my own.

At least one thing I can thank my father for is his discipline and dedication toward work that he built in me. Those are the only good memories I have of him when he used to take me to his offices and manufacturing plant alongside him.

There are times when I wonder if, subconsciously, I'm still trying to earn his approval.

Or trying to compete against him.

"Ouch, shit!"

The loud curse yanks me back to the present and I'm momentarily awestruck, staring at Bianca as she skips on one foot to go settle down on the couch. She came from the direction of the stairs on my right and can't see me since her back is to me as she walks by. Just like last time, she's wearing almost next to nothing, dressed in sleep shorts and a cami with one strap falling dangerously low on one shoulder.

What the hell is she doing in the middle of the night?

The girl is strange, I swear.

I ignore the jealousy that flickers in my chest, knowing she wore this outfit for Niall and probably came from his bedroom. *She's not mine*, I remind myself. Nonetheless, I keep seeing the vision of her lying underneath him, kissing him… fucking him.

The male pride and ownership in his eyes when he yanked her into his arms after catching us so indecently close, filled me with rage. *She's mine*, was the message I'd gotten loud and clear.

Suddenly, I wanted to steal her from him.

And as I stare at her, the idea sounds tempting. Nothing will hurt his ego more than me stealing his prized possession.

The room is dark so she doesn't see me lurking in the shadows just a few feet from her. She can't hear the illicit and dangerous intentions forming with each second that passes. Nor do I make my presence known, content on watching while she's unaware. Oblivious. Beautiful.

Some of the light from the stairway drifts into the living room, casting a soft glow on her profile while her body is slightly turned away from me. I breathe quietly, not wanting to alert her to my presence yet, while sipping from my glass of whiskey I poured earlier.

I'm guessing she hit her foot in the dark and I wince, knowing that always hurts like a bitch. I would find it funny that it made her upset enough to curse out loud but I can't see past the haze of lust she's cast on me.

The adorable yet fiery woman intrigues me.

Abruptly, she stands up and my fingers tighten around the glass when she bends over, giving me a view of her tight ass as she searches for something on the couch. Once she finds it, she straightens and I realize it was her phone. She's about to turn around and leave when it rings loudly, startling her.

"Ro!" she says, her hand coming to rest on her heaving chest. "You scared me."

"Why am I awake?" she repeats incredulously to whoever is on the other end before plumping down on the couch. "Why are you? You're calling me in the middle of the night."

I shouldn't be eavesdropping on her private conversation but my house, my rules. It's not my problem she's lost in her own little bubble. My grin is devious because after tonight, she'll think twice about letting down her guard at my place.

Relaxing my back against the counter, I cross my legs as I continue listening to her. She has the softest voice I've heard with a touch of breathlessness. I adjust my cock when I imagine her voice becoming deeper as she whispers my name while I have her beneath me.

"God no, I didn't run into his hot stepbrother."

My attention snaps back to her and my lips tilt to one side as she calls me hot, even if it's in infuriation. Hmm, so she's been thinking about me too.

The truth spreads unfamiliar warmth to my chest.

"I don't need to see his smug face again, knowing he's seen me practically naked."

My grin widens as she huffs a breath, trying to hide her embarrassment, and the slight hoarseness in her voice. I bet she's imagining our encounter just like I am. Only in my head, it doesn't end with her running away.

"Niall says he's a manwhore." *Asshole.* "And that I should stay away from him."

I bet he did.

"I already hate him for ruining my night." Her tone is angry and she mutters, "He's the reason I'm still a virgin, Rosa."

Holy fuck. A virgin. Hence, the fuck-me lingerie that night.

How the fuck hasn't he slept with her yet? Does he have a malfunctioned dick or something? And why does it make me feel relieved?

If she were mine, I wouldn't let her leave my bed until she begged me for mercy. I'd be fucking her night and day until her throat was hoarse from screaming my name and her body spent. She certainly wouldn't be complaining to her friend about how unsatisfied she is sexually. With all that fire and sass, she'd be a wildcat in the sheets. The things I could do to her... my cock jerks in my pants just thinking about it.

I'd honestly be doing her a favor by taking her from Niall.

"Niall is not a dud in bed, Rosa," Bianca snaps. "I'm not going to cheat on him just because I'm horny. You know what? Bye. I don't even know why I'm having this conversation with you. Go annoy Nova."

As soon as she ends the call and rises from the couch, I put down my glass on the island. The sound echoing in the silence freezes Bianca in her tracks. With a startled gasp, she turns in my direction until my cold eyes collide with her vivid

SCANDALOUS GAMES

ones.

Her nervous swallow is audible and music to my ears.

I wish I could see the color on her cheeks that I can feel radiating from her as she realizes I overheard her whole conversation. She remains stunned for the longest seconds while the tension in the room thickens.

Her unmistakable shyness feeds the primal beast in me.

I continue silently staring at her as she tries to gather a semblance of courage. I'm curious to see if she'll confront me head-on or pretend the last few minutes didn't happen. Perhaps she'll scurry away to Niall's bedroom.

However, something tells me she isn't one to run away.

"It's impolite to eavesdrop," she scorns, despite the slight hitch in her breath.

When I don't say a word, her confidence falters. Her hands fall from her hips as I straighten to my full height and slowly round the island. Each step I take, she takes one back, but my strides are longer and it's not long until I reach her.

Her eyes fall down to my chest, then lower farther, and when she bites the corner of her lip, I want to groan. As if remembering she shouldn't be checking out her boyfriend's stepbrother, her gaze snaps back to my face.

"Wh-what are you doing?" she whispers when I crowd into her personal space. "Dash?"

Fuck. I've never loved my name more than on her lips.

Her soft curls fall down her back as she tilts her head back to maintain our eye contact. Our chests brush when I lean forward and her lips part, eyes going wide like she's afraid I'm about to kiss her.

I can't resist smelling her fruity scent before I pull back. When she sees me holding my suit jacket that I dropped earlier, her mouth snaps shut. A pink blush darkens her cheeks and I smirk, making her nostrils flare adorably.

She can deny it all she wants.

Fight her instincts all she wants.

But the truth is… Bianca is attracted to me.

And soon, it's going to be Niall's downfall and… *hers.*

"My advice," I speak, staring down at her as I step back, "dump Niall or you'll die a virgin, kitten."

Chapter Thirteen

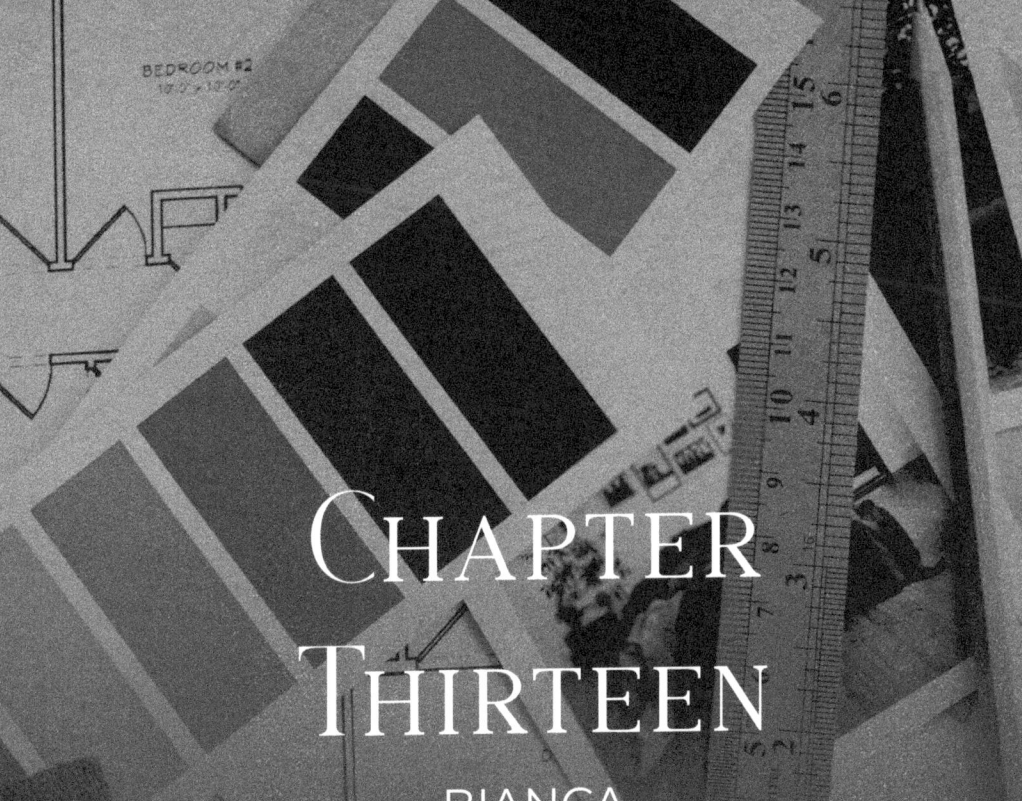

BIANCA

(PRESENT)

Stay away from Justin.

Two days and his roughly growled warning is still haunting me. I've never ran as fast as I did that afternoon once he opened the door. The stark possessiveness in his tone frazzled me so much, especially the foreign reaction it caused in my body. It left a wicked throb in my pussy and I fucking hated it.

He's the last man I should lust after.

No. I don't desire him.

It's only because it's been a while since I've been fucked. Been a while since I've been so close to any man, and that's all this is. A case of horniness.

Maybe I should have a one-night stand. They aren't messy, are they? I'm sure I can manage to sleep with a guy without going on a few dates first.

Then why not fuck Dash, a tiny voice taunts, and I take a deep breath.

Stop thinking about him. I mentally scold myself.

Besides, I'm mad at him for ordering me to stay away from his best friend as if he has any right. The underlying message is as flashy as his massive ego that if he can't have me, nobody else can either.

I swear I was so utterly speechless when he accused me of seducing Justin.

SCANDALOUS GAMES

And how dare he threaten to call my dad!

That was taking it too far. The only reason that kept me in his office was my job and the slight fear of him going forward with his threat. Knowing him, I knew he wasn't bluffing.

It was a miracle and also my experience dealing with asshole clients that made me go through with the rest of my meeting. Once I shift into that headspace, hardly anything affects me. The project is actually good and will add a lot of value to my portfolio. The excitement outweighs my annoyance with the man himself.

I survived him once. I'll do it again.

The loud ringing of my phone pulls me out of my musings as I sit in my home office. When my sister's name flashes, my mood sours. She had texted me a couple of times but I ignored them, not wanting to talk. Until now, she felt resentment toward me; but now, it's building in my chest. I have lunch with my parents tomorrow and I'm dreading it like the plague. Knowing I can't avoid Arya any longer before she notices, I pick up the call with a calming breath.

"Hey, Arya."

"Bi-Bianca," she stutters.

My fingers tighten around my phone when she sniffles, and my senses sharpen. "What happened, Arya? Where are you?" She sobs harder, making me worried, and I demand, "Talk to me, baby. Why are you crying?"

"Aryan br-broke up with me," she replies, hiccups lacing every syllable.

My chest hurts at the pain in her voice, and I softly ask, "But why? I thought he loved you."

"He does and that's why he did it."

"What do you mean? I don't get it," I pry, confused.

"After I talked to you that night, I realized how unfair I was to you." I sit back in shock, not at all expecting that, and continue listening. "I can't ask you to sacrifice your happiness for me by asking you to get married when you're not ready. You deserve to find love whenever it may be."

"Oh, sweetie. But I still don't understand why you two broke up."

"I told Aryan the same and we decided we'll find another way to convince our parents. That's why I was trying to reach you but you didn't return my texts. Then today, Aryan came to my house and said we need to break up because our families will never agree. It's best to part ways now than later when it'll hurt worse."

"Arya," I mumble as a tear leaks down my cheek.

"I-I begged him to stay but he wouldn't listen." She cries harder as she speaks, "But he left anyways. I ca-can't live without him, Bianca. I love him so much. You remember how I told you I wished to find my soulmate? Well, he's the one, but I can't even have h-him."

At moments like these, I wonder why we ever let ourselves be vulnerable to one single person. To give them the power to dictate our happiness.

Even when it seems perfect, it always leads us to heartbreak.

Love is nothing but messy and painful, and I'm proven right once more. The only difference is I have the power to fix it this time. It will be so easy to let my sister wallow in hurt after she told me I no longer have to help her. I have the chance to walk away unscathed, yet I can't. Because I'll regret it like so many choices in my life.

Besides, she's my little sister who I've held in my arms as a baby and vowed to protect and cherish, no matter what.

"Call Aryan and tell him he made a mistake," I say, hiding the tremble in my voice. There's nothing but silence for the longest seconds like my words shocked her or something.

"What!?" she whispers. "Why would I do that?"

"Because I've decided to get married, Ari." Just like that, I seal my fate. "I was going to tell you after I talked to Dad tomorrow."

"Are you serious?"

"Yes. So talk to Aryan and tell him not to worry about our parents."

"Oh my god!" she gasps and the happiness mixed with astonishment is evident in her tone. "Did you meet someone? Tell me it's not because of me and that you genuinely want to get married, Bianca."

"Of course, Arya," I lie as numbness sinks in. The taste of it is like poison in my mouth. "Let's just say your words gave me the push I needed."

"You mean it?"

"Yes." I sigh. "Now go win your soulmate back, baby sis."

"Thank you! Thank you! Bee. I love you."

"Love you back."

I'm about to hang up when she yells, "But wait… you didn't say if you're seeing someone."

The urge to say Dash's name screams inside me but I hold myself back. I wish I could've gone with Iris's plan because it would've solved everything. Maybe I should've tried harder to convince him, but it's too late now.

"I'll tell you everything once I've talked to Dad. Okay, Ari?"

"Fine. Maybe we can meet for dinner?"

I relax when she doesn't push. I have a feeling it's because she's eager to call Aryan. "Yeah… Dinner sounds good. I'll let you know. Bye."

Once she hangs up, I drop the phone on the desk and fight the urge to scream. Or cry. Or disappear. I can't pick, and instead sit with my head between my hands as I come to terms with the decision I've made. I console myself that I'll be fine. Maybe if I say it enough, it might become true.

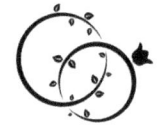

The crisp night air caresses my skin and sends a shiver down my naked back in the black minidress I'm wearing. I'm standing at the entrance of The Mirage. The gentlemen's club I visited with Rosa the last time.

My mom always said that one should never make hasty decisions when angry or when emotions are all over the place. Like mine are tonight. Because they only lead to terrible regrets, and a burden like that is heavy to carry.

SCANDALOUS GAMES

In spite of knowing it myself, I'm unable to stop as I'm about to make one more.

It's not the only lesson I learned, though. Sometimes when you've lost one battle, you need to fight another to feel strong. It's a human instinct to do so when you're pushed into a corner, and I don't know about others, but it's always helped me.

I'm risking a lot coming here. A last bold attempt. If it goes like I hope, I might just come out winning.

Well, that's if I'm allowed inside. Or my efforts to doll up will all be in vain.

I hand my keys to the valet before confidently striding toward the gates, even though deep inside I'm a nervous wreck. After the last time, I expect a security guard to appear at my side and ask me to leave or, worse, run into Nova who will surely tattle on me to Rosa.

Instead, I'm greeted politely by the guard as he opens the door, and I keep my expression neutral and confident like I have every right to be here. At a gentlemen's club.

I channel my inner Rosa and boldly walk up to the bar and settle on a stool. When the bartender approaches, I order, "One gin and tonic please."

Once he places the drink in front of me, I take a sip and let the alcohol burn down my throat. Warmth spreads through my body once it settles in my stomach. Sometimes a girl needs liquid courage, and I certainly do if I want to face Dash.

After the phone call with Arya, I could feel my walls closing in on me and panic rise inside my chest. I couldn't stop picturing what my life will turn out to be like with a strange man who I'll call my husband, with no way out. The claustrophobic feeling grew and I knew I had to try convincing Dash one last time.

Despite our mutual animosity, if he agrees, I trust him not to betray me. He may be threatening and arrogant, but I have a feeling he's a man of his word.

I'm just praying he's here tonight since it's a Saturday and I can pretend to run into him. It would be so much easier if there was something he could get out of this too. So the fake arrangement is beneficial to us both. Sadly, there isn't and that's why this makes it so much harder.

Most men have the inner instinct to be a woman's knight in shining armor. I saw it that night in Dash's eyes when I came crying to him after breaking up with Niall. Maybe it's still lying in a dark corner inside him and I can entice it to come out.

But if he asks me to beg—which he might, since he's also an asshole now—I won't do it.

There has to be a line where it becomes pathetic, and begging is it.

I stare at the wall and pray to the angels who'll listen and send me a hint or a way to accomplish my plan.

"Is the drink that bad, beautiful?" says a voice I know all too well.

I turn and look up into Justin's eyes as he hops onto the empty stool beside me. Of course, he's here. Thank fuck! I at least didn't run into him this time.

"My drink is fine," I answer with a smile.

"Then why are you scowling at it?" he asks jokingly.

Huh. I didn't realize I was thinking so hard. "I wasn't."

"If you say so, beautiful."

He's always in a cheery and flirty mood, it seems. Suddenly, I recall Dash's words that it's all a mask to hide his true feelings. If that's true, then he's a great actor. I wonder if it gets tiring to wear it all the time.

I'm the kind of person who wears her emotions on her sleeves. Sometimes, it can be a weakness when you don't want the other person to know your hidden thoughts.

"So what brings you here tonight?" he questions curiously while pointing at the bartender. I watch as the bartender brings Justin his drink—a glass of expensive whiskey—like he's done it many times. Hmm... Justin must come here a lot.

"Do you live here in the city?" I avoid his question by asking my own. He doesn't miss it but lets it go to answer.

"No, I don't," he replies, sipping his drink. "I came to visit Dash and was supposed to leave last week, but my plans changed. I take it that the meeting went well since he hired you?"

"He told you?"

"Wasn't he allowed to?" he queries.

"Nothing like that," I utter. I'm wondering if Dash also mentioned his threat. "He doesn't seem like the type who talks much, except to bark orders."

He chuckles low and I shrug innocently. Shaking his head, he smirks as he agrees, "You're right. The man is a workaholic, so it's become second nature to him."

"So I should expect him to be demanding and overbearing while we work together?"

"I'm afraid so, but something tells me you can handle him," he muses before leaning slightly closer to me. "My turn to ask questions now, beautiful. Are you here to see him?"

My cheeks heat at the bluntness of his question and going by the satisfied grin on his face, he already knows the answer. His closeness has me thinking of Dash's accusation followed by the threat he issued. However, when I accused him of being jealous, he denied it and taunted me instead.

Out of nowhere, an idea forms in my brain, which just might backfire on me if gone wrong. I also know my instincts have never steered me wrong. *Except once.* Besides, when your back is against the wall, you have nothing to lose.

Keeping my eyes pinned on a smug Justin, I slowly take a sip from my glass. Inching closer, I softly say, "Actually, I was hoping to see you."

Justin looks stunned for the first time and I have to hide my smile. It doesn't take him long to recover and the flirty expression brightens his blue eyes.

"Is that right?" he lowers his voice, running his tongue between his teeth. His tone indicates he knows I'm lying but he decides to play along.

I don't care as long as it ends up in my favor. "Yes, and you wanna know why?"

His head tilts and he shrugs. "I won't lie, I'm curious."

"Because Dash threatened me to stay away from you," I reveal while flipping my hair back. Finishing my drink, I boldly declare, "And no man tells me who I can and can't date."

SCANDALOUS GAMES

"So you want to make him jealous?"

"No. I want to teach him a lesson that his threats don't scare me." Rising from my chair, I ask him, "So the question is, are you in or not, Justin?"

"It's not even a question, beautiful." He winks and stands up, grabbing my hand as he leads me inside to the main area. "In fact, I'm more than happy to."

Chapter Fourteen

BIANCA

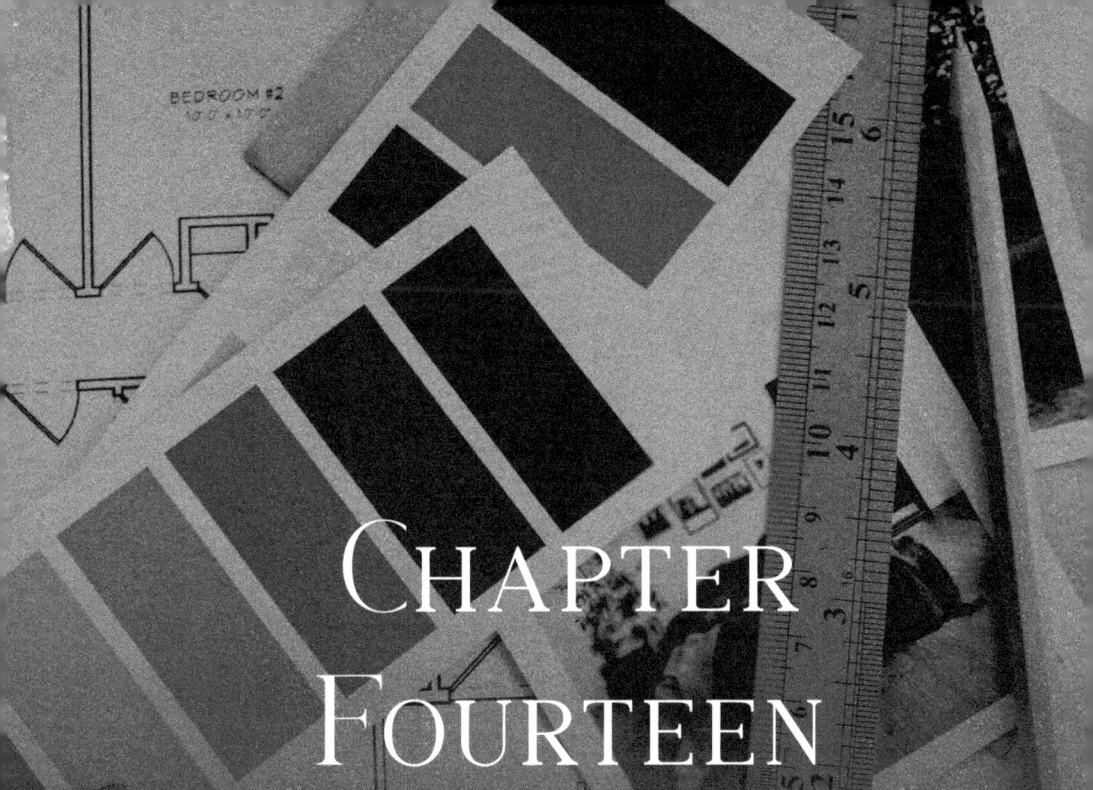

The club is still as beautiful and sexy as I remember. My eyes take in the large crowd gathered in the sitting area as men have their drinks while women sit on their arms. Their greedy fingers grip the women's thighs, some bold enough with hands underneath their skirts. Unlike last time, the debauchery is not contained to the private rooms.

It takes me only a few seconds to realize there's a party happening tonight.

Thick desire and anticipation pulses in the room. The hungry gazes, the low hum of people talking. It causes heat to rise in my belly while curiosity burns in my veins.

When I notice a makeshift stage in the center, I look at Justin questioningly, "Will there be a performance?"

His arm circling my waist pulls me closer to answer over the music and chatter. Laughter dances in his eyes like I asked something funny. "Yes, but not the kind you're thinking, and first there's going to be a bidding."

My gaze widens and I nervously ask, "Bidding for what?"

"Women."

I shudder racks through my body, unable to believe I heard him correctly. It explains why all the men are so eager and lascivious. "Isn't that illegal? Do the women know?"

SCANDALOUS GAMES

"It's all consensual and the women are aware they'll be sold for the night. Women love the fantasy while the men love the chase and the competition," he explains with a seductive grin. "The illegality of it only adds to the thrill, beautiful."

When I look around, I notice the same excitement in the women's gazes too, and I realize Justin isn't lying. They want to be up on that stage and bought by men. "So the bidding will be happening on the stage?"

"No. That's for later when the man with the highest bid fucks the girl he bought in front of everyone."

"Oh my god!" the words spill past my lips before I can stop it. Just when I think these men can't get any more depraved, they do. The shock slowly evaporates when another emotion takes root inside me and I go completely still as I blurt out, "Is Dash participating too?"

"He's done it before," replies Justin, his sharp gaze focused on my reaction. "Though I doubt he'll be doing it tonight."

My brow furrows at the insinuation and I laugh, "Why? Because of me?"

An unknown emotion flickers on Justin's face before it's gone. He pockets his hands casually and speaks in his carefree tone, "He will deny it but he wants you, Bianca."

"I-I don't believe you." I shake my head and he remains quiet.

Justin has to be wrong because if he isn't, then shouldn't Dash have said yes to my proposal? I was handing myself on a platter to him, not that I would've let him have me. Then there's also the jealousy I felt behind his threat. The madness in his eyes before he ruthlessly denied it. Could it mean that he actually wants me if I want to believe Justin?

A sudden rush of confidence bursts through me because my plan might just work. Otherwise, I'm screwed.

"Why else would he order you to stay away from me, beautiful?" he counters smugly.

"Because ever since we met again, he's enjoyed making my life hell."

Justin's shoulders shake with silent laughter and the corners of his mouth tilt up while I roll my eyes. "You're not so innocent yourself, Bianca. I've seen you challenge him back twice already. Once he sees you with me, you can expect another attack from him too."

That's what I'm counting on.

I'm lighting a fire and if I'm not careful, I'll get burned too.

I should feel guilty for using Justin without letting him know, but I don't know him well enough to trust he won't out me to his friend. But where the fuck is Dash?

"When will the bidding start?" I ask instead, not wanting to look too eager to find Dash. I'm unable to ignore the slow awareness telling me he's close and the longer I don't see him, the faster my heart beats.

As much as I want him to agree to be my fake husband, I have this need to shatter his control that has only grown over the years. I want to feel it crack and crumble.

Mostly, I ache to prove him wrong.

To make him admit he's a liar.

SIMRAN

To torture him until he admits that he's jealous at the thought of me with another man.

"It's already begun," Justin answers and I glance around, frowning at the crowd. "Where?"

"I'll show you." He takes my hand and walks toward another door I missed last time. Each step makes my spine tingle with nerves and something else I don't want to name. It's one of those moments where every sense feels heightened. The rush of stepping into the forbidden and unknown.

Justin grips the doorknob and slides it open, silently waiting for me to amble in first. My breath gets stuck in my throat at the sight in front of me as I halt in the middle of a step. I forget about Justin walking close behind me while I glance at the six women standing on separate platforms.

All of them are beautiful and naked. Locked in a mirrored glass box.

Like prized dolls for the men to stare and bid on them.

I'm so consumed by them that the rest of the world blurs as a vision of myself in the same position rocks me to my core. It's the natural curiosity to imagine, coursing through me as I wonder what it would be like.

Do they feel powerful or cheap? Hot or uncomfortable? Feel the need to run and hide?

I know I would run and as if I manifested it, I suddenly feel like turning and never returning. The room shrinks like someone sucked all the oxygen and replaced it with iciness and smoky mist.

His presence feels like a caress, the dark aura emanating from him before I see him. Every second moves in slow motion as I glance around, my eyes searching for him under the soft lights. I know that his eyes are already pinned on me, watching and relishing in my torment as he remains hidden.

His gaze feels enraged.

Foreboding.

Salivating.

And I can't decide which scares me more.

Small movements from my right side cause me to look there just as Justin's hand presses into my back. Time ceases when wild and stormy green eyes clash with my brown ones. They darken to frightening degrees when they land on his best friend's fingers circling my waist and pulling me into him. I swallow when I realize I bit more than I bargained for. A mistake I'll pay for dearly.

Dash lurks in the shadows like a predator.

His black Armani suit hugging his tense, muscular shoulders as he straightens to his full height. A glass of whiskey held between his long fingers while his thumb circles the rim back and forth. His expressive eyes—constantly taunting me—assess us while the rest of his face is hidden.

I don't need to look to know his lips are flattened into a thin line as he plots his attack.

Because it will come.

One thing I haven't forgotten is that Dash hates being defied. And I have defied him.

SCANDALOUS GAMES

Openly.
Daringly.
Fearlessly.

It brings a heady bolt of power in me while pissing him off immensely. It's screaming from his wide stance and the slow rising of his chest. Except even angry, he's controlled and calm, and his outwardly cool reaction ignites the opposite in me.

When he takes a small step, the soft lamp in the corner brings his handsome face to focus. He makes a deliberate show of sipping his drink while his lazy gaze travels over every surface of my body. I try to ignore it, but my skin reacts to his perusal and my lips part like he's stolen all my air with only a single glance.

His lips tilt the longer I—*strain to*—stay still, locked in a battle of wills with him.

Each second that passes, the more confident he becomes.

Our gazes are in a silent challenge to see who breaks first.

Instead of backing down, I decide to poke—no, *attack*—the beast by leaning against Justin's shoulder until no inch separates us. His arrogant smile falters when I bring Justin's hand to the top of my naked thigh and rest it there. I smile victoriously when his eyes drift lower, breaking our stare-off.

I don't scare easily, Dash, my eyes say with a lift of my chin when he looks up.

"Game time, beautiful," Justin whispers in my ear right before Dash crosses the room to us in a flash.

I forgot momentarily how scary and intimidating he looks up close. His size always makes me feel small even though I'm not compared to other girls. His expression hardens into steel as he stares unflinchingly at his friend while completely ignoring me.

"What the fuck is she doing here?"

"I invited her," replies Justin smoothly, unafraid.

A muscle clenches in Dash's jaw and I'm offended at the blatant way he disregards me. Like I'm not standing right here.

"He doesn't speak for me." His face whips to mine and there's no masking his emotions. The calm now wholly swallowed by the storm, while Justin's arm is the only anchor keeping me steady.

"I'm going to deal with you in a minute," he grits out in a hard voice. *"Alone."*

My pussy clenches at the lowly spoken promise and threat, all rolled into one. I blame the betrayal of my body on the sensual and salacious vibe in the room and not because of the hulking man glaring down at me.

"You're not my keeper, Dash."

"Be glad. Because if I was, you'd be chained to my bed twenty-four seven. It's the only thing stopping me from throwing you over my shoulder and stealing you away."

I gulp when he says that loud enough for Justin to hear. He can't mean it, *right?*

"Bianca isn't going anywhere, Dash," Justin warns, and I snap out of the trance Dash's words put me in. "She's my date, not yours."

"She's not even your type, you asshole."

Ouch. I hide my wince by holding my chin high and step closer to Dash. I don't shrink away from the full intensity of his undivided attention, and taunt, "I thought you never get jealous? Does this mean you lied?"

I smirk when he goes still and see Justin's proud smile from the corner of my eye.

A cruel smile graces Dash's mouth as he retorts, "Don't assume I don't know the game you're playing, kitten. Throwing yourself at Justin won't change my decision."

"Let me help you see past your big ego since you're obviously blind. I don't need you," I lie boldly. "And if I want to throw myself at Justin, there's nothing you can do about it. News flash… You're not the only man."

Dash's nostrils flare but he remains quiet while Justin steps in his path and demands challengingly, "Do you want her, Stern?"

I feel other people's curious eyes lingering on the three of us, especially on the two men. They both have equal height. Justin is slightly leaner, but no less intimidating in this second. He and Dash stand in a heated stare-off while a silent conversation takes place between them.

I yearn to question them because it's obvious that it's about me.

Dash looks like he's seconds away from punching his best friend but decides against it. Instead, he points all this aggression toward me and without looking away, sneers in a low tone, "No. You can have her."

With one scathing look at us, he turns and walks out of the room. And so goes my hope of convincing him. I underestimated the control he has over his emotions.

They are sealed way more tightly than I fathomed.

As impenetrable as a steel vault.

Chapter Fifteen

DASH

I'm going to murder my best friend.

Then I'm going to teach that little cocktease a fucking lesson for disobeying me. I should've known she wouldn't listen. After all, the sole purpose of her existence is to torture and turn my life upside down.

I swear if I tell her not to jump off a cliff, she'll do it just to piss me off. Almost like deep down she knows I'll be right behind her. Chasing her. Catching her. Never being able to resist and always making me question my morals.

Bianca isn't just dangerous.

She's as lethal as death.

My own sweet demise.

It won't be tonight, though. She'll learn not to test my limits, especially when I tell her to follow through with my orders. To never lie to me either.

I don't believe for a second she isn't here for me, no matter how much she denies it. While that clarity brings me satisfaction, the second brings trouble. Because she wasn't the only one who lied, I did too when I said I wasn't jealous.

Every inch of me is brimming with envy and possessiveness.

She doesn't realize the wounds she's opening up.

The moment she had stepped inside the room, I noticed her, looking breathtaking and sexy in her little black dress. Too little because like before, it showed more skin and curves than it concealed. I bet she doesn't have dresses in her wardrobe that won't entice and infuriate me at once.

Entice because I crave to rip it off her.

Infuriate because no other man is allowed to gaze at her but me.

I was seconds away from taking out the eyes of every man in the bidding room. It didn't matter that there were six naked women on display, Bianca had ensnared everyone's attention with a single glance. So, when I saw none other than my best friend grab her like she was his, my vision blackened in rage and a foreign emotion.

She intentionally chose him, knowing I'll react.

Her gaze was smug and satisfied when they swung to mine. It was the silent challenge in her bright eyes that made me pause and return that bold stare.

Only for the dirty vixen to up the stake.

Of course, I couldn't let her think she won so I walked away, leaving her to Justin. I told myself he wouldn't touch her but I'm doubting it now as I observe the two of them.

I seethe while they sit closely at the bar, drinking and talking. My hand clenching around my second glass of whiskey when she softly laughs at something he whispers to her. It looks so genuine that I'm taken aback. Never has she once smiled at me the same way.

All I ever received are her damn sass, defiance, and dares.

I decide I'm going to make Justin's death as painful as possible. The bastard is getting close to her despite knowing the truth and just how badly she ruined me years ago. For the longest time, I didn't care that she was innocent and blamed her with my cold, black heart.

Then, I erased her from my memory until she no longer existed.

As I watch her and feel the familiar feelings ignite, it's history repeating itself. Yet there's no stopping it. No one has ever been able to escape, so neither can we.

Nevertheless, I won't be the only one going down this time.

Bianca will be beside me as I take us both down the rabbit hole.

She remains beautifully unaware of my intentions as she continues flirting with Justin. But I know she feels my hard stare on her even though she can't catch me in the dark. Every so often, she glances in my direction and every time she fails to find me, a frown pinches her features.

The gesture was similar to that in the past when I stalked her from the shadows.

A wicked game of hide-and-seek.

I'm curious to see how far she's willing to take her little dare of making me admit I'm envious. It's a test of both of our limits until one of us snaps. I know I'm hanging on by a thread yet I want to torture myself a little bit more.

The longer she teases me, the harder her punishment is going to be.

I'm sipping my drink when a woman approaches me, the one I was planning to bid on before Bianca arrived. The only reason I was doing it in the first place was because I wanted to forget her and not because I was actually interested in the woman.

I thought a good dirty fuck would make me forget the one I truly craved.

What a fool I was.

SCANDALOUS GAMES

No one has ever been able to compare to her.

"Hi," the girl whispers shyly. She must have seen me watching her in the glass box. "Can I sit with you?"

When she slightly moves closer, the light from the lit sconce slides into my booth. She mistakes my silence for a yes and takes a seat beside me. Her full breasts, which are now covered underneath her short dress, graze my arm as she leans into my side while her hand lands on my thigh.

She certainly didn't look so bold when she stood naked.

I grab her wandering hand and I'm about to tell her to fuck off, when soft brown eyes meet mine across the room. Bianca's gaze lowers to where I'm holding the other woman and hurt flashes in her eyes for a second before it vanishes.

It's enough for the damage to be done.

"Fuck," I curse when I see defiance flash across her face as she mistakes our closeness for something else. A provocation.

She slowly rises and leans forward to whisper in Justin's ear. He nods and goes to pay the bartender while she turns to face me.

I narrow my gaze in warning because I know the mistake she's about to make. It's too late because she's already made up her mind. With a pleased smirk and a shake of her head in haughty disapproval, she breaks our eye contact and goes to defy me yet again.

Turning to the woman, I shove her hand away like she burned me but by the time I look back, both Bianca and Justin are gone. Uneasiness and darkness filters in my veins at the vision of him caressing and pleasing her. Touching her in places where I marked my claim years ago.

The girl calls my name from behind as I push past her. It might as well be white noise. A single goal consumes me as I march toward the rooms in the back. My instinct says I'll find them in the same room she found me.

Except tonight, I'm the one following her like a stalker.

The lights dim, indicating it's time for the winning couple to consummate for the hungry audience. I can't seem to give a fuck about it as I enter the hallway on my right. The few people lingering in the hallway all make their way to the stage until I'm alone.

A low moan pierces my ear just as my gaze locks on their silhouettes. My fingers curl into fists as I close the distance. Each step feels a little too late.

I halt as I round the corner.

Red.

It's all I see and feel running in my veins. Blazing hot jealousy boils inside me, the flames igniting and making me want to burn her with it. Such a petty emotion yet it makes grown men crumble. Makes them want to destroy the world, kill each other. I claimed myself to be above it but, as it turns out, I'm no different.

Only when it comes to her.

First, it was because of my stepbrother and now... my best friend.

She stills for a fraction of a second, sensing my presence like she was waiting for my arrival. If I wasn't so attuned and staring so closely, I would've missed it. Ever so slowly, hooded brown eyes slide to mine and roam over me before turning away.

The action, conveying without words that I'm unwanted.

Replaceable.

That I'm interrupting her slutty little rebellion.

I try to remain impassive and cold but I'm not made of stone, no matter how hard I try. My body vibrates with violence as she sits on Justin's lap while his fingers grip her thighs, thumb rubbing back and forth. Every part of her body that he touches, I want to replace and mark with my teeth, imprint her skin and make her scream.

Until I'm the only one she feels.

Justin doesn't seem to notice me while caressing her soft skin. And why wouldn't he? The bastard has the sexiest woman alive writhing on his lap. And I served her ripe to him for the taking.

My first and last mistake.

He stays still in a trance, while she boldly grips his shoulders and grinds on his leg. The friction against her cunt makes a loud moan escape from her lips as she throws her head back. I can't tell if she's actually aroused by him or putting on a show for me.

I'll bet my soul on the latter.

Well played, kitten.

Her bared throat is begging for my hand to be wrapped around it, as I cut off her airway for being so close yet out of my reach. For making me feel like I'm dying. I just might if she doesn't stop taking her pleasure from my best friend.

I lose the last of my senses as her head lowers like she's about to kiss him. The fucker won't be the first to taste her lips before me. An intimacy she never allowed me. Like I didn't deserve and had to earn it.

My stepbrother sure as hell didn't deserve it, yet I saw her give him dozens of kisses.

It was tortuous. An inescapable nightmare.

It's the same feeling rising like a tide as her small hands cup Justin's face. The thread holding me together finally snaps and I bark a fraction of a second before their mouths are about to touch.

"Enough."

Chapter Sixteen

DASH

Both of them halt, their lips still inches apart as my voice cuts through the air.

"Get away from him, kitten."

I exhale only when she leans away from him but continues to move her hips slowly. My fists clench when one of the straps of her dress falls dangerously low on her slender shoulder.

"You're interrupting us again, Dash," she retorts, without looking my way.

Fucking brat.

She will pay for every second she remains glued to him.

Justin finally meets my furious gaze with a smirk of his own and shrugs innocently. I'll be dealing with him later. That is *if* he comes out of this alive. Taking a threatening step forward, I harshly order her again, "Get the fuck off his lap before I kill him because of you."

She stills but doesn't move to follow my command despite the threat I have every intention of making a reality. Something she foolishly and defiantly ignores as she meets my gaze while Justin intelligently stays quiet. His amusement, however, is unmistakable.

"Kitten," I warn, my voice on edge.

"Stop growling orders at me." Her head whips toward mine and she says angrily,

SIMRAN

"I am not yours."

Time freezes as her claim leaves a ringing in my ears. *Such wrong words to utter, kitten.* Even Justin tenses from the corner of my eye, knowing just how dangerous of a trigger they are for me.

In a flash, I'm across the room. She doesn't get a chance to react before I'm hauling her off of his lap. Her small fists connect with my chest. They don't even penetrate past my clothes and I capture them in my hand in a vise grip.

I drag her farther inside the room, away from him.

"Leave," I tell Justin, who wisely listens and doesn't argue.

Bianca stares at his back like he betrayed her before her eyes flick back to mine, breathing fire. Underneath her gaze lies a drugging blend of lust and satisfaction, like she was waiting for this moment. Yearning for me to snatch her from my best friend.

To fight the only person I call family.

I can't decide which one of us should be more scared. Her for the destruction she has coming her way if she wisely doesn't stay away, or me for being so weak and self-sabotaging when it comes to her.

As I stare at her, I'm as impressed as I'm mad that the little vixen took it this far. When in reality, I should be disappointed that I lost so easily. My control is as slippery as sand at this point.

None of it compares to the rapture running in my veins at having her all to myself. But then she opens her mouth, spoiling my momentary bliss.

"You ruined my date."

That damn haughty lilt to her voice gets me every time. Freeing her wrists, I grab her ass and pull her onto her tiptoes. Our harsh breaths fill the narrow space.

"What part of 'stay away from him' did you not understand, kitten?" I demand, leaning into her face and crumpling her dress between my fingers. The material is so soft and thin that my hands twitch to tear it off her. "And stop calling it a date when we both know the truth."

"What part of I'm not your business didn't you understand?"

"That's where you're wrong, kitten," I growl. "You are my fucking business."

"Since when?"

"Since you crashed back into my life." A dark shiver runs down her spine that I feel underneath my palm. Inching my fingers up, I wrap my fist around her silken hair and yank her head back. "So when I tell you to do something, you obey."

"Or what?" she taunts.

I push her backward and throw her on the couch instead of replying. I'd rather show her I'm a man of action and my threats aren't empty.

Her excuse of a dress rides up her thighs, giving me a glimpse of her lace panties. But when I stare at her, all I see are Justin's hands on her skin.

And the vision of her pussy grinding on his lap.

Him breathing the same air as her.

My face must betray my violent thoughts because she licks her soft lips while backing away. I predict her move at the same second she jumps and runs in the opposite direction. I catch her around the waist, her back colliding with my chest

SCANDALOUS GAMES

as I carry her with one arm to the couch.

Addicted to her scent, I inhale roughly while taking her earlobe between my teeth. The sound of her soft whimper shoots straight to my cock when I bite down hard. "Run again and I'll fuck you on that stage after I catch you."

She shudders violently as if the vision I painted is thrilling her.

"Yo-you wouldn't."

"You let another man touch you, Bianca. Maybe you'll like it when they watch you too," I murmur, licking the column of her throat.

When she doesn't answer, I push her face down on the couch and spread her thighs to situate myself between them. Her hips buck against my hard length pressing into her tight ass. Pulling her head up with my grip on her hair, I demand, "Tell me... do you want to be fucked in a room full of strange men? Their lusty eyes on your cunt as it stretches around my cock, and your tits shaking from the force of my thrusts while they wish it were them instead? Answer me, kitten."

I tug at her hair when she closes her eyes. Her tongue wets her bottom lip before she utters, "Says the man who wouldn't even let me get close to his best friend."

My cock hardens painfully at her sassy taunt while my stunned silence makes her bold.

"The same man who threatened to murder him if I didn't get away. You become mad when I talk to other men, Dash, let alone touch. And you're telling me that you can handle them seeing me naked, writhing and moaning your name, when you all but think I belong to you?"

There's a tightening in my chest when she whispers the last words because a part of me knows she'll never be truly mine. The reminder feels like a stab in my gut. Maybe I can have her for just one night despite knowing it'll never be enough.

I have to purge her out of my system.

"You don't belong to me," I angrily reply.

She isn't deterred and pushes her hips into mine. "Then let me go back to Justin."

"No." The sound emerges from deep inside me.

"Make a choice, Dash, because I'm sick of your mind games. At least with him, I know what I'm in for."

"Fucking hell, Bianca."

"Admit you were jealous," she demands, her confidence rising as she feels my stubbornness crumbling. Where the fuck has all this sass come from? It both turns me on and makes my blood run cold with annoyance.

When she grinds against my dick and moans loudly, I dip my head between her shoulder and neck. I bite her collarbone when the scent of her arousal hits my nostrils.

"Dash," she cries when I suck harder instead of freeing her skin from between my teeth. Like a masochist, the pain only ignites her desire. It doesn't seem to distract her because she whispers, "Say you lied about not wanting to fuck me again."

"Damn it, woman," I curse, pushing off of her.

I run my hands through my hair, trying to stay strong and not give in to her pull. Once I say it out loud, she gets all the power and there will be no taking it back. She turns on her back and I wait for hurt to flicker in her face but she stares back softly, like a breathing temptation and a seductress.

"Does admitting the truth scare you, Mr. Stern?" she taunts, head tilted.

If she knew the half of it, she wouldn't be seducing me with her come-hither eyes, dress shoved up to her waist and soaked panties on display. Her pussy is so bloody wet that the material outlines her folds. My mouth waters to part her slit and lick her juices.

It's starving to know if she still tastes the same.

"How far were you planning to take it with him, kitten?" I ask, lifting my gaze to hers.

I observe her as she chooses whether to answer me or continue her little agenda. It's like we're stuck in a dance of tango, circling and circling but neither of us giving in fully.

The push and pull.

The thick tension, killing us both slowly.

"You shouldn't have stopped," she says with a tilt of her lip and shrugs. "Because now you'll never know."

"You were going to kiss him," I state, the accusation cutting through the air.

Slowly, her gaze lowers to my mouth and her tongue peeks out to bite the corner of her lips. When her pupils dilate like she's helplessly wondering what I'll taste like, I draw closer to her.

A moth to a flame.

A predator to its prey.

A thirsty man to an oasis.

When I rest my hands on either side of her hips, crowding her, she stares at me from below and muses, "Maybe, and then I would've let him fuck me…" A low growl escapes my lips, which makes her smile. "Or maybe I knew you'd chase him away before I could, Dash."

My cock jerks painfully at the sweet purr in her voice and I grab the backs of her spread knees and yank her to the edge. A surprised yelp spills from her mouth as I slap them wider and lower to my haunches.

"You're really proud of yourself, aren't you, kitten?" I hum, placing soft kisses along her left thigh.

"Of course," she teases. "I brought you to your knees."

"And that gives you power?"

"Doesn't it?"

"Not even close," I whisper just as I dig my teeth into her skin where Justin held her. Back bowing from the pain, she cries out and grips my hair, pushing me back. I enjoy the bite of her fingers pulling at my strands and suck the spot on her thigh hard.

I'm savage as I do the same to her other thigh while she chokes out, "Dash… Please."

The way she screams sounds like she's in pain but the wetness leaking and glistening on her panties say the opposite.

SCANDALOUS GAMES

I become dizzy from the scent of her arousal, her moans, and the way her whole body writhes. The sight of her soft tits shaking so wildly as she shakes side to side, makes me imagine them doing the same when I make her ride my dick.

"Fuck... Dash. I can't take it anymore."

"Yes, you will because neither could I while seeing you in his arms since the second you walked in with him," I growl, my voice not sounding like my own. "Every part of you that he touched, felt, enjoyed... I'm going to mark with my teeth."

Blush darkens her high cheekbones as she gazes down at me and licks her lip before murmuring, "He didn't touch me anywhere else."

Her voice is a little breathless and inviting.

"Didn't he, though?" I arch my brow and cup her pussy tightly. "You rubbed your cunt all over him, Bianca." Her eyes widen in fear and arousal as I push her panties to the side and lick my lips. "I ought to mark you here too."

"Don't you dare."

I tsk when she attempts to close her legs and place my shoulders in between, so she can't close them. An electric shiver courses through her when I lower my mouth to her core, hovering but not touching. She moans when I inhale deeply despite the slight embarrassment I sense in her.

"Remember this the next time you dare to test me." I grunt and lick her slit before I bite it hard enough so she feels the sting and still craves it. Her juices taste like an expensive candy I could become addicted to.

Jesus. Her flavor is just like I remember.

"Oh fuck. fuck." She thrashes wildly. "Dash... Ah."

I'm taken back to that night as I suck on her pussy lips until they're swollen and reluctantly pull away before I forget it's her punishment, not pleasure.

When I look up, her hand covers her mouth to keep from moaning or screaming my name. I crawl over her body and when I lower her arm, I become stuck on a lone tear that escapes down her cheek.

She watches, mesmerized, as I lean down and kiss it away. When I pull back, we've both traveled back to seven years ago when I replaced all her tears with soft kisses until she melted in my arms.

The moment feels awfully sweet and romantic but I'm none of those things. I never will be. So before we fall into dangerous territory, I shove her wrists above her head to give her the only two things I'm capable of.

Pain and pleasure.

I watch her pupils dilate as I trap and hold her immobile. Her nipples harden into tight peaks that beg for my mouth. With my free hand, I trace around her tight bud and slowly slide my fingers lower until I'm met with the soft skin of her thigh.

"Dash," she whispers, restless and horny.

I tease and rub back and forth before inching them underneath her dress. I stop just short of her wet heat, leaving her in torment. I groan when I feel wetness on her inner thighs. The little cocktease got so wet tormenting me that it dripped out.

Deep down, I know it's all for me.

Still, I won't be satisfied until she says it.

"Were you wet for him, kitten? Did you leave a spot on his thigh when you were grinding like a slut?" I demand, my dirty words arousing her. "Is he walking around with your scent on his skin?"

"I... I... don't know," she lies and whimpers when I pinch the inside of her thigh.

"Or was it because of me? Did your cunt weep at the thought of torturing me, maddening me? Did you wish it were me instead?"

A deep blush covers her cheeks while each inhale and exhale of her breath brings our lips closer. I yearn to kiss and ravage her mouth because it was the one thing she didn't allow me that night. The taste and softness of her lips.

The rush of our tongues dueling.

Oh how I craved to steal the kiss that she kept denying.

"Why do you care, Dash?" Her voice sounds almost hurt while her eyes glint sharply. "You told Justin to have me. Don't get mad that I let him when you all but pushed me into his arms."

My heart aches to tell her I didn't mean it but the words won't come out. I shouldn't care about her damn feelings. I bury my conflicting emotions by hardening my expression.

"You started this little game, kitten." My taunting voice causes her to grit her teeth and she pushes against my hold. I pinch her again until she stills but breathes harshly. "Now, I'm going to make you regret it."

"The hell you will."

"I told you there will be consequences if you don't listen."

Her legs kick out when I pull us up with my grip on her arm. I smile as she tries to slap my hands away but I easily maneuver her onto her knees. Her wrists once again trapped behind her back.

I circle my arm around her heavy tits and pull her flush against my chest. Slapping her thighs, I part them wide until cool air caresses her exposed cunt, making her tremble. Inching my fingers between them, I rip her useless panties with a flick and circle her clit twice.

"Fuck!" she moans like she hasn't been touched in ages. It makes me curious.

"When was the last time you were fucked, kitten?"

"None of your business," she forces out past the pleasure coursing through her. Her favorite words while the exact opposite for me. Despite it, I don't miss the slight embarrassment in her tone.

I smile when I realize the truth, feeling relieved and thrilled at the thought.

"How long since you had a cock inside you?" She doesn't answer, so I still my fingers rubbing on her slit, and coax, "Your pussy is screaming it's desperate to be filled. Tell me, baby."

"Fuck you, Dash."

Slap. Slap. Slap.

Her cries of shock and pleasure drown my ears when I spank her pussy rapidly. My cock hardens even more at the wet sound her pussy makes as it connects with my palm each time. My pleasure spikes when the evidence of her enjoying the harsh slaps lands on my fingers.

"Oh god!" She pants in shock, body going lax. When I flick and pinch her sensitive clit, she tries to shut her legs, but it only traps my hand.

SCANDALOUS GAMES

"Such a perfect girl taking her spanking so well."

"You fucking asshole! I can't believe yo—" *Spank.* "S-stop doing that."

"Keep bad-mouthing me and I won't stop," I scold harshly. "You still haven't answered my questions, kitten."

"Oh, so you can skirt the truth but I can't?" Most girls would give in after a harsh spanking, yet the one in my arms keeps asking for more with her steel determination.

"You don't know the floodgate you're opening, Bianca," I warn. "Or the monster you're inviting."

Unafraid and bold, she arches her back and raises her hand to wrap around the back of my neck while the other sneaks over mine resting over her pussy. I almost come in my pants when she guides my fingers to her entrance, pushing the tips inside, and whispers, "I already let you in a long time ago, Dash. It's too late for the warning, don't you think?"

The feeling when you realize you're in real trouble yet can't do shit, it's the same rushing through me at her confession. Before I can thrust my fingers inside, she catches me off guard and shoves my hand away, slipping from underneath me.

She steps out of my reach, shaking her head when I make a grab for her. It'll take nothing for me to yank her back but the expression on her face holds me back. I watch as her lips purse and she says, "But I'm still going to end this little game. You don't get to interfere in my life and then not tell me the reason."

"You know what's funny, kitten?" I rise to my full height and stalk closer, making her neck tilt. "You want me to admit my feelings yet you yourself won't give me the full truth."

I smirk viciously when her confidence falters. We both know she's not just here to prove me a liar and punish me in her own perfect way.

It's another last attempt to make me her fake husband.

A bold plan but fuck if it's not working.

Our gazes remain locked in a silent war as I wait patiently for her to either deny or simply walk. I gloat thinking I have all the power, but I fume when she crushes it with a finality.

"You're right... somewhat," she says, smirking. "I'm still going with my plan, but I didn't come here for you. I was going to ask Justin, an idea you gave me, by the way. But making you jealous... Well, that was just the icing on the cake."

"You're lying."

"I'm still going to ask him."

"The fuck you will," I growl, my mood darkening. "Come. Here."

"No." She shakes her head and turns around to leave.

Once again I'm thrown back to the night I saw her for the first time in my bedroom and then watched her leave with Niall—just like right now to someone else. An urgency like never before spreads through me and every single thought turns to dust except the thought of not letting her walk away.

"I wasn't jealous seeing you with him, Bianca." My guttural and raw voice stills her just as she reaches the hallway. "I was in pain."

I cross the distance and take her hand in mine, slowly turning her around to face me. Tilting her head back, I cup her cheek and let it all out. "Every single smile, every word, every touch that you gave him freely made me see and bleed red. It was a constant battle inside my head to not care, to not stare and not have you all to myself."

Everything I say is the truth, except I wasn't talking about Justin.

And she doesn't even realize it.

"Dash."

"But I still can't marry you," I utter. "Even if it's fake and a sham."

Chapter Seventeen

BIANCA

His rejection—once more—douses cold water all over my burning body. The splash, stinging twice as painful.

I don't understand why this refusal is hurting more now than the last time. It doesn't matter that I was prepared. Yet it keeps burning me from the inside out.

All because of his overwhelming confession.

The raw honesty leaves me too stunned to speak except his name. I sought after the truth, chased it ruthlessly the whole night and instead of feeling victory, I feel loss. Yeah, he admitted to being jealous and I should be reveling in it, but the emotion it held was so much more.

Or maybe I'm just imagining it.

This is Dash. Cold and unemotional. It has to be another one of his mind games.

He continues to stare intensely, watching my face for a reaction, but I slowly back away, making his hand fall to the side. The moment breaks, a wall building between us, and with it comes his perfectly practiced mask.

I hate how easily he puts himself back together and buries his emotions like a flip of a switch. The only evidence of the last few minutes is the wrinkling of his suit and hair in disarray from when I pulled on the strands.

While I'm still struggling to erase it and calm my wildly beating heart.

SIMRAN

With each second, his iciness starts soaking into me, making goosebumps rise on every surface of my skin where he savagely left his marks in places that are still throbbing.

Even if I want to forget all about tonight, I can't because I'm going to be feeling him for days. If it was his intention, he succeeded.

My body keeps tingling whereas my mind is rapidly accepting the consequence of his denial and the only reason I came here in the first place. Desolation sinks in that despite everything going my way, it didn't lead to the conclusion I ached for. I'm once again stuck with the saddest and painful reality of marrying for real.

I feel so silly for pinning all my hope on Dash.

But mostly, I'm disappointed in myself.

I'm torn between wanting to save the rest of my dignity by telling him I didn't actually come here to sway his decision before he cruelly answered. I open my mouth to say the same but I can't find it in me to lie. He knows me too well and I would rather stand by my choice than deny and run like a coward.

I also know we can't go on like this.

The frustrating push and pull, the fight and the taunts. Especially ending up alone in the dark corners and *almost fucking*. It has to stop and I only see it happening one way.

"We can't work together, Dash."

There's a lingering pause when I hold my breath and it whooshes out of me when he nods while pocketing his hand. "No, we can't."

My mood sours even more at him agreeing so casually. It leaves me surprised because I honestly expected him to disagree or fight or threaten me like he's done till now.

And why does it sting yet again? And why do I keep expecting him to suddenly have a humbling heart when mine isn't even on the table?

If he's giving mixed signals, then I'm not doing any better.

I'm just as much at fault as he is.

"I'll find you a replacement or give recommendations for your project on Monday," I say, unable to handle his intense stare and silence.

"Bianca," he sighs.

"I'm leaving," I say, cutting him off. "Goodbye Dash."

He made his choice and the last thing I need is pity from him, which I can sense pouring off him. His lips press into a thin line and it only makes him look hotter instead of repulsive.

"I'll walk you out," he says firmly. "Come on."

I step back and shake my head. "No, thanks. I know the way well by now."

He ignores my words and grabs my hand roughly before pulling us in a different direction to the one I came in. I protest, tugging my hand, but he tightens his grip and stares down at me. "The crowd tends to get wild on a party night, so there's no chance I'm letting you leave alone. Got it?"

"But you're going in the wrong direction, Dash."

I trail after him, trying to keep up with his long stride as he explains, "There's a private elevator. I'm taking you there."

SCANDALOUS GAMES

As soon we reach it, he presses the button and tugs me inside when the door opens. The enclosed space feels ten times smaller and cozier with just us two as it begins to ride upward. My heart races uncontrollably when he continues to hold my palm in his big one. His thumb is grazing back and forth, almost like he's unaware and can't help himself.

He does it so effortlessly like he's been doing it for years.

With each pass of his calloused finger, I'm lulled into a trance and warmth spreads through me. He keeps staring ahead, expression locked so I can't read and steal his thoughts.

Does he realize gestures like these only fuck with my head?

They throw me for a loop and I'm left confused with my body's reaction. Still, I can't find it in me to yank my hand away.

Afraid of drawing attention and interrupting the soft touch, I take in our reflection in the mirror instead. My lips look swollen from trying not to scream, cheeks flushed as if I was fucked to within an inch of my life, while my hair is no better. But what causes a low throb in my core are the purple hickeys his lips left on my thighs.

I trace them with my fingers before I can stop myself, not caring about the fact that he could be watching.

Just like that, my mind wanders back to his possessive touch, the dark raging desire in his gaze as he growls and punishes me. The pleasurable pain when he ruthlessly bit my pussy. The action was savage and barbaric yet I wasn't appalled.

It only heightened the ecstasy I felt and had he not stopped, I would've come just from it. And just when I thought it was over, he spanked my pussy. Hard. Viciously. Mercilessly. The sharp sting spreads into heat, and I bite my lip when a whimper tries to escape.

The sudden urge to close my thighs has me shifting nervously on my feet.

I had never known a man could become so consumed with lust and madness until him.

That jealousy could be such a powerful drug.

After experiencing this side of him, I feel robbed that he didn't dominate me like this the night he took my virginity. He was commanding and possessive back then too, but there was also a reverence in the way he claimed me.

I'm so lost in my treacherous thoughts when I realize his thumb has paused and as the haze wears off, I'm met with his piercing and knowing eyes. They lower to where I'm clutching my dress and I instantly let go.

My cheeks heat at getting caught red-handed for having dirty daydreams about him.

Before I can make any more mistakes, the elevator stops and opens to the lobby. Perfect timing. I breathe easy and take a step but he pulls me back, blocking my way.

I frown when he says, "Wait."

My lips part as he carefully removes his suit jacket, his muscles making my mouth water. I hate the treacherous thought that saddens me at not getting the chance to explore his hard body. He was always in good shape but now he's become impossibly broader and a hardened version of his younger self.

SIMRAN

Does he still roam around shirtless at his house? The question sparks from the memory of him doing it in the past. Every time I ran into him when I used to visit Niall, Dash was always walking around half naked. Sometimes, I believe he did it to torture and annoy me on purpose.

A satisfied smirk would stretch across his lips each time he caught me staring.

I blink and focus back on him while trying not to melt when he wraps his jacket around my shoulders. His scent envelops me in an invisible embrace while the rest of me is dwarfed. Instead of letting me go immediately, he untucks my hair from beneath the collar so it spills down my back.

Grabbing the ends in the middle, he pulls me closer and tilts my face with his finger on my jaw and rasps, "My marks on you are only for my eyes. Understand?"

"Okay," I mumble.

Only after I've agreed, did he move aside and take me outside of the building while holding my hand once more.

Okay. He has to know he's being sweet. For a man who claims to be a monster and against marrying me, he's sure being romantic and protective.

Curious eyes in the lobby stay hooked to us as we make our way to the valet stand at the front. The young guy on duty sees me and approaches with a smile as if he recognizes me from before. However, as soon as he notices Dash stepping in his line of vision, his gait falters and a terrified expression shadows his features.

I can't see Dash's face but intimidation and fury roll off him in waves. My eyes widen when he says in a dark tone, "Eyes off her, if you'd still like to keep your job."

"M-Mr. Stern," the valet stutters. "Sorry. I didn't know she was with you."

"I'm not," I mutter and step around Dash so I'm not standing behind him. Narrowing my gaze, I tell him, "He was being polite. Something you ought to learn."

"My impoliteness wasn't an issue when you were soaking and riding my fingers, kitten."

My cheeks tingle in embarrassment when he says it loudly, making sure the other guy hears. Looks like it's working because he is now staring awkwardly at his shoes as if it's the most interesting thing in the world. Dash arches his brow arrogantly while crossing his arms, and informs me with a tilt of his head, "And I was polite when I didn't offer to kick him out of the city for smiling at you."

"Your definition of polite is really screwed, Dash."

"As long as it keeps other men away from you."

"Oh, yeah?" I chuckle mockingly, shaking my head. "How's that gonna work when I'll be married soon?"

A muscle tics in his square jaw while his pupils darken dangerously. "You won't be my problem then," he replies before barking at the valet, "Bring her car around."

His broody attitude makes me want to throw his jacket at his face but I hold back the urge. Only because it's cold outside and not because I secretly crave to have a keepsake of his.

Or that his scent is far too addictive. Smokey and all him.

And definitely not because his gaze keeps flickering down my body every few seconds.

SCANDALOUS GAMES

The longer it takes for my car to arrive, the more the air crackles around us as we stand alone on the quiet street. The half-moon plays peekaboo from between the clouds and I wish I could enjoy the beauty, but my mind begins to worry about tomorrow.

I wish for time to come to a standstill.

Wish for the night to not end.

Because once morning comes, my life will forever change. Just like the moon... Pretty from afar but filled with black scars upon closer inspection.

The smooth rumbling of my car pulls me back to the present and Dash places his palm on my waist to guide me forward. The valet lets the engine run and steps out. The jacket falls down one of my shoulders as I bend to get inside.

Dash's fingers graze my bare collarbone when he rights it before it can fall off completely, making my breathing quicken. His hand lingers a little longer before he finally straightens and shuts the door.

Without a goodbye or a backward glance, he turns around and walks out of my life.

Even when I lay down on my bed hours later, his scent and marks still linger on my skin.

Chapter Eighteen

BIANCA

Sundays always reminded me of cozy and happy memories. It used to be my favorite day of the week growing up because it was the one day where my whole family, including my grandparents, would spend time together. It could be going on a day-long trip, a movie night, or simply a picnic in the park.

Arya and I would wake up early and excitedly in the morning and help Mom with the preparations while Dad would finish his important meetings so he wouldn't be disturbed later.

It continued to be a tradition—the one I actually loved—until my grandparents passed away in an unfortunate accident. The tragedy hardened my dad.

Our Sundays went from being together to everyone being in their own separate rooms.

Their deaths caused a crack in our family that could never be filled or repaired.

Today, the same premonition courses through me as I drive to lunch with my parents. I can already envision the matching disapproving scowls on their faces for avoiding them for weeks. In truth, I've been mentally preparing myself. I just know my father would give me a lecture. My mother, on the other hand, will most likely guilt-trip me with passive remarks.

They aren't bad parents and I do love them with all my heart, but it becomes

SCANDALOUS GAMES

hard to get along when our thinking and values are poles opposites apart. They see the world as black and white and fitted in a box. If you dare to step outside of it, it's wrong and unacceptable.

The moment I tell them I'm ready for marriage, only then will they finally be proud of me.

Just how sad is that?

I remind myself that I'm doing this for Arya once I reach the upscale family restaurant. I had sent my mom a text so I know they'll be here already since the place is closer to their house. Parking my car, I grab my purse and stride to the hostess stand.

Families and a few couples sit on tables around me and their soft murmurs, blending with music, prickles my ears. Usually, the ambience, poolside view, and open sky brightens up my mood but right now, it isn't.

The cool air coming from the pool on my right teases my arms and I'm glad I wore a halter neck and frayed denims so my legs are covered. I didn't expect the weather to be a little chilly this morning. The hostess guides me to my dad's private table which is always kept reserved for him on Sundays.

My shaky hand automatically drifts to my hair to push it away, but I bring it back down, knowing Dad hates it when I'm fidgety. One should always be calm and composed, no matter the situation. At least, that's what my father drilled into Arya and me.

It has helped me more times than I can count but when I'm overstressed, the bad habit sneaks in.

"Bianca, beta." My mom's soft voice greets me as soon as I round the corner.

As always, she is elegantly dressed in a light blue pantsuit without a hair out of place. My dad is sitting beside her with his coffee in one hand and tablet in another. He's never not working and the effect is starting to show by the stress lines marring his forehead. Even so, he doesn't seem to show any signs of slowing down.

"Hi, Ma." I smile and lean down to hug her while she remains seated. Turning to Dad, I greet him, "Good morning, Papa."

"How nice of you to finally find time for your parents, Bianca."

"Veer," my mom scolds at his disapproving tone.

"I'm sorry, Papa." I sigh, taking a seat across from them. "I was busy with work. I thought you'll understand."

"I always make time for my family."

The urge to remind him that he may have been with us physically but his mind was always stuck on business has me biting my tongue. Instead, I take a sip of my water until the impulse washes away.

"Enough about work," says my mom, trying to lighten the mood. "Did you hear Saranya's older daughter got engaged? I hear the boy is from a good business family."

No 'how have you been, Bianca?' Or 'why have you been distant lately?' And 'did anything exciting happen to you?'

It only ever circles back to marriage, whether it's about mine or any daughter of one of her random friends. Lately, it's all she wants to gossip about as if it'll entice or guilt me into saying yes. Like it's a race I'm losing.

If she knew that it only takes Arya's heartbreak to convince my mind to marry, she would've done it a long time ago.

My dad, who usually avoids partaking in her gossip, says, "He was interested in our Bianca and would have been a perfect match. At this rate, hardly a good match will be left for you."

The last part was directed to me and it takes years of practice not to shrink under his gaze. He even rests his tablet on the side so I don't miss the severity of his statement. My mom nods her head in agreement from beside him.

It's like being faced against two determined bulls with no chance of survival.

I feel like I'm reduced to a prized possession that they can't wait to get rid of. Oftentimes, I wonder if I'm just a liability to my father that he wants to pass forward before I lose my value. And right now, it seems like his comment is proof enough of that.

The most hurtful is them, especially Mom, not even caring to ask if I'm ready or if there's a reason behind my reluctance. All that matters is their reputation in society while my sentiments are irrelevant.

Well, it doesn't really matter now anyway.

Their lifelong wish is about to come true.

"Your father means well, sweetie," Mom explains before asking, "Did you see the profiles of the boys I sent from Priya Aunty? There are some great matches. Maybe you could meet one of them."

Priya Aunty is a matchmaker my parents hired despite me saying no several times to search for the love of my life. She's another woman besides my mom who's even more eager for my marriage. After all, I'm the only one standing between her and a hefty fee if she succeeds in her matchmaking.

At least, one of us will be having a happy day because until now, I had no intention of touching that list.

"It's actually the reason I wanted to meet you both." My tone instantly sparks an excited glint in my mom's gaze. Though she tries to hide it, it's unmistakable. My dad, on the other hand, only watches with an unreadable expression. "Well, I've decided t—"

I trail off when a shadow falls over our table, stealing my parents' attention.

"Hi, wifey."

The low and husky voice raises goosebumps on my arms and my heart stops beating for a second when I look up to meet Dash's soft green eyes. The color is so light under the morning sunlight that I'd be able to see my reflection if he was just a breath closer.

His hair, which is slightly longer in the middle, falls onto his forehead, softening his edges only marginally, while my own eyes devour his dashing and masculine beauty in a three-piece suit. Navy blue, which only brings out the color of his eyes, seems to be his favorite color.

Black sunglasses hang from his suit pocket while his muscles are barely confined and hidden beneath his expensive clothes. I'm still admiring every little detail about him when his words hit me like a freight train.

SCANDALOUS GAMES

He called me wifey. Wifey! What the fuck!

Wait… Did he change his decision?

My eyes widen both in shock and confusion, much like my parents, whom I can sense are going through the same emotions as me. Well, minus the drooling over Dash part.

"Dash." His name is a breathless whisper on my tongue.

As if he can sense my inner turmoil from my voice, he takes the lead before I blow our cover. I try to process what is happening internally, but many freaking questions seem to be fighting to come out to the surface.

"Sorry I'm late, my love," he softly speaks before bending down to take my palm and kissing the back of it as he sits down on the empty chair beside me. The movement is effortless and natural like we've done it a million times. "Still getting used to the traffic."

My love. Jesus. Is this how he flirts when he's being nice? I have to be dreaming that this is the same man I've been chasing and fighting my lust over the past few weeks. The man from yesterday might as well be a figment of my imagination.

A disillusion.

A dream.

The smile on his rugged face feels way too real. The possessiveness in his eyes, too tangible. His acting skills are too genuine.

I can't decide which version of him made my heart race faster and my skin shivering.

"Who is he, Bianca?"

"Why is he calling you his wife?"

My dad and mom ask at the same time as they gather their bearings. His voice is an angry lash while hers is a bewildered whisper. Their gazes, however, hold the same horror.

"I'm Dash Stern. Your daughter's fiancé," Dash confidently replies. Our joined hands are resting on his thigh while he lays his other arm on the back of my chair. His fingers lazily graze my upper arm while I stare between him and my parents mutely. "Nice to finally meet you, Mr. and Mrs. Chopra."

My dad bristles, nostrils flaring, and ignoring him as he demands from me, "Is this true? When and why did you get engaged without telling us?"

"Very true and real, sir," Dash replies, unperturbed by my dad's blatant disregard of him. His voice, proud and unflinching. Laced with an unspoken message saying he's not so easily dismissed. He pauses until my father meets his gaze before continuing, "I'm afraid it's all my fault. I proposed to Bianca last night because I couldn't wait to make her mine. The heart wants what it wants, timing be damned."

"And you didn't think her parents' blessing mattered?" my dad questions.

"It's her heart and the rest of her life I'm after. She's going to be my wife no matter what." The possessiveness in his words floors me. He deliberately lets his declaration simmer in the air before adding, almost as an afterthought, "With all due respect."

My father doesn't visibly react but I feel him sizing Dash up silently. His expression settles into the one he poses in front of his colleagues and rivals alike.

Make no mistake, he is angry having been spoken back to by Dash, but there's also no denying he's just as impressed.

Had Dash cowered—an impossibility—he wouldn't be sitting here. I've seen most men shrink in front of my dad, so a stranger standing up to him is a true show of integrity and strength in his eyes. Especially if the said man is going to be his future son-in-law.

Even if it's fake and until Arya is married.

Although this is only the tip of our carefully crafted lie, we would be under the laser focused microscope of my family, who will be searching for the tiniest of cracks. A tear, to be exact. It'd be nothing short of scandalous if we got busted.

"Bianca," my mom sharply says, yanking me back to the present. "Tell us this isn't true."

I'm taken aback by her sullen mood, and guilt settles in the pit of my stomach when I see hurt flash across her eyes.

"It is." My voice sounds scratchy and raw like someone squeezed my neck too tight. I can't believe I'm the one losing my shit and flailing like a fish out of water instead of Dash, even though it was my magnificent plan. "I thought you'd be happy, Ma."

"Happy? I feel like I don't even know my own daughter." She replies, her bob cut swinging as she shakes her head in bewilderment. "You've been against the idea of marriage since the start and now you're telling us you're engaged? You didn't even have the decency to tell us you're seeing someone. Your father and I have raised you better than this."

Dash tenses beside me at my mom's harsh scolding while tears sting my eyes.

Embarrassment rolls through me as he witnesses the moment with a front-row seat. I've never felt so small in my entire life. My fingers instinctively tighten around our hands on his thigh and there's a pang in my chest when he squeezes back.

The small gesture gives me little strength as I face my livid mother.

I'm not the least bit shocked when Dad remains quiet. Of course, he agrees with her and honestly, I expected this reaction from him. Definitely not from my always-polite-and-sweet mother, whose pride and poise never allow her to have an outburst in public.

I take a hold of Dash's other hand on my bare arm when he leans forward to speak in my defense. I can't decipher if his instinct to stand up for me is all part of the loving fiancé act or if it means more.

Don't be stupid, Bianca.

Of course, it has to be all for show. Because the alternative is too hard to swallow and I'd be crazy to imagine he actually cares for me.

I have to give him credit for his acting skills. He has me fooled for a second.

His whole body remains coiled tight as I answer my mom, "I didn't plan this with the intention to disrespect either of you, Mom. I'm even more hurt that you're making me feel guilty for falling in love and insinuating that I'm incapable of choosing a worthy man for myself without your help. And I definitely don't like you insulting my fiancé, whom you haven't even tried to get to know first or spoken two words to."

She reels back in shock, mouth agape at seeing me stand up for myself. Something I have never done against my parents, much less for someone else. Whoever said that courage comes from the unlikeliest of places or... a *person*, was spot on. Dash was the last man on earth I would've expected to be that someone for me but strangely enough, he is.

Also, a tiny part of me doesn't want him to see me as weak. Someone with no backbone.

Or without a mind of her own.

The need to pat myself on the back is a more welcome feeling than the one from a few seconds ago. I'm even more surprised that feigning that Dash means more to me wasn't as foreign or tough as I pondered. Or that instead of it leaving a bad taste in my mouth, all it left was a strange warmth in my bones. Maybe we're both natural liars and I can do this after all.

Pretend I'm madly in love with a man who infuriates me.

Pretend I'm his devoted wife when we can't even stand each other.

Pretend he's my forever when we already have an end date.

"You're right, kid," says my dad, shocking me and Mom. "But you have to understand that it's a lot for us to process since you've sprung it out of nowhere. Your mother has been dreaming of this day to come, just not quite like this. It'll take time to accept it."

"I know, Papa." My shoulders slump. Still, he's not suspicious so that has to count.

The small trace of softness vanishes from his face as he turns to Dash. "How long have you been seeing my daughter?"

Fuck. My mind blanks and panic swells in my chest because I know we're not prepared for an interrogation. Something we could have avoided had he not decided to make his surprised grand entrance.

I gasp silently when his large hand curls around my thigh to seize my nervous tapping, away from my parents' eyes. The tips of his fingers dangerously and indecently close to my pussy.

It distracts me from my rapidly beating heart as I focus on his voice. His words, yanking the ground from beneath me and tilting it on its axis.

"Seeing isn't the word I'd choose." His gaze softens. "I've been in love with Bianca for as long as I can remember. Though it took her a while to finally see me and confess she feels the same."

I stare at his profile speechlessly when my mother asks, "When did you two meet?"

"Seven years ago."

"For the first time, yes," I add before he can mention Niall and reveal more. "We stayed in touch until he moved here and I couldn't deny I wanted him."

"So this is a whirlwind romance?" My mom's lips purse in distaste. "Your marriage doesn't stand a chance. I don't approve of this."

"Approve?" I jerk back, aghast. "It's my life. My future."

"You won't have my blessing."

SIMRAN

"Meera." My dad sighs, laying his hand on my mom's curled fist on the table. "Let's all calm down."

The rough scrape of the chair pushing back on my right stills all of us. I whip my head to the side just in time to see Dash get up, eyes thunderous while the rest of his face remains impassive.

My mouth drops open when he tugs on my hand until I'm standing in the crook of his arm and declares, "We're leaving."

Chapter Nineteen

Dash

Jesus. What the hell am I doing?

Bianca had made the plan sound like a piece of cake, except she forgot to mention her parents are complete assholes. No wonder she is willing to have a sham marriage.

I should walk the fuck away from this dysfunctional family without another look back.

The rational side of my brain, warning me that this is an unnecessary complication. That it was a mistake coming here. I shouldn't give a fuck and stick to my decision that I told Bianca last night.

But I just fucking can't.

She has got her claws inside me yet again. It's etched so deep, that there's no pulling them out, consequences be damned.

Because when it comes to her, I've never been rational. It isn't even in the spectrum of feelings she makes me long for. Only a twisted obsession that aches to consume her alive and me with it.

Her vulnerability triggers a deep seated impulse to be her hero when I've only ever been the villain.

A monster hidden in plain sight.

Her inevitable downfall.

Staying away is as much for her sake as it is for mine, yet I can't not help her. Not after witnessing firsthand how badly her uptight and demanding parents treat her. Disbelief, I expected, even a bit of anger at finding out, out of the blue, that their daughter is engaged, but not so much vehemence pouring from them. Their pride was way more important to them than her happiness.

I guess Bianca and I have a lot more in common than I thought.

The pain and sadness radiating from her was plain as day and when I saw her shoulders slump—the movement barely noticeable—from my periphery, I wanted to wrap her in my arms. And I'm not even an affectionate type of man.

I destroy and burn those around me.

I don't do soft things, yet I was willing to for her.

Because her behavior is jarring and so uncharacteristic to the Bianca I've come to know. My kitten has a backbone and fire. She's fierce and compelling.

In one fell swoop, my decision was made and sealed. I understand now more than ever her resolve and urgency to go through with this insane plan. If I wasn't convinced already, the temptation to take her parents down a notch undoubtedly did.

Bianca's stunned gaze hits the side of my face while I glare down at her mother, whose hand flies to her mouth.

"I don't like anyone upsetting my fiancée." My voice is cold. "Which is all you've done since I sat down. When you're ready to talk calmly, call us. But know this, I am going to marry her, with or without your approval."

"No daughter of mine is marrying without her family by her side," her father grunts, who has been silently assessing whether or not I'm worthy of his daughter.

He is going to search for everything there is to know about me the second we leave. Once he does, he'll be calling me himself. Because I did my research, too, before coming here and I wasn't surprised when I learnt he wants to marry Bianca into a family which will also benefit his business empire.

Something I can tell Bianca isn't aware of.

Meeting his challenging stare, I reply, "I suggest you make up your mind soon before it's too late."

"We'll talk about this later, Bianca," her dad says, making her body go rigid.

"Let's go, kitten," I whisper softly in her ear.

Her gaze flits to her mom who turns her head away and it takes all of my strength to not curse at the arrogant woman.

How can she treat her own blood this way?

I lead Bianca away from their table and she mutely follows. I don't say a word, sensing she needs space to gather her courage. I stiffen when she tugs her hand from mine and murmurs, "I need to go to the restroom."

Without waiting for my reply, she wanders to the back but not before I witness a tear drop down her cheek. I push my hands in my pockets and pace back and forth while telling myself not to go after her.

I don't need to keep up the act of a loving fiancé when we're alone. No need to tangle myself more into her mess than absolutely necessary. Maintain my distance.

Despite all these thoughts running rampant in my head, my feet carry me toward her.

Like I said, rationality out the window. Nonexistent.

The corridor is empty near the restrooms and not giving a fuck, I blaze past the door into the women's room. I come to a halt when my irresistible obsession comes into view.

She stands alone in front of the mirror looking so small and sad. Her shoulders, shaking slightly in silent sobs. The pain is so strong she doesn't even notice my presence for the first few seconds. It's when I click the lock in the place that she stills and looks up at my reflection.

Those pretty eyes widen before she hastily hides them beneath her hair while fingers push her tears away.

"Dash. Go away." A hiccup in her voice.

I stride closer and turn her around. When she doesn't put up a fight, concern flares inside my chest. Pushing her hair back until her stunning face isn't hidden, I tilt her chin up with my fingers. She closes her eyes, lips pressed together while I rub those tears away.

Despite us being in the similar position in the past, a tremor racks her body like she doesn't expect softness from me. Only difference is, she didn't carry such baggage on her small shoulders.

Could it be because she's still heartbroken over Niall? It can't be. Seven years is a long time to be stuck over the first breakup. She has to have moved on.

My heart is incapable of loving anyone.

Her words ring in my ear, leaving a chill in their wake.

"Dash," she whispers when I stay quiet for too long.

I squash down my stinging emotions and the memories that surface as I stare down at her. Thick black eyelashes flutter slowly around red-rimmed eyes yet it doesn't take away from her beauty. She's like one of those women who look prettier after they cry, cheeks tinged with a blushing hue, nose and lips slightly pink.

Or maybe I'm biased.

I don't reply to her and lean to my right to grab a tissue paper, wet it slightly under the water, and bring it to dab under her eyes. A little bit of mascara spills from the corner and I clean it without smudging it further. Her cheeks darken even further, and her lips part as her eyes roam over my face.

"Wow… Got nothing to say? No insulting remarks or threats," she teases. "Don't tell me my parents left you scared."

Her attempt at lightening the mood doesn't suppress my rage. "You don't want my opinion, kitten."

"Your scowls betray your thoughts, Dash. Might as well say it out loud."

I throw the dirty tissue into the bin and crowd her against the counter. Her palms lay flat on my chest, curling into my shirt. "Your parents are selfish pricks and don't give a shit about you. I wouldn't be surprised if you were adopted. 'Cause it's the only explanation that makes sense as to how you're related to them." Her jaw drops at my harsh words and I arch my eyebrow. "Liking my thoughts now?"

"They love me in their own way," she mutters. I can't tell who she is trying to convince.

SIMRAN

"They made you cry."

"Angry and frustrated tears." A small shrug. "The topic of marriage is kind of a touchy one."

"I think they have lots of expectations and don't like it when you go against them."

"I'm their eldest daughter. So, of course, they do."

"It's neither healthy nor right," I bluntly say. "Burdens like these only end in one way. Your soul crushed and the feeling of never being enough because you'll never be able to live up to their expectations. Especially if you put your own happiness first."

Her stare sears me when I inadvertently reveal too much, immediately regretting it. The empathy in her eyes feels like we just crossed a boundary. There was a time I yearned to let her in, and allow her to see the parts I kept hidden beneath my rough exterior like she's doing now.

But we're seven years too late.

I may still crave her, obsess over her, but I don't want her in my life any second longer than necessary. While we're together, I'm going to sate my craving for every inch of her until it's quenched.

Claim her tight little body in every obscene, filthy way. And as many times as I want.

Lure the kinky seductress in her out to play until she's ruined for other men.

Then as soon as our little arrangement is over, I'm going to be the one to walk away from her life.

With my heart and secrets intact.

Chapter Twenty

DASH

The sound of someone banging on the door, followed by an impatient voice, pulls us apart. Even though we haven't been doing anything naughty and are fully clothed, Bianca breaks the connection between us and turns red with embarrassment at having been caught.

She does look flushed at our close proximity and no, it's not just because of the crying.

"Oh god! You need to hide," she whisper-yells while pushing me backward. "Go into one of the stalls."

She grows frustrated when I don't budge. It's funny that she thought she could in the first place. Doesn't she realize she's a tiny thing compared to my size?

"I'm not hiding."

"She'll see you," she utters while staring at me like I've grown two heads.

"And?"

"She'll think we… we were…"

"We were what? Fucking? Kissing?" I smirk, stepping closer and tilting my head. "Having a taste of your sweet cunt, or maybe I had you on your knees sucking my cock. Hmm… either one sounds believable, considering the flush on your cheeks."

The heat and lust shining in her eyes has my dick twitching inside my pants. It would be so easy to undo the string holding her top together. A single tug is all

SIMRAN

I need and I could suck her hard nipples in my mouth. Slide my hands inside her panties and make her scream my name.

I should've fucked her last night when I had the chance. I wonder if my marks are still on her thighs and if she thought of me when she saw them in the mirror. Her mouth parts to retort, but gets interrupted when the woman outside yells.

"Uh, hello? Shall I call someone for help?"

"No!" Bianca yells back before rushing to say, "Just a minute please."

"Which excuse is it going to be?" I ask.

"Why can't you be embarrassed like a normal person?" she grumbles with her hands on her hips.

"Why the fuck would I be embarrassed for being alone with my wife?" I counter.

A shiver runs down her naked spine, which she tries to hide by tilting her chin up high. "I'm not your wife yet."

"That'll soon change and then you'll be Mrs. Stern."

"Who says I'll be taking your name?"

I harden my gaze and cross the distance. Yanking her onto her toes, I circle my fingers around her throat and growl, "The marriage may be in name only but you will be wearing my ring, taking my last name, and sharing my bed. Your pussy will only know my cock, your lips will only feel mine, and your pleasure will belong to me. Understand?"

"There will be no fucking."

"Oh, kitten," I tsk, smiling darkly. "There will be. Lots of it. Every day and night." Trailing my lips over her jaw to her ear, I whisper, "You will beg, scream, moan, and won't step outside of my house until I'm satisfied you'll feel me in your cunt when I'm not with you."

When she sways, I let her go and step back with a satisfied smirk. Her pupils are dilated as she parts her lips, and my cock swells further when she shifts on her feet.

Looks like the dirty vixen likes the promise.

I leave her stunned with her panties soaked, and walk outside. I run into the woman waiting in the hall, whose eyes bug out upon seeing me before she peers inside in confusion.

Striding to the lobby, I scroll through my messages and emails on my phone while I wait for Bianca. She and I have a lot to discuss about our fake arrangement to make sure it succeeds. Mainly to work on her terrible acting skills.

In hindsight, I should've called or texted her first. However, when I found out she was meeting her parents, I didn't think—I just drove here. The restlessness I felt at the fear of being too late was so foreign yet familiar.

The shocked look on her face as she saw me standing at her table earlier followed by stark relief was worth the traffic rules I broke. It was amusing to watch the play of emotions swirling on her face when I called her wifey. Something I plan to call her as often as I like, just to see the blush darken her cheeks.

And it's not because I secretly love the ring to it.

The sound of footsteps coming closer yank me to the present and a frown crosses Bianca's features when she finds me waiting. She peers up once she's standing in front of me.

SCANDALOUS GAMES

"Why are you still here?" she questions, confused and dazed.

I slide my phone inside my suit jacket and answer, "I'm taking you to my place so we can discuss our marriage in detail, wifey."

Again, that damn blush.

"You and your nicknames." She huffs with a shake of her head. "Why can't we go to my place?"

"Scared to be alone with me?"

"Hardly."

I chuckle low. "You live too far and my hotel is near."

"How do you know where I live?" Suspicion laces her tone and her expressive gaze narrows.

"I asked someone in your office."

"What?" She gasps. "They're not supposed to share that information."

"I'm persuasive," I retort with a sigh. "Now, are you done with the twenty questions?"

I think I liked her better when she was crying and not sassy.

No you don't, asshole.

"Just one more."

"Ask fast before I throw you over my shoulder and take you."

"How the hell did you know I was here?" She bites her lip, looking too fucking adorable. "You're not stalking me, are you?"

"No. I'm not, kitten," I say with a roll of my eyes before grabbing her hand and guiding us out. "I went to your apartment first to tell you that I'll help you with this farce, but the doorman told me you weren't home. He also shared that you come here weekly for lunch with your parents, so I drove straight here."

"Oh!"

I stop at the valet and when I turn to her, I find her watching our joined hands raptly. A soft faraway look on her features. Instinctively, my thumb rubs back and forth before I realize it feels too intimate. Romantic. Protective.

I'm none of those things.

A pang hits my chest as I jerk my hand free but I ignore it. "You drove here?"

"Yeah," she whispers, meeting my gaze. "I'll follow you in my car."

"Okay."

I get out of my car just as Bianca pulls up behind me and does the same. She walks confidently with her shoulders straight. Thick hips swaying side to side enticingly as she meets me halfway.

"You haven't bought your own place yet?" she asks curiously.

"I haven't found the one I liked yet."

"Will you be moving here after your merger with Kian's company?"

I place my hand on her back instead of holding hers like I want to as I guide her to the entrance of the Taj Hotel where I'm staying. I always prefer this hotel whenever I'm traveling because of their ambience and quality of service.

"Yes. But only for the first six months until I only need to visit the branch for important events and annual meetings," I reply. "Kian will mostly be managing it."

"Oh, okay." She nods.

My brows pinch together as I wonder if I imagined the note of worry in her tone.

We take the elevator up to my suite on the eighteenth floor and the whole ride she remains silent and deep in thought. At this moment, I wish I could read her mind. I crave to know everything she's feeling. Her secrets. Her dreams.

I ache to ask if she still loves to watch horror movies despite the fact that they give her nightmares. If she still eats snacks in the middle of the night. Or if burgers and fries are still her favorite.

All the silly habits I remember from when she used to stay over with Niall at our house. I knew her better than my stepbrother did just watching her from the shadows.

The elevator dings and opens to my private hallway. Bianca's gaze widens in awe as takes in the floor-to-ceiling glass wall on either side with the view of the city below. She steps inside and a gorgeous smile lights up her entire face.

"This is so stunning."

Not more than you, I want to say but I hold my tongue. "Come inside once you're done drooling, kitten," I say over my shoulder as I walk to the kitchen and take two water bottles from the fridge. Grabbing a glass, I pour one into it just as she rounds the corner observing the space. I've noticed an inquisitive look deepens her features whenever she's in a new environment. Like her inner designer can't help herself.

When her gaze lands on mine that's watching her intently, nerves and shyness dance in her dark pupils as she stalls on coming closer. Her foot kicks to the side while her teeth bite the corner of her bottom lip.

My hands ball into fists to keep from tugging it free and replacing it with mine.

I badly need the kiss she owes me.

"I thought you said you weren't scared of me," I tease as I rest my hands on the kitchen island, tapping my fingers slowly. Better to keep them busy, so I don't lose the fight to close the distance and touch her.

Fire flares in her big brown eyes as she puffs, "I am not."

"Come here." My deep voice puts her into action and she fills the gap, sitting down on one of the stools. I pass her the glass and command, "Drink."

"I'm not thirsty."

"Not even after all that crying?" I raise an eyebrow. "Have some."

Her fingers inch forward and wrap around the crystal as she takes a sip, and I hide my smile when she finishes more than half of it in one go. Stubborn girl.

I can already tell the coming months are going to be entertaining as hell.

Usually, I hate the thought of anyone being in my space since I'm an extremely private guy. I wait for the same dislike to appear for having Bianca here, knowing we'll be living together for the foreseeable future. Yet the feeling never comes.

SCANDALOUS GAMES

In fact, I'm eager and thrilled at the prospect. The urge to do it soon, growing stronger with each passing second. On one hand, I'm desperate to avoid any morsel of intimacy while on the other, I'm craving it all the same.

What would it be like to wake up next to her every morning? To come home to her every night? Is she yearning for these rituals too? Or will she resist?

I shake my head. Of course it'll be the latter.

My kitten has claws, which she enjoys bringing out around me. Even in between the moments of shyness and softness like right now.

Her back straightens as she tucks her hair behind her ear. I sense a question swirling in that pretty little head of hers before she even whispers it in a breathy and curious voice.

"Why the sudden change of heart to marry me, Dash?"

Chapter Twenty-one

BIANCA

Don't look down. Don't look down. Don't look down.
I chant repeatedly to resist the urge to lower my gaze to his muscular chest and wide shoulders. Which is hard, since he's standing at a perfect angle and even sitting on a high stool, I barely reach his neck.

Who even has a body built like a damn brick wall?

It should be illegal. Maybe I should file a petition and do all of us women a service. Especially when it makes it difficult to have a serious conversation. Honestly, I'm not sure how to go on, now that he has said yes to my proposition.

Until yesterday, I was simply focused on convincing him, which seemed like an impossibility since he was so adamant in kicking me out of his life. Worse, I kinda liked the chase.

Tormenting and teasing him...

I felt powerful knowing I could wield such strong emotions from a man as commanding as Dash. The high is like floating on cloud nine.

Hence, I never gave the rest of the plan much thought, like how we're going to make this work. After today's lunch, we'll have to make sure it's solid if we want to make it believable to my parents. My mom made her stance very clear and by now, she would have convinced Dad against us. Although I sensed he was adjusting to the idea of Dash and me living a life together, Mom's rejection threw water all over it. He will scrutinize us while plotting to manipulate me into ending my relationship.

With our mad exit, the ball is in their court because I won't be calling them.

In my head, I had let myself and my stupid best friends convince me the fake relationship was a slick plan while the only hurdle would be to find a man. Turns out, it's the least of my problems and was only the tip of the iceberg.

Fuck! Why does everything have to be so complicated in my life?

I peer at Dash under my lashes and wonder if we need a contract or something. A non-disclosure agreement? You know, like in those rom-com movies. Because if I have any chance of surviving him, I need to set boundaries. Rules that keep us—mainly him—from crossing the lines because they are already blurring.

It stirs a low throb between my legs as I imagine us sitting in a dark conference room. Him laying all his deviant demands and seductively asking in a low voice...

Do you want to be my whore, kitten?

Fuck! Where did that come from? Stupid sex-starved brain.

I bury the unfiltered and filthy vision and manage to focus on him without blushing and betraying my naughty thoughts as I wait for his answer. It has been burning inside my head and rose to the forefront while my drive over here.

Dash isn't surprised at my sudden question, rather looks like he was waiting for it. The green in his pupils darkens as he keeps them pinned on me. The full intensity of his attention is so striking and feels like the caress of a wind. You don't see it but you can feel it.

The piercing gaze steals all the oxygen from my lungs.

It scares and excites me all the same.

See... blurry lines.

"Does it matter, kitten?" he counters with a slight tilt of his head. "I already said yes."

"It does to me." My gaze narrows. "You all but threw me out last night."

"I was a perfect gentleman. I escorted you to your car." Amusement dances in his sharp eyes and I swear I want to throttle him.

"Again, your definition of 'gentleman' is screwed," I counter before smiling sweetly. "I'll buy you a new dictionary."

His lips twitch, causing my heart to stammer, but soon his face becomes intense and serious. I don't even realize I leaned closer to him until he does the same on the smooth marble between us. I would move back if I knew he wouldn't take it as if I'm scared.

"There are certain rumors floating around me. I need to change my reputation as a playboy bachelor if I want to continue working with the government. Marrying you puts them all to rest."

In other words, it's just another business deal to him.

My shoulders slump in disappointment and I lower my gaze now I know that I'm just a calculative move to clear his name. God! Here I thought he was actually human and had a semblance of good inside him. Maybe this is better. I wouldn't owe him anything.

"But that's not why I said yes."

SIMRAN

My head snaps back to his and the darkness staring back at me makes my spine tingle and goosebumps rise on my skin.

"It's not?" I whisper, my mind racing a mile a minute.

"I said yes because I'm selfish when it comes to you, Bianca. The thought of another man calling you his wife, fake or not, makes me want to end their life. You may never give your heart to me but I won't let anyone else have it either."

"Because you want my heart?"

His eyes become playful and lustful as he smirks, "I haven't decided yet."

What the hell does that mean? And why does it make my pulse race?

He pulls back and straightens himself while leaving me stunned and staring at the empty space. Meanwhile, he walks out of the kitchen and down the hallway. I don't follow because I'm still reeling from the effect of his bold statement.

It should be scary, the ease with which he basically conveyed he wants to have his cake and eat it too. Apparently, his possessiveness and domineering attitude knows no bounds. And I invited it with welcoming and open arms.

I'm stuck on the rumors he mentioned when he returns a few minutes later with his suit jacket and vest gone. His forearms flex as he rolls the sleeves and my mouth drools at the veins in his arms and the light dusting of hair. Though he appears relaxed, his hard edge cannot be tamed.

Intense and broody might as well be his middle name. Surprisingly enough, I've only seen him smirk or be mischievous with me. Otherwise, he has his carefully practiced cold mask in place.

I don't want to admit how it makes me feel.

The green flecks in his eyes lighten as they land on mine and he nods toward the drawing room. "Let's talk."

Hmm, I might have to do something about his bossy orders if we're going to be in a pretend marriage. No matter how my pussy betrays me by finding it a turn-on, I won't put up with it. Making my way over to the couch where he's already lounging, I walk past him to sit as far away from him as possible, only to go tumbling down on his lap as he tugs on my arm without any warning.

Circling my waist, he shifts me until I'm sitting with my bent legs on either side of his hips and my hands resting on the couch behind him. The same male satisfaction flitters across his face every time he has his way with me and ends up winning.

I swear my protests have no effect on him whatsoever.

They might as well be invisible.

"You seriously need to stop manhandling me, Dash." I glare down at him, irritated only half-heartedly with him. Not that I'll admit it.

His brow arches mockingly as he teases, "Is that any way to talk to your fiancé, kitten?"

"I'm not wearing your ring yet," I retort, waving my left hand in front of his face.

He catches it in his big one and traces my ring finger, his pupils becoming heated as they travel back to mine. "I'm well aware and I'll rectify that soon."

"Wait... you're not actually going to buy me a ring, are you?" He stares back as if

SCANDALOUS GAMES

it should be obvious. He can't be serious about spending money on an engagement for a fake marriage. Knowing him, the expense wouldn't be cheap. I try pulling back but his hold tightens, so I shake my head. "Uh-uh. No way. I'll just wear one from my collection."

"No."

"You'll be wasting money."

"I'm a billionaire, in case you don't read the newspaper," he replies with a smug grin. When I open my mouth to argue, he cuts me off. "I'm buying you a diamond ring and it's final, kitten. If I have to force you to wear it and glue it to your finger, I'll do it."

"You're insane."

"Only when it comes to you." As if reading my regretful thoughts he adds, "And too bad you're stuck with me." Still holding my hand, he switches the topic. "So how do you want to proceed with the plan? Should I expect a court marriage or a big wedding? When do we announce it? Though I should warn you, it won't be long before the media catches wind of us."

I catch only half of what he says, because all I can feel are his muscles flexing beneath me. Hard as steel yet warm and comfortable. They are so fucking distracting and it doesn't take long for flashbacks to visit me. I don't stand a chance of a serious conversation if we stay pressed like this.

"Do I really need to be on your lap while we discuss this?" I complain.

"How else are you going to get used to my touch?"

"I'm plenty familiar with your *touch*." My tone is annoyed, to which his grin widens. "More than it's required in front of my parents, unless you plan to manhandle me in front of them."

"If the situation calls for it, I might," he says, making my eyes widen.

"Be serious, Dash."

He relaxes his back against the plush couch, his fingers gripping the tops of my thighs as he shrugs his big shoulders and confesses, "I like having you close, kitten. Get used to it because it will be happening a lot."

I cross my arms and lift my chin as I match his bossy tone. "Well, in that case, we need to set some ground rules."

"Afraid I'm all about breaking rules." He smirks, his tongue running between his teeth as his predatory gaze lowers to my chest.

I look down to see my breasts pushed together and my nipples poking through the material of my top. With a huff to hide my burning cheeks, I bring my hair forward to cover my body's arousal to his proximity. His expression screams it's too late.

"Tell me your rules," he demands instead of opposing when I don't budge.

I hold a finger up for each of them. "No bossing me around. No touching me when we're alone. No more mind games. This arrangement will be strictly business, Dash. If you can't agree, then I'm walking away."

Silence stretches once I'm finished laying down my terms and I feel the undercurrent of tension in him, but I hold my stance. As important as this is for me, considering it's my last resort, I wouldn't do it unless I'm an equal in this, which

SIMRAN

means he can't call all the shots.

If I continue to let him treat me in his domineering and territorial way, lines will get blurry. It will only be a matter of time.

While my heart is safely locked inside the cage, so will be my body. If I allow him to touch me, I'll become addicted because in two short weeks, I'm already halfway there.

He may act all obsessive and infatuated now but once I'm out of his system, he'll walk away while leaving me a crumbling mess. I won't let it happen. *Never again.*

"Are these rules really important to you?" he finally asks, voice devoid of emotion. I nod anyway and my stomach hollows when with one single move, he picks me up and sets me down beside him.

I'm too stunned to react because he does it so fast. At first, I'm afraid he's rejecting me and I've pushed him too far until he meets my gaze with his steady ones. Something calculative, lurking beneath them.

"Okay. Although I can't promise to not be demanding, because it goes against my very nature, I will give you a choice in the final say. As for not touching you…" His eyes turn molten as they run over me seductively. "I'll do it because it won't be long before I have you begging for it."

I swallow the nerves because he's taken my rules as a challenge. Instead of giving me safety, they make me feel anything but. Only Anticipation. Arousal. *Thirst.*

Still, I somehow manage to mumble, "I won't beg."

"You did last night."

"Last night was a fluke."

"And you also did seven years ago," he growls, voice deep and guttural. "And if I were to play with your wet cunt right here, you'll do it again. It's the only reason you're insisting on this stupid rule."

His words light up my body and it takes all my willpower not to squirm and clench my thighs together to stop the ache. I hate the tremble in my voice when I reply, "Whatever helps you to follow it."

The smirk on his face widens at the breathlessness and stubbornness in my voice. I take a relaxing breath, assuming he's done, until he speaks again, "And I have one condition too, kitten."

My hackles rise because it feels like a trap. Except, I don't know how I lost or how I'll pay for it. At least his list isn't as lengthy as mine, so I hesitantly ask, "What?"

"You will move in with me."

"But I already have my apartment," I say dumbly. The whole reason I chose him was to avoid the entire living together situation because he won't be in the city half the time. He himself said so. Besides, where the hell am I going to move into? He doesn't even own a place.

Unless he's planning to shift to mine.

Hell no. I've already experienced living with him back when I stayed with Niall. It was torture of the worst kind. And I won't have anyone to use as a buffer to avoid him.

"This is nonnegotiable." His tone is firm while his face is calm. "Besides, you'll

SCANDALOUS GAMES

only have to shift to the thirtieth floor."

My jaw drops at the revelation. "You bought an apartment in my building?"

"No. I bought the whole building." The smile that stretches across his full lips is nothing but devilish. "Like I said, we'll be living together, no matter what."

It really hits me at this moment that I've made a deal with the devil.

An insane, devious, and sinful devil.

The control I fought for a second ago might as well be an illusion. "When did you do that and how? You might be rich but you can't make something like this happen so fast."

"Like I said, I'm persuasive and it also helps that I'm best friends with Justin," he explains but leaves me more confused. He must sense it because his head tilts in astonishment and he probes, "You do know who he is, don't you?"

"Um… No." I frown. "Am I supposed to?"

"Heard of Merchant Properties?" he asks and I nod because, of course I have. They are the biggest real estate dealers and developers in the country. "Justin is the CEO and the son of the founder, kitten."

"He's Justin Merchant?" My voice goes high-pitched, making Dash chuckle. "I thought he was a recluse and an antisocial."

"He prefers the term *selectively social* and he's not the recluse the media likes to paint him as. He tends to avoid them and they don't like it."

"Wow," I mutter to myself. To think I had no clue who he was this whole time. I'm still distracted and musing over Justin also being a billionaire when Dash interrupts.

"Do you accept my condition?"

After the initial shock, it's actually convenient if I think about it, and it only seems fair since he met my demands too. "Yes."

"Good." His tone is victorious. "We'll move together tomorrow."

"Tomorrow?"

"Yes. Is that a problem?"

Other than the fact that I'm not prepared to be in such close proximity to him constantly and without barriers. I've been alone for years and now I have to share my home with a man I will soon call my husband. My future is turning out to be full of surprises.

"I thought we'd wait until we're married," I finally reply, hoping he'll take the excuse.

"I'm not spending another minute apart from you." His deep voice is a promise and a warning. "You're mine now, kitten."

Chapter Twenty-two

DASH

"I'm guessing congratulations are in order, Stern," Justin mocks, slapping today's newspaper on my desk. There's a photo of Bianca and I standing outside the restaurant, holding hands and staring at each other, on the front page with the bold title "Wedding Bells are around the Corner."

"And an engagement gift too."

"Asshole," he retorts before falling serious. "Is it true or just another media ploy bullshit?"

"What have they written?"

"They're apparently labeling you a knight in shining armor after someone saw you rescuing Bianca. The person overheard you threaten her father, then announce you're her fiancé. I'm guessing some poor waiter sold the story for some extra cash."

The media has become nothing less than a god these days with their eyes and ears missing zilch once they've caught you in their crosshairs. No corner in the world you can hide from them. So, it's no surprise to me that they caught Bianca and I, and wrote the gossipy article in less than three days.

At least they had their facts somewhat correct.

"Sounds about right." I shrug at Justin, leaning back in my chair. "Veer Chopra is a fucking prick and treats his daughter like a commodity. Me threatening him was an exaggeration, though."

SCANDALOUS GAMES

"Men like him see everyone as a threat if it involves their daughter," Justin sneers before fixing his inquisitive gaze on me. "Speaking of daughter, when did you fall in love with Bianca and what possessed you enough to propose to her? Just this weekend, you were at each other's throats."

"It's just a temporary business arrangement."

"Care to elaborate?" he asks, one eyebrow raised.

"Details don't matter. She wanted a fake husband so I said yes when she asked me."

"You mean, she played you into saying yes?" He laughs out loud. "Is that why you went all ballistic on my ass that night, because you thought she was gonna ask me?"

"Shut up, dickhead."

"Fuck! That woman is a savage."

His amusement grates on my nerves, making me grit my teeth while he continues to snort. If he wasn't my only best friend, I swear I would have buried him six feet under the ground a long time ago.

Once his laughter dies down, he stares at me thoughtfully for a few seconds before speaking, "Are you waiting for me to tell you it's a bad fucking idea?"

"I'm not going back on my word."

"She's your brother's girl, Dash," he reasons, speaking in a placating tone.

The words still enrage me none the same and I grit out, "Ex-girlfriend. He cheated on her, remember?"

"Does she know the truth about Niall?"

I stiffen, guilty and disturbing memories replaying inside my head. It's not often I think about them since they're a chapter of my life I've tried hard to forget. Living in the past has never helped anybody.

"No," I finally answer. "And I'm not going to."

"You can't keep it from her." His tone is hard and forceful. "She deserves to know before finding out from someone else, which she will once your lives intertwine as a couple."

"Our relationship isn't real for me to confess my sins of the past to Bianca. It's none of her fucking business anyways."

I ignore his disappointing and sympathetic look boring into me. Besides, it's not as if she's asked me about Niall, which tells me she wants our history to remain just that. There's no need for rehashing the ghosts of the past when it's what neither of us want.

Because the alternative will have her ending up hating me.

And I'm not going to destroy us before I've even had her.

"You're making a mistake," he warns darkly. "But since you're once again blinded by your lust for her, I suggest you be careful and don't break her heart."

"It won't come to that." I shrug. "I'll be out of her life before then."

His head shakes like I'm in denial. What can I say? Sometimes denial is bliss.

Justin is worrying for no reason. Though I don't fault him for trying to be a good friend. I'll just have to prove him wrong that I won't let lust cloud my judgment, unlike last time. The sound of my phone pinging saves me from continuing this taxing conversation and I grab it to read the message.

"I have to go," I announce, standing up as I button my jacket and put my phone in my pocket after texting the driver to bring my car around.

"Where?" Justin questions, doing the same.

"I'm moving into my new apartment today."

"I'm coming with you."

"Don't you have your own company to run?" I taunt. "I invited you for a weekend and not for you to practically move in, dickhead."

He rolls his eyes, wrapping his arm around my shoulder as we walk out of my office. "Is that your not-so-subtle way of telling me to fuck off? I thought we were BBFFs, Stern."

"BBFS?"

"Boy best friends forever."

"The fuck!" My lips curl in a wince. "What illegal stuff are you smoking now?"

"You don't like it?"

"If you say you do, I'm throwing you over the roof."

"What's wrong with it? My niece taught me that one last night on video call."

"You being a grown-ass man, for starters." I toss his arm from my back as we step inside the elevator and turn to him. I mutter under my breath, "And you call me an idiot."

"So I guess 'I'm Joey to your Chandler' is out of the question?"

"Did you hit your head somewhere?" I jibe while getting annoyed by the minute. That's the thing about Justin. One second he can be imparting wisdom like a priest and the next, joking around like a goof.

"Besides, it would be the opposite," I throw over my shoulder as we reach the lobby. "I get more pussy than you do."

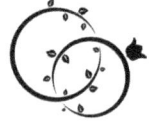

***

We arrive at Bianca's apartment building just in time as the movers from my hotel. I had plans to move two days ago but both hers and my work clashed. She took half a day off and thank fuck, because I wasn't waiting any longer. Had she not, I might have just kidnapped her from her office.

Justin steps beside me as we enter the lavish lobby and I'm pondering whether or not to tell him the real reason why I was so adamant in buying this place when he beats me to it.

"What's so good about living here?" he muses. "I thought you weren't interested in buying a house in the city."

"This is more convenient."

He eyes me suspiciously at my lackluster tone. "You haven't been acting yourself since you met Bianca, Dash. It's concerning."

"You're imagining things with all the free time you suddenly have on your hands."

SCANDALOUS GAMES

I have half a mind to shut the elevator door in his face since apparently, he's in a really chatty mood today. Usually when he acts like this, something else is bothering him, so he creates diversions to avoid dealing with it until he's ready.

He leans on the far side and smirks. "You haven't fucked another woman in the last two weeks despite being at The Mirage on most nights. And let's not forget, you're an engaged man when you've basically been the preacher boy against marriage your whole life."

"Why do you keep forgetting it's fake?" I growl, exasperated.

"Keep telling yourself that."

Not bothering to answer, I stare at the number of floors going up while praying we don't run into Bianca. Hopefully, she's not back from her office yet so I don't have to deal with a smug Justin and feed more gasoline to the fire.

The elevator finally stops in front of the private lobby, leading to the penthouse, and both of us stride inside. I notice a few big boxes lying on the side waiting to be unpacked when high-pitched voices followed by laughter from around the corner fills the apartment. My eyes close as all my hopes are quashed because I recognize one of the voices as Bianca's.

Justin stalks in the direction of the noise while I trail after him and I hear his low intake of breath, before his feet come to a halt. My curiosity is piqued at his reaction and when my gaze lands at the view, I'm as stunned as him while my cock twitches as Bianca's perky ass stares back at me from the floor.

God! Is she trying to kill me?

Possessiveness flares like an old friend that Justin is also enjoying the same view. Her tiny denim shorts ride up her ass cheeks and I want to spank it before covering it up from another man's gaze.

The girls—Bianca, Rosalie, and another one, whom I don't recognize—remain oblivious to our rapt presence. Their tangled limbs are everywhere that it looks like they're having an orgy, only they're playing a game of Twister. Who fucking plays it in the middle of the day? Or at all?

"I know for a fact that you can spread your legs wider than that, Iris," grumbles a frustrated Rosalie. "Stop cheating."

"Fuck me!" curses Justin under his breath, looking in awe at the women. I can only imagine the dirty fantasies he's picturing in his head. Bianca better not be in one of them.

The girls are so loud and arguing among themselves that they don't hear me when I clear my throat. Bianca has her ass up high while bent over Rosalie, their lips almost touching, and I want to yank her to my side because I don't like anybody touching or getting close to her besides me. Apparently, all humans fall into that category.

"Can I join, ladies?" Justin asks loudly, ignoring me.

They all go down in a heap at his flirty voice before two pairs of wide eyes and a set of glaring ones meet ours. Bianca is still leaning over Rosa with her head turned to face us and when our gazes lock, color darkens her cheeks before shifting to Justin.

I glare at him when I catch him staring at what's mine. "Take your eyes off her ass."

"Fake? Yeah right," he mumbles low, so only I can hear his taunt.

"When did you guys arrive?" I hear Bianca question.

"Ever heard of knocking, trespassers?" Rosalie demands at the same time.

"Ro!" I hear the third one hiss to her hellfire friend.

"This is my apartment, Rosalie," I reply in a bored voice.

"And Bianca's," comes her smug response.

"It's not mine, Ro," answers Bianca with a roll of her eyes when she mistakes my silence as offended. Not that I care when I actually like calling it ours, which it is for the foreseeable future.

"Of course it is, Bee. What's his is yours now," she says matter-of-factly, then quirks one eyebrow at me. "Isn't that right, Mr. Fiancé?"

My hungry gaze is on Bianca when I rasp, "Whatever she desires, it's hers."

We are suspended in an intense stare-off while Bianca tries not to blush and fails. It gives me the moment to take in her unabashedly and notice her messy bun, the slope of her neck bare under her off-the-shoulder-top, and not an inch of makeup on her stunning face.

This is what I'll come home to every night.

"You're moving in together?" Justin's loud voice steals her attention.

I mask my expression into boredom because I've already shown more than I want to and can feel her friends observing my every move like a hawk. As much as I'm glad she has protective friends, I really wish they would leave and take Justin with them. I'm already regretting bringing him in the first place.

"They are." Again, Rosalie answers before I can and explains, "See, that's what happens when two people get engaged."

"You have a mouth on you," he taunts, irritation flashing in his eyes.

Rosalie is unaffected as she tilts her head and scoffs, "Next you'll tell me I have a nose, eyes, and ears."

I hide my chuckle at her retort and while they continue to bicker, I stalk toward Bianca who watches them with an amused expression. It immediately transforms into fervor when I step in her personal space, crowding her against the table behind.

"Miss me, kitten?" I tease, resting my hands on her sides.

"Your I'm-the-boss-of-Bianca personality? Not at all."

Her fake indignation and breathless voice pulls a low chuckle out of me, making a shiver run down her spine. It's as unmistakable as her intoxicating scent. A wayward curl falls into her dark eyes so I tuck it behind her ear with my finger. She leans into my touch before retreating like she realized it at the last moment.

It fills me with satisfaction that she's as affected by our proximity as I am.

"Dash," she whispers, and I instinctively lean closer to her tempting lips.

Her nervous swallow has me tracing my finger down her ear to her collarbone, where her pulse is pounding rapidly. Goosebumps rise on her silky skin, making me want to press my mouth there and suck until I taste them on my tongue.

"Yeah, kitten?" I rasp, staring into her dilated pupils.

"You're touching me."

"I am." I continue tracing my finger back and forth on her bare shoulder.

SCANDALOUS GAMES

"The rules."

"What about them?"

"You promised you wouldn't break them." She tries to sound strong but her voice falls into a breathless whisper.

"No touching when we're alone," I repeat her rule before smirking. "We're not alone, kitten."

Her gaze narrows dangerously but she ends up looking adorable. She tries to cross her arms in a defiant stance but the tight space only puts her flush against me. It only maddens her further while pleasing me.

"Loophole or not, it's still breaking it," she complains.

"Your mistake, my gain."

Ignoring our friends' loud presence behind us, I inch my hand lower to the hem of her thin top and slide it underneath to dig my fingers into her waist. A tiny gasp escapes her mouth but it's enough to distract her as I shove my hand in the waistband of her jeans.

"Dash!" She moans when my palm cups her ass and I squeeze while her panicked eyes stare over my shoulder. No need for her to worry though, she's perfectly hidden from their view.

As if I'll let them see the flush on her skin and eyes drowning in desire.

"I'm a breasts man, kitten, but seeing you bent over with your ass staring at me, I wanted to fuck you right then and there." Her whole body vibrates, eyes going round, and I roughly palm her ass, pulling apart her cheeks until she rises on her toes to escape my touch. "If we were alone, I would've bent you over the nearest surface, tied your wrists with my belt behind your back, and slid my cock in your cunt until you fell apart for me."

"Too bad you can't touch me when it's just us," she sasses despite the haze of lust. Her nipples harden and poke against her top, betraying just how much she likes my fantasy.

"Don't for one second think just because I can't touch you, that I can't have you begging for me to fuck you, kitten."

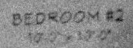

Chapter Twenty-three

BIANCA

His challenging and arrogant promise leaves me fuming and my imagination running wild. My mind, fantasizing all the filthy ways he could seduce me. The confidence that lies underneath his tone that he can have me begging without laying a finger on me is irritating.

I especially hate how my body is attuned to his every command, every dirty word spoken, betraying me by melting at his husky voice.

Before I can respond with a comeback, Rosa speaks from behind him.

"Hey, Bee, we have to leave."

I sidestep from behind Dash's hulking frame, instantly missing the warmth of his touch as his hand slips from my shorts. Of course, only he would find a loophole and use it to his advantage. I can't actually believe he had the nerve to grab my ass with our friends standing a few feet from us. It's my fault, really. Didn't I sense a trap when he agreed so easily? Should've listened to my gut.

He's unashamed, arrogant, and wicked.

And apparently even in public, I'm unprotected from his devious ways.

Justin is nowhere to be seen when I look around the room while Iris and Rosa stand beside each other with an apologetic expression. Well, Iris does while Rosa's face is pinched in pure annoyance. The one she wears when it's anything related to Nova.

SCANDALOUS GAMES

"I thought you were gonna stay for longer?" I remind her and she shrugs.

"My mom wants me to go look at wedding venues," comes Rosa's disinterested answer. "Apparently, not all of the money in the world puts you high on the waiting list."

"And I'm meeting Nathan," adds Iris.

I feel Dash's body heat and his musky scent before he presses against my back and leans forward to whisper a taunt in my ear, "And you say being alone with me doesn't scare you."

"Shut up." I glare at him, making his lips twitch in amusement. Facing my two grinning friends, I roll my eyes before moving closer as I tug them both out of the room. "I'll walk you both out."

"Shall we start calling him *jiju*?" whispers Iris. Rosa snorts behind her hand.

"Oh, you find it funny, Ro?" I snapped before smiling sweetly. "We can call Nova *jiju* too if you like it so much."

Her mouth flattens into a thin line. "You wouldn't."

"Stop, you two," says Iris in a cool voice before stealing my attention by fanning her face. "Dash is superhot, Bee. I understand now why you gave your virginity to him."

If I didn't know Iris was wholeheartedly committed to Nathan, I'd be jealous of her awestruck voice. Then I remember I have no claim on Dash, despite our mutually beneficial arrangement. He might play the act of the doting husband in front of the world, but he's free to secretly fuck whomever he wants.

Which won't be a hardship for him since he's all about discreet affairs.

As soon we reach the door, they turn to me expectantly before Rosa bluntly asks, "Are you going to fuck him?"

"What? No," I say, affronted. "I don't want him."

"Is that why you let him grope your ass when we were inside?" Rosa smirks. My cheeks flame and it's all the answer they need. Turning to Iris, Rosa says, "I told you."

Great. I just gave them ammunition to tease me mercilessly.

"Let's not forget you seduced him at the club," adds Iris to which Rosa nods.

"Because I wanted him to agree to the plan," I exclaim. "I wasn't going to fuck him."

"Keep telling yourself that."

I shake my head as I huff, "I'm not going to sleep with a man who has dirty threesomes on a daily basis. He's a manwhore." I could not sound more judgmental.

"Only means he'll be exceptional in bed," winks Iris. He was my first yet I knew deep in my bones he was the best. The men later in my life only proved me right.

Rosa simply shrugs and pitches in her two cents, "It's not like you'll fall in love with him. Just enjoy the free orgasms and say goodbye once Arya is married."

"Get out, you both." I shut the door on their laughing faces and breathe a deep sigh.

There's no more denying that I'm physically attracted to Dash and my body craves his rough touch, the fantasies he paints and his deep, dominating voice when he's turned on. Knowing he's my ex's stepbrother and made it his mission to uproot my life in the past doesn't make me desire him any less.

However, it's not enough for me to have sex with him again and cross the line into dangerous territory. Our connection only brushes the surface and no matter how much I ignore it, I've never been the girl who has meaningless sex. Especially with a man who infuriates me half the time.

I'm not going to give in to the pull that breathes like a live wire between us.

He and I are forbidden and always will be.

Our history is too complicated to be anything but.

And being around Dash also brings up the memories of Niall, in spite of the cage I've locked them in. Mostly, the anger and the pain that he never once called or tried to win me back, let alone apologize for cheating on me. When I had caught him, he hadn't even pulled out of the girl even after seeing me standing there with tears streaming down my face.

All I remember is running and ending up outside Dash's bedroom.

I stupidly thought I had moved on from Niall's betrayal but when you've never found closure, the scars never fully heal. The wound may try to seal itself but all it takes is one scratch for the stitches to come undone.

It's not that I'm still in love with Niall. Because over the years, I realized he was never the one for me. It's the ugly damage it's caused to my teenage heart that I haven't been able to repair. Every time I tried to date in the past, a flicker of doubt would make itself home inside me like a slow poison and kill everything.

Separating from him and looking back on our relationship, little snippets or memories showed me he wasn't as perfect a boyfriend as he pretended to be. There were times he would belittle me in subtle ways, disregarding my feelings, but I could never see past the lovesick fool he had made me.

My first heartbreak became my ultimate downfall.

It hardened the layers around my heart until I stopped letting anyone in. Sadly, they're still as strong as ever. They've covered my heart so deep that no one can ever rupture it.

The idea of love… feels like a hopeless dream. Because all it brings with it is a chaos of sadness and loathing. All I know is, I never want to be the pining, love-obsessed girl I once was.

"Kitten."

Upon hearing Dash's soft voice, I turn around from gazing out the floor-to-ceiling glass wall to face him. His expression is pinched in concern and burning curiosity while the rest of him is impassive and cold.

"Yeah, Dash?" I ask, clearing my throat.

Jeez! How long was I zoned out? I ponder as he continues to stare intensely. Can he tell I was wondering about his stepbrother? It makes me wonder whether they still hate each other. Do they still talk? Or if he bragged to Niall that he and I slept together? Niall was petty enough to do it, had the situation been reversed.

Most importantly, do I even wanna know? It'd be nothing less than opening a can of worms. Maybe it's safe to continue to ignore the elephant in the room. The less deep we go into our shared past, the easier our coming days will be.

Or you're just not courageous, my mind taunts viciously.

SCANDALOUS GAMES

"Do you need help moving your stuff?" he asks. I expel a sigh when he doesn't grill me about my earlier thoughts.

I focus on him and frown. "I've already moved all my necessary things, Dash."

"The master bedroom upstairs is empty."

"Yeah. I left it for you and took one of the bedrooms down the hall on this floor."

His gaze narrows dangerously and his forearms bulge when he crosses them in front of his wide chest. "What is wrong with the master bedroom?"

"Umm… nothing."

Every corner of his penthouse is more stunning, spacious, and lively than mine. The stairs on my right curve and lead to the floor upstairs. As soon as I took the tour, my mind was bombarded with all the ideas I could implement to spruce this place up and make it perfect. Of course, the master bedroom is the best of all rooms with a glass wall on each side of the four-poster bed and a balcony in the front.

Since Dash owns the apartment, I couldn't be selfish and steal it by calling dibs. Trust me, I was tempted. Instead, I chose the one downstairs, far away from his. So I really don't understand why he's suddenly in a pissy mood at having it to himself.

He takes a threatening step forward and tilts his head as he demands, "Then how come your bags are in the other bedroom, wifey?"

"If you think I'm sharing a room with you, you're delusional, *my fake husband*," I announce the second the meaning behind his words register. It's not as if someone is coming to visit us and check the proof of our relationship.

I gulp, my back hitting the wall as he crosses the distance between us and cages me in. Bending to be as close as possible while keeping his promise of not to touch me when alone, his breath fans across my lips as he growls, "I didn't ask you to move in because I needed a roommate, kitten. You're going to be my wife soon and there's no way you are allowed anywhere but in my bed."

"Did you even listen to my rules?" My anger rises at his commanding tone, trying to have his way. Lifting my chin, I remind him, "No bossing me around."

"I told you I'll give you a choice. So either you shift your stuff upstairs or I'm bringing mine down to yours."

"That's not a choice, you asshole."

"I only had one condition and so far, you're not holding your end of the bargain, kitten."

My breasts brush against his wide chest as I exhale a rough breath. The urge to push him away rises but I ignore it because it will mean touching him. No way am I giving him the satisfaction.

"It wasn't mentioned that I had to share the bedroom with you, Dash. I moved in like you asked. So, really, it's your fault," I say in a breezy tone.

Instead of making him fume like I intended, he becomes eerily calm. I sense the devious wheels turning in his head and my insides tighten into a tensed ball when a tiny smirk lights up his face.

"You say being alone with me doesn't scare you but your actions say otherwise."

"For the last time, I'm not scared," I snap.

"Then prove it."

The manipulative, bossy bastard simply shrugs and his eyebrow arches arrogantly as he waits for my answer. Like he doesn't already know that I never back down from a challenge, especially from him. I'm torn between telling him to stick his "then prove it" up his ass and proving him wrong. The latter half of me wins.

"Fine. I'll share the master bedroom with you." *And annoy you into regretting it.* I keep the promise to myself. When he continues to breathe down my neck, I sigh, "Will you step back, please?"

"Anything for you, wifey."

"Then stop calling me wifey."

"I'm just practicing," he replies with an innocent smirk.

"Don't kill him," I mutter to myself as I shove past him and walk away. His amused chuckle, following and taunting me down the hall.

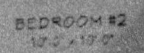

Chapter Twenty-four

BIANCA

The evening comes way too soon until it's time for dinner. However, it's only because his mighty ass demanded I finish moving my clothes and other items to his bedroom upstairs by the end of the day. I'm pretty sure he secretly loves seeing our clothes arranged together in the closet more than I do. For a man who despises intimacy except while fucking, he sure likes to make me an exception.

It does strange things to my already confused head.

Last I saw, he was busy talking on the phone in another room, which I'm guessing will be his home office since the movers brought in and placed a sleek wooden desk inside, along with a matching chair. It was the only new furniture since the rest of the apartment was fully furnished. Though I wouldn't mind replacing a few things.

While he's gone, I order us both some food. Chinese for him and a burger and fries for me. It will take another half an hour for it to arrive so I sit at the dining table, pull out my laptop, and work on a project I'm behind on. I took half a day off today with the moving and all, so I now have a lot of emails to catch up on.

I'm a few minutes in when my phone starts ringing and Arya's name flashes on the screen. Looks like Mom finally discussed it with her if she's calling. Everything happened so fast that it slipped my mind to tell my sister myself. Last time we talked, I didn't reveal much.

"Hi, Ari," I chirp, picking up the call.

"You got engaged to Dash Stern?" she screeches in a high-pitched voice.

"Did Mom tell you?"

"Mom? What, no," she denies. Her tone sounds taken aback. "It's all over the news, Bee. One of my colleagues showed me a tabloid with you standing beside Dash. How come you never told me you're dating a freaking billionaire? Why would you keep it a secret?"

I'm still processing the news of an article being out there to hear the rest of her words. Thanks to my dad shielding us from the limelight, the media has never paid much attention to write some gossip story about me. It means Dash is probably the reason there's one out there, which is going to make my dad pissed.

Another complication I didn't need.

And shouldn't Dash have warned me that the fucking paparazzi stalks him? Just how famous is he? So many questions, not a lot of time for answers.

"Bee? You there?" Arya's voice pulls me back to focus on the present.

"Yeah. Yeah, I'm here."

"So it's true then? You and Dash? Do Mom and Dad know?" she asks in rapid fire succession.

"Yes. We had lunch with them on Sunday and announced the big news."

"Was this the reason you told me to win Aryan back?"

The relief and giddiness I hear in her voice when she utters his name strengthens my resolve and reminds me why I'm going through with this charade in the first place. Love really makes us do stupid things.

"Of course, Ari. I told you everything will turn out fine. Once I'm happily married, you can ask Dad for yours and Aryan's next year."

"How did he take it when you told them?" Her tone is hesitant and low. "Was Ma happy?"

I wonder if I should share the whole debacle and tension at lunch because Arya has never been able to understand my complicated relationship with our parents. More often than not, she sides with them and honestly, it's not her fault they get along. But that doesn't mean it hurts less. Their values and desires simply align.

"They're not talking to me."

"Seriously? But why?"

"Because I chose the man myself and didn't tell them before becoming engaged." I sigh, a headache slowly forming. "It's like I can't win with them. The article will only make them madder."

"They're being silly. Dash is better than any man they could've picked for you, Bee," she consoles. "I'll talk to them."

"Don't you dare," I immediately counter, shaking my head even though she can't see.

At my firm tone, she mutters, "Fine. But we're meeting this Sunday and you're telling me all about your secret whirlwind romance. I can't believe you hid it from me. God! I have so much to ask you."

If only she knew the truth. "Sure, Ari. I gotta go. My dinner's here."

SCANDALOUS GAMES

"Congratulations, by the way," she replies in a singsong voice. "Bye, Bee. Love you."

I hang up just as the doorbell rings. Shutting down my laptop, I walk to the front door and return to the kitchen while carrying the food bag. The smell of the burger, enticing and lifting my troubled mood.

As I rest it on the island, my phone notifies me about a text message. Curious, I make my way to the dining table and I pull up short when I see it's from my mother. Arya better not have ignored my warning and talked to her.

> MOM: Your father and I would like to have dinner with you this Sunday. Bring your fiancé. We'd like to meet him too.

"Well, damn," I mutter. Maybe there's hope, after all. But first, I need to confirm, so I text Arya.

> ME: Did you talk to Mom?

Her reply comes instantly.

> ARI: Of course not. You told me not to.

The sounds of footsteps approaching has me tucking away my phone and I face away to take out our food, plates, and two bottled waters. I'm a bit nervous at the thought of living with a man for the first time. Suddenly, it hits me that this is too intimate, as if we're a real couple even though it's fake.

Still, it's nerve-racking. I'm not even trying to think about when I'll have to sleep beside him on the same bed. I could just sneak to my old apartment once he falls asleep. Then in the morning, I'll return before he's awake and he'll be none the wiser.

Hmm... It could totally work.

Satisfied with my little plan, I turn around. "I hope you like Chinese because—"

The rest of the words get stuck in my throat and all my thoughts scatter while every nerve ending in my body comes to life at the sexy vision before me. I swallow the drool threatening to fall out of my mouth while my eyes try to decide where to stare at first. Looking away is an impossibility and breathing seems secondary.

Because Dash is standing shirtless in our kitchen.

His ripped muscles look carved from the finest stone and chiseled to perfection. Muscular seems too tame a word to describe his veiny forearms, broad chest, and eight-pack abs with the happy trail leading to the bulge beneath his black sweatpants.

Sweet mercy! Who fucking needs eight-pack abs?

I swear if sex appeal had a name, it'd be Dash Stern. Don't get me wrong, Dash is powerful and magnetic in his pristine thousand-dollar suits but the half-naked him is a sight to behold. Sexy. Sinful. Irresistible. Freshly showered with his hair still wet, pants dangerously low against the V of his hips—he's mouthwatering. My fingers itch to dig into the cuts and planes of his hard abs to explore every inch of him for hours.

What will it feel like to have him pressed against my naked skin?

My stomach hollows and I have the strong urge to squeeze my legs to ease the ache that his perfect physique ignites. It's like my brain has stopped functioning because I can't rip my eyes away and stop staring like a sex-starved creep.

Is he going to flaunt his body in my face every day? How the fuck am I supposed to resist him? It's like I'm taken back to seven years ago when he roamed around shirtless in his house. Silly of me to think he would've changed.

Dash clears his throat. I blink and wrench my gaze to his. My cheeks redden when I find a smug smirk gracing his too handsome face. His green irises, sparking with lust and delight at my stuttering and salivating state.

My head tilts back on instinct when he approaches behind the counter and I'm enveloped in his smoky scent with a hint of aftershave. The breath whooshes out of my lungs when he crowds me from behind and leans over my shoulder to check out the food.

"Smells delicious," he whispers in my ear.

"It's from a popular restaurant."

"Wasn't talking about the food, kitten."

I blush like a schoolgirl while he pulls away, his fingers ghosting over my waist just shy of touching. It takes me a few seconds to recover and meet his gaze as he helps me set the plates and carry the water to the table. The muscles in his back, rippling and flexing with each step, and I want to cry at the sensory torture.

If this is his plan to seduce me without touching, I'm afraid he'll succeed.

Following him, I sit across from his seat and avoid his piercing gaze by busying myself in pulling out the fries and burger. He fills his plate with his own food but unlike him, I can't concentrate on anything except his naked chest or his hair falling on his forehead, giving him a boyish look.

"You keep staring at me like that, wifey," he says in a low, husky voice before hooded eyes meet mine, "and I'd be tempted to make a meal out of you."

My hands pause halfway to my mouth and I act aloof and annoyed while my body hums in pleasure. Ignoring it, I shrug and snap, "Then go wear a shirt."

"Or you could take off yours so I have something to look at too."

"Nice try." I laugh, rolling my eyes.

His low chuckle reverberates down my spine and then we both dig into our plates. The second I bite down on my burger, I forget all about Dash and his distracting body while my taste buds sigh in pleasure. I don't know what they put in the bread and the patty that has me addicted.

Who gives a fuck if it's unhealthy when it tastes like heaven?

The sudden loud scraping of a chair has me freezing and focusing on a tensed

SCANDALOUS GAMES

Dash standing over me. "What?"

Shaking his head, he grabs his plate and walks past me while muttering something like, "Death of me."

Moody asshole. I finish eating my dinner before I remember my mom's earlier text. Turning to him while he stands with his back to me, I ask, "Did you read the article about us?"

"Yes," he answers swiftly.

"Why didn't you warn me?"

He whips around and his broad shoulders move as he shrugs, "I told you there are rumors going around about me and it has put me under the media's radar. Usually, I only have to worry about them back home."

"What rumors?"

His gaze sharpens. "You're telling me your friends haven't filled you in?"

My guilty face says it all but I don't shy away as I ask in a nonjudgmental voice, "Is it true?"

Gripping the marble counter on each side, he leans back and crosses his legs as he quirks an impassive eyebrow. "You think I'm capable of killing a man, kitten?"

"No." I'm surprised by the conviction I feel down to my bones. Dash can be described as a lot of things but never as a remorseless killer. He certainly wouldn't jeopardize his business by being hotheaded. I can tell he's relieved at my answer because the furrow in his brow disappears. "I can't be sure about my parents, though."

"It's not their opinion that matters to me."

The sincerity in his voice has me feeling all gooey inside and special. "You really don't like them, do you?"

"They haven't given me a reason so far."

"Well then, it's going to be one awkward dinner." I wince. When he stares, confused, I explain, "They've invited us for dinner this Sunday."

"Do you believe they changed their mind about us?"

I rest my chin on my steepled fingers as I answer, "I think it's a test to judge us as a couple under their terms and territory."

"They want to see if we're really in love," he softly says and I nod. "Then you might want to hone your acting skills. You're terrible."

"I am not," I snap, offended.

He pushes off the counter and walks to where I'm sitting and accuses, "You almost gave us away last time."

"Because you came out of thin air announcing we're engaged."

"I still think you can do better," he throws over his shoulder as he walks out of the kitchen. "I can't be saving your ass every time, kitten."

He's out of my view before I can respond with a smart-ass remark. Come Sunday dinner, I'll show him just how *in love* I can be.

Chapter Twenty-five

BIANCA

I stay downstairs and distract myself with work until I can no longer avoid going to the bedroom. It's futile for me to hope that he's gone to sleep without me, but I can't be certain unless I check for myself. He didn't once come back to demand I come to bed, which felt like a real possibility. After all, bossing and tormenting me is his favorite pastime.

I have half a mind to sneak to my old apartment. However, I don't want to give him the smug satisfaction if I were to be caught.

Maybe that's what he's counting on. He would love that, wouldn't he?

I glance at the stairs and with a sigh, switch off my laptop before gathering the courage to confront our bedroom situation. God forbid he accuses me of being scared of him yet again. As I switch off the lights, unfiltered questions run through my mind.

Did he ever have a girlfriend? Did they share an apartment?

Did I ever cross his mind?

I stop my train of thought when they enter into dangerous waters. Of course he wouldn't have reminisced about me. I was just his stepbrother's naïve girlfriend. The girl he had to put up with in his house and glared at most of the time. Sometimes, even save her from trouble when her boyfriend was too busy getting shit-faced.

SCANDALOUS GAMES

It was at that moment I realized Dash wasn't as cold-hearted and cruel as Niall claimed. Despite his hard outer shell and perpetual glower, he was protective and affectionate.

His callousness was a layer of defense from the world.

In some ways, he's still the same. Mysterious and secretive as he was before, one can only tell if they look closely. Since we ran into each other, he has stolen and invaded my life while keeping his guarded. Despite me wanting to keep our arrangement as impersonal as possible, he ruthlessly tore through the line and took more than I bargained.

He knows my deepest fear and my complicated relationship with my parents, while I know nothing about his. Even Niall wouldn't tell me anything except warning me to keep my distance.

No matter how much I deny and resist, there's a burning curiosity inside me to know the man Dash Stern is. I want to dig beneath his heartless exterior, uncover his secrets and unmask the real him that he hides from everyone.

He knows my weaknesses, my vulnerabilities, and I want to learn his.

As his wife—even a pretend and temporary one—it's my right. At least, that's the lie I tell myself.

The hallway is dark and quiet until I see light spilling from the door to our bedroom as I get closer.

So, he's awake...

With my chin held high, I push inside, only to find the huge bed empty with the lamps on each bedside providing some lighting in the room. I glance around for signs of him, when the cold breeze hits my bare legs.

That's when I see Dash sitting on the balcony, working on his own laptop. It's a little after midnight so I'm shocked to catch him working so late. I never stay up this late unless I have a meeting the next day or I'm behind on my projects, which is my excuse for tonight.

Then again, I don't run a billion-dollar company.

He doesn't even notice my presence until I'm standing right behind him. The light spilling from the laptop screen flits across his concentrated face. His shoulders are hunched and his lips are pursed as he types away. I'm contemplating whether or not to disturb him when he speaks up, startling me.

"Did you need anything, kitten?"

"It's really late, Dash," I softly say. "Do you often work till this hour?"

"Yes," he answers without losing the momentum of his rapid typing, and it's enough to reveal he's a workaholic. And come to think of it, I've noticed him constantly on his phone either texting or conversing. Just like my dad. He couldn't bear to be away from work even for a second and I'm well aware what it did to him and the unfeeling man he became as a result.

At this rate, Dash is halfway on the same track.

And I don't like it.

"It's unhealthy," I scold, before inching closer. "Come to bed, Dash."

His fingers pause instantly and the energy around us shifts and cackles as he raises his green eyes to mine. Underneath the moonlight, they glow like two jewels and appear darker. For the first time, he appears flabbergasted before a soft expression transforms his rugged features. I become breathless and shy under his unwavering stare, like he's trying to look into my soul. And pulling apart the pieces until he reaches my core.

I desperately wish I knew what he was thinking right now.

"Am I dreaming or did you just invite me to bed, wifey?" he teases. His husky voice, feeling like a warm caress. The nickname, holding more intimacy underneath the starry sky.

"To sleep. Don't get any dirty ideas," I warn in a light tone.

"Impossible." He smirks. "All I have are dirty ideas when it comes to you. Some downright filthy."

I blame the shiver that dances down my spine on the cool night breeze. "Just come to bed, please."

I'm ready to snatch his damn laptop when he sighs and nods.

"I have one important email to reply to. How about you get ready for bed and I'll meet you inside?"

"Fine."

Returning inside, I pull out my favorite pair of sleep shorts and a loose cami from the closet and go to the bathroom to change. Since I'm super tired, I'm tempted to skip my nightly skincare routine but the fear of an unwanted pimple popping up has me rejecting the idea. It took me years to finally find the correct routine that suits my skin and it's been a blessing. Quickly brushing my teeth and combing my hair, I skip back to the room.

My eyes immediately connect with Dash's just as he's straightening up from the bedside table and I feel naked when his gaze roams down the length of me. My nipples tighten underneath my thin top and I regret skipping my bra because I almost forgot I won't be sleeping alone from now on.

Holy fuck.

I swallow when I notice he's only wearing boxers and see the outline of his huge dick as it slowly hardens before my hungry eyes. Never has a man's thighs made my pussy quiver but his muscular and powerful ones have me lusting. The man has no ounce of fat in his body, I swear.

He's perfect everywhere with his striking and sinful physique to complement him.

And he's all mine.

Temporarily.

"Unless you want to be bent over this bed and fucked raw in the next two seconds, I suggest you stop staring at my dick," he growls in a guttural tone, raising goosebumps on my skin. "Your stupid rules be damned."

His eyes are livid and glowing with intense need when mine snap to his. I'm rooted to the spot while observing his tensed and bunched muscles as he roughly breathes. It's as if he's fighting really hard not to act on his promise. Possessed and ensnared by him, my mind flashes to the night at the club.

The way he took control of me without my permission, the rough sting of his teeth as he marked my skin... and bit my pussy because I rubbed against another man. The naked possessiveness and madness in his eyes scared and exhilarated me at the same time.

God! Would it be so wrong if I fucked him? Just once so I can end this torture.

"Fuck, kitten! You're killing me." He groans, stepping closer as if pulled by an invisible thread. It snaps me from giving in to my body's urges and making a mistake. Sleeping together will only complicate our connected future.

"You're not sleeping in that, are you?" I mumble, ignoring the need in his voice.

I watch his jaw grind as he calms himself down before the primal look vanishes and the mischievous yet stern Dash is staring at me. The bulge in his boxers doesn't seem to be in a state to calm down as easily. Neither does the throb in my clit.

"No." His answer makes me sigh in relief. It lasts for a second before he smirks. "I sleep naked."

I bite my lip, imagining his hard length pressed against my back all night before shaking off the naughty train of thought.

Focus, Bianca.

"Tonight, you won't," I throw back with resolve before threatening with a shrug. "Not unless you don't want me to share a bed with you."

He reacts by recoiling and snarling, "Don't tempt me into tying you up."

"I dare you." I lift my chin and don't budge from my demand.

"Fine."

I smile when he relents and whips the covers off before settling down on the bed. His eight-pack abs tightens and taunts me as he lies down on his back. Lifting slightly on his elbows, he watches me crawl into the bed and his tongue peeks out to lick between his teeth when I unintentionally give him a view of my cleavage as I bend.

I shoot him a glare when he chuckles low, and turn onto my side, giving him my back as I draw the blanket over me. The mattress dips slightly when he shifts and a minute later, the room is blanketed in darkness.

"Goodnight, wifey."

"Night, dear fake husband."

Minutes pass and sleep doesn't come as I wriggle, trying to find a comfortable position, but my body can't relax. The mattress feels weird and scratchy despite being so soft and pillowy and made of the finest wool. It always takes me a while to get used to a new bed or a new place, which is frustrating.

Plus, I'm hyper aware of Dash on my side, so close that I can feel his body heat, hear every even breath he takes while his scent drowns and suffocates all my senses. Every little nerve ending under my skin tingles and sparks to life until sleep is all but erased.

I jump when he sighs loudly and whispers in the dark, "Weren't you tired, kitten?"

"I miss my bedroom," I whisper back. "And I forgot my cuddle pillow."

"There are literally four right here," he mocks.

"My old one is my favorite, okay?"

My pulse skyrockets when his calloused fingers grip my small wrist. One small tug and I'm plastered against his side. I'm too stunned to mutter a protest when he nestles me in the crook of his arm and shoulder while draping my left leg over his until I'm lying halfway on his warm and shockingly comfortable chest.

"Here, cuddle me."

For the longest of seconds, I'm still as a statue and concentrating on my rapid pulse, like my heart is in my throat. I'm grateful for the darkness so he can't see my blush forming on my cheeks. Every hard ridge and texture—it molds and fits against my curves.

I'm about to call him out for touching me when the tip of his finger traces up and down my spine teasingly while the other palm caresses the back of my thigh with his thumb. It is so soothing and pleasant that my eyes begin to feel heavy.

"So you're a cuddler, Dash?" I mumble, halfway close to passing out.

"No, I hate it. Now, go to sleep."

He denies it, yet holds me so tight that our heartbeats sync and beat the same rhythm. The desire to pull away doesn't even penetrate my mind. Instead, I curve my arm around him until I fall into a dreamless slumber.

Chapter Twenty-six

BIANCA

Remember when Dash said he was going to buy me an engagement ring? Well, he forgot to mention one tiny detail—that it will involve an eight-hour trip in a private jet across the world. Because here I am in the capital city of fashion and romance—*Paris, France*.

I forgot the number of times I pinched myself to make sure I wasn't dreaming. Or hallucinating. Or gone plain crazy.

Yesterday, all I received was a simple text saying to pack my bags. It was easy to assume he was flying me to his home since he mentioned in passing I would need to attend charity functions and social gatherings with him after the news of our engagement broke all over the country. After Nova and Rosalie, we're the next "it" couple and everybody wants private details of our whirlwind romance.

It's been an overwhelming experience, to say the least.

One editor of a top magazine wouldn't stop hounding me for an exclusive interview despite me refusing several times. At least I wouldn't have to worry about her now. I don't know how Rosa does it, honestly.

Throughout our flight, Dash smartly evaded my prying questions about our adventure with a knowing smirk on his face. The controlling asshole had even paid the crew members to not reveal our destination.

The maddening part—I couldn't even yell or complain at him under the crew's watchful gaze because, to the public, we're a head-over-heels-in-love couple. A fact my dear fake fiancé took full advantage of by sitting me in his lap, with intimate caresses that left my cheeks flaming and squirming on his thighs.

It was distracting, tantalizing, and sinful agony.

And no, I didn't secretly revel in it. *Lies.*

However, it was satisfying to see shock contour his ravishing face when I played along and called him darling breathlessly until I was certain he was going to fuck me then and there. The primal and salacious expression full of savage lust left me floored and winded.

Then to punish me for my secret rules holding him back, he marked the column of my throat by biting me savagely. He did it where everyone could see and sat back with a satisfied smirk for the rest of the flight, stealing possessive glances at the hickey.

He must have been a predator in his past life, because the man is obsessed with marking me with his teeth like a savage.

However, my anger had all but evaporated the second we landed. I stepped out and was greeted by the driver in a French accent saying, *"Bonjour, mademoiselle."*

I swear I staggered in my heels when I learned we were in Paris. The beautiful city I've always dreamt of visiting when I was young and smitten with after binge-watching Hallmark romance movies. I would fantasize about walking on the bridge over the Seine with the love of my life and follow the tradition of love locks.

What can I say? The young Bianca was a hopeless romantic. Utterly naïve and trusting.

A faint memory of me confessing this to Niall assaults me.

There's no way Dash could know, right? Because when I peered at him, as always, his face was a veil of secrecy. Obscure and unfaltering.

Though at the moment, it's staring at me in soft wonderment, a faint smile on his mouth.

"I can't believe you brought me to freaking Paris," I yell for the hundredth time, still unable to believe it. I sound like I've never been on an international trip before.

I twist in a circle around the large living room of our one-bedroom suite because—Dash is clingy and has separation issues. Or so I tell myself every night I slip into bed and hug his warm body until I fall asleep. Each time I ask if he still hates it, his gruff answer is yes, yet he doesn't push me away and neither do I.

Three days of us living together and I've already become addicted to him.

From afar, he captivated me, but now that we're close, he has me hooked.

We're staying at a luxurious five-star hotel, the name to which I couldn't even pronounce. Though, Dash faced no qualms. Apparently, he took French in college and actually paid attention.

If he plans to ghost me here, I'm in serious trouble.

The ceiling is so high and arched, leading to another room as I stride farther inside while Dash follows behind. I'm gazing and admiring every inch of this place while his gaze is transfixed on me, like my reactions are more entertaining and amusing. I can feel the heat of it, searing into my back like the caress of warm sunlight on a stormy day.

With a whirl, I turn around to face him, wide-eyed and smiling.

SCANDALOUS GAMES

"Would you like me to pinch you again, kitten?" he teases and raises an eyebrow before sauntering closer. His gait, slow like a panther. "Or I could spank your delectable ass while you stare at the Eiffel Tower from the bedroom balcony?"

I back away, remembering the sting of his palm and how I felt it with every step I took the next day. One of the most erotic experiences of my life that taunts my mind every now and then. "You'd be lucky if I let you near my ass again, let alone spank it."

He stops inches away, hands inside his pockets, and taunts in a husky voice, "Why? You soaked my hand when I spanked your cunt. I can still hear the wet sounds your pussy made and your cry of pleasure."

My fingers tighten in my skirt while I stand with false bravado instead of squeezing my thighs. Cocking my hip, I taunt, "Now you can live with the memory and die a happy man."

A haunted look flashes in his pupils but it's gone just as soon as it appeared. Slowly, his gaze lowers to my parted lips and rises back to mine before he confesses, "I'll die a happy man only after I've tasted your lips and stolen the kiss you owe me from seven years ago, Bianca."

Hearing the sound of my name on his lips for the first time, said in that low and smooth baritone, lets me know the seriousness behind his confession. His mad and tormented face, when he thought I was going to kiss Justin, reflects behind my vision.

Never had I seen a man look so desperate yet ravenous for a simple kiss. As if it was the difference between life and death. Even if he hadn't intervened, I wouldn't have kissed his friend, not after the way Dash was staring at me. Like my kiss was something special.

Something to be treasured.

Something belonging to his lips only.

And even though he can steal it under the pretense of our fake relationship—he never once has. He could claim my mouth as rightfully as he touches and holds me, yet he hasn't.

But I know he's waiting. Aching. Not for the perfect moment. But for something else entirely. That's deeper. Darker. Shattering.

"How can I owe a kiss to someone I believed I'd never meet again?" I softly demand.

"Yet here you stand, soon to become my wife."

"Only in name. Don't forget that."

His eyes glower. "As if you'll let me."

The vehemence in his tone has me taken aback and my heart thumping erratically. Naked fear and the urge to run away stabs me at the insinuation he wants more. The reason I chose him hinges on him being unemotional, heartless, and not believing in the idea of love. It's the only way this'll work.

The physical attraction, I understand, but beyond it, just the thought scares me. He can't blur the lines and tilt my world, my heart, upside down. I won't allow it. The domineering and heartbreaker Dash I can handle, but him in love and fascinated with me—I won't survive him.

My intuition is telling me it'd be ten times worse than the last time.

"Don't make the mistake of falling for me, Dash," I warn. "This—us—can never be real."

"Isn't that supposed to be my line?" He smirks, despite the fire burning in the depths of his green orbs.

"I'm not the one flying my fake fiancée to Paris to buy an engagement ring."

He doesn't even flinch and stares hard, the intensity of it invasive and laser sharp. So nerve-racking, like he's trying to peer down to my very marrow and is succeeding.

"Why are you so scared of love?" His tone is laced with curiosity without any judgment. He's trying to understand me.

My natural instinct is to defend and deny, like I always have to myself and to others. So much so the lie spills without even trying. Leave it to Dash to crack the chain because around him, I've never been anything but vulnerable. So the truth easily falls, raw and crooked.

Everything comes pouring out.

"Love doesn't scare me, it's the aftermath. The inevitable heartbreak, the tears and the agony, and the worst part comes later when self-doubt creeps in, the apology that never comes to give you closure. The shattered pieces that would never fit again and the ghost of heartache that haunts and blackens the light and the good," I profess, a sad laugh spilling from my lips. "I never understood why the people in my world pretend their home is perfect when it's rotten inside, it's because happily ever afters don't exist. But unlike them, I would never resign myself to the same fate."

"You're still the same eighteen-year-old girl, Bianca." His voice is devoid of emotion, and I flinch. "You may not love him anymore but you're letting him hold all the power even seven years later."

He doesn't need to say Niall's name because the familiar dislike is alive in his eyes. Another emotion flickers in them but I can't name it and it's gone in a flash. However, I can't focus on anything but his cutting accusation.

The expression in his depths is the one I've been prey to countless times whenever we ran into each other in the past. Like I'm a silly, weak girl.

If I want to protect my heart by never falling in love, it isn't a weakness.

It certainly doesn't mean Niall still has a hold over me.

"You're wrong," I growl angrily. "Says the man who hasn't been in love, let alone had his heart broken. So what the fuck do you know, Dash?"

My back hits the wall when he crosses the distance and grips my jaw, tilting my face to his. His grip is firm yet soft as he stares into my angry eyes while staying as calm as a deep ocean.

"I don't know what love is but it's not because I'm running or hiding from it—unlike you," he says, his voice cold as ice. "So, I certainly wouldn't fall for you, kitten. As for flying you here, I like to spoil my woman and as long as you're mine, I'll continue to do so. Don't mistake it for anything more."

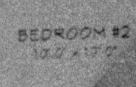

Chapter Twenty-seven

BIANCA

"You're in Paris? Without us?"

"He took you to Paris?"

Rosa and Iris scream on the screen when I reveal where I am, making me wince, and I lean away from the phone until they calm down and stop cursing at me. As soon as I was alone in the bedroom, I video called them, not caring it was midnight back home. They picked up on the second ring, both wide awake.

Rosa glares at me for leaving her behind so I focus on Iris, whose eyes are comically wide like a cartoon character.

"Yeah. He wanted to surprise me," I tell them, trying not to melt into a puddle before I remember his harsh words from earlier, "and buy me an engagement ring, even though I said no."

"Does he not know we have stores here?" huffs Rosa sarcastically. "And did he forget it's a fake engagement?"

"I think it's romantic," sighs Iris dreamily. "Just imagine the things he'd do if he were actually in love with you."

These two are like an angel and devil perched on my shoulder.

I snort a laugh. "Do not romanticize him, Iris. He does these extravagant gestures for all the women he dates. Or should I say, *sleep* with. I'm just another girl in a long list."

"So that's the reason for the sullen face?" queries Rosa suspiciously.

"We had an argument and he left without a word."

"Did he hurt you?" Rosa demands. "I still have the tape from the club. Just say the word and I'll teach him a lesson."

"Whoa! Relax, Ro," I answer until the murderous rage melts from her eyes. "First, delete that damn video. Second, we both said mean things to each other. And also, we don't wanna give him a reason to leave me in a foreign country."

My attempt at a joke fails when they continue to stare back at me with concern. Iris looks thoughtful, before asking softly, "What was the argument about?"

My mind replays the whole conversation and my stomach tightens with guilt for being harsh with him when he was only trying to understand my point of view. Dash has always been a blunt and direct person and never sugarcoats his thoughts. A fact I both hate and love.

"He said that I'm letting Niall's betrayal affect my future," I answer, settling back comfortably against the pillows on the huge fluffy bed. "That I'm scared to trust another man. You guys don't think that's true, do you?"

Their faces mirror matching sadness and hesitancy as they fall silent for several seconds. It's Rosa who speaks first and with caution, as though she doesn't want to hurt or offend me. Suddenly, it feels like an intervention.

"I've known you my whole life, Bee, and for as long as I can remember, you've always been the girl who believed in fairy tales, Prince Charming, and growing up to someday have your own family away from the fakeness of our world. I loved the fact that you were bold, open, and unafraid. Loved the fact that you still believed in love despite your family history. And then suddenly, that part of you died the night you broke up with Niall."

She pauses to take a deep breath, like the memory is as hard on her as it was on me, and tears sting my eyes. Her own wet gaze meets mine as she continues, "It was so hard to watch you become a shell of your former self for months. I hate him so much for breaking your heart and your ability to trust another man. Every time I've seen you date someone, you slowly pull yourself away the second it starts to become something more. You've built these walls around your heart so high, that stops you from giving someone a real chance."

People say no one forgets their first love, when the truth is it's the heartbreak that no one forgets. And when the reason is your boyfriend cheating on you after promising you're his entire world, the betrayal is bone-crushing and scarring. If you're young and already believe the world is a cruel and pretentious place, then it's simply impossible to get over.

Cheating doesn't just wreck your relationship, it ruins all the future ones.

The feeling of not being good enough for someone, despite giving them every ounce of you is an ugly and twisted emotion.

The fear makes a permanent residence in your psyche, whispering and taunting. Once the trust is broken, it's twice as hard to rebuild and no matter how hard I've tried, something always holds me back.

It's easy for people to preach about being tough, to not let the past hold you back—but it's easier said than done. Teenage heartbreak is toxic for a reason.

SCANDALOUS GAMES

"None of them really fought hard to stay, Ro," I finally whisper to her and Iris. "Maybe I want a man who's strong enough to break those walls. Because I don't have it in me to give my heart to just anyone."

"At some point, you'll need to ask yourself if those walls are actually protecting you or becoming the chains holding you back."

I mull over her shockingly deep words that resonate inside me. I don't know if I'm ready to face the truth, though, when it seems like my life's becoming even more complicated lately.

"Would it be so bad if you fell in love, Bee?" Iris asks with a sad smile.

"Kitten."

I look up into Dash's face as he stands in the doorway, holding what appears to be a large bakery bag hanging from his hand. His expression, soft and pinched in apology.

Yes.. My mind whispers. *Yes, it would be bad.*

"Is he back?" Rosa's mad voice draws my attention. "Let me see him. I have a warning for that arrogant asshole for literally kidnapping you."

My cheeks turn pink in embarrassment when her loud voice floats to Dash, whose lips tilt into an amused smirk. I peer down at my phone to see Iris rolling her eyes at Rosa and stifling a laugh. The depressing mood, now lifted from their faces.

"Gotta go. Love you both," I whisper to them and cut the call before Rosa can say any more or threaten Dash with bodily harm.

I straighten up and sit with my hands in my lap while trying to appear outwardly calm, even though my insides are crumbling at how sexy he looks. He looks like royalty with his broad shoulders encased in a crisp winter blazer that tapers into a lean waist and hair mused as though he ran his fingers through it too many times. Dashing, and did I mention sexy?

He could give French men a run for their money.

Mad, Bianca. You're supposed to be mad at him.

However, I'm forgetting the reason why I should be mad as he stands there silently, waiting for me to speak.

"Well?" I arch my eyebrow.

His lips twitch slightly before he strides inside and once close, stares down at me.

"Do you know your nose scrunches when you get mad?" He taps the tip of said nose as he tells me this. "It's cute."

"Is that why you do it often?"

"Sometimes."

"Asshole," I retort, and he smiles.

The color of his eyes darkens when he becomes serious after a moment. "You were right."

"What?" I whisper, stunned, my heart rate dropping.

"That our arrangement isn't real and has an end date, where you and I go our separate paths," he murmurs, his knuckle tracing over my jaw lightly. "It wasn't my place to say those things and it won't happen again. Let's just enjoy the time we have here."

My emotions are a mix of relief and disappointment, when it shouldn't be the latter. The conversation with my friends is still laying heavy in my mind and now that he's coming in with a truce, my thoughts are a jumbled mess. I'm so confused that I don't even know what to say at first. He may regret saying it but he still means every word he said.

"Was that an apology?" I tease, burying my complicated feelings.

"No." He says, dangling the bag in front of my face. "This is."

I take it from him and hurry to uncover the contents, my mouth watering as soon as I lift the lid and see four different flavors of pastries, macarons, mousse, and cupcakes. Each more pretty, colorful, and delicious than the last, and even the aroma is dizzying.

Does he expect me to eat it all? This will easily serve more than a few people.

"I didn't know which flavor you liked, so I got a little bit of everything," he explains gruffly. I can feel his piercing eyes watching my face for every little reaction.

"Red velvet," I answer, picking up one of the cupcakes. "That's my favorite."

A low moan slips past my lips the second I bite down on the creamy top before I can stop it. Never have I tasted a dessert so exquisite in my life.

"Oh my god! This is so good." I sigh in pleasure.

His rough inhale steals my attention and our gazes lock. They are pinned on my mouth and I lick my bottom lip on instinct. I touch around my lips with my finger in case I have cream left on my face and become embarrassed when I feel some.

With a shrug, I go to lick it off but the next second, my wrist is captured by Dash and I stare, dumbstruck, when he brings it to his lips and sucks it into his mouth. It leaves an unbridled chain reaction over my body. My nipples tighten painfully and my pussy clenches, aching to feel his tongue when he licks my finger.

"It is good," he rasps in a dark and rough voice. It's as chocolaty as the cupcake in my hand.

Then, all too soon, he breaks the connection by dropping my hand and cloaking his sharp features into his famous broody mask. Like he didn't just soak my panties a second ago.

Left my skin covered in goosebumps.

Made me breathless.

Needy.

Dripping.

"We leave in two hours," he informs, backing away. "I'll be in the living room working, if you need anything."

Without another word, he turns his back to me and leaves.

I'm so in over my head.

Chapter Twenty-eight

dash

O bsession is like a disease.
Incurable.
Poisonous.
Addictive.

The deadliest thing about it is that it never goes away, not completely, and simply fools us into believing we have absolved ourselves. Love, one can grow out of, but never obsession. It fades into the background, disguises and submerges in a dark recess of our mind until destiny collides you with the heart of your obsession.

And then… you're fucked.

Bianca became the heart of my obsession seven years ago.

The fact that she was my stepbrother's girl and young and pure didn't stop my obsession from growing deeper and more twisted. It had begun with the need to ruin my stepbrother. Instead, it ruined us all. She and I drifted apart until she became a ghost of my past. I thought it was the end.

Years later, we clash once more and with it, blooms the sick fixation from its dark corner. Now, it's deadlier because there's nothing holding me back from making her mine.

Nothing except the truth.

This utter fascination… or *mania* I have for her has a scary dark side. The man

SIMRAN

I become is vindictive, destructive, and villainous.

I want to resist the intangible pull between us but being around her constantly, it's damn near fucking impossible. And if I let myself have her—like I've always longed—I'll crush her already broken and fragile heart.

I'd rather die a thousand deaths before I hurt her.

So, I let her believe she's just another woman, when the truth is she's the first and only one I've dated—fake or otherwise—in my miserable thirty-five years of existence. The only woman I've wanted to spoil. The only one to make me delirious with lust and possessiveness.

Even though it's unhealthy and dangerous to continue this arrangement of ours, I can't walk away. Bringing her to Paris wasn't a spontaneous decision, it was quite the opposite and left me staggering as well.

It's like my mind's floodgate has opened and every little memory I possess of Bianca, whether good or bad, is resurfacing without my control. I was sitting in my office when one of her private conversations with Niall flickered in my mind. It was hazy and incomplete, but her soft voice expressing her dream destination being Paris had stuck to me ever since.

Despite warring with myself that I shouldn't give a fuck and it was a terrible idea, my hands had already been typing to my assistant to book our flight. After seeing the breathtaking look in her eyes, I knew it was worth it. Though the engagement ring was just an excuse, my real intent to bring her here is entirely deviant.

The wait, almost killing and heightening my excitement for tonight.

I had gone to check on her in the bedroom a while ago, only to find her sleeping peacefully. The jet lag must have made her tired because even though I had ordered her to rest on the plane, she had stubbornly refused.

I'm not going to lie, it was entertaining and arousing as hell to mercilessly tease her.

We arrived around twelve and now it's a little after three, which means I need to wake her if we want to make it to our appointment at the jewelry store. While she had slept, I had gone through my important emails so I wouldn't be disturbed for the rest of our stay unless it's urgent. Switching off my laptop, I walk in the direction of the bedroom.

She's still out, lying on her stomach with her right leg hitched high so her black thong is peeking out. In an instant, my dick is hard and begging for attention from her. It would be so easy to slip that tiny lace down her thighs or just shove it to the side and wake her up with my cock inside her.

Because I can still taste her on my tongue from that night at the club.

Can still hear the sounds she made and how she grinded her pussy against my mouth, silently begging for more.

She has no clue how I'd jerked myself off as soon as I'd gotten home while it replayed in my head. Especially her teasing voice whispering... *I already let you in a long time ago, Dash.*

Truer words have never been said.

As though she can sense my presence subconsciously, she turns onto her back and gives me a view of her stunning face. The features, so striking with a natural blush to her sharply cut cheekbones. My favorite part are her sharp brown eyes, now closed but when gazing at me, they reveal every emotion in her heart.

Every inch of her is perfect and delicate.

Every inch of her—*mine.*

Inching closer, I tuck her hair behind her ear and she leans into my palm with a sigh. The simple gesture, spreading warmth and rising protectiveness for her through my chest. I trace her lip with my finger, then lower it to move along her collarbone where I can see my love bite sitting proudly.

Something had come over me when she'd called me darling and I'd lost it.

I'd almost begged her to say it again because it felt real, like she meant it.

If I don't fuck her soon, I'm going to lose my sanity. She has already driven me to the edge and I'm constantly distracted with the filthy visions of her my mind conjures. Visions that if I told her, will have her bright red and running for the hills.

Her defiant glare when I boss her around makes me want to fill her mouth with my cock shoved down her throat. Every time she walks around in tiny shorts and a loose shirt falling off one shoulder, I want to bend her over the nearest surface and fuck her without mercy. And just when she thinks it's over, I want to do it all over again until she forgets her own name.

It's not even close to the other depraved filth I want to do to her.

Like treating her as my whore after the way her eyes begged me that night. That soft, curious, and innocent curiosity tightening her body had me spellbound. She awoke a primal fiend inside me that craves to corrupt her. And had her friend not interrupted, Bianca would have said yes. It was on the tip of her tongue and I could taste it.

Those stupid rules of hers are the only things holding me back. However, it won't be long before I have her begging. Besides, it's fun to watch her squirm and resist me as much as it is torture.

"Kitten," I murmur, cupping her cheek. "Wake up."

She stirs slightly, eyelids still closed, so I nudge her a bit harder until she mumbles incoherently in her sleep. With a smile, I tickle her until she bats my hand away before turning to the other side and grumbles in a raspy voice that goes straight to my cock, "Go away."

I chuckle under my breath. Resting my hands on the bed's edge, I bend and brush my mouth against her ear, whispering, "If you're not up in the next two seconds, I'm going to wake you with my tongue in your pussy, wifey. And once I start, it's going to end with you riding my dick."

As if her body is linked to my voice, her eyes fly open a second before she sits up and I move just in time so our heads don't collide. Soft brown irises drop to my lips before slowly rising to my eyes and her cheeks darken.

"Are we late?" she asks, looking distracted.

I can't help but tease, "I'm almost disappointed you woke up. I wanted to take off that little thong you're wearing with my teeth."

She blushes harder and looks away before sliding off the bed on the other side.

If she wasn't sluggish, her mouth would have hurled an insult for touching and staring at her flimsy panties when we're alone. My smirk widens and I arch my eyebrow at her silly attempt of putting some distance between us. All it would take is two strides for me to crowd her into a corner.

"When do we have to leave?"

I take mercy on her and answer, "In an hour. Get dressed."

Nodding, she searches around the room so I point toward the closet connected to the room, "In there. I unpacked our clothes."

Mumbling a thank-you, she briskly walks inside while I go out to make arrangements for a car to drive us around town. When I return minutes later, she's coming out of the bathroom in a robe. Her naked thighs teasing me with each step until I'm sure I'll die if I don't touch her soon.

The thick tension, mounting with each passing day until one of us cracks.

It's almost becoming a game of wills.

I quickly take a shower and get dressed and even though she went first, I'm still ready before her. Deciding to check my emails, I wait for her in the living room. The merger my company is working hard on is finally about to pay off despite the trouble brought on by the investigation.

Kian Singhania, my new business partner, confirmed over email that they agree with the terms and conditions. Doing business with him will further strengthen my reputation and put rumors to rest. It also means I'll have to leave for home soon and my chest constricts at the thought of leaving Bianca behind. Moving in with me is not something I can coerce her into. Her whole life is built here and my city doesn't exactly hold good memories for her.

"Dash."

Her soft-as-a-petal voice pierces through my musings and I suck in a breath when I take her in from head to toe.

Fuck. How many purple dresses does she own?

Each meant to drive me crazier than the last. The one she's wearing today leaves little to the imagination despite covering her curves and reaching to the end of her legs. Molded so deliciously like a second skin, that I'm pondering how she got it on. Hair twisted in a bun with a few silky tendrils framing her face. Her neck is bare and I narrow my gaze realizing she covered the hickey.

In a flash, I'm in front of her, yanking her head back before she can react. I pull her flush against my chest by gripping her ass just as I bend down to suck where her neck and collarbone meets.

Her fingers grip my coat as she yelps, "Dash!"

I soothe the sting with my tongue before pulling back to meet her hooded eyes. "Did I say you can hide my mark?"

"The last time you said it was for your eyes only."

"Anywhere else, I mind," I growl before circling her nape with my fingers and rubbing the fresh mark. "But here—I want every man who dares to lay their eyes on you to see my marks."

She glares even as her hard nipples press against me. "Stop acting like a caveman."

SCANDALOUS GAMES

"Stop driving me mad." *And being so beautiful.*

"Don't look at me like that." Her voice trembles and limbs shake.

Not loosening my hold, I press against her hips and let her feel my hard cock until her eyelids flutter. When she doesn't push me away, I walk her backward until her spine collides with the wall behind her. I bring my mouth close to hers until we're breathing the same air. "Like what?"

"Like I'm yours."

Leaning my forehead on hers, I slide my grip from her neck to cup her cheek. "Would it be so bad if you were mine, kitten?"

She goes rigid and a shutter goes down, and I know I've lost her.

"Yes."

That single syllable holds so much finality it crushes me. Nobody ever gets to me. I've learnt to keep my emotions locked tight, except for her. Because she makes me feel every toxic and silly human emotion. At this moment, I feel unworthy. A feeling I felt all my life growing up, and it fucking bleeds. Stings like she ripped me apart.

Slowly, I let her go and put space between us. Hardening my expression into one of casual boredom, as if I didn't just bare myself to her a second ago, I speak, "The car is waiting downstairs."

"I don't have a coat," she hesitantly informs me.

I briskly walk to the other room and return with a garment bag, handing it to her without a word. She grabs it and methodically opens the bag, revealing an expensive dark purple full-length winter coat that matches her dress. I can tell she loves it from the way her gaze softens and sparkles as she runs her fingers over it reverently.

"When did you buy this for me?" She says in awe, stunned.

Instead of replying, I check my watch and coldly bark, "Let's go."

Hurt flashes across her face, but I ignore it and turn around to leave. Her footsteps follow only after I've reached the door.

If she wants to continue this arrangement like we're strangers, then her wish is my command.

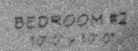

Chapter Twenty-nine

BIANCA

The whole ride Dash doesn't spare me a glance or say a word. The small distance as he sits on the opposite end in the back seat feels oceans apart. His cold demeanor and silent treatment, throwing me off balance and making me question the choices I've made in the past few weeks. I knew I fucked up bad when he didn't pull me close or tease me with his touch, which he loves to do in public.

The most daunting thing about all of this is, I secretly miss it, that I never really hated it as much as I pretended, and I didn't realize how much I became used to it.

And isn't that what I wished for?

He's been nothing but thoughtful and supportive in his own domineering way ever since he agreed to marry me. And all I've done is fight and argue with him. My first impulse seems to be defiance when it comes to him.

It's like my mind is subconsciously listening to Niall's warning from long ago.

I don't want Dash to think I'm not grateful for everything he's doing for me. Standing up to my family, having my back as though I'm his to protect when he could just stay to the side and do only what's necessary. He doesn't have to care for me behind closed doors, yet he's done it since day one.

And now, I've gone and ruined it with my insecurities.

The iciness—close enough to indifference—seeping from him could chill the

SCANDALOUS GAMES

hottest of deserts. My body feels cold and shivering despite wearing the beautiful woolen overcoat he got me. *In purple.* My favorite color. It's simple yet chic and fits me perfectly.

When was the last time anybody gifted me something? I can't even remember.

My eyes are drawn to his profile which is just as sexy as the rest of him. That chiseled jawline under the light scruff could cut glass while his mouth that always had a secret smirk for me, is now set in a firm line. The all-black suit stretched over his muscular frame sending off untouchable and fuck-with-me-and-I'll-destroy-you vibes.

Till now, I believed he had his walls up and was keeping me isolated. Oh, how terribly wrong I was. This is what it feels like to be on the outs from him.

The silent, vacant, and inscrutable Dash Stern with the arctic chill in his bones.

One second, I was in the shadow of his warmth and suddenly, I'm thrown aside and put with the rest of the measly humans. My life split into two conflicting worlds.

If we could go back in time, I never would've answered him. The raw sincerity, the longing in his voice when he uttered that question, shook me to the core. There's no way he could want me beyond our arrangement, right?

All my fears and demons came swimming to the surface and I blurted out yes as I retreated into myself. It was second nature to me. Just like Rosa revealed. Living with the truth that there's something broken inside me, a piece that would never fit into place and leave me warped, is a sad burden. It's continuously weighing me down and I never felt its heaviness as tangible as I do now.

By some miracle, if I wasn't as afraid of letting someone in, there are a million reasons he and I can never be anything but two people bound by a painful history. A history I've tried so hard to forget and run away from.

As we drive down the roads of Paris with its picturesque beauty and vintage yet modern architecture, I reminisce about a future that could've been.

Perhaps, Dash and I could have fallen in love in another lifetime.

A lifetime where our past didn't exist.

A past without guilt.

Without thorns.

The intense ride ends after what feels like ages, when in reality it was an hour despite the traffic. The driver opens the door for me while Dash steps out from his side and I'm crushed when he doesn't react as the strange man takes my hand to help me out. He quietly waits by my side until I right my clothes and guides us inside the luxury jewelry store, which appears to be closed from the outside.

The guard at the door holds it open for us and I'm proven right when I notice that it's empty except for the two of us and a beautiful woman welcoming us with a polite smile. Her blonde hair is sleek and shiny as it falls down her back in waves and she steps forward, then greets us.

"Good evening, Mr. Stern." I notice her eyes stay on Dash a little longer but it's enough for jealousy to flare inside me. Next, she turns to me. "Miss Chopra. So nice to have you both here. I'm Chloe and I'll be helping you today. If you'll follow me, I'll show you the pieces I've set up for you in the back."

SIMRAN

As we follow her, I'm struck by the ambience of the store and the gorgeous diamond pieces adorning each of my sides. Each one, more mesmerizing than the last. The two chandeliers alone are made of intricate gold patterns. I thought I had seen luxury but this is in a whole other league.

"Are we the only ones here?" I whisper to Dash. Since we came during the day, I thought at least a few customers would be inside shopping.

Dash doesn't miss a beat as he replies smoothly, "Yes. I wanted privacy."

My goodness. Is this real?

Who books a whole store just to shop privately and just how rich and powerful do you have to be for them to actually consider it? In a whole other country, no less. Well, the answer is becoming a billionaire. The sky's the limit once you are one, apparently.

I feel like I've stepped into the body of Vivian from the movie *Pretty Woman*. Except, I didn't grow up poor and I'm definitely not a prostitute.

If I'm being honest, though, I can't seem to enjoy any of it with him being a moody jerk. I have the insane urge to shake and yell at him until he goes back to being mischievous and possessive. Knowing his famous control, he either won't react or easily manhandle me into submission. That's if I'm able to move him in the first place. My strength is no match for his.

The back of the room is way prettier and classier than the one we came from and notice that it has less pieces on display. These pieces, however, look more expensive and one of a kind. We are seated on a comfy sofa in front of a round glass table and soon, two glasses of champagne are served. Dash refuses while I grab mine.

I'm here so I might as well enjoy myself. Everything else revolving around this trip has gone downhill since we arrived. And yes, I know I'm to blame. Another video call is due with my best friends to take their help to turn this trip around. I glance briefly at my broody fiancé and I do something I never would've until yesterday or even this morning.

"You sure you don't want a sip, darling?" I softly purr to Dash, laying my hand on his thigh. His green eyes flash with a primal warning.

Bingo.

His muscles bunch and tense underneath my fingertips and I slide them an inch higher, feeling emboldened, before rubbing my thumb back and forth. Deftly gripping my wrist, he rests it back to my side.

"I'm good." His voice is cutting.

No kitten or wifey. Just two dry words with no emotion. Except, his piercing gaze doesn't lose its edge, betraying the fact that I'm getting under his skin. A heady rush of power courses through my veins. Holding his unwavering stare, I casually take another sip of the fruity champagne and slowly lick my bottom lip. I smile when he tracks the movement with quiet intensity.

Feigning nonchalance, I shrug. "As you wish, my love."

As graceful and predatory as a panther, he grips my jaw and brings my face back to his before I can turn away. I'm held in place by an invisible thread and notice a little too late that he's taken the glass from my hand until he brings it to my parted

SCANDALOUS GAMES

lips.

"Drink." I obey without a single thought and he issues another command, "Don't swallow."

In a trance, my body realizes his intention before my mind catches on. Strong hands pull me closer and his lips lock on mine, drinking the liquid straight from my mouth. Our lips touch for a fraction of a second before he leans back, leaving me dizzy.

My legs press together as a rush of wetness, different from the alcohol, runs between my folds until I'm nothing but a puddle at his feet. It wasn't long enough to be a kiss, yet it felt like one and was enough to imprint the feel of his soft lips on my soul.

A non-kiss that stole my breath away.

I should've listened to the warning.

When I focus on him, I half expect him to be smug and satisfied for ripping the semblance of control I thought I had but if possible, he looks even more dangerous. Barely restrained. Instead of running away, I want to drown in him until he breaks me apart.

"Miss Chopra."

My gaze connects with the woman and I want to vanish into thin air. I can't believe Dash did it in front of her because it's written all over her face she saw the whole thing. Should I even be surprised? He's shameless and confident.

"Yes," I speak, my voice hoarse.

"I would like to show you a few pieces based on what Mr. Stern detailed. If there is anything specific you'd like, do let me know," she informs, her voice professional. Pulling the first piece, she sets it in front of me and continues, "This is a two-carat diamond with an oval cut and yellow tint, which is very rare."

The ring is simple yet stunning and before I've finished admiring it, she pulls out another piece while Dash sits beside me quietly. I can feel his attention on my face, capturing every emotion with his hawk-like intensity.

As I try each ring on my finger, I fall in love with them all, yet my heart is not completely in any of it. My conscious, saying I cannot let Dash purchase any of these for a fake fiancée. There's no way I'd let him spend an obscene amount of money and I don't give a fuck if he's a billionaire or a king of his own universe. The woman he falls in love with is the one who deserves it.

And it will never be me.

Just as I'm about to tell him my thoughts, I'm struck by the sight of the next piece the lady sets down. My throat closes when I see the lightest shade of violet I've ever seen on a diamond. Blinding, rare, and mesmerizing. Every little detail from the cut to the pattern about it is meant to draw eyes.

"It's stunning, isn't it?" Chloe smiles. "It's from our yet-to-be-launched collection and when Mr. Stern said he wanted a diamond with a purple tint, I had to show this and now I can see why. It's a three-carat round brilliant-cut ring."

"It's beautiful," I whisper before politely asking, "can I have a minute alone with my fiancé, please?"

"Of course."

As soon as we're alone, I turn to him. "I want to leave."

"Why?" he asks in an infuriatingly calm voice.

"Because I asked."

"Why?" he repeats in the same baritone.

"You're not buying me a ring," I declare with as much steel as I can muster. "Especially one where the cost could feed a small country."

"Know what I think, kitten?" His frame straightens from his casual posture before he picks the ring I was eyeing and grabs my small wrist in his rough palm. With his hold firm and tone velvety smooth, he says, "You secretly enjoy pushing me just so I make good on my promise."

I'm stuck staring at his lips when I feel him slide the ring on my left hand. It fits fucking perfectly like it was custom-made for me. I tug my hand as my pulse kicks up but he tightens his hold. "Take it off."

"Remember what I said?" I swallow as his words flash in my mind. Bold and unbending. The emotions I have no business feeling wrap themselves around me when he coaxes, "Say it, kitten."

"I'll wear your ring even if you have to force it on my finger."

Still holding my hand possessively, he demands. "Whose wife are you going to be?"

"Yours."

"Whose last name will you take?"

"Yours, Dash," I whisper, my fight crumbling with each declaration.

"It means you belong to me, Bianca, and as your husband, if I want to buy you a thousand rings, you won't fight me." He growls roughly before yanking me into his arms and gripping the back of my neck. "If I wish to spend my fortune along the way, you can't stop me."

"Why? Because you like to spoil the women you're with?" I throw his words back at him. The jealousy and hurt I shouldn't feel, swirling together. "I'm not your flavor of the month you can throw money at and think I'll be impressed and fall at your feet. This is nothing but a mutual—"

"I swear if you tell me this is fake one more time, I'm going to bend you over my knee and spank your ass until everyone in this store knows you're mine."

My mouth closes at the warning pulsating from every inch of him. My stupid body rejoices and shivers, desperate from his rough touch. I push at his chest, desperately wanting to get away because he's messing with my head. All my senses become jumbled around him. One second, I want to push him away and the next, I'm falling under his spell.

I lower my gaze to his chest and demand, "Let go, Dash."

"Look at me."

I shove harder but he's like a mountain. Resolute and relentless.

"I said, look. At. Me."

The force and plea in his words have me obeying him before I can stop myself.

"I lied, kitten. I don't date nor have I spent time with any woman in the past. Period. I especially don't spoil them and the most they get from me are orgasms before I'm out of their lives." His voice is raw and eyes peering down to the broken

SCANDALOUS GAMES

girl inside me, he cups my cheek. "Ever since you crashed into my life with your fierceness and sass, I've done everything except what I used to do. Because when I'm around you, no one else exists for me. And when I'm without you, you're the only one I ache to see."

Is it possible for your heart to soar and beat out of your chest? Because mine will at any second if he continues to hold and stare at me like the world around us is nothing but smoke and I'm his center.

Who would have thought this man would evoke hope inside me?

Make me wish for a dream that felt so far-fetched? And until yesterday, terrified.

"Dash," I whisper.

His thumb silences my lips. "Until the day our arrangement lasts, you're my woman and I'm going to worship you like you deserve. When this ends, I'll be out of your life once again. The only difference is, I won't be your one and only regret."

Chapter Thirty

BIANCA

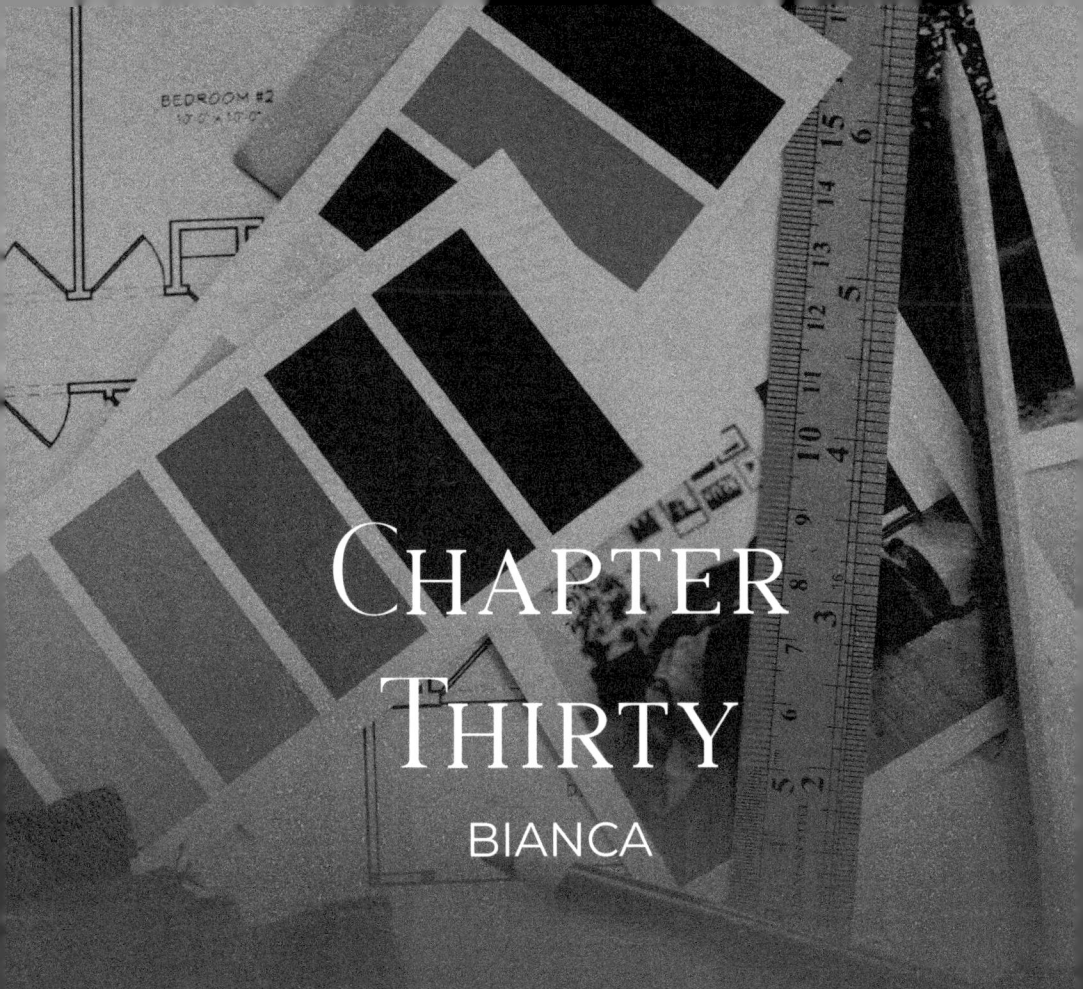

I let him buy the beautiful ring, but it's not like I would've been able to stop him.

Especially after his confession. It's replaying on a constant loop in my head and the words sink into my skin with deeper clarity with each second that passes. Had it been any other man, I would've ran for the hills from even that small touch of intimacy. Instead, I feel free and content, not suffocated.

Perhaps it's because he said he'll let me go, like he knew I needed that assurance. Except, my reaction to it was odd and something I'm not ready to face or admit just yet.

Throughout the entire ride back to the suite, I kept stealing glances at my hand as the shiny diamond blinks against the soft sunlight. We sit on the opposite ends of the back seat again but without the iciness and gloominess. Instead, a low pulsing tension is simmering in the air between us, charged with all-consuming lust because of the unforgettable non-kiss.

The memory of his lips, like a ghost against mine.

Just how will it feel if he actually kissed me? Will he be aggressive and dominant as he is every time we've come close to fucking? Or will he be soft and teasing?

I don't know which excites me more.

I shiver when calloused fingers caress my forearm, pulling me from my musings.

SCANDALOUS GAMES

Frowning, I notice our car has stopped but we're not outside the hotel. Hundreds of tourists surround us as they walk the vibrant and aristocratic street of Paris along the Seine while the Eiffel Tower stands tall along the bank.

Never have I seen utter beauty so close. I really hope we have time to visit the Eiffel Tower.

"A little sightseeing, then we'll go back," says Dash. I grab the door handle to step out when his voice halts me. "Wait."

He elegantly steps out first, followed by the sexy move of buttoning his suit jacket the moment he stands tall, before rounding the car to my side. Our chests brush when he helps me out with my hand braced in his and I inhale sharply, his smoky scent drugging me. My left hand instinctively lands on his chest as I find my balance and we both look at the ring at the same time.

His mark of ownership.

It feels surreal and dreamy.

My sharp intake of breath is audible while his grip around my waist tightens, sending a shiver racing down my spine. I tilt my head and I'm struck by the savage possessiveness darkening his features. The dark lust lurking in the depths of his beautiful eyes. The shutting of the door breaks us apart and I put some space between us until it's not just him I'm breathing.

"I'll bring the car around when you're ready to leave, Mr. Stern," informs the driver before disappearing into the crowd.

"You wanna walk or eat first, kitten?" Dash asks, tucking me into his side with his arm around mine. It only feels natural as I lift my right hand and interlace our fingers together.

Both of us, aware of the intimacy yet we don't pull away.

"I want to roam around a bit," I answer.

No way am I wasting time on food when there is so much to see. Who knows when I'll get another chance? My job as an interior designer pays really well but it'll be a long while before I can afford a trip on my own to France. The second I got it, I stopped living off my parents, which was my foremost goal as soon as I graduated.

"Have you traveled here before?" I curiously ask Dash, who shows me all the different spots, a little story behind each landmark like my personal tour guide. His memory is really sharp and keen and more often than not, I become lost in him rather than the view.

"Twice. Both times for business conferences," he admits. "I made time to explore the city on the second trip."

Dash always had wanderlust and would often travel on a weekend-long trip as far as I can remember. It was obvious it was his way of de-stressing from the chaotic world. Either he spent his time working alone or with Justin in the past. Now that I think of it, it seems lonely and sad.

Suddenly, I'm curious to learn more about him.

"Isn't traveling your hobby?"

His hand, which was playing with my fingers, pauses and as he peers down at me, a lock of his hair falls on his forehead. "It was."

It's my turn to stop on my tracks. "When was the last time you went on a vacation?"

"Just told you."

"The business trips don't count."

"My last trip was to Vietnam when I was twenty-four."

"You're serious?" I gasp. That's ages ago. "But you can travel anywhere you desire. Why haven't you?"

"Having the world at your fingertips isn't always a blessing, kitten. It often becomes a burden and takes sacrifices to continue. When you have no one, your work becomes your entire world."

"It's okay to take a break, Dash," I tell him softly. "You already work too hard."

"It's all I have and I can't afford to take a break, nor do I want to."

"Is it worth having premature gray hair?"

His lips kick to the side at my sarcasm. "I'll still be handsome. Besides, women love an older guy. You're ten years younger than me and I make your pussy wet, don't I, kitten?"

I shush his mouth and hide my blushing cheeks from passersby. "You can't say that in public, Dash."

His fingers curl around my wrist and he lowers it, but doesn't let go. Mischief dancing in his forest green eyes, he teases, "What? That you love getting your pussy spanked or that your cunt tastes like the sweetest drug men would die for? Or that the taste of it still haunts me as much as the feel of it stretching around my cock?"

Holy fuck. Damn his filthy talking mouth—and my pussy that suddenly feels empty and quivers for him. Having him inside me was both pleasure and sweet pain. I had felt him for days after. Every dirty, sordid deed he did to my body is etched into my skin.

Yanking me closer until I'm standing on my toes and our lips a hairbreadth away, he speaks smugly, "Is that too indecent to say in public?"

"You're shameless," I insult him, only for it to come out throaty and breathless.

"You have no idea, sweetheart." Tucking me into his arms again, he pulls us in the direction of a restaurant with outdoor seating. "Let's get you fed, wifey."

Despite the rush, we get a table in a nice little corner with a direct view of the Pont des Arts bridge and the Eiffel Tower. Dash sits across from me and he's a handsome view himself. Hair tousled and his suits well-fitted that it's obvious they are custom-made and my favorite are the ones where he also wears a vest, like the one today. So prim and proper, and a striking contrast to his dirty talking mouth and seductive eyes.

Who knew men in suits were my kryptonite?

I gaze around me while Dash orders for us in fluent French. Each syllable, raising goosebumps on my skin because of how sexy and confident he sounds. The silence as we wait for our food is serene and comfortable. My gaze is drawn to him every few seconds while something from our conversation pricks at the back of my mind.

"Dash."

"Yeah, kitten?"

"How is your dad? Are you close with him?"

SCANDALOUS GAMES

His shoulders immediately tense and the calmness evaporates from our table before his gaze flies to mine. The detached and impassive man staring back at me is unrecognizable, as though I'm peering into a stranger's face. My stomach hollows upon realizing I touched a nerve.

"He died two years ago from cancer," he replies, with not a trace of emotion. It's as if he's declaring a mere fact. I'm shocked he even answered. "And no, we weren't close."

"I'm sorry."

"You never knew him."

"I'm still sorry for your loss and that you had to go through it," I say, hoping I sound soothing. "It's never easy to lose a family member, no matter if you were close or not."

I stare blankly at the menu while regretting why I even asked. I had to go and open my mouth just when his mood lifted. No wonder he's a private person. I feel terrible for believing he was intentionally hiding information about his life. I'm even more startled when he speaks again.

"I had a father but never a family, Bianca." His voice is firm and once our gazes collide, he continues, "My mother died giving birth to me and rather than just her, I lost both my parents that day. My dad dedicated any love he had left to the army while I grew up with nannies that I lost count of while moving from one city to another. Most kids' childhood memories are of family trips, bonding over sports with their dad, and all I have are of packing my bags every few months, sometimes even weeks, saying goodbye to yet another city while staring out the window of a train. My father was a cold and rigid man who believed emotions were for a lesser man and I was a burden he had to carry around. The only reason I know he's gone is because his lawyer sent me his will."

The man he describes is nothing like the one Niall told me about. He worshiped the guy and said he was the father he never had. It's disturbing to hear a parent could neglect their own son while being everything to another.

Was this the reason behind the animosity between Niall and Dash? It's like I'm seeing the past replay in a new reality that I couldn't have predicted.

Tears sting my eyes. One escapes and emotions clog my throat as I listen to every heartbreaking word he says. However, it's not pity but only sadness I feel for the little boy who never had a loving family. My parents have flaws but at least they gave us a home filled with equally happy and sad memories. Unlike him, I was never alone.

Dash is not as invincible and ruthless as I made him out to be.

Just like me, he's guarded, imperfect, and has demons in his past he hides beneath his rough and sharp edges. Nevertheless, he is also strong, intelligent, and has made a name for himself when most would have drowned in sorrow.

"It's his loss, Dash," I fiercely tell him. I don't know if it makes me a bad person but I hate his dead father. My heart freezes when Dash's gaze softens, like he didn't expect it and he continues to stare with such intensity that every noise fades into the background.

"You might be the only person who believes that, kitten," he says in a hollow

SIMRAN

voice.

Just then, the waiter arrives with the food and our connection breaks. The haunting look, now gone, and I take it as a sign he's done sharing for today. But no matter what, I can't erase what he said at the end. It's sad to think he believes he doesn't deserve to be his father's son, when it should be the opposite.

I promise myself I'll show him how wrong he is. The same way he's unknowingly made me want to let go of the past.

The rest of our lunch passes by smoothly without any more heavy talk and it's pleasant. From the scenic beauty, the people, to the freaking weather, everything about Paris is breathtaking and unforgettable. The atmosphere feels magical and I've never felt the love in the air more potently than here, in Paris, as I glance at cute couples, and families enjoying themselves.

It gives me hope for the first time in years, reminding me I was a hopeless romantic for a reason. Maybe that girl is still alive inside me.

As I wait for Dash while he's gone inside the restaurant, my eyes land on a young couple a distance away as they walk on the bridge. The boy has his arm around her shoulders as he whispers to her. At the same time, he shows something in his other hand, which makes the girl smile bright. She shakes her head at whatever he said but he looks adamant, making me highly intrigued. I watch as he guides her to a corner and I smile in awe when he sneakily places what has to be a lock, not afraid of the fact that they're breaking a rule. I don't know whether to be worried or laugh at their boldness. Nevertheless, it's beyond cute.

Love is crazy... I tell myself.

I'm so lost in them, I don't even notice Dash coming back until he says, "Shall we go, wifey?"

I turn to him after the couple disappears while hoping I didn't get caught at my day stalking. He stands tall and broad, peering down at me and it's like a rush of déjà vu to the first time he surprised me and called me wifey.

It's only been a week and he has managed to turn my world upside down. He came into my life like a tidal wave. Stealthily and powerfully. One minute, I was single, and now I have a fiancé that I share a home with, who apparently loves to spoil me rotten.

"I'm starting to get annoyed with the fact that you keep sneaking up on me, Dash," I grumble.

He chuckles low, making me desperate to hear the sound of his actual laugh. "I obviously need to do a better job of having your attention on me constantly, especially when you're alone."

As if he isn't already haunting my mind twenty-four seven. It's become a sickness I want no cure of. I'm as aware of him as the beating heart inside my chest.

Grabbing my hand, we make our way to the car and just as we reach it, he lets me go. I frown when he starts walking backward.

"I forgot something," he informs me. "Wait here."

Almost ten minutes later, he returns and as he jogs toward me, women ogle him like they want to lick him up. Once he's by my side, I flash them my ring finger with a satisfied smirk. They look away with embarrassment written all over their

SCANDALOUS GAMES

cheeks.

"Kitten," Dash rasps, amusement and desire in his voice. "Did you just give them the finger?"

I shrug innocently. "Just being a possessive fiancée."

"Yeah. I'm sure that's all it was," he teases, fully aware I was jealous.

Thinking we're leaving, I unlock the car door, only for him to push me against it. My breasts flush against his chest as he cages me in his arms, dwarfing my small frame. It used to intimidate me, but now I feel protected. Elbows bent, he lowers his head until our lips are shy of touching, then speaks in a rough voice, "I asked if I could kiss you that night and you said no."

The hot memory ignites a throbbing feeling in my pussy. "I know."

"Is it still a no, kitten?"

"It is." He goes quiet and stares until I become breathless. I whisper his name in a plea, "Dash."

"Then I won't ask, I'll just take."

Shock paralyzes me as his lips descend on mine and he does as he promised. He takes, like he has every right. He takes, like my mouth was made to be kissed by him. Hungrily. Savagely. Thoroughly.

He doesn't just take, he steals. My senses. My oxygen. My thoughts.

Every. Fucking. Thing.

And I let him.

Until we forget where he begins and I end.

His animalistic growl vibrates straight to my clit and my whimper is swallowed by him. Tilting my face the way he wants, he dominates my mouth and I kiss him back with fervor. Desperation. Greed.

It doesn't feel like we're playing a game to fool the world.

It feels real.

He feels like *mine*.

"Dash." I moan when he pulls my bottom lip with his teeth before diving in again like he's starved. I rise on my toes to let him in deeper and his hand snakes down to my throat possessively. When he squeezes a tiny bit, I become dizzy.

Wrenching his mouth back, violent and hungry eyes devour mine before lowering to my swollen lips. Tracing my bottom lip, he growls, "This is how you show that I belong to you."

Chapter Thirty-one

DASH

Bianca tasted like mine.
She felt like mine.
And fuck… She kissed me back like I was hers. And I never wish to stop. All I want is to sink inside her skin, and run in her bloodstream like she's etched herself into mine. The irresistible vixen met me—tongue to tongue, teeth to teeth, and with a passion that rivaled my own.

Sweet. Heavenly. Fatal.

Because one taste isn't enough. Just as I was always afraid of. And had we kissed back then, it wouldn't have felt half the way it did today.

That fucking kiss was a culmination of seven years of obsession, lust, and possession.

I finally understood why everyone gushes about Paris. It's because there is something powerful in the air that makes men and women lose their minds alike. With lust. With need. With *love*.

The kiss may have been fueled by jealousy and possessiveness for the first few seconds, but it twisted into something deeper by the end. It wasn't the only moment that fucked with my system. It was the conversation where I ended up sharing parts about my life I've not told anyone, including Justin—someone I consider as close to family as possible in my fucked-up brain.

SCANDALOUS GAMES

At that moment, as she sat across from me and looked so beautiful, I was afraid my heart would stop beating if I looked away for even a nanosecond. I spilled all the sordid details of my turbulent and empty childhood.

Being vulnerable has never been my strong suit, I only ever thought of it as a weakness and something I was incapable of. A human need beneath me. Yet one look in her eyes and I bared my soul, including the shattered pieces I carried around in my heart.

The single thought running along the lines of: I wanted Bianca to see every part of me. The good, the ugly, and the twisted.

I needed her to know she wasn't the only person broken by her past, because so was I. Expect hers is partly my fault. And if I were a better man, I would confess to her. But it would come at the cost of losing her forever.

It's something I can never do, not when I've just found her again and because I'm selfish. Besides, if I told her now, she'd shut me down faster than we could end up together.

This may have begun with the need to get Bianca out of my system and quench my desire for her, but I was only lying to myself. Deep down, it was always about making her mine. Unlike my ex-stepbrother, I won't let her slip away from my grasp.

But with our complicated past hanging over us, will she ever truly be mine? She doesn't know the part I played that night or the ruckus that happened after she left. So how do I keep this woman without losing her before I even have her?

The doorbell rings just as Justin's warning resurfaces and I push it down as I make my way over. Unlocking the door, I grab the package I requested to be brought up from reception. Anticipation builds inside me as I head to the bedroom to give it to Bianca, where she went to hide, saying she needed a bath.

I know the kiss affected her as much as it did me and it blurred the lines she was adamant not to cross. It's too late now and I won't have her pulling away, pretending it never happened.

Or worse, call it another regret.

Besides, the lines were smudging from the moment I said yes. So before she can build her walls up and pretend I don't make her heart race faster than any other man, I simply won't give her a chance.

Sometimes a man has to play dirty to have the woman of his dreams. Lucky for her, decency never existed in my bones. Tonight, I'll show her just how indecent I can be.

Every city has two worlds and while Paris in daylight is vibrant and romantic, the one after midnight is all about debauchery and forbidden pleasures. Until tonight, I've never been more thrilled to explore than with Bianca at my side. I want the curious yet innocent vixen in her to come out to play.

Knocking once, I enter the room and notice she's still in the bath and the door is slightly ajar. My pulse kicks up with awareness and I know it has to be a mistake because there's no way she'd leave the door unlocked. Not while she's naked, wet, and with me close by.

Unintentional or not, she invited the predator that wants her flesh.

Me.

The vision of her lithe body glistening under the shower, fingers tracing her soft skin, flashes behind my eyes and sends shock waves down my spine. I drop the box on the bed, take off my suit jacket, and after loosening my tie, I stalk toward the bathroom.

Steam slightly spills into the room and my gait falters when a tiny moan pierces my ears. My nostrils flare and my senses sharpen when another sweet moaning sound reaches me and any restraint I had twists into a ball of savage lust.

Bianca doesn't hear me over the sound of running water as I enter without her permission or a warning. The first thing I see is her silky hair sticking to the length of her arched back as she stands sideways while one of her hands moves in a steady rhythm between her legs.

Eyes closed, lips parted, with one hand against the tiles holding her up as she pleasures herself, renders me glued to the spot and my cock rock hard. Sharp, piercing need builds to yank her into my arms, but I hold back and continue watching her, mesmerized.

Her heavy tits shake with every rough inhale and exhale, and dark pink nipples pebble and point upward, just begging to be sucked and bitten. I want to look everywhere at once—her pussy, her nipples, her fingers as they rub between her drenched slit. But my gaze is drawn back to her gorgeous face. Her soft lips are still swollen from our kiss and I just know she's thinking about it as she plays with her cunt.

I don't make my presence known and continue to stare as she brings her other hand to cup her right breast before she squeezes and it spills out of her small palm. If she'd been performing for me, I would've ordered her to squeeze harder and pinch her nub until pleasure mixed with pain. I would've teased and brought her to the edge without falling over and over until she was mindless and delirious for an orgasm.

My cock begs for attention at the fantasy and vision before me but I ignore it. I lean back against the counter and feed the voyeur in me as the woman of my wet dreams brings herself to pleasure.

So sexy that I want to blind every man on the planet.

Beautiful and wanton as she fingers her tight pussy.

Naïvely oblivious to her fiancé's devouring eyes watching her raptly.

I wish I could see every inch of her juicy, pink cunt, stretching around her small fingers, but it might just send me over the edge. The thought vanishes as soon as her wrist moves faster, her moans get louder, and my vision darkens when I see the flash of my diamond ring on her finger.

Fuck. I squeeze my length because I never imagined it would be hot seeing her touch herself with the hand wearing my ring. A mark claiming she's taken and belongs to me. The harder I stare, the more I ache to have that same hand wrapped around my girth.

Just when I thought I couldn't be more turned on, she goes and sucks on her finger that was inside her pussy a second ago.

Dirty little vixen.

SCANDALOUS GAMES

My kitten is as depraved and filthy as me and I want to corrupt her even more.

Precum leaks from the head of my cock as she circles her hard nipple, pinches and pulls, before returning it to her wet heat. As if tethered to me by an invisible thread, she turns toward me, baring every fucking inch of her. My eyes zoom in on her rapidly thrusting hand as she rises on her toes when the pleasure becomes too much.

I cannot look away while I feel my heartbeat in my ears and I breathe silently to not alert her. She's so lost and consumed that she probably wouldn't have heard me if I had called out her name. The second her spine goes rigid and her panting grows louder, I wrench my gaze back to her face to memorize the look she wears when she falls apart.

"Yes… yes… yes," she mumbles incoherently, and my world stops when she whispers, "Dash."

Her orgasm rains down on her.

She crashes and splinters into pieces under the wave of pleasure.

My harsh exhale and her soft whimpers fill the space. And just like that, I'm a goner for Bianca. She sealed her fate when she called out my name.

Her chest rises and falls with each calming breath as she comes down from her high. She looks like an effervescent dream, skin flushed and glistening from the water. Except, I wish it was my cum covering her. Then she'd be perfect.

The sound of my footsteps shifting closer yanks her back to reality and her hooded gaze clashes with mine. She swallows as a pink hue darkens her cheeks. When her eyes land on my cock pushing against my pants, her bottom lips curl between her teeth.

"You're breathtaking when you come, kitten."

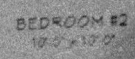

Chapter Thirty-two

BIANCA

Oh my god.

He watched me make myself come. And while I called out his name, no less.

I flush even harder at his praise.

Fuck. I begin to hyperventilate while he stands a few feet away with his eyes digging into me in his unnerving ways that make my skin tingle and light up again. Despite coming harder than I've come in a long while, my pussy is ready for another orgasm. One delivered by him.

With his tongue. His fingers. His huge cock that got hard watching me.

None of my brain cells seem to be functioning because I don't make a move to shy away or cover my body. I just stand there, the steam creating a cloud around us while water teases my back and lets him soak in every crevice and inch of me.

Realizing my intention, his jaw sets, eyes darkening savagely, as he runs them all over my body slowly, teasingly, and hungrily. He looks angry but I know he's fighting his restraint to not touch me while we're alone. But suddenly, they are the last thing on my mind.

Because after that mind-blowing kiss, the rules went out the fucking window. He all but eviscerated them with every swipe of his tongue, every swallowed moan, and each rough bite and suck. Just as I feared, his kiss was just like him.

SCANDALOUS GAMES

Aggressive.
Passionate.
Filthy.

There are a million reasons for us to desire anything more from our scandalous arrangement, yet they all dissolve into nothingness as I hold his stare.

Except the large bulge straining his pants, there's no telling he's affected.

I study him carefully, hoping to see a telltale sign that he's affected. He has since discarded his Jacket and vest, revealing his strong forearms, which were straining against the silk of his shirt that he fills out perfectly. The collar, still sharp while his tie hangs loose, giving him a ravishing look and the difference between us only heightens my awareness of him and skyrockets my arousal. As if he's testing me, he remains silent.

Every part of me he caresses and peers at with his ravenous eyes, I feel marked. Possessed. Claimed.

"It was a private moment, Dash," I say, shutting off the shower behind me. "Not an invitation to watch like it's your personal porn show."

Pushing open the sliding door completely to get out, I grab a towel and make a show of rubbing and drying myself, Dash watching every move. I've never felt so bold except whenever I'm under his spell. Like he calls to the inner naughty girl inside me who loves his undivided attention and seeks the thrill in pushing him.

"The door was left open, kitten," he states in a husky voice. With his head tilted, he taunts, "And you taught me it's always an invitation. Don't mistake me for a gentleman."

Tying the towel around me, I close the gap between us until we're standing inches apart. Running my finger over the button of his shirt, I rasp, "I never did."

I run my tongue between my lips when his hands curl against the marble counter, so I slide mine lower and trace his belt, not purposely touching his dick. The temperature becomes hotter despite the chill and droplets of water sticking to my skin.

Calm and commanding, traits he wears like a second skin, Dash makes no attempt to stop or push me away. Without my heels, I barely reach his shoulders and even in my vulnerable state, I feel powerful because the desire shining in his green orbs fills me with confidence.

That doesn't mean I'm unaware of the fact that he can snatch it away if he wishes. And the fantasy of him taking away my will until I'm under his dominance and mercy is an addictive rush. When I softly brush over his hard length, he finally speaks.

"What do you think you're doing, kitten?" he says in a low, harsh voice.

"Feeling my fiancé."

"No touching when alone, remember?"

"You're not allowed to, but I can."

"That's not how it works."

"They're my rules," I murmur. Staring up at him under hooded eyes, I rest both my palms flat on his abs that are like steel and inch my hands upward, feeling every hard ridge through his shirt. Rising on my tiptoes, I lick the seam of his lips and whisper against them, "What I say goes."

"Teasing and taunting me with your body makes you horny, doesn't it?" he growls before capturing my bottom lip between his teeth when I try to move back. Pulling until I whimper, he lets it go with a pop. "I bet your pussy is dripping with your juices and orgasm."

I'm enjoying my free rein over him far too much. Unable to stop myself, I make quick work of opening his top three buttons and pull so I can feel his warm skin underneath. Every night when I sleep in his arms, I have to fight the urge to trace his abs with my tongue and explore every muscle. Every granite inch.

It's a different kind of hell when your mind and body are at war.

One screaming he'll wreck me if I let him fuck me, while the latter taunts it's a blasphemy to resist such a fine specimen like him.

The sane choice would be to pull back, walk away, but when you're still buzzing from a powerful orgasm and the man who sent you over the edge in your fantasies is standing pressed against you, madness becomes your best friend.

Drugged from his masculine scent and his hardness pressing against my stomach, I give in to the long-awaited need and lean down to press a kiss on his chest. His rough exhales ruffle my hair and send a shiver down my spine, leaving goosebumps in its wake.

His pleasured grunt excites me and I lightly bite, desperate to hear it again. The sound is raw, gravelly, and throaty. My body comes alive with a need so sharp and intense, it steals my air. Placing kisses everywhere, my mouth tastes skin until I trail my lips to his ear.

"Wanna know what I was imagining when I made myself come?" I whisper in a teasing tone.

Wild and turbulent eyes connect with mine when my head is wrenched back and his other hand wraps around my neck before he arrogantly demands, "What was I doing to you, kitten?"

"Your cock in my mouth and fucking my throat raw."

"You want to suck my dick?"

"Yes." I moan, becoming dizzy under his tone and his possessive hold.

"Will you take every inch like a good girl?"

"Yes."

"And will you swallow every drop of my cum?" he rasps.

"Yes. I want your taste on my tongue, Dash." I nod rapidly, delirious with need. Even I am unable to recognize the girl dirty talking back to him.

Inching his fingers lower, he plays with the knot of my towel, which has miraculously stayed on. It causes delicious and teasing friction against my nipples, and amplifies my lust.

"Then beg for my cock like a good little girl, kitten," Dash commands.

"What happened to making me beg without laying a finger?" I taunt instead, ignoring the protest of my body that craves to fall to my knees and worship him. His eyes flare in challenge and warning just before he lets go.

I swallow thickly when his hands lower to his waist and unclasp his belt. Instinctively, I take a step backward and the corner of his lips tilt dangerously and

SCANDALOUS GAMES

deviously before he slowly pulls the expensive leather through the loops.

The belt hangs low as he lowers his hand to the side before promising, "I will make you beg and then I'm going to fuck the sass right out of your mouth with my cock."

"You like my sass."

"I like good girls even better, especially in the bedroom." I don't even make it half a step before his arm snakes forward and he loops the belt around my neck, yanking me against him. Crisscrossing the end and holding it in his grip, he tugs me closer to his mouth without us touching. "I don't need my hands on you to have you under my command and mercy, kitten. My belt or my tie works fine too."

My clit throbs and I can hear my pulse pounding in my ears as he keeps his eyes pinned on mine while clasping the belt and tightening the noose to control me better. There's no guessing his dirty intentions beneath the hard stare. He could be fantasizing about choking me or pushing me down to my knees and I'd be none the wiser.

"What are you doing, Dash?" I whisper, scared and turned on at the same time.

"Drop. The. Towel."

I hold the knot tighter but one savage look from him and I obey by uncurling my fingers and letting it puddle at his feet. My nipples harden immediately, aching for his mouth.

I'm taken back to the past when he licked and played with them to distract me from the pain of having him inside me for the first time. Nothing had felt as amazing as the feel of his tongue and his lips. I could have come alone from that stimulation and his cock throbbing inside me.

"Good girl," he praises, and it washes over me like the teasing caress of a wind. "Want to know how I would have made you come if you'd let me?"

"How?"

His gaze drops to my breasts and he licks his lips before speaking in a husky tone, "I would have first teased and tortured your tits with my tongue, sucking on your dark nipples, knowing it makes your body come alive, and just when they become sensitive, I'd bite and pull on them with my teeth until you gushed for me."

A shiver runs down my spine and I arch my back, silently enticing him to just do what he said, rules be damned. His lips tilt into a smirk but he doesn't take the bait. His demand, loud and clear that unless I beg, he won't. His restraint is as annoying as it is hot.

"Cup your tits and squeeze hard, Bianca," he sharply orders. "I want to see them spill out of your hands. Or…" I hold my breath. "Say please so I can have my mouth on them."

"You want a taste?" I tease, then grab my breasts before circling my nipples with my thumb, and a pleasing moan slips past my lips. I tighten my grip and meet his eyes. "Then come get it because I'm not saying please."

"Is that your way of telling me you're desperate for my touch, kitten? Because your eyes are begging for one thing while your mouth is saying another."

"Then listen to my mouth."

"I'd rather fuck it."

Yes, please, is on the tip of my tongue and because he can read my dirty mind, I almost scream it when he uses the end of the belt and slaps my right breast.

"Dash," I whimper, rising on my toes.

"Pinch your nipples," he growls. "Rough and hard so it stings."

The authoritative timbre to his tone has me pinching my nubs and just as I let go, he spanks me again right on my sensitive left nipple before paying the same attention to the other. The sharp pain vibrates from my breasts straight to my clit, and I feel the building of another orgasm.

Fuck. He knows my weaknesses all too well.

When I still don't beg, his calm teeters on the edge. A gasp slips past my lips when suddenly he interchanges our positions without touching me and my back is pressed against the counter roughly.

Our faces inches apart, breathing in each other's air, he rips me open with his words and I still. "Stop being so scared of being vulnerable, kitten. The rules, the defiance, it's all a layer of defense to make yourself feel in control. So if you think I'm going to fall for it and touch you like I so desperately want just to give you the satisfaction of winning, you're wrong. If you want me, then know I won't demand any less than all of you, Bianca. Unafraid, vulnerable, and sweet."

My eyes close against the onslaught of feelings wreaking havoc on me and I feel bare to the bones that he saw beneath my layers so easily. I want to hate him but I can't. I want to give him what he wants yet I'm nervous.

Staring at me with awe and desire, he lowers his voice to a seductive timbre and says, "Say yes, so I can soothe the sting on your nipples with my tongue. Say yes please, so I can trace your tight pussy with my fingers, circle your clit, and fill you up. Beg me like my good girl, so I can finally touch my future wife the way I'm desperate to. Surrender your body to me or tell. Me. To. Stop."

None of us move an inch and I can hear my rapid heartbeat between us. His desperation mirrors mine and I lose the wordless fight, dooming our fate. "Kiss me again, Dash. *Please.*"

We clash. Lips to lips. Chest to chest. Soft against hard. Like two lost and broken souls.

His hands rip and throw the belt away before greedy hands circle my waist to press me against him harder. He does this while his mouth takes mine savagely, no holds barred and fucking me with his tongue. I bite his bottom lip and pull at his hair at the nape of his neck and he reciprocates by squeezing my left breast so painfully, it only makes me crazier.

Nothing else matters except him.

As promised, he tears his mouth away to bend and take my abused nipple in his mouth before sucking softly while lavishing it with his tongue. He flicks the swollen and sensitive nub again and again until I squirm in his hold.

Pushing his head down harder when he moves to the other breast, my head falls back when he circles my areola before swiping at the tip and sucking it deep. His other hand explores the rest of me, caressing and teasing, pulling and digging, making my pussy throb.

His touch feels familiar, like coming home, yet nothing like the last time.

SCANDALOUS GAMES

"Fuck, Dash." I moan, crying out when he sucks too hard. "Too much."

My grip slips from his hair when he raises his eyes to mine and a carnal smirk takes over his entire face. "I haven't even started, kitten."

Fuck. Me.

Like I don't already know. The man still has his clothes on while I'm naked and will probably need another shower after he's finished with me. That's if I don't pass out from the sensory overload alone.

Straightening to his full height, he spreads my legs to press his cock against my bare pussy and threads his fingers in my hair to hold me captive. "You wanted to meet my rough and dark side. It's too late to back out now, because I'm not letting you go."

"I don't want you holding back, Dash," I boldly confess.

His piercing gaze brightens with dark possession a second before he steps back. Just like that, his carnal and deviant side comes out to play.

"On your knees."

Chapter Thirty-three

DASH

I need Bianca more than I need air.

The second she decided to play this little seduction game of hers, all my good intentions of waiting went up in flames. Now, as I watch her lower herself to her knees, soft brown eyes shy and excited, and her beautiful body mine to own, I want to keep us locked away forever.

"Take out my cock, kitten."

A full-body shiver racks her at my command and nervous yet eager hands unbutton my pants before lowering the zipper. The sound, echoing and heightening our arousal with every breath. I watch her face for every little reaction, from the way she bites the corner of her lip as her hands fumble with my briefs to her dilated pupils burning with anticipation.

She's fucking breathtaking.

The hitch in her breath, followed by a soft gasp, is audible when my dick springs free, almost slapping against my lower abs and her gaze widens. It has the reaction of precum leaking from the tip and I have to swallow my groan when she licks her lip innocently.

"Lick it clean." I thread my fingers in her hair while wrapping my other hand around my shaft and bring the leaking crown to her parted lips. Her tongue sneaks out to lick and I tighten my grip to still her. "Eyes on me when I have my cock

SCANDALOUS GAMES

inside you. Whether it's your mouth, your cunt, or that tight fucking ass."

Shyness flickers in her gaze but she holds my unwavering stare and the second her lips close around the tip and she licks the slit to taste my salty precum, I've gone to heaven. Sliding my fingers to the back of her neck, I push her head down until she has no choice but to accept every thick inch.

I don't hold back and keep thrusting slowly until I'm at the back of her throat. She sputters and chokes, her drool dripping from the corner of her mouth, and she has never looked more beautiful. A tear slips down her cheek, and her hands dig into my thighs, but she doesn't fight and lets me dominate her.

"Such a good girl, choking on my dick," I rasp. "Suck and feel what you do to me, Bianca. How hard you make me just by being you."

Pleasure courses through my spine and I pull out before thrusting back into the hilt and without asking, she sucks again, wrenching a groan from me. Slowly, her body relaxes as she becomes used to my rhythm, deep and long. Each time I slide inside her mouth, it's more amazing than the last. I'm loving her soft submission as much as her sass when she's taunting and fighting me.

"Fuck. Just like that, kitten." She moans around my shaft, wet with her saliva, and the sound travels straight to my balls. When her fingers sneak underneath to caress them, I become a savage. Her tits shake when I grab her head with both hands and thrust hard.

"Such a hot—" *Thrust.*

"Wet—" *Thrust.*

"Mouth." *Thrust.*

She whimpers, eyes closing at the intense throat fucking and I almost spill in her mouth when one of her hands slips between her legs. "Sucking my dick made you horny, you filthy girl?"

I palm her tit and slap the side of it before pulling at her nipple because I can't seem to get enough of them. She has the hottest fucking pair of tits that taunt me every time she's around me, especially when I have to sleep with them pressed against me all night long.

"Dash," she mumbles in protest when I pull out and rub the crown around her lips.

"I've wanted to do this from the moment I laid eyes on you in the club." *In my bedroom.* I lightly slap my dick against her cheek and she gasps. Her hooded eyes meet my heated gaze, coaxing a growl from me. "Resisting not to shove you down to your knees and fill your sassy lips with my cock and my cum."

"Fuck my mouth, Dash."

Damn, she's perfect.

"You like getting your throat fucked, you dirty little tease?" She nods and I smile at her eagerness. "Beg for it."

"Please let me feel your cock." Her breathless whisper is music to my ears.

"Show me how wet it makes your pussy," I demand while pushing the head of my cock past her lips. She takes me deeper and raises two of her glistening fingers with her juices. "Coat my balls with your wetness and don't touch yourself unless I tell you to."

SIMRAN

Her eyes flash with defiance at my cruel demand but her submissive side wins.

"Open your lips wider, kitten." My voice is guttural. "You're going to swallow every drop."

Everything ceases to exist, except the feeling of being in her warmth and my desperate need to come, which has been building for the last few weeks. I push my pulsing cock and thrust like a man possessed by the woman of his obsession, kneeling and taking everything I have to give. I fuck her rough and hard like I promised, finally claiming her like I wanted to seven years ago.

My harsh groans and her soft whimpers fill the space, and I feel my balls tighten. The rapt desire in her eyes, the flush on her cheeks, and her face a mess from tears and spit sends me over the edge. Two more violent thrusts and my body locks tight as I jerk in her mouth while she greedily drinks every jet of cum.

"Your mouth is going to be the death of me, kitten." I grunt and she smiles, licking her lips. "I'm going to want to kiss and fuck it all the time now."

She blushes and I lean down, picking her up before setting her perfect ass on the beside the sink, making her hiss at the coldness. Before she can complain, I crash my mouth on hers, push my tongue inside, and kiss her hard. Her arms circle my neck while her legs wrap around my waist and she grinds her cunt against my cock until I'm hard again.

The sweet taste of her mixed with my cum has me kissing her deeper and I run my hands down her back before grabbing her ass. Her shocked whimper is drowned by the hard spank I land on her ass before squeezing so she feels the sting.

"Fuck, Dash," she whines against my lips. "You really love spanking me, don't you?"

My response is another hard spank.

"I love my marks on you," I grunt, tilting my head to suck on her neck. Pushing my hand between us, I cup her pussy and trace my middle finger over the seam of her slit before pushing inside. "You're so fucking dripping. I should've known you'll like it rough."

"I shouldn't like it so much," she whispers and our eyes lock. "I shouldn't like you."

"Your cunt does," I growl before I shove two fingers in her wet hole. "And so do you, Bianca."

"Ahh… fuck!" she cries out when I press down on her clit with my thumb. It's still sensitive from her earlier orgasm.

"I warned you to walk away." *Thrust.* "Twice." *Thrust.* "You should've run, kitten." *Thrust.* "Because I'm going to make you mine."

Her walls clench around my plunging fingers and she hurtles over the edge with a scream. I watch her face, mesmerized as she comes all over my hand, riding wave after wave of her climax. I circle her throbbing clit until the last tremor racking her body subsides and she falls apart in my arms.

But I need one more and this time, I want it on my tongue.

The sound of my voice, talking to order room service from the phone beside her head, has her eyes snapping open. My own drop to her swollen lips, the corner shining with remnants of my cum, and I lick the spot and shove my tongue inside

SCANDALOUS GAMES

her mouth before pulling back to focus on the call.

"I need extra towels in our room." Bianca frowns before it twists into nervousness when I smirk. Her lips part to protest but I pull my fingers out that were still inside her and push them in before motioning for her to suck. Focusing on the person on the call, I say, "Ask them to wait in the living room and they're not to leave unless I tell them."

Blood rushes to my cock when her tongue laps at my fingers, like she's enjoying her taste. I narrow my eyes when she bites the tip just as I put the phone back in the placeholder.

"This is the second time you've bitten me, kitten," I taunt, pulling out my wet fingers.

Her face is pure innocence as she replies, "I thought you like it rough."

"I'll show you just how much, but first," I slap her thighs wider, lower to my haunches, and bring her ass to the edge as I bend my mouth to her messy cunt. "I'm going to make you scream while eating this pussy that belongs to me."

"But you just called someo—" she trails off, her head dropping when I lick her center.

Her fingers grip my hair just as there's a knock on our suite door, followed by the sound of footsteps coming in. Bianca startles and tries to jerk away but I grab ahold of her thighs, pinning her down. Ignoring her, I push my tongue between her wet folds and trace from her clit to her tiny rosebud, groaning at the sweet taste of her arousal.

"Dash, stop. Someone's here," she whispers in a half moan, half gasp. "Ahh... They'll hear."

"Why do you think they're here?" My voice is dark as her eyes meet mine. Circling her clit twice, I take it between my teeth and suck. She shudders and gushes on my waiting tongue. I lap at her juices before growling, "They'll hear me pleasuring my woman."

"You're going to ruin me." Her voice is nothing but a whisper, as she becomes lost in her desire while I become consumed with eating her pussy like I'll die if I don't.

Maybe I do want to ruin her.

Until I'm the first and last thought on her mind.

Until she's ruined for all other men.

Spreading my fingers on each side of her tiny waist, I use my thumb to open her folds until her tight cunt is on display for my eyes. "Such a pretty pink pussy," I admire, blowing on her clit. Pushing my middle finger in until her walls suck it in, I growl, "It's mine. Say. It."

"Yes. Yours!" she cries out as I thrust.

Using her juices as lube, I push my thumb in her ass. "Did you let another man in this ass after I claimed it that night, kitten?

"No, Dash. Only you."

"Good girl." The feeling is indescribable knowing there's a part of her only belonging to me, touched by just me. "Because I'm going to fuck it again without mercy."

I smile when she clenches down on my fingers at my dirty promise.

One of her hands slaps against the mirror behind her while the other grips the edge of the counter harshly. Her feet dig into my back as I finger fuck both her holes and flick her clit with my tongue and teeth until she rides my face with abandon.

"I'm going to come."

I fill her cunt with one more digit and scissor inside her, thrusting against her G-spot. Her walls lock down, clenching and pulsing. Shoving my fingers to the hilt, I still and just as I feel her getting close, I spank her clit and she shatters.

"Dash!"

I prolong her orgasm by slowly thrusting and lazily licking her juices as she fills my mouth. She's a sight to behold as her body jerks with every spasm, eyes closed and lips parted.

Pulling out of her reluctantly, I tuck my cock— which protests when I don't fuck her even though I badly want to—back into my briefs. It's the only mercy I could give her, because I already worked her too hard. Besides, the night is still young.

Taking her in my arms, she trustingly wraps hers around my shoulders and nuzzles my neck. The feeling of contentment takes me by surprise and it's so foreign that I'm left scared at the thought of anyone stealing it away.

Bianca is making me feel things I don't deserve. That I believed a man like me would never receive in this lifetime.

When I set her down in the shower, she pulls back and peers at me with a shy smile that pulls at my heartstrings. The soft and satisfied look on her blushing face, filling me with pride and possessiveness.

"Please tell me there's no one outside." She whispers, afraid of anyone hearing.

It's too late now.

"Probably, kitten." I pull her hands away when she hides her face in them. "Don't tell me it didn't turn you on, knowing they could hear everything I did to you. The proof is on my tongue."

"I can't believe you." She rolls her eyes, making me chuckle.

I cup her cheeks and press a kiss on her pouty lips. "You did ruin all the towels, kitten. How many could you possibly need? You're so tiny."

"I did not."

"Take a shower and come outside," I order, kissing her one last time. "I'm nowhere done with you."

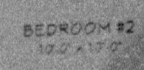

Chapter Thirty-four

BIANCA

I stand in front of the full-length mirror and don't recognize myself. The dark blood-red gown drapes over my curves, the bodice built like a corset with the sweetheart neckline in black lace ruching while the fitted skirt, with a slit going up to my thigh, flares out to the floor.

Sliding my curled hair over one shoulder, I twist and gasp again at the back of the dress. Two strings, which were made up of numerous tiny diamonds, crisscross and adorn my bare skin, the deep cut dipping to the top of my hips.

Royal, sexy, and bold.

It's the feeling running through my veins at having been surprised by Dash yet again. My gaze had zoomed in on the large black box sitting in the middle of the bed when I came back from my second shower. I was contemplating whether or not to touch it when he had entered the room and declared he bought it for me to wear tonight.

My mind was still reeling and glowing from what happened in the bathroom to do anything but nod at him mutely in acknowledgment. The corner of his mouth had lifted knowingly before he himself went in to shower, leaving me alone with my racing heart.

My daily quota of sass around him had apparently run out while I was seducing him.

I thought for sure a set of sexy lingerie or some kind of sex toy, even a combination of both, might be waiting for me inside the box decorated with a plain black bow. We're talking about Dash here. The man is as kinky as they come. So, my wild guess could totally have been a possibility.

However, I was pleasantly stunned with the gorgeous gown and the fact that he got my size right. First, the coat, and now this—I'm quite impressed with Dash.

Perhaps this was his seduction plan all along.

I mean, what can I say? A girl can dream.

The sound of footsteps approaching pulls me out of my musings just as the energy in the room shifts and sizzles with tension. I hear his sharp inhale when he sees my back a second before I see his reflection behind me in the mirror.

Silly girly butterflies dance in my stomach when our eyes lock. His caress on my skin is like a thousand bolts of electricity.

Instead of killing me, I feel alive.

No words are spoken for a while as we absorb each other in. As always, he looks magnificent in his sharp and pristine thousand-dollar suit with his hair styled back. There's no mistaking his sharp cheekbones, chiseled jawline, and trimmed beard. The black bow tie, completely different from his usual style, makes his appearance undeniably sexy. Something about it is making me all hot and bothered.

As we stand together, our outfits beautifully complement each other.

His raw masculinity, making me feel feminine and soft in all the right places.

I meet his intense gaze when he presses closer and rests his palm on my lower back. I feel the shape and callousness of each long finger heating my skin with just one innocent touch. These little caresses, heated glances, drive me wild almost as powerfully as coming on his tongue when the deviant beast beneath his calm veneer dominates me.

He has to do nothing but be in my vicinity to have my panties soaked.

"Having dirty thoughts about me, wifey?" He smirks.

I blink back to reality and school my features. "You wish."

"I better be the only man making you blush like that."

The jealousy dripping from his rough growl has me smiling and I turn around to face him. His arms circle my waist and he rests his palm possessively on my ass.

"Or what?" I challenge.

His nostrils flare. "Or else I'll fill you with my cum, so every time you walk and it drips down your thighs, you'll know who you belong to."

"You're giving me all the more reason to do it, Mr. Stern."

"Then how about this?" he growls, yanking me flush to him. "If you think about another man, let alone touch him, then the rumors about me killing a man *will* become true."

"Dash," I gasp, speechless.

"I've already lived through hell watching you in another man's arms while wishing you were mine, Bianca. I won't survive it again."

His confession tilts my reality and my heart feels like it'll beat out of my chest. He doesn't need to say it but I know he's talking about Niall. Dash desiring me all those years ago isn't something I could've imagined in a million years, if that's what

SCANDALOUS GAMES

he's implying.

He felt so out of my league with his broody glares and quiet intensity that I was sure he hated me for living in his home with his stepbrother whom he despised.

"You wanted me?" I ask, whispering and searching for the truth in his face.

"How could I not? You're perfect, kitten. But you were in love with Niall."

"You hated him."

"Because all you ever saw was him, while I all ever saw was you." Our foreheads touch when he bends and cups the back of my neck, his thumb tracing languidly. "It took seven years and a fake relationship but I finally have you, for however long it lasts."

The last part is said for my sake but I know he doesn't mean it. It's written in his piercing gaze he intends to keep me and for some bizarre reason, it doesn't frighten me.

Today has been nothing but an emotional roller coaster.

The adrenaline is still pumping in my bloodstream and as long as we're here, the last thing I want to do is sort out my new and messy new feelings. I want to live in our flirty bubble a little longer because once we get back home, reality will be waiting for us.

"Where are we going, Dash?" I ask curiously instead.

Does Paris have opera shows? The way we're dressed, I feel like we're going to one.

"It's a surprise," is all he says in my ear before kissing the side of my neck and straightening to his full height.

My skin tingles where his lips were. It's like he knows all my secret spots that are meant to madden a woman with lust.

"You're not even going to give me a hint?" I half complain.

"It's a party."

"Really? I couldn't tell."

He chuckles. Intertwining our fingers, he pulls me out of the bedroom and together we walk out of our suite, then to the elevator. Inside, he cages me in the corner and runs the back of his knuckle down my arm, raising goosebumps in its wake.

"You look like a dream, kitten." His voice is husky. "I can't take my eyes off you."

Just one compliment and he turns me all mushy inside. "You look handsome too, Dash."

"Want to know what I love most about this dress?" he says, low and rough. With one hand resting above my head, the other moves from my arm to the top of my thigh visible through the slit, and he glides the pad of his finger up and down.

"What?" I whisper, anchored by his stare.

"That I can touch this anytime." His roaming hand inches underneath my skirt through the slit and he cups my pussy, grinding against my clit. I bury my face in his chest as he traces a single finger between my folds over the thong until it's soaked with my wetness.

"Dash." I moan.

"Take off your panties."

I shiver at his demand and stare at him with wide eyes. "Why?"

"Because I want your cunt bare all night long." He drags the tip of his finger to my center and pushes in, making me clench involuntarily. "If I'm in the mood to play with it, I want nothing in between. So take it off or I'm ripping it."

His hand disappears and he waits, stern and patiently.

A trill courses through me and I do as he asks while my cheeks flame. I feel naughty as I inch my fingers underneath and slowly glide the thong down my thighs. Dash watches raptly while I pray the elevator doesn't stop at a random floor, getting me caught. The second it's off, he takes it from my hand and slides the lace inside his pocket.

The move, sexy and possessive.

"Good girl."

I shiver.

Those two words of praise should be illegal on his tongue.

I'm thankful the elevator stops before he can make another dirty request. Once again, he takes my hand in his as we walk to our car waiting outside.

Every step reminds me of my nakedness underneath the dress and the second cool air caresses my pussy outside the hotel, I inhale sharply. Dash smirks and I narrow my eyes in warning.

It has no effect on him.

"Feeling cold, kitten?"

"Shut up."

He chuckles low and helps me into the back seat before doing the same. As we glide into the traffic, I'm entranced by the nightlife in Paris and gaze out the window the whole ride. Stars glitter in the sky while the moonlight lights up the history buildings and I wish we could stay here forever.

I was worried my trip would be sad and unmemorable. Should've known Dash wouldn't let that happen. He doesn't even realize it but he gave me an unforgettable experience at my dream destination.

Whenever I think of Paris, I'll always think of him too.

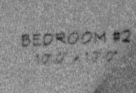

Chapter Thirty-five

BIANCA

Have you ever felt like you've entered another realm? A world you heard whispers about but never truly believed it existed. The legendary tales of debauchery and luxury that felt far-fetched.

Tonight, I have a feeling I may just find out, if the discreet building we're standing outside is anything to judge by, especially the two hulking bodyguards perched on either of the gates. Both dressed in all black, they look intimidating, and my curiosity of the place rises tenfold.

Awareness prickles at the back of my mind that Dash has brought me to a club. Memories of the last time we were together at one rises to the surface and it feels like forever ago that we would only watch each other from afar. This place itself doesn't feel the same. The vibes are subtle, luring and mysterious.

Much like the man on my arm.

The moonlight casts a shadow on his profile, highlighting his perfect jawline as he nods at one of the two men, who lets us in without a word. We step into an eerily silent and a dimly lit corridor that surprisingly doesn't look creepy and dingy.

I tighten my hand around his. "Where are we, Dash?"

"Sanctum." He caresses the inside of my wrist, on my pounding pulse, soothingly.

Intriguing name. "Have you been here before?"

"No. You need to bring a date or be a couple to enter."

"Did you bring me to a sex club?" My question comes out breathless. I narrow my gaze suspiciously and maybe even with slight jealousy. "And you were never tempted to bring a woman the last time you visited? You're known for having threesomes at places like this."

Dash stops and faces me just as we reach another door and tucks a wayward strand behind my ear. "It's a kink club, kitten. It's for couples to explore and experience their sexual fantasies in a safe and clandestine world where nothing is off-limits. And like I said, I've never come here before, because until you, I never wanted to."

"What's so special about me?"

"Moments and memories are special but you, kitten," he pauses, his thumb grazing my bottom lip and eyes full of softness and bewilderment, "you're extraordinary." Bending down, he kisses me once. "Rare." *Kiss.* "Beautiful." *Kiss.* "And mine."

My heart somersaults at each press of his lips and goosebumps rise on my flesh with each endearment. My mind, on the other hand, screams it's a dangerous game we're playing and to not let my guard down around Dash.

It's one thing to call me his, when we're in the throes of passion but when it's said during intimate moments like this while sober and with so much clarity, it terrifies me.

Learning he wanted me in the past has changed our dynamic completely.

I wonder if I would have asked him to be my fake husband if I knew the truth. The answer comes easily and I know we still would've ended up here together. Because my attraction to him and our chemistry was undeniable the moment we ran into one another.

Even before I saw Dash that night, I was gravitated toward him.

Then I craved him the second I saw him.

And had he not brought us here, I never would've known just how much. I'm not merely attracted to him, I actually like the man he is. That truth is the scariest of them all.

"I'm never going to have threesomes, though," I tease when he leans back.

"Good. Because I don't share and you'd just be signing their death warrant."

"But you'll let others watch?"

"We're not here to fuck, kitten," he reveals in a dark note. "I brought you because I know you like to watch other people fuck, it turns you on when they lose their inhibitions and put their bodies on display while consumed in dirty lust. I saw it in your eyes that night, and if it wasn't for your innocent curiosity of voyeurism, I never would've met you again."

"I-I'm not a voyeur, Dash," I whisper in denial while ignoring the dampness between my thighs and that intoxicating rush of thrill.

Charming and seductive as a devil, Dash circles his fingers around my neck and tilts my face until I can't hide from him. Then coaxes in a dark and low voice, "Is that why you couldn't look away when Justin fucked that girl's throat?"

"I don't know," I stammer, closing my eyes.

His fingers tighten, stealing my oxygen, and I'm met with a fierce gaze. "I haven't

SCANDALOUS GAMES

forgotten the pleasure on your face or the disappointment when I wrenched your gaze away from them. It's seared into my brain. Tell me it didn't turn you on when I was fucking that whore while you stared from the shadows."

I shake my head, biting my lip, because damn it, I couldn't pull my gaze away. It felt wrong and forbidden and I didn't want to stop.

"Don't deny the truth, kitten. Once we go inside, your wet cunt will prove you a liar." His body shoves mine against the door and faster than I can react, his hand pushes underneath my skirt as he growls, "Say it or I can find out for myself right here."

"Fine. Yes," I murmur, aching to feel his fingers against my core. "I liked it."

His eyes glow with lust and satisfaction. "Nothing makes me harder than knowing you're a kinky little girl with a penchant for voyeurism, kitten. I want to know your every depraved desires, your filthiest fantasies that you dream of when you lie awake at night."

"Why?" I can't help but rasp out.

His mouth tilts in a savage smirk. "Because they're mine to make true."

"You'll make me an addict."

"I'm already yours."

Steadying me on my feet, he tucks me to his side and finally knocks on the door. A second later, it opens, revealing an elegantly dressed woman, who greets us from a few feet ahead. I notice two more closed black doors on either side.

"*Monsieur and mademoiselle*," says the woman with a flirtatious smile. "Welcome to Sanctum."

I give her a polite smile while my insides feel like jelly. I'm too busy admiring her simple black gown while Dash gives our name until we're ushered into the room on our left where we're asked to check in our phones as they're not allowed inside.

Unlike at The Mirage, there will be no sneaking into this club.

Once done, we are taken down to yet another corridor and two more doors when I hear the sound of soft acoustic music playing. It's in French so I don't understand the lyrics but the woman singing sounds sensual and soft.

My eyes widen in surprise when I realize she's performing live and clad in a sexy Bordeaux dress which appears see-through under the spotlight. I half expected to walk into an orgy but inside, rich couples in pairs or groups dine together around private tables, laughing and flirting. Huge chandeliers hang from the ceiling while the low lighting gives an intimate ambience.

"Would you like a drink first, kitten?" Dash asks, bending to whisper in my ear.

"Yes, please."

I'm going to need alcohol, even if it's one drink, since there's a limit for what tonight has in store for us. I won't lie that not knowing anything isn't adding to my arousal. My body is already thrumming with need. An unquenchable thirst.

Mostly because of the presence of Dash beside me.

I feel insatiable despite having two mind-blowing orgasms.

He and I are seated in a booth in the corner, hidden from prying eyes, and instead of sitting across from me, Dash slides in by my side. The impeccably dressed waiter comes and takes our order, leaving us alone. Dash leans and stretches his arm behind me, playing with my curls while his other hand traces up my naked thigh.

"What are you thinking, kitten?" he curiously murmurs.

"I can't believe I let you talk me into going commando."

He chuckles and I squint my eyes playfully. "Here I thought you'd be nervous."

"Oh, trust me, I am."

"Why?"

"Because ever since I met you, I've done everything opposite of my nature," I confess and he stills, fingers pausing on my skin. "I've never chased a man yet I ran after you, asking to be my fake husband. Every time my life has gotten messy, I always find my way to you, even when I thought I hated you, and you say yes every time. Out of all the people in the universe, you've managed to become my savior. Twice."

"Don't mistake me for your savior, Bianca," he says, his voice ominous and unflinching. I shiver when his fingers circle the back of my neck. "It will be your downfall. I'm not your knight in shining armor, I'm just a selfish and possessive man who has no moral compass when it comes to making you mine. I claimed your virginity because even if you couldn't be mine, I'll always hold a permanent piece of you that will only belong to me. It's just your bad luck that fate wound you into my arms again."

"Are you going to ruin me?"

"I will."

"Why?" I whisper, inching closer when I should be running away.

"Because it's all I know."

He says it so brokenly and definitively that I feel my heart crumble. Undeterred and probably reckless for not running away, I cup his face. Bringing his lips down to mine, I whisper, "I think it's too late for a warning."

"Is it?"

"Yes. Because I'm already ruined." I crush my mouth against his and kiss my not-so-knight in shining armor.

Because being ruined by him is already a thousand times more exhilarating than being broken by a man I believed to be safe and good.

Bad luck with him is more enticing than any good fortune.

Chapter Thirty-six

BIANCA

Rich velvet. Mirrors. Glittering lights.
The playroom beyond the dining area and deeper into the club is jaw-dropping and an otherworldly sight. I feel like I've stepped into an erotic fairy-tale land with stunning scantily dressed women and elegant and handsome men.

Dash told me that it's the oldest club in Paris and used to be a secret society for the wealthy and the elite. Even now, it exists only for high-profile politicians, businessmen, and celebrities. Except, it is not as secretive as it used to be.

Sanctum is simply a labyrinth of dark, mysterious corridors, and chandelier-adorned rooms. There's another bar inside for the patrons, who came to fulfill their curiosity of the dangerous atmosphere.

Dash appears to be at home here with the confidence and grace of a majestic beast while I look like I'm an innocent prey caught in his clutches. Unlike the guests outside minding their own business, everyone in here is admiring and staring at the newcomers with curious gazes, and some flirting before disappearing into dark corners.

Women's hungry eyes dart to Dash but when I peer at him, his gaze is pinned on me.

My heart flutters inside my chest with happiness.

SIMRAN

I let go of my bottom lip, which I was biting nervously and as though he has a sixth sense and can feel my pounding pulse, he pulls me in the direction of the curved staircase, leading upstairs to *les boudoirs*.

Every step heightens my nerves, sharpening my senses and anticipation until I can hear my own heartbeat in my ears. Every sound and every person fades into white noise and blurry figures the higher we climb. My fingers, which are holding my skirt so I don't trip, tighten when I sneak a glance below. I suck in a sharp breath because from above, I can see couples that I couldn't see from the floor making out from some of the mirrors.

Fuck! How did I not notice them? Why did I think any corner of this place would be innocent? We haven't even reached the main room of sinning, yet I'm beyond turned on.

My attention is stolen by Dash who stops and twists toward me, his piercing eyes hooded and bright like the chandeliers around us. He doesn't miss my spying and curious gaze and roams his over my heaving breasts, spilling over the neckline, to my cinched waist in my corset that makes every breath lightweight, and finally to my naked leg.

Nothing gets past him and his lips tilt upward, knowing I'm wet just from that tiny peek. He says he wants me to confess to all my desires and fantasies, but without a single word, he knows them all better than I do.

He peers to the deepest, darkest parts of me I didn't know I had hidden.

By the time our gazes collide after his close perusal of every inch of me, I'm a wanton mess of lust and it leaves a trail of blazing fire on my skin.

The flames burn higher to the point where it's suffocating when he speaks in a guttural tone, reading my sinful thoughts. "You're not allowed to touch yourself for the rest of the night."

My pussy clenches at his commanding voice.

"And you're not allowed to come."

"And if I do?" I can't help but sass.

His mouth lifts in one corner but it's a cruel and threatening kind of smirk. And god, it only sharpens his sharp cheekbones and rugged features. I instinctively take a step back when he circles me, trapping me against the railing behind.

Arms on either side of my waist, he leans over my small frame and threatens, "If I catch you stealing another orgasm that's not on my fingers, my tongue or my cock, I'm going to take you to a private room, tie you spread-eagled on the bed, and wrench so many orgasms from your horny little body that you'll beg me to stop while wishing you didn't disobey me."

"Is that supposed to scare me?" I arch my eyebrow, half tempted to ignore his rule.

"Ever heard of forced orgasms, kitten?" he taunts, his gaze sadistic, and I swallow. "The first two, maybe three, are pleasant like your body is floating on a cloud until your clit becomes swollen and so sensitive that every touch tethers over the fine line of pain and pleasure. Just when you feel you can't take any more, the orgasm builds slowly, powerfully, that you can't help but fall over the edge. As soon as it ends, I play with your pussy all over again until you're in an endless circle of

SCANDALOUS GAMES

lust and madness. You're not ready for it yet, but disobey me and I won't show you any mercy."

"You're insane."

"Still don't want to run away?"

"No." *Because I'm just as insane.*

"I wouldn't let you anyways," he promises darkly. Stroking my cheek with the back of his knuckle once, he pulls away and waits for me to walk ahead.

Two dark enclaves at the end of the hallway beckon us. Suddenly, my dress feels too tight as we approach them, the unknown thrilling and scaring me at the same time, and then I hear the telltale noise of soft moans and deep grunts amidst the sound of bodies slapping.

Unable to take the suspense any longer, I turn to my right and come to a stop just past the threshold. Dash's body heat presses into my back just as his intoxicating scent envelops me. His hands grasp the sides of my waist and his fingers dig into my flesh as he pushes us deeper into the room while staying quiet.

"Oh my god!" I gasp, unbidden and shameless. "This is…" I trail off.

I feel like I've stepped into a land of writhing masses, an erotic scenery.

There are four smaller viewing rooms with glass walls with couples inside having sex in threes and fours. It's a mating of hard cocks claiming the women's pliable bodies. Some getting nailed by two men at the same time. The ecstasy on their faces, vivid and stark.

It's dirty, raw, and hedonistic.

The rest of the enclave is adorned with long and wide couches where some watch the orgy with a spellbound fascination while others are in different stages of getting undressed, making out, and even having sex.

My cheeks warm when my wide eyes inadvertently clash with a woman's just as the large bearded man behind her bares her small breasts to the entire room. I'm unable to look away when he takes her erect nipples between his fingers and pinches, making her moan. Her sounds, drowned by the cries of others.

I realize with a startle that I'm brazenly staring at a naked woman with her boyfriend, just a few steps away. I instinctively shut my eyes, embarrassed and shocked and *hot*.

"No. Watch her," Dash growls in my ear.

Pressing himself harder against my back, he lets me feel the shape of his hard cock and bites my earlobe when I don't immediately obey. As if the beautiful girl was waiting, our gazes lock again. Hers are hooded while mine are shy and entranced.

Dash collars my neck from the front so I can't look away and I know he can feel every intake of breath through my parted lips. His thick and pulsing shaft, adding to the erotic thrill.

The sexy, bearded man reveals his woman's naked body by pulling down her dress the rest of the way. He's fully clothed in a dark gray suit, straining to contain his bulging muscles as he wrenches her hands behind her back, and pushing out her chest for every person to see.

I would've been jealous if I didn't know that Dash's hardness was because of my reaction to all the sex happening in every corner, and not because of the naked

SIMRAN

bodies of strange women getting fucked.

A little bit of my nerves vanish as seconds tick by and it hits me that the couple I'm watching is getting off on our close and vivid attention. A wave of desire rushes down my spine as I stare at his free hand, which is inching from her breast to her pussy, spreading her folds. He traces her center with his middle finger and my breathing turns shallow.

When I look up, she licks her lips, watching me raptly, and I know she's getting off on both the stimulation of her partner's fingers and displaying her naked body. To the crowd. *To me.*

"Dash," I murmur, pushing my hips against his until he groans. Feeling emboldened and desperate by the scent of arousal and the screams of pleasure, I grind my hips against his.

"Are you wet, kitten? I bet you are," he grunts, his fingers squeezing my throat. "I knew you'd love it here. Do you like the show they're putting on for you, filthy little girl?"

I stifle the whimper climbing up my throat, unable to describe the feeling and put it into words. Not that I need to, when he can feel my shallow breaths, the tremors racing up my spine, and my fingers clutching his arms so I don't fall.

I blink, focusing on the couple once more. The man whispers something in her ear while she stares into my eyes and I still as she boldly cups her breasts, pulling and pinching her nipples. My own harden into painful nubs, seeking friction, and I shift restlessly when the man pushes two fingers in her pussy to the hilt in one savage thrust, making her cry out.

"Touch me," I plead, shocking myself.

"No," Dash denies.

Meanwhile, the man drives his fingers inside her with a ruthless speed and I feel my own walls clench on thin air, needing to be filled by Dash's fingers urgently. The rougher he gets with her, the higher my lust climbs.

My mind screams for the man to just fuck her and I don't recognize my inner voice.

Why am I loving it so much? I never knew I had a voyeur kink and it's better than any fantasy I could have had, obliterating all the others.

"Please, Dash."

"Bad girl," he tsks, grabbing my hand that I didn't realize I was inching between my thighs. "No touching, kitten."

I'm so embarrassingly wet that I could feel my arousal trickling down my thighs.

Circling my waist and holding my wandering fingers hostage, I shudder, feeling his lips suck on my pounding pulse, swirling his tongue teasingly. He tortures me by not caressing where I need him the most and just then, the man pinches his girl's clit with his fingers still inside until she shudders her release.

Our connection breaks as she jerks in his hold, head thrown back, and I feel every tremor as though it's my own. Her blonde hair cascades down her back and while she's in the throes of her orgasm, he picks her up and lays her over the couch before bending forward aggressively to eat her pussy with fervor.

Memories of Dash's mouth on my pussy invade my mind.

SCANDALOUS GAMES

I'm unable to take any more. My clit throbs and the familiar ache builds in my core, just out of my reach. My gaze shifts to another couple—a woman riding a man with abandon, as he spanks her ass on each thrust.

My dirty mind imagines riding Dash's cock, making him spill inside me.

He must have the same thought because his hand lets mine go to cup my left breast and squeeze, rubbing my nipple with his palm.

I'm turned on like crazy but so is he. Hard. Long. *Thick*.

The couple I'm watching becomes a trio as another guy joins them, bending the girl and shoving himself inside her without warning. My eyes feel heavy lidded as the threesome gets rougher and harder in front of me.

"It won't ever be you," Dash growls, tilting my face toward his. "No one but me is allowed to touch you."

I pull him down by cupping the back of his neck and lick the seam of his lips before whispering against them, "Yes. Only you, Dash."

He affirms my words by pushing his tongue inside my mouth and kissing me deeply. My toes curl at the violent aggression in each swipe and suck of his lips. The world disappears until all I feel is him. His strength, his scent, and his possessive touch, anchoring me to him.

I seek his mouth when he draws back with a dark smirk.

He's intentionally tormenting me, believing he has all the power just because he told me not to touch myself. However, he isn't the only one who knows how to bend the rules to their favor.

Two can play this game.

Staring into his eyes, which narrow when I take his wrist still gripping my breast possessively, I inch it lower over my abdomen. Without pausing, I slide it farther down and slip it underneath my skirt, and I sigh in pleasure just as I press his fingers against my wet pussy.

"Kitten," he warns, inhaling sharply.

Uncaring if anyone stares, I push his finger between my folds and whine in frustration when he doesn't take the lead. I want the same dominance and passion from our hotel bathroom.

"Did you forget what I said, little brat?"

I stare back innocently. "You said I can't touch but nothing about *you*."

"Are you that desperate you can't wait?" he taunts.

"Can't you feel how wet I am?" I press his hand harder, making his jaw clench and gaze turn primal.

"But it isn't because of me, though, is it, kitten?" he says, wrenching his hand from mine before roughly dragging me into a dark corner, away from lascivious eyes. I gasp when he shoves my arms above my head and tilts my jaw. "You're soaked because of watching that girl come."

"Are you jealous?" Shock laces my voice.

"I am."

"You're hard," I accuse.

"Because of you and the raw pleasure on your face as you gazed at them." His voice is thick with lust and envy. "Because the filthy vixen inside you turns me the fuck on. But it also makes me insanely jealous because I want to be the only man driving you crazy just like you do me. I need to be the only one making your cunt wet and have you begging. I want to possess you, Bianca."

A scary shiver runs down my back hearing his confession. My stomach flips while his words wrap around my heart. "No one drives me mad more than you, Dash. Not one person in here makes me wet with just a single look. So stop torturing us both and *please* make me come."

My answer must satisfy and banish his jealousy because he wedges his thigh between my legs until my pussy deliciously rubs against him. Then he asks with a salacious growl, "You never answered my question, kitten."

"What?" I murmur, seeking more friction.

"Do you want to be fucked like *my whore?*"

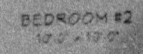

Chapter Thirty-seven

BIANCA

I freeze with my wrists held captive by his strong hands and under his penetrating and waiting eyes. His question, lingering in the air between us as his gaze reverberates down my body, causing goosebumps to rise on my skin.

Unfiltered fantasies that I buried in a dark corner after the first night he uttered it to me, rises to the forefront and assaults me once more. My traitorous pussy becomes slick when I imagine the nights I spent alone in my bed, touching myself to the thought of him calling me his whore.

I shouldn't want a man to call me that, right? It's demeaning and humiliating.

Then why does it arouse me so much?

Yet I can't deny the dirtiness, forbiddenness, and tabooness behind it that thrills and pleases the inner dirty girl inside me.

As if Dash can hear my inner battle and torment over my confusing feelings, his gaze softens and he bends. His breath flutters my hair as he whispers in my ear, "It's just you and me, kitten. Tell me… Yes or no."

"Yes." It falls from my mouth and there's no taking it back.

My closed eyes flash open when Dash pulls back, crushes my waist between his palms, and grinds my pussy against his muscular thigh. He keeps thrusting my hips back and forth until the texture of his pants rubs on my clit. The friction, too intense, and I'm shameless, not caring I'll leave a wet patch on his thigh.

"Fuck... Yes!" I encourage, sighing with pleasure at the fact that he finally ended the torment.

Primal need darkens his sharp features and he demands, "Say you're my whore."

Our eyes meet as I lick my trembling lips.

"Say it, kitten."

"I-I'm your whore."

His grip becomes painful and he uses me like a rag doll, grinding and rocking me against his thigh until an ache builds in my stomach. I clutch onto his shoulders for dear life, loving every second.

"Pull aside your skirt and show me that wet cunt making a mess of my pants."

Grateful he dragged us to a dark corner, I hastily obey his brazen demand and display my sex for his carnal gaze. My cheeks redden when I follow his stare and notice my pussy lips spread wide, exposing my clit and my juices sticking obscenely, darkening the color of his expensive pants.

"Is that all for me?" he teases, spreading my legs wider.

Embarrassed and shy, I go to cover myself when he wrenches my hand back to the side.

"Good little whores don't hide themselves."

I grab his shoulders just as he picks me around the waist and walks somewhere behind me to take a seat on a couch I didn't notice before. It's in a private nook, still shading us from others in the room. I moan when he flicks my clit with the pad of his thumb. Once. *Twice.*

"More," I beg when he stops.

"My little whore wants to come?"

"Yes, please." His fingers flex. "So badly."

Lust clouds my brain every time he calls me his whore in that rough timbre voice of his. He says it so possessively, reverently, illicitly and sinfully. I hate how much I love it coming from his lips.

Fingers threading in my hair, he propels me forward, and bites my bottom lip before issuing another command, "Ride my thigh like you would my cock and make yourself come. Keep that pussy on display. I want to see that needy little clit grinding against my leg."

You know what I didn't realize all those years ago about Dash? That he is nothing but a savage beneath his bespoke suits.

With a mouth filthier than the devil's.

His mind, deviant than a sinner's.

And I just might come from his filthy words—wicked enough to send me over the edge of ecstasy—alone. My hooded eyes stay locked on his as I shift my hips. Dash, on the other hand, simply rests his palms on them, feeling every slow thrust. The desire shining in his pupils as they flick between my thighs and my face has me riding him faster.

Under his attention and hold, I feel owned and possessed.

"Dash," I whisper, feeling the familiar tide rise in my core. I dry hump him harder, chasing it. "I'm so close."

SCANDALOUS GAMES

I jerk when I hear the front of my dress tearing and my breasts bouncing free. He *ripped* my dress.

His lusty eyes devour my naked breasts, as they bounce with every thrust. Dash gives me his vicious grin at my wide eyes and I cry out when he twists my nipple. Punishing the other, he growls, "Whose filthy whore are you?"

"Yours," I whimper.

His palm slaps my breast and I buck against his leg violently. "Want more?"

I can do nothing but nod as I almost reach the peak, the pain from his spanking mixing with the pleasure heading closer.

My voice is hoarse when I beg like the needy whore he's turned me into, "Again."

"Where?"

"My pussy."

Spank.

Spank.

Spank.

My vision blackens, and light flashes behind my eyes as I fall apart, riding wave after wave of endless pleasure. The orgasm, pulling a loud scream out of my lips that Dash swallows, crushing me with his mouth.

I'm panting heavily, breathing his air, when he presses a soft kiss and whispers, "Mine."

I blink my eyelids open and he pushes my hair behind my ear. I pull back and my cheeks flame when I remember my naked breasts and torn dress.

"I loved that dress."

"And I love your tits," he says, staring at my swollen and red nipples. I hiss when he flicks them. "And I plan to buy you a thousand more dresses."

"You'll probably ruin those too."

"We're leaving," he announces abruptly but his need mirrors my own.

I lower my gaze to his cock straining his pants and my body comes alive again. God, I'm a horny and insatiable mess. "You didn't come."

"I'm not done with you." He smirks. "I'm going to fuck you in our hotel room where only I can hear your screams."

He smiles seductively, seeing the excitement on my face, and I bite my lip while blushing. His gaze darkens and he sets me to the side before shrugging off his jacket and putting it on me. I stand on shaky legs, happy to get out of here and desperate to have Dash inside me. So he can claim me again.

I frown when he doesn't do the same and sits with his legs spread.

"Dash."

"Get on your knees." He arches one eyebrow arrogantly, points at his thigh, and orders, "Clean the mess you made, kitten."

The sticky, wet mess I left on his thigh stares back at me and I swallow, unable to meet his eyes. My legs tremble and my fingers tighten around his jacket that smells like him. My heavy breaths push my stinging and hard nipples against the material of his jacket that dwarfs my small frame.

"Lick it with your tongue," he says with more force. "Now."

SIMRAN

Stepping closer, I lower myself to my knees between his spread legs. The bulge of his cock taunts and teases me and I can't believe he's had me in this position twice in one day. Only this time, I'll be tasting myself.

His piercing eyes—that I dare not meet—sends an electric shiver down my spine. It twists into a full-body shudder as I feel his fingers thread in my hair so he can watch my lips inch closer and my tongue peek out to follow his filthy demand. He jerks my head back before I can.

"Eyes. On. Me."

Another tremor racks my body at his low and throaty command. Slowly, I raise my gaze to his face, green pupils a dark pool of lust.

I lick where my juices shine on his pants. His grip doesn't ease, so I do it again and again until there's nothing left of my orgasm. Except, I've only made more of a mess. When his cock twitches, I'm tempted to suck him again but I know he won't allow it.

Besides, I need him inside me more.

I sit back, staring at him softly, and he traces my lips saying, "Good girl."

Next second, I'm in his strong arms, being carried bridal style out of the club. We're at the staircase when I worry I might be too heavy for him, so I speak, "Put me down, Dash. I can walk."

"How many times do I have to tell you that I like you in my arms, kitten?"

I shut my mouth instantly, hiding my blushing face in the crook of his neck. Peering over his shoulder for a second, I'm not the least bit shocked at the curious and smirking faces as they watch Dash take me away. Their knowing expressions telling they know I'm about to get fucked by the domineering man.

He isn't even out of breath by the time we exit and our car is already waiting for us. Only once I'm secured in the back seat does he let me go to slide in himself.

"Drive," he barks at the driver.

The ride back to the hotel is quiet but thick with tension. My body is coiled so tight that I'm afraid of touching Dash for fear the thread holding us together will snap. I'm hyperaware of my half-torn dress with my breasts naked underneath his jacket and my bare pussy that is still embarrassingly wet from the remnants of my climax.

I sneak a glance at Dash and find his fists clenched with one resting under his jaw as he stares out the window. I squirm in my seat when the blinking lights hit the obscene bulge running down the inside of his pants that he isn't even trying to hide.

How did I even fit him in my mouth?

The sound of a low growl yanks my attention back to his face and my heart races faster, having been caught ogling his cock. If we were alone, I would've been sitting on his lap and riding his cock right this second. His locked expression saying the same.

The driver must sense our urgency and Dash's growing intensity because he drives faster down the street and my stomach flips when we finally arrive.

"Wait for me," says Dash as the car stops.

I watch his tall frame step out and round the hood to my side, carefully helping

SCANDALOUS GAMES

me out so I don't mistakenly reveal my half nakedness. Though, my face must betray my sinful thoughts.

Few seconds later, Dash and I step into the elevator.

It stops at our floor.

His control unleashes and the suit jacket is tugged down my arms.

"Go to the balcony and be naked," he commands as soon as we step over the threshold of our suite. "I want to fuck you under the stars."

His hulking figure stalks forward while he loosens his tie. The effortlessly sexy move slows down my steps.

Everything about him screams sex god.

So unfair.

"Don't make me wait, kitten." He throws his tie before flicking the top button of his shirt open. "You've already made us wait long enough. It took every restraint I physically possessed to not wake you with my cock inside your pussy every morning or fuck you at night until you passed out while you wore those tiny shorts meant to drive me crazy."

His roguish gaze rakes down my hand clutching my torn dress like it offends him. Shoulders bunched so tight and broad, he looks ready to attack. Another two buttons undone and his chest teases me, with a light smattering of hair that makes him look masculine and sinful.

"Balcony. Now," he growls.

I run.

His footsteps follow, unhurried and confident. Like a hunter knowing his lamb is caught and captured. One glance in the mirror in the bedroom reflects my glowing face, aroused gaze, and flushed skin. I let my beautiful gown fall around my feet until I'm standing in only my high heels.

Stepping over the crumpled dress, I walk naked to the open and dark balcony. In the distance, the Eiffel Tower glows like a jewel while the wind is just chilly enough to harden my nipples. A thrill courses down my spine as I step farther, eager for Dash's arrival, when a hint of a moan teases my ears. I halt and search to my right, finding no one on our neighbor's balcony and thinking my mind is hallucinating after being at the club.

But the voices come again, a little louder and unmistakable, making me freeze. To my left, I make out the silhouette of a couple making out, and my heart thuds.

Looks like somebody beat us to our idea.

I don't pause to watch despite the sick rush because all I'm craving is Dash.

Without another look, I hurry inside before I'm caught staring but pull up short when the object of my desire sucks all the oxygen out of the room as he steps into the bedroom. I forget the world around me as my gaze flies to his bare upper body, consuming every tight muscle of his chiseled eight-pack abs with my unblinking eyes.

Each ab looks carved out from stone.

I think I just died and went to heaven.

The cut dips and the planes of his chest are a mouthwatering sight as my eyes follow the happy little trail disappearing into his unbuttoned pants, which is hanging indecently low. I finally understand why women drool over that infamous V because Dash's is lick-worthy.

I can't believe he's mine... My mind lays its claim.

Our eyes lock at the same time.

He crosses the distance and my brain finally functions. I blurt out softly, "Dash, we sho—"

"What did I tell you, kitten?" he cuts me off, his expression hard.

I take a step back while fighting not to lower my gaze. "I-I'm naked."

"And where were you supposed to wait, brat?" He invades my space.

I open my mouth to lie when our neighbor decides to take their make-out session up a notch. Dash's lips tilt while I was hoping he didn't hear.

"It's your lucky night, kitten," he rasps before arching one eyebrow. "Why are you inside?"

I shake my head at his illicit intention. "We're not at the club. They'll see us."

"Then you'll just have to be quiet."

I squeal when he picks me up, leaving me no choice but to wrap my legs around his waist. Our skin connects, and my nipples rub against his hard pecs, the light chest hair causing friction, and I moan. My nails dig into his flexed forearm as he yanks my mouth to his, kissing away my protests until I melt in his embrace.

His hand grips the back of my neck tightly so I can't pull away when I run out of air as he tastes my lips and every corner of my mouth with his tongue.

"You're so goddamn sweet, my wifey," he groans against my lips before diving in again. "I can't decide if I love the taste of your kisses or your tight pussy more."

Cool air caresses my naked back but the heat from Dash's skin keeps me warm and his kisses leave me drowning that I almost forget about the oblivious audience. Wrapped in his arms, I no longer seem to care. Only a single need remains on my mind.

"Please fuck me, Dash," I whisper, licking his bottom lip before I suck it. His taste, better than any alcohol. "I need you."

My head drops when he exposes the column of my throat, kissing and biting. He's rough and unapologetic as he marks me with his teeth. I'm going to be wearing nothing but his hickeys if he doesn't stop.

I tug at his hair and stare into his lust-darkened face.

My eyelids almost close in pleasure when he circles my nipple until it's painfully hard before sucking it into his warm and wet mouth. I watch, mesmerized, as he laps and lavishes at my breasts until they're glistening with his saliva.

It feels so goddamn good that an ache rises in my lower stomach. I whimper when he takes the tip between his teeth, biting down like an unhinged savage.

"Don't make a sound," he barks.

Impossible. "I'm going to come."

He takes his mouth away before growling, "You're coming around my cock, nowhere else."

"Yes, please."

My pussy brushes against his length when he slides me down his body before roughly turning me around and pushing my front against the thick brick railing.

SCANDALOUS GAMES

He's hidden us in a corner so we can gaze at the now half-naked couple having sex, but they can't see us.

It feels ten times more taboo and wrong than at the kink club.

But we're too far gone to care.

Our mutual thirst for each other, leading our actions.

Dash shoves my legs apart and twists my long hair in his fist, pulling until my back bows, and grabs the front of my throat. The sound of the other couple reaches us like a sinful symphony.

"You still want to be fucked like my whore, sweetheart?" Dash grunts.

"Yes."

"I don't show them any mercy."

"I can take everything you give me."

"Even if I said it's your ass I want to fuck?" he says darkly, viciously.

I shudder, both in fear and desire. I must be losing my mind yet again if I want him to take my ass. Still can't believe I let him claim it years ago despite giving my virginity to him too. I truly gave him every piece and firsts of mine that night.

He stole them all like a thief in the night.

Something about him possesses my mind and my heart. Like a dark spell.

His hand squeezes my neck, yanking me out of my musings. "Ass or pussy, kitten? My cock is aching to pound into you."

"Fuck my ass."

"Beg me like my pretty little whore."

I lick my lips, my pussy leaking as I push against his erection. "Please fuck my ass, Dash. However you want. Please, darling."

My endearment unleashes the beast in him and he bends me while slapping my ass cheek. *Hard.* "Keep your eyes on them while I fuck you."

Chapter Thirty-eight

DASH

Never in the last seven years did I think I'll have my beautiful Bianca in my arms again.
Naked.
Bent over.
Begging for my cock in her tight ass.

I keep her face tilted forward and trace the back of my knuckle down her spine to her red ass cheek. Her body trembles beneath mine and she shudders violently when I slide my finger between her cheeks to her tiny rosebud.

Circling it slowly, I dip my digit lower to her dripping cunt, and swirl it in her wetness before rubbing her asshole again. She's clenched so tight that I'm afraid I'll come as soon as I push inside.

"Spread your ass cheeks," I growl. "Show me where I'm going to put my cock in."

"Oh god."

"God isn't making you sin, kitten." I slap her pussy, making her moan. "I am. So it better be my name you scream from those lips."

"Dash!" she cries out when I pinch her clit. Once. *Twice.*

Her moans turn ragged. I lean over her body and push my wet finger in her mouth, effectively silencing her. Like a greedy little girl, she sucks them, tasting herself.

"Stay quiet unless you want to be gagged."

Her head shakes.

"Open your ass for me," I order impatiently.

The cries of our neighbors get louder and I know it's only making Bianca hornier because the evidence is on my hand that I press against her gushing pussy.

However, my attention is solely on her.

No other woman turns me into a sex-starved man like my kitten.

I draw my gaze to her hands as she brings them behind her and pulls apart her cheeks for my hungry eyes. The shake in her fingers is unmistakable as is the scent of her arousal in the air. I run my tongue between my teeth as the moonlight and the soft light drifting from our bedroom shows me every inch of her dark pink asshole, glistening from her juices that I rubbed in.

"Good girl," I praise, wishing I could see the soft look that crosses her brown eyes every time I utter them. She's always so feisty, but not when I have my hands on her.

Then she's the perfect submissive girl I crave her to be.

There's no stopping me when I lower to my knees, intertwine our fingers, and spread her wider before licking her hole with my tongue. Nothing has tasted as divine as her desire. She pushes her hips harder against my mouth, chasing and seeking her pleasure.

I tilt her hips higher and scrape my teeth across her clit until she's dripping on my waiting tongue. My beard, scratching against her soft skin, and it makes her grind harder.

"Such a needy little whore." I grunt, loving the shiver crawling up her spine.

I knew the moment I saw her, she was going to be perfect. The minx in her begging for my depraved desires. No other man will know that she gets off on being treated like a wanton whore. *Only me.*

She wisely stays quiet as much as she can under my moving lips as I eat her pussy like an unhinged psycho. I need her so wet that I can slide in without hurting her. Let her feel only the pleasurable pain as I stretch her forbidden hole with my thick girth.

Holding her still, I spit on her tiny rosebud before slowly inserting my middle finger. The wetness makes it easy to push past her resisting muscles and I'm knuckle-deep. Her breaths turn shallow as she adjusts to my invasion and I kiss her skin soothingly.

Still, she's nowhere ready for the size of my cock.

The sick fuck in me loves it.

I slide my other hand to her pussy and flick her clit as I push another finger inside her ass. Scissoring inside her, I shove a third finger in and she tries to fight.

"Dash, I feel so full." Her voice is nothing but a helpless whisper.

I rise to my full height, pull her flush against my chest, and thrust my fingers in and out. Forcing her to accept everything I'm giving her. I whisper filth in her ear, aware how it makes her melt in my arms.

"You will feel full when I have my big cock inside you, kitten."

Her nails dig into my forearms as I wrap it around her tits while finger fucking her faster and rougher. She rises on her toes but I'm relentless.

"Breathe for me, baby," I rasp, punctuating my words with a thrust. "I'm going to fill this ass with my cum. Then watch it drip out of your gaping hole." *Thrust.* "I'm going to mark you as mine."

"Y-you're going to fuck me bare?"

"Yes." My cock jerks.

"Tell me I'm the only woman you've fucked bare, Dash," she demands possessively instead of telling no, and it fuels my lust while the head of my cock leaks with precum. "You're the only one I ever would, kitten. I want nothing between us. You want that?"

"Yes."

I kiss her cheek as I whisper, "Guess you're stealing my first too. You love that, don't you?"

"It's only fair," she teases and it turns into moans when I slam my fingers hard.

I pull them out just as I feel her clench harder. No way is she coming on my hand. Bending her at the waist, I push my pants and boxers lower and take out my angry dick. The head purple with an intense need to fuck like I've been wanting to do all night.

It was torture knowing she was bare underneath her dress and I couldn't fill her.

Neither of us even realizes the couple is long gone and I'm glad because I need to hear her scream my name as she comes around my dick. She's going to get it rough and hard. Pleasure with pain.

I step between her thighs and spread them wider with my legs, her sexy high heels glinting in the dark. She still has her hands keeping herself open, even though I can sense her nervousness beneath her false bravado. The first time I was gentle, slow, but I know she doesn't want that now.

Tonight, she wants to be *owned.*

Our sighs of pleasure are mutual when I dip my cock between her wet folds, lubricating my shaft with her juices. The purple crown presses against her clit and I slap it with my tip, making her moan loudly.

"Fuck, Bianca. So wet." I trace her up and down. "So soft." I push just the head in her cunt. "And *tight.*"

Her walls clench around me and I lick my lips as I stare at where we're joined. Her dark pink asshole slightly open from my fingers. The sight of her like this forever imprinted in my head.

"Dash… Please," she begs.

Pulling out, I aim the head against her tiny rosebud and push. Her body resists and my jaw clenches as I fight the urge to shove to the hilt. I replace her hands with mine and pull apart her cheeks so I can stare vividly as I slowly but relentlessly thrust inside.

"Relax, kitten," I coax. "Let me in."

"I forgot how big you are, Dash."

"Keep talking like that and I'll forget to go slow."

SCANDALOUS GAMES

"Maybe I want that," the filthy girl taunts and I drive hard on the next thrust, sliding a few inches of my shaft past her tight ring. She cries and tries to jerk away but I tighten my grip around her hips.

"You fucking take it," I say through clenched teeth and thrust, pushing in another inch.

"Ahh..."

"Is this what you wanted, kitten?"

"Yes. Use me, Dash. *Harder.*"

Fuck. Her mouth is going to be the death of me. I pull out until the head is grazing her entrance and plunge to the hilt. Her wail of pleasure and pain, echoing in the dark. Her walls have me in a death grip, the feeling so intense I have to close my eyes. My cock throbs inside her as I hold myself in, simply enjoying the amazing feel of being inside her.

It's when she wiggles and whimpers that the savage need overpowers me.

With an animalistic growl, I begin to pound into her mercilessly, forcing her to accept every punishing thrust.

"Scream my name, Bianca."

I raise my hand and bring it down on her ass. I grip the back of her neck with one hand and hold her hip with the other as I fuck her ass like a madman. As if I've never been inside a woman who tears apart my control with a bratty insult or when she begs me like she's my precious little whore.

"Dash!" *Thrust.*

"Who do you belong to?"

"You." *Thrust.*

"Who's my little anal slut?"

"I am." *Thrust.*

I watch her hole swallow my wide shaft and wink when I pull out completely. I spit on it, making it dribble inside before plunging my cock in her. Sliding my fingers in her long hair, I tilt her head back and reach her pussy with the other to thrust in her empty hole until she's filled.

"To-too much." Her voice is hoarse. "I can't."

I lean over her helpless body and bite her earlobe before growling, "Yes, you will. This is how I like to fuck, kitten. Rough. Hard. Unhinged. Merciless." She clenches around me and I feel her body tense. I smirk before taunting, "Look at your pussy choking my fingers. You're going to come, aren't you?"

Her response is to whimper, lips parted.

"Are you gonna come with my cock in your ass, kitten?"

"Make me come, please."

I pick her up with my cock still inside her ass and carry us into the bedroom before I bend her over the massive bed. She turns her face to the side and I push her arms above her head, holding her immobile.

"Don't move your hands," I order harshly.

Thrusting into her, I flick and rub her clit at the same time. Every time I bottom out, I pinch and flick her bundle of nerves until her moans become longer. I keep the pace punishing, my balls slapping against her cunt, and I feel her body lock tight.

"That's it. Come for me, kitten," I rasp. "Choke my dick."

"Yes. Yes!"

I flick her clit before spanking her reddened ass. She falls apart, back bowing as her fingers twist in the sheets and her whole body jerks as the orgasm rains down on her. My eyes watch her, mesmerized.

Before she can come down from the high, I cover her back with my chest and circle her throat. The dirty sound of skin slapping fills the space but it's the wet squelching sound her ass makes that wrenches the orgasm out of me.

"Fuck. Look at this dirty little girl milking the cum out of my cock." Like a savage, I bite down on her collarbone and mark her as mine. "I'm never letting you go, Bianca. Going to fill you up every night until there's no doubt left in your mind."

"Dash!"

My name on her trembling lips prolongs my orgasm and I hold her tighter while my cock jerks with every spurt of cum from my balls until I'm spent. Our harsh breathing, filling the quiet space.

A sense of rightness spreads warmth through my chest and I go still when Bianca turns her head toward mine while cupping my face with her palm.

Her lips touch mine in a lazy, wet, and sensual kiss.

And everything I did tonight becomes nothing because in those few seconds, Bianca completely *owns* me.

Chapter Thirty-nine

BIANCA

"This absolutely beats the view from the Burj Khalifa."

I stare at Rosa while she stares in awe at the picture of Paris as seen from the Eiffel Tower. The expression on her face, almost comical since nothing usually impresses her. Even if it does, she never has the look of wonderment as she does now while we sit in my old apartment, along with Iris.

"Let me see," says Iris impatiently, trying to snatch the phone from Rosa's death grip.

"The picture will not disappear if you wait for a minute," retorts Ro, putting the phone out of Iris's reach, who scowls at her.

I definitely missed their mindless bickering.

Iris turns to me and wiggles her eyebrows suggestively. "You fucked him, didn't you?"

I blush at the vivid memory while trying not to fan my face or ruin another pair of panties. Never imagined I would get off on the things he said and did to my pliable body.

Rosa doesn't even look up from my phone as she mutters, "Of course, she did. She's practically glowing like a virgin who discovered dick for the first time. Better question to ask would be… How many times did he make you come?"

"Oh. Shut up, Ro," I grumble.

"That many, huh?" She smirks.

"I lost count," I sheepishly answer, covering my face with my palms.

Iris loudly claps and hoots, "Ah ha... I knew you liked Dash, Bee. It was obvious from the way you eye fucked each other whenever you were in the same room."

"You only saw us together once."

"One time was enough to know he's smitten with you."

"So, keep the groping to a minimum, please," Rosa requests. "I have no interest in a live porno."

If she only knew the things I saw and did in Paris. I still can't believe it sometimes or get it out of my head. I probably never will.

"Again, it only happened once," I snap, rolling my eyes. "And you weren't supposed to see."

"Show me the ring again," exclaims Iris.

Rosa turns with a big grin just as I raise my left hand, the purple diamond sparkling. Iris takes my wrist and fingers the cut, tracing reverently.

"This must have cost a fortune," she mutters.

"Awful lot of effort for a fake relationship," says Rosa suspiciously. "Don't tell me you caught feelings for each other in such a short time."

"Of course not," I hastily counter, scoffing at the insinuation. "We fucked because we're attracted to one another and he bought the ring to make our relationship as real as possible when we meet my parents tomorrow. That's all there is to it."

After spending another extra day in Paris and sightseeing at more local spots, Dash and I returned. Since we were both jet-lagged—well, I was, while his workaholic ass went straight to work—from our long flight, we had to postpone our dinner plans with my family. Of course, my mom didn't take that too kindly and conveyed as much when I called. Alas, nothing can be done about it.

"As long as it's a fake relationship with benefits, I say have fun." I focus on Rosa while Iris wears a neutral expression. I can sense her disagreement from a mile away. "It's a risky situation you're in and if one of you wants more, it'll get messy."

"There's nothing to worry about."

Except I feel like I'm lying to my friends... *to myself.* The time we spent in Paris, the parts about his life he shared, has shown Dash to me in a new light. I always thought of him as an arrogant, possessive, and cold man but he's so much more—thoughtful, mischievous, and protective.

He's still no less possessive and domineering. I mean, he confessed he desired me when I was with Niall and then is constantly calling me his, with an intense clarity in his piercing gaze.

But men say a lot of the things in the heat of the moment, right?

The earth-shattering kiss—it felt too real, like he was marking me as his.

However, as I listen to Rosa's warning and Iris believing Dash is smitten with me, I'm slightly regretting giving in to him. I know I shouldn't have broken our rules. It was for this exact reason I made them in the first place.

Now, I don't know where he and I stand. God, I'm so fucking confused.

It's been three days since we've been back and both of us haven't had a chance to spend time alone since we're catching up on our respective workloads. I haven't

SCANDALOUS GAMES

even seen him sleep, quite honestly. He's been holed up in his office and even if he's home, he's either on his phone or attending online conference meetings. Always gone in the morning by the time I wake up and then I'm asleep by the time he returns.

Strangely enough, I don't like that.

"How are you going to tell your parents you're having a court marriage?" asks Iris, pulling me back to the present.

"Or that you're doing it the day after tomorrow?" adds Rosa.

I shrug. "I'm just going to rip the Band-Aid off. I don't want to give them a reason to try to sabotage my relationship with Dash. So, the sooner we marry, the harder it will be for them to not accept it."

"That's wise."

The next two hours pass by in a blur as I tell them all about my adventures, minus the kinky club in Paris, and catch up with their lives. Rosa informs us that her parents are trying to force her to marry Nova by the end of this year, who for some reason is in agreement. So, now she's trying to figure a way out of it. We don't arrive at a solution by the time they have to leave.

It's ten at night when I take the elevator to our—I mean *Dash's*—apartment, and I don't expect him to be home. Hence, my surprise when I find him in the kitchen, cooking no less, with his shirtless back to me. I blink twice to make sure I'm not hallucinating.

"You're home early," I state dumbly after a pause. My heart, suddenly galloping in my chest.

He twists to face me, roaming his lazy yet burning gaze over my messy bun, thin cami top, and loose lounge trousers—which are baring my belly button—to the tip of my toes. I don't miss his lingering pause on my braless breasts, making my nipples harden instantly.

Jesus, I'm needy again.

I pretend I haven't secretly missed kissing him and the all-consuming way he does it.

I pretend that despite him coming home late every night, I don't feel him slide into bed and pull me into his arms right after he whispers that he still hates cuddling. As if he knows I'm listening and I have to hide my smile.

Maybe I give it away when I curl my body tightly around his warm one. Don't know what I'll do if he sleeps naked like he warned me.

"I didn't know you cooked." I nervously fill the silence when he stays quiet.

Rounding the counter, he stalks to where I'm lurking in the doorway while wearing every woman's kryptonite—low-hanging sweatpants that leave little to the imagination. Like mine wasn't already corrupted by him.

"Dash—"

His lips descend on mine, stealing my breath away. My back collides against the wall, my hands gripping his wrists as his cup my face and he kisses the ever-loving hell out of me. He pours three days' worth of tension, longing, desperation into one single kiss.

Like I'm not the only one who missed the mere press of his lips against mine.

The insistent flick of his tongue against the seam of my mouth, followed by the teasing glide as he tastes every corner with a low groan, betrays his satisfaction.

Our breathing is heavy, ragged, and harsh once he pulls back. The green flecks in his eyes, lighter than I've ever seen, as he gazes softly into mine. It triggers something in me and suddenly, Rosa's words from earlier flick through my hazy brain, shattering the momentary bliss.

"The rules." I attempt to put some distance between us but my words come out hollow, no real power behind them. He sees it for the feeble and pathetic excuse they are.

"Fuck your rules, kitten," he curses, low and rough. "We play by mine now."

Before I can argue, he kisses me hard again, shutting me up until I forget my own name.

"Don't confuse Paris with Vegas." His thumb rubs my bottom lip. "Everything that happened there between us isn't staying there. You gave me your body and I'm not returning it. *Not yet.*"

Wrapping his large hand around my hand, he tugs me toward the kitchen and doesn't stop near the dining table like I expect. Rounding the island, he turns, grabs me around the waist, and sets me down on the counter in one swift and strong move.

The strap of my cami top falls down one shoulder and my chest expands when he tucks it back into place. The heat from his fingers, burning my skin and lingering after he removes his hand. Every little thing he does, especially the domestic kind, like greeting me home with a kiss, draws me deeper into his orbit.

Until I don't know if I'm sinking or flying.

Either is dangerous to my heart.

He gives me his back as he goes back to cooking on the stove and speaks casually, "Do you like biryani?"

Instantly, my mouth waters while my semi-functioning brain observes my surroundings and doesn't miss the delicious aroma of herbs and veggies along with rice simmering in the cooker before Dash covers it to let it steam.

"I do."

"Good to know burgers aren't the only thing you eat," he jokes.

"I have other favorite dishes I enjoy, just so you know."

"Tell me one."

My mouth parts before I close it. I swear, literally nothing comes to mind and he turns to glance at me with a smug smirk. So, I blurt out randomly, "I love…fries."

"That's a snack."

"I also like pizza." My face scrunches as I say it, making his shoulders shake with silent laughter. I throw my hands in the air as I sigh, "Fine. I have an unhealthy obsession with burgers."

I start to slide off the counter but he's in front of me in a flash and halts my progress with his hands on my thighs. He towers over my frame even with the added height as I sit on the counter and my neck strains as I maintain eye contact with him.

His eyes dance with mirth and warmth, like I'm a fascinating creature fallen

SCANDALOUS GAMES

into his lap.

"You're sexy when you're mad and too adorable when you're annoyed."

"Both of which you make me feel plenty."

He leans forward, inching his fingers up my inner thigh and closer to my sex before drawling, "They make you *plenty wet* too, kitten."

The loud whistling sound of the cooker saves me from his wandering hands and I come to my senses. His eyes promise it's not over before he reluctantly pulls away. The muscles in his forearms flex as moves to a cupboard to take out the wine glasses, which I didn't know we had. Then he opens the refrigerator to grab my favorite red wine I always keep at my place.

"Set the plates, wifey."

Stupid, idiotic butterflies take flight. I couldn't ignore them even if I tried.

Dash has two moods around me, which I can guess by the nicknames he calls me. I'm his wifey when he's playful and seductive but when he's overcome with dark possessiveness and deviant desires, I'm his kitten.

And god, how they both affect me equally.

There was a time when the latter used to annoy me. Now, it's the polar opposite.

My heart flips at the affection they hold, even when he's growling in the smooth yet rough timbre of his voice.

Dash quirks a perfect eyebrow when I sit like a statue. I jump and quickly move, not before I notice his hungry gaze lock on my bouncing breasts underneath my top. *I'm playing with fire*—says his expression.

No skipping bra. I make a note to myself.

We fall into comfortable silence. The air, thick with our unmistakable chemistry. Every once in a while, our arms will brush as we move around each other. My breathing would quicken whenever he presses against my back in a disguised move to grab small things, cornering me between his wide chest and the cold marble of the kitchen island..

The familiar feel of his body takes me back to Paris when he bent me over the bed, held me immobile, and fucked my ass until I came all over him. With a shaky breath and an inner curse, I stand at the opposite end.

His tiny and innocent little actions are confusing my head and driving my libido insane. Our close proximity is a twisted game of foreplay. And it's made it harder to resist him now that I know what's waiting after his cold control snaps. Endless pleasure.

The dirty, gritty, savage kind.

It's when we finally take a seat at the dining table, opposite each other, that I manage to get my insatiable body under control. Steam billows out when he uncovers the pan with precision. My nostrils are hit with the delicious aroma of perfectly cooked rice mixed in a rich dressing.

It's going to be yummy, of that I have no doubt.

Everything this man does is nothing less than amazing, like failure just isn't an option for him. It feeds the curious part of me that finds him fascinating. That little glimpse he bared has arisen an addict that craves another hit.

His slightly curly hair falls onto his forehead, highlighting the slope of his

Roman nose and pronounced cheekbones as he pours us both wine. My fingers itch to push it back so his eyes—which are my favorite part of him—aren't hidden.

I shove the urge down because it's what a girlfriend would do.

We're not together.

He's my soon-to-be fake husband.

It's all pretend.

A sham.

Despite the facts—or should I say *warnings*—circling my brain, my lips have a mind of their own and I curiously ask, "Who taught you to cook?"

His hands don't pause as he fills my plate with food and his head tilts an inch, indicating he heard my question. He doesn't answer immediately and lifts his eyes to mine. Sliding the plate across the table toward me, he replies in a melancholic voice, "Rani Aunty." Filling his own plate with twice the amount compared to mine, he elaborates, "She was one of my nannies when I was twelve and the only one whose name I remember. Mostly because she was the first one who made an effort to get to know me. I was determined to keep her at arm's length, never talking because, what was the point, they all left eventually, or I did. Except, my stubbornness had nothing on hers."

There's softness and a boyish smile on his usually broody face as he continues, and I raptly listen and hang on to his words.

"I would usually lock myself in my room but one day, I decided to hang out in the living room, giving her the perfect opportunity. She came and sat with me, then randomly began telling me stories about her own kids. It was a one-sided conversation where she didn't push me to participate. To her, my listening was victory enough. The love in her voice for her family struck me hard because it sounded like a world I thought of as a myth. For weeks, we continued our odd ritual where she regaled me with stories and I listened until one day, I couldn't help but reply with a sarcastic remark."

His lips tilt, a faraway look crossing his eyes as though he's living the memory. Entranced, I watch him. "I can't recall the exact words I said but the happiness on her face is imprinted in my mind. I began spending more time with her and since cooking was her hobby, most of it was spent in the kitchen. So, she forced me into helping and then taught me a few recipes. Days later, I found her husband had taken another job that required her family to uproot and she wanted me to have something to remember her by. She was with me the shortest yet I was close to her."

I can just imagine a young Dash feeling abandoned once again and it causes a sharp pain in my chest. A flash of that same hurt flickers, darkening his features before it vanishes. He doesn't have to say it for me to know she felt like a mother to the lost and lonely boy in him.

He drinks a long sip of the wine and returns his attention to the food but doesn't eat while I seem to have forgotten about mine.

"Eat, kitten," he says, lightening the mood. His voice, however, is tense.

I take a bite and an involuntary moan escapes my lips. His gaze heats momentarily as we stare into each other's eyes.

SCANDALOUS GAMES

"You didn't stay in touch with her after she left?" I ask cautiously, hoping it doesn't end in a sad way.

He chews another bite, swallows before nodding. "I did. She called me every month. She felt more like family than my own father ever did."

"So you still talk to her?" Hopefulness lingers in my tone. "She must be so proud of you."

"She passed away six years ago."

The spoon clatters on the plate as it drops from my grip.

Again, no trace of emotion. His voice is frigidly impassive whenever he talks about someone close to him dying tragically. Always so matter-of-fact, it's frightening.

"I'm sorry to hear that."

His chair scrapes across the tiled floors as he abruptly stands, his plate half eaten. Wiping his mouth with a napkin, he downs the wine and excuses himself, "I have an important call to attend. Don't wait for me."

Before I can process the sudden one-eighty of the night, he's gone.

My own appetite lost, I sit alone, staring into space for a few long minutes before composing myself and carrying our unfinished plates to the kitchen. I busy myself by cleaning the space and scold myself yet again.

Why do I have to always push him harder than he's willing?

He gives an inch and I end up taking a mile.

Switching off the lights, I make my way to the bedroom and like the first night, he's working on his laptop in the balcony. Only this time, I'm conflicted to disturb him, unable to judge his mood. Instead, I enter the bathroom and get ready for bed.

He hasn't moved when I slide under the covers. The bedside lamps shining in the otherwise dark room allows me to gaze at him while I lie on my side. The glow of the laptop screen reveals his profile and as if he can sense my presence, our eyes meet across the small distance.

My breathing accelerates and I hold his gaze, wishing I could read his mind. Hoping I could take away the pain he felt his entire childhood. However, I'm no better.

Because in the end, I will be leaving him behind too.

Chapter Forty

BIANCA

The bright sunlight pouring through the windows jerks me awake. The rumpled bedsheet and the lingering smoky scent of Dash is the only proof he slept last night. I check the time on the bedside clock and notice it's eight in the morning.

Damn. I must have not heard the alarm.

Last night's conversation is still heavy on my mind as I rise from the bed, stretching my arms and legs until I feel marginally human. I'm distracted by the thought of the impending dinner tonight with my parents, when something from the corner of my eye catches my attention.

A handwritten note sits on the nightstand, trapped under my phone. Curious, I pick it up, my eyes widening when I finish reading Dash's message.

Our court appointment is today.
Be ready at twelve in the afternoon.
I'll be there to pick you up from the apartment…

What the fuck? The arrogant bastard didn't even sign his name below. Yeah, because that's the part I should be focusing on at this moment—his manners.

Getting married today? Hell no. Didn't we decide on tomorrow? How dare he

SCANDALOUS GAMES

change it without discussing it with me first? My parents are going to be pissed yet again if I tell them I got married without informing them, just like my engagement. It's like Dash is doing it all on purpose. He's been steamrolling our arrangement right from the beginning like a controlling fuck.

But does a day early make a difference? Am I making a big deal out of nothing? my rational side whispers. Of course, I am not. It's merely the underlying fact that Dash cannot continue to make all the decisions. I let the annoyed and inconvenienced side of me win.

I'm fuming as I dial his number and he picks up on the second ring.

"Kitten, I'm in a meeting," he says as a greeting, sounding occupied. I hear murmurs revealing he's in a room full of people.

"I read your note."

"And?"

God, give me strength. "May I ask why?"

"No."

I glance at the ceiling, counting to five while trying not to snap.

"We were going to see how it went with my parents. This was supposed to be the last resort," I remind him, in a high-pitched voice because he clearly forgot that tiny detail.

"I thought us marrying was the whole point of our deal."

"It was... *is*."

"Then *may I* ask what the problem is?" The hint of sly amusement is unmistakable.

"Why didn't you tell me last night?"

"I left you a note."

Should I be thanking him then that he didn't spring this up on me at the last second? Because that's what I hear from his infuriatingly composed tone.

"Are you having second thoughts, kitten?" He lowers his voice and asks. "You nervous?"

My back freezes and the reality of what I'm about to let happen hits me at the speed of a bullet train. Because once I marry him and sign those papers, there will be no going back. I'll be deceiving everyone around me. Yet I also know it's the only option I have.

Still, I can't accept my nerves in front of Dash. He's the epitome of confidence. Except when he's talking about his emotions.

"You should've asked, Dash," I say, summoning all my strength. "Just because I don't run a billion-dollar company, doesn't mean I'm not just as busy."

"I would never assume that," he replies, his tone indicating I didn't offend him. "Which is why I checked your schedule first."

"You went through my calendar?"

"Yes."

"On my laptop?"

"Where else would I check?" He sighs.

"How do you know my passcode?" My tone is aghast.

"Zero zero zero hardly constitutes as a password, kitten. A toddler would have

SIMRAN

cracked it." He scoffs, maddening me. "You also have the same one on your phone. Bit useless, if you ask me. And before you ask, yes I saw the photos you took of me in Paris."

I flush red from head to toe and shake my head at his lack of boundaries. Why did I expect he would have them in the first place? The joke's on me. And yes, I couldn't resist clicking pictures of him when he wasn't looking.

Never let good sunlight go to waste… is my mantra.

"Triple zero is a perfectly safe and strong password since nobody expects one to have it these days."

"Says who?"

I narrow my eyes because he's obviously trying to distract me with this pointless conversation. The voices I heard earlier are now inaudible as though he switched rooms.

"Did you leave your meeting?"

"I don't like others listening to my private call with my fiancée who's having cold feet."

"I am not."

"Good. I'll see you at twelve then."

"My dress isn't ready yet," I lie like a fool.

"I don't care what you're wearing as long as you're there and signing the papers, kitten." I can just imagine his firm expression and now I've run out of possible excuses. As if he can feel my struggle, he softly coaxes, "It'll be okay. You're doing this for your sister. Look at it this way, the sooner you do, the sooner she gets her wedding. Then you can happily get rid of me," he jokes and a chuckle spills past my lips.

"I couldn't get rid of you if I tried."

"No, you can't, wifey." I shiver at his possessive growl. "But it'd be fun to see you try."

Instead of going to the office, I take the day off work to avoid creating unnecessary gossip at work. Explaining to my boss my relationship with Dash—her client—after the media spilled the news all over was more than enough. I had to make up a whole other story as to why I didn't tell her the day she revealed he was my new client. Thankfully, she didn't ask many questions once I told her Dash is a private person and that in a way, I'll do a great job since I knew all about his likes and dislikes.

"Do you need me to kidnap you?"

I glance at Rosa in the mirror, who moves along Dash's side of the closet and messes his color scheme in a disarraying pattern.

"Would you stop with his clothes?" I scold before answering her. "And no. I would rather not be a runaway bride. Might I add he's doing this for me, not the

SCANDALOUS GAMES

other way around."

Her wandering hands open his drawers next and she switches his socks with the ties. Poor Nova is going to have his hands full with her.

"I still think we should have a secret signal if I need to rescue you."

"Why didn't I call Iris?" I mutter to myself.

"Hey! I heard that."

I smooth my purple lace top before putting on the white jacket that I paired with my ankle-length silk pants and high heels. My curls bounce when I whirl toward Rosa, who is scowling. "How do I look?"

"World's first fake bride."

"Ro!"

"You look stunning, as always, Bee." She bridges the gap between us and rights my collar. Tugging my hair like she used to do when we were kids, she softly asks, "Are you one hundred percent sure you want to do this? We could always find another way."

I intertwine our hands and shake my head, smiling reassuringly. "I'm good, Ro. We've come too far to back out now."

"Promise me that if you ever feel it's too much, you'll let me know."

"I promise."

"One last question and a very important one."

"What is it?" I probe, worrying at her serious expression.

"Which terrifies Dash more? Snakes or guns?"

I exhale a relieved breath and roll my eyes. "Seriously, Ro, what are you planning now?"

"I need to know for my 'if he ever hurts you' speech."

"Oh god!" I don't know whether to laugh or be scared.

"At the moment, I'm terrified of you, Rosalie."

Both of us jump at the said man's amused voice. Dash leans his shoulder on the doorway with one hand in his pocket and the other rubbing his jaw. His stormy eyes flare with desire when they lock on mine and slowly take in every inch of me, leaving goosebumps in their wake.

"You're late, Mr. Fiancé," mocks Ro, unperturbed by his presence.

"Always a pleasure to meet you, Rosalie," he retorts before straightening to his full height and informs us, "I called out twice for Bianca."

I tuck my hair behind my ear and wince. "Sorry. We didn't hear you."

Crossing the distance, he takes up all the oxygen in the tight space until his scent is the only thing I'm breathing. None of last night's sullenness remains in his steady gaze, his mask back in place as he pulls me into him.

"You look beautiful, kitten," he whispers only for me to hear by bending down.

I blush like he said something naughty, making Rosa grin and raise one eyebrow questioningly. Her amusement evaporates when he wraps his arm around my shoulder.

"Why are you touching her? You don't have to be her caring fiancé when it's just us."

Dash's lightness succumbs to possessiveness in a flash. He stares her down as he

SIMRAN

replies in a calm veneer despite the hard expression on his sharp face, "As much as I like your threats and protectiveness for your best friend, that's where I draw the line. The only way I'm not touching her is when she tells me no."

I tense, expecting Rosa to lash out with another sharp insult or threat, but she leaves me flabbergasted when she smirks with something akin to satisfaction. Dash is too busy glaring to notice he played right into her hands by giving her the reaction she was searching for. Though, I also have no idea, except I know she's up to something.

Before the situation escalates, I step forward to tug my smug best friend out of the room, only to not make it far before I'm yanked back against a hard chest.

"What did I just say, kitten?" Dash raises one eyebrow as I peer at him.

I feel like I'm in a tug-of-war between him and Rosa.

"That you're clingy," I tease innocently. His lips lift on one side.

"Okay... I'm going to wait outside before you both make me puke."

Dash holds me hostage as Rosa walks out of the closet, leaving us alone and in a flash, I'm pushed against the wall with a starving man leaning over me.

"I can't wait to call you Mrs. Stern," he rasps, tracing his knuckle down the front of my throat as I swallow. "Then when we get home, I'm going to make you scream my name."

My fingers dig into his shoulders and I whimper as he licks over my pounding pulse and bites down hard. Heart racing, my body hums to life when he softly rubs the spot he marked with his teeth.

"Perfect," he compliments with a primal look in his eyes.

I almost stumble when he pulls back as though he was my anchor and grasping my small hand in his strong one, he leads me outside. His hickey sits proudly on my collarbone as I sneak a glance in the mirror. So, I slide my long hair over my shoulder, only to startle when a low rumble emanates from Dash. Immediately, I drop my arm back to my side.

"Don't make me tattoo my name where you can't hide it, kitten," he warns. "I want to see my mark on your flesh when I make you my wife."

In a few hours, Dash Stern will be my husband.

Husband. Fuck.

The rush that courses through my veins is maddening. Rosa is waiting near the elevators and the three of us step into the cab as it descends. My inquisitive friend doesn't miss our hands intertwined like lovers or the bold hickey on my neck. My collar doing fuck all to hide it.

Surely, he can't be serious about tattooing his name, right?

Who am I kidding? Of course he is.

"Justin is driving with us," announces Dash, pulling me out of my musings just as we reach the ground floor.

"Are you also coming with us, Ro?" I question my friend, who remains in the elevator.

She shakes her head. "I'll follow you in my car since I have to leave right after."

"Okay."

In the lobby, Justin is waiting for us, dressed in an impeccable suit, but he's not

SCANDALOUS GAMES

alone. Even more astounding is his expression, void of his signature flirtatiousness that he wears like a badge. In its place is a dark mischief and dangerous intrigue as he stares down at a girl who's glaring and yelling at him, her finger aimed at his chest.

She's younger than me and I recognize her as one of the tenants from my building. Their stance suggests they're in an argument while she's throwing daggers at him with her eyes. As we get closer, I hear the end of her sentence, spoken in an angry voice, "I'm going to be homeless because of you, you selfish, inconsiderate, rich prick."

Wow. She could give Rosa a run for her money in the cursing department. And here I thought of her as sweet and shy.

"You have another week to search for a new place," replies Justin in a placating tone.

It backfires because she glares harder at him with her hands on her hips. "What you're doing is illegal."

"Selling my own building?" He clicks his tongue. "Afraid not, spitfire. So, I wouldn't go around suing me if I were you."

The girl notices us approaching and embarrassment hits her cheeks when she realizes we heard everything she said. What I don't understand is why she said she'll be homeless. Wouldn't I have received a similar notice if our building was getting emptied?

"This isn't over, asshole."

"I dare hope not." He looks strangely smitten with her, despite the hate on her face.

With one last icy look, she pushes past us and disappears into the elevator.

"Somebody finally didn't fall for your charm. I thought the day would never come," taunts Dash with a chuckle, making Justin glare.

"It's your fault, you fuck."

"What did you do, Dash?" I demand, slapping his chest with my free hand.

He peers down, gaze softening. "Nothing, kitten."

"Hmmm, I don't believe you." Turning to Justin, I ask, "You tell me."

"After he bought your building, he asked the tenants living in the floors below to find a new place. Something about privacy. Now, that girl hates me for selling the place to him in the first place. Although, that detail shouldn't have been privy to her."

Dash scowls at Justin for outing him and at my upset expression. Now, his best friend is the one looking smug and with a whistle, he exits the building.

"Kitten."

"You need to give her place back."

"No."

I lift my chin. "Yes."

"It's too late now." I open my mouth to reply, but a yelp leaves my lips instead when I'm hung upside down over his broad shoulder. He spanks my ass. "We'll talk about this later. Right now, I have other pressing needs like making you my wife."

"You bossy jerk."

SIMRAN

Spank.

"Keep running that mouth and I'll carry you into the court just like this." I shut my mouth and close my eyes when he whispers pleasingly, "Good girl."

Chapter Forty-one

DASH

After the two most tortuous and slowest-moving hours in history, my beautiful obsession has finally become my wife. *Mine.* The vivid possessiveness that flares inside my chest is both a welcoming and scary feeling.

Bianca Dash Stern.

The three words I never imagined to hear as the registrar declared it in front of our best friends. I ended up doing the single thing I vowed never to do. Marriage. The bane of my family's existence. Yet the feeling is nothing short of spectacular and long awaited. My kitten doesn't realize the floodgates she's opened, letting me in and sealing her fate, signing papers that make us belong together.

Because to her, the vows are nothing but meaningless words. A necessary ritual. While they are everything to me.

I meant each word down to my soul as I said them looking into her chocolaty brown eyes. A man who never believed in marriage, thought of it as nothing but a curse. Yet today, I'm desperate and tempted to believe they're a blessing in disguise.

It's becoming a lot harder to pretend the need to get her out of my system has twisted and molded into something deeper. *Darker.*

I wonder if I'll ever be able to let her go when the time comes.

My fingers tap incessantly on the steering wheel as Bianca and I drive to her parents' house in the evening. The day has been a hectic one and I had to postpone two of my afternoon meetings because I didn't want to leave her alone while she wallowed in the guilt eclipsing her heart.

Despite her parents being selfish and dictatorial, she's still tearing herself up over lying to them. It's unfathomable to me to understand because I could never pledge my loyalty to my father after the shitty way he treated me right till the moment of his last dying breath.

He broke and turned the empathic side of my heart cold and callous.

Her mom and dad are not in the same spectrum as mine yet it's harder for me to see them as anything but. I'm staying over for dinner for as long as it's considered polite before stealing Bianca away and making her forget all the worries of today.

I stroke my thumb over her racing pulse as I keep our hands locked while driving with the other. Touching her has become a necessity for survival, like breathing and eating. I might've had qualms about intimacy in the past but they've all but eviscerated in the aftermath of Paris.

"They make you uncomfortable at any point, I'm taking you back to our place," I declare over the low music playing in the interior of my car. The smell of rich leather mixing with her addictive perfume.

Glittering lights of the high-rise buildings shine on her stunning face as she twists in her seat to face me. Her tongue swipes along her lower lip whenever she's deep in thought as my words register in her overthinking brain.

"They're not as bad as you think, Dash," she counters with a frown. "We can't have another scene like last time."

My expression tightens at the cavalier way she speaks, like it's a common occurrence. "Standing up for you isn't making a scene. I would do it again in a heartbeat."

It's her who soothes my rising anger by caressing my hand until I relax marginally. "Just try to get along with them. Please, for me?"

"As long as they don't upset you, I will."

Knowing it's as much control as I'll budge, she acquiesces and turns to gaze out the passenger window. We stop at a red light and I can't resist sneaking another glance at her curled hair framing her face and the delicate slope of her neck to the sight of her cleavage taunting me with the swell of her full and luscious tits.

Wearing a demure floral dress, she still looks like a sinful angel I crave to corrupt with my devious desires. It had taken all my restraint not to fuck her as soon as we were announced husband and wife, and then later when she strolled out of the closet.

"Is your sister's boyfriend coming tonight?" I ask, speeding when the light turns green.

"Arya said Aryan will be there."

"How much have you told Arya about us?"

"Not much more than what my parents know." A cute scowl mars her features as she reveals in a not-so-nonchalant tone, "Although, she knows more about you than I do and she didn't even have to google your name."

My lips tug to the side as I detect the underlying note of jealousy and I hide it by rubbing my jaw. "Impossible, kitten."

"Umm, yes. She does." She scoffs. "Even religiously follow every article written about you."

Another red light and I turn to her, capturing her chin in my hand as I put an end to all her useless doubts. Hell, she knows more about me from the last month than Justin does after knowing me since we were teenagers.

"She doesn't know that *you* make me weak in the knees just by merely existing. She doesn't know I feel more alive with you in a single breath than I have my entire life." Staring into her hooded eyes, I rasp, "She doesn't know my favorite flavor is the taste of your lips and my favorite pastime is making you blush. Or that even though I only had you once, you're the best I ever had. You, kitten, are the only one to witness the weakest part of me. So, yeah, you couldn't be more wrong if you thought there's another person on this planet who could know me better than you do."

Leaving her stunned and speechless for the first time, I drive into the traffic once more. A brief glance shows me the pink color darkening her cheeks and trailing down to her chest, making me wonder just where it ends.

Another half hour later, we reach her childhood residence that is nothing less than a lavish mansion in a big, gated community. There's a big circular driveway we round as soon as the guard at the entrance lets us in. It's another glaring reminder of our polar opposite upbringing. Ironic how we still bear the same emotional scars.

Bianca wrings her hands in her lap, betraying her nerves as she gazes ahead.

Unlocking the car, I slide out and round the hood to the passenger seat before opening her door. Her head tilts as soft eyes meet mine and I offer her a reassuring hand, more than happy to be her strength. I can see the thoughts running rampant in her pretty little head as she prepares to reveal our surprise wedding.

If I were a better man, I would feel guilty for not waiting until tomorrow and for putting her in this position. However, the thought of going another day without completely making her mine left a sour taste in my mouth.

I also wouldn't lie that I needed the control that I felt slipping when I revealed another memory to her last night back into my life. It brought back old, vulnerable feelings I prefer to keep buried.

Her small hand wraps in mine and I hold it tight as I lead us to the front door. Before we can knock, it opens with a flourish by none other than her mother, who has a fake smile perched on her lips. I take it for the red flag it is and put my guard up while Bianca is none the wiser. She's as impeccably dressed as though she's hosting a party, not a simple dinner.

"Hi, Mom." The love in Bianca's voice is unmistakable, filled with longing.

"Here I was waiting for you to cancel yet again."

My shoulders tense at the taunt delivered in a sickly sweet tone but she's not fooling anybody. She purposefully ignores my presence, like that could offend me. So I don't greet her either. She would need to have my respect first before anything she does bothers me. Bianca squeezes my hand, sensing my darkening mood without even looking.

"I told you we weren't in the city," replies Bianca.

Her mom purses her lips. "Where were you?"

"Are you going to let us in first?"

As soon as we enter, I hear footsteps before a girl with a bright and excited smile rounds the corner and immediately, I recognize her as Bianca's little sister, Arya. Her boyfriend, Aryan, trails closely behind with undying devotion lightening his eyes that he has locked on his bubbly girlfriend.

"Bee!" she screams in a singsong voice while running toward Bianca with open arms, as though they are meeting after ages.

Instantly, my wife's entire face lights up like the Fourth of July as she braces for the impact of her hug. I have to steady her hips so they don't tumble to the floor. My eyes lock with Aryan over their shoulders and he has the same amusement dancing in his gaze at our girls.

"I missed you so much, Ari."

"I can't believe you went to Paris without me." Arya pouts.

"In her defense, she didn't know either," I answer for Bianca, whose cheeks tinge with wicked memories I'm remembering as well. I focus my attention on Arya and introduce myself politely, "I'm Dash. Bianca's told me lots of things about you."

"I'm Arya. So nice to finally meet you, *jiju*," she says, wiggling her eyes mischievously at Bianca, who blushes even harder than I thought possible at the last word. She's going to turn into a tomato at this rate. "Although, I'm upset she kept you hidden from me."

"Again, not her fault," I tease and circle Bianca's waist from behind. "In her words, I'm clingy so I steal all her time."

Arya's features soften in awe as I play the doting husband. I have to stifle a laugh when Bianca stomps on my foot in a warning. But I'm having too much fun to resist riling her up. Sadly, she has no choice but to play along.

"You two are the cutest."

"We're not," protests Bianca. I mouth over her head "we are" which makes Arya laugh. Bianca glances at me suspiciously. "Did you deny it?"

"I wouldn't dare, wifey." I tap her scrunched nose.

The energy in the room shifts in a hot flash as soon as her mother reappears again and speaks, "Come on, girls, your father is waiting. Both of you can gossip later."

Arya and her boyfriend are none the wiser of the tension between Mrs. Chopra and me. This is going to be one long, agonizing dinner if her husband doesn't have a better mood. I tell myself I'm doing this for Bianca and strangely for the other couple, who couldn't look more in love as their eyes keep meeting every few seconds.

The girls walk hand in hand ahead of us while Aryan matches his steps with mine. He's nothing like I predicted with his nerdy glasses, an untucked button-down shirt, and denim jeans. I'm shocked he's even allowed in the vicinity of Arya by her strict father. The man wouldn't let just anybody near his daughter.

Aryan's handshake is firm as he introduces himself. His tone jovial as he smiles,

SCANDALOUS GAMES

"Welcome to the family."

If only the matriarch of the family felt the same.

Or the truth about Bianca's sacrifice for his future.

Veer Chopra is still as intimidating as ever with the rigid set of his jaw and a few more frown lines than the last time I saw him. He pockets his phone he was reading from before smiling affectionately at his two daughters. A far better greeting than the one Bianca received by her passive-aggressive mother.

I hide my shock and steel my spine when he approaches me next and offers his hand that I take in a firm handshake. I'll bet all my net worth he did his due diligence on me, deciding I'm worthy of his elder daughter.

"Dash." His voice is smooth.

"Mr. Chopra. Thanks for inviting us," I reply, putting aside my pride to make a genuine effort. After all, everything rides on him and I would never jeopardize anything for Bianca, if I can help it. "I would like to start fresh."

"Let's have a chat before dinner," he declares. "I want to know all about the man my daughter has fallen in love with."

My gut says he knows plenty and it impressed him enough to change his tune. Otherwise, I wouldn't have been able to step inside his home. I'm just waiting to hear what his view is regarding the nasty rumors surrounding me.

He turns to Aryan next, which gives me an excuse to walk to Bianca's side, who has her inquisitive gaze pinned on us instead of listening to what Arya is saying to her.

"What did he say?" she questions the moment I'm in front of her.

I cup the back of her neck and place a soft kiss on her forehead comfortingly. Instantly, she relaxes and sways into my body. "Nothing for you to worry about."

Chapter Forty-two

DASH

"So you married my daughter today."
Hardly many people catch me off guard or surprise me, yet this man has managed to do it twice in one hour. My mistake for underestimating him because I didn't expect him to find out so soon. Though I keep my shock concealed by schooling my features in a blank mask. His ties go far wider than I predicted, which he confirms as he continues.

"Nothing happens in this city without my knowledge, especially when it concerns my daughters," he explains, sitting in his high-back chair in his office while I sit with my legs crossed across his wooden desk. "Did you really think I wouldn't find out?"

"I was counting on it." My pleased voice makes a muscle tic in his jaw. "I had already told you my intention that day."

"A very bold move on your part, son."

I hold his scathing stare with one of my own and shrug. "Once I know what I want, wasting time isn't in my nature. Bianca was always meant to be mine."

"You're smart." He gives a non-sarcastic laugh, pointing his finger at me. "You knew I would ask you to end it with her, so you beat me to it by wedding her, well aware I'll have to accept it in front of the world unless I want to be humiliated."

He's looking for a malicious reaction that he won't find from me. It's astonishing he's more concerned about his own reputation than Bianca's happiness or wishes. Had she truly fallen in love with someone else and brought him home, she would have been in for a rude awakening.

"Do you not trust your daughter's choice?" I counter.

"A murderer is hardly a suitable choice now."

Years of restraint holds me back from snarling and acting impervious as he attempts to rile me up. The ugly rumor is like a black mark painted on my back that I can't scrub off my skin. Nobody gives a fuck that there's no single evidence connecting me to my rival's death or that I have an alibi at the time the murder occurred.

"The court says otherwise."

"Kian is a man who knows how to pull the right strings. He wouldn't let anything stand in the way of his ruthlessness and tenacity to beat his father by building his own empire. The merger is as important to him as it is to you." Leaning back in his chair, he waves his hand in dismissal and threatens, "Besides, my concern is Bianca's safety and well-being. Men like you always have a few skeletons in the closet and with the business you're in, you're bound to have enemies."

He doesn't miss my fists curling as he implies I could harm Bianca or let another human being hurt her. However, I also can't deny his apprehensions aren't entirely misplaced.

The defense industry is a game of monopoly with old and corrupt players who don't take kindly to new people entering into their territory. Threats, intimidation, manipulation are all done to hinder growth, all of which I experienced and survived myself.

"No one is hurting my wife." *Because her worst enemy is her husband.*

"What about your past?" He arches one eyebrow questioningly.

A tingling sensation forms behind my neck, an awareness prickling in my gut at his probing tone. "What about it?"

"It was clean. Too clean."

Of course the bastard investigated my past. Though, he would not have found the truth. I had made sure no one knew of my father's second family or my ties to them. Ensuring I cut and erased them after that god-awful night.

"In my experience, it's always a red flag. So should I be worried about my daughter?"

The lie falls easily from my lips, tasting bitter and as though I've practiced it a thousand times. "My wife knows everything about me. The good, the bad, and the ugly. So, if you're doubting her integrity, then you don't know her at all."

His gaze narrows and sharpens. "I'm protecting her and I have every right as her father."

"Yet you haven't asked the most important questions."

"What could be more important than her safety?"

"Do I love her? Do I make her happy? How much does she truly mean to me?" I shake my head in disgust as I throw my words in his arrogant face. "All you've done since we sat down is worry about your own reputation rather than what she wants. Maybe it's exactly why she didn't tell you about us sooner."

SIMRAN

His jaw grinds and a vein pops in his forehead but I'm not finished. I smile cruelly, the one I give my rivals, and lower my voice as I shatter his illusion of control. "I wonder if she'll even want your blessing if I told her you tried to marry her off to her best friend's fiancé, Nova, despite knowing he's already engaged. Imagine how badly your respectable reputation would be tarnished if it was made public that you basically tried to sell your daughter for some measly profits."

"She'll never believe you." I laugh in disbelief at the bastard not even attempting to deny it. It's going to crush Bianca if she ever finds out.

"Are you willing to find out just how much?" I threaten. He remains intelligently quiet and I rise to my full height, sneering down at him. "Don't for one second think I won't destroy you if you ever try to sabotage my relationship with Bianca or dare to steal the smile from her face. I meant it when I said no one hurts my wife, not even her own family."

With one last scathing look, I leave his office. If he's smart, he would take my warning seriously.

BIANCA

I'm a ball of nerves as I watch Dash and my dad make their way to his home office after all of us mingled and had a few drinks. I'm half tempted to follow and eavesdrop but my sister's excited voice keeps me rooted to the couch.

"Ooh… Looks like Papa is taking him for *the talk*," says Arya as she air quotes "the talk".

"You think?" I mutter absentmindedly.

"Oh yeah. He had one with Aryan, too, when I began dating him."

I'm alert now. "What did Papa say to him?"

"Aryan never told me. He did look like he pissed his pants," she reveals, half wincing and half laughing. "Not that you have anything to worry about. Dash is intimidating as hell, even more than Dad."

That's what I'm afraid of. Dash is mischievous, teasing, and protective, but it's a side he has reserved for me. A layer I glimpse when it's just us together. While the other side of him is cold, scary, and vicious, which becomes tenfold around people he can't tolerate and doesn't respect.

Unfortunately, my dad is one of those people.

You put two angry and prideful bulls together in a tight space, one is bound to come out bloody. They have had a rough start, which is troublesome for our already precarious situation.

Meanwhile, Mom's rude and sour behavior was easy to dismiss as she played the gracious host, walking back and forth between the kitchen and drawing room. It was blatantly obvious Dash isn't her first choice for me, without her even giving him a chance.

My eyes dart every so often, waiting for him and Dad to return. Only for anxiety

SCANDALOUS GAMES

to strike the longer they don't. Then again, it's only been a few minutes. Tell that to my wildly beating heart.

Please let them get along, I pray to the angels above.

"That's a big fucking rock," gasps Arya, when I tuck away a curly strand behind my ear with my left hand. It's a welcoming distraction from my chaotic thoughts. Stealing my hand, she admires my ring. "Is that a purple diamond?"

"Mhmm. I didn't even know they existed." It glitters when the light hits it just right.

I won't lie, it took me a long time to get used to the weight. I'm always extra careful to protect it, considering it's the most expensive piece of jewelry I own. More like borrowed, since I will return it to Dash once our arrangement ends.

"I'm really sorry, by the way."

"Why?" I counter, honestly confused.

"I wouldn't have said those things to you if I'd known you were dating someone." Her expression pinches in apology. I notice she's cut her hair even shorter, so now it reaches her shoulders and it makes her look even younger. "I shouldn't have butted into your life, regardless. Forgive me, please?"

"Stop being silly, Ari. I love you and I could never stay mad at you."

The pure relief and joy on her face pulls at my heartstrings. Her gorgeous smile is the most important thing to me in the world. It makes all the risks worth it. No matter the tumultuous emotions Dash is evoking inside my broken heart, I cannot let it deter me from my goal.

"So have you both picked a date for the wedding?" asks Arya with exuberance, eyes brightening. "Gosh! We have so much to plan—and shopping. And let's not forget the bachelorette party."

My stomach drops and nerves dance beneath my skin as I wince because I'm about to pour cold water all over Arya's building enthusiasm. Was I asking too much that I wished for the same reaction from my stubborn parents? Disappointment and anger swirls inside me, and I push them down.

"I married him today at the courthouse, Ari." My words don't register as she continues to ramble.

"I'm thinking Jaipur for shoppi—" she trails off as soon as my news penetrates. Her shocked gasp is audible as she stares at me, dazed. "Wait, what?"

I open my mouth to shush her when another voice rumbles from behind us.

"You're married!"

My mom's outrageous cry startles us both while my eyes widen like saucers as they clash with hers when I look sideways. I hurry to rise and approach her cautiously. Red blotches form on her cheeks as she reins in her anger.

"Let me explain, Mom."

She dramatically presses her palm against her chest, shaking her head at me. "My own daughter didn't think to invite her mother to her wedding. And at the courthouse. How am I going to show my face to my friends?"

I close the gap between us, only for her to halt me with her hand. I explain in a soft tone, "We didn't want to wait and I didn't think you'd want to come. And why would I? You haven't spoken more than two words to my husband."

SIMRAN

"This isn't the Bianca I raised. Disrespectful and selfish."

I flinch while tears gather in my eyes. Arya rushes to my side and intertwines our arms. She speaks strongly and with a firmness I didn't expect while defending me. "Ma! Why would we be against it? Dash is perfect for her, and so what if she didn't want to have a big wedding?"

"Lower your voice, Arya," admonishes my mom while I stand mute, feeling gutted at her displeasure. All because I didn't marry the man she wanted. Turning to me, she declares, "I do not accept this."

"Afraid the papers make your opinion irrelevant."

Dash appears in my peripheral vision, walking with a thunderous expression aimed at my mother. The unadulterated relief that falls over me is both unexpected and staggering at his mere presence.

Like nothing can touch me if he's by my side. This man—*my husband*—has made me feel more protected in the last month than I've ever felt in my entire life. Not even when I was hopelessly in love with Niall.

The second Dash is near, I'm pulled into his warm embrace, making Arya's hand disappear. I lower my gaze, not wanting him to see the tears yet again at my mom's behest but as always, he misses nothing when it comes to me.

Tilting my face, he rubs the tear that escapes free with his thumb. His sharp gaze twists to my mom, who glares at us with her chin held high.

His voice is chilling as he speaks, "I warned you last time not to ever upset Bianca. Apologize to my wife."

"Dash!" I gasp at the same time my mom does.

"How dare you?"

At the commotion, my dad and Aryan aren't far behind. Immediately, they sense the tension in the room and the rage pouring off of Dash. Outwardly he's contained, but only I know he's teetering on the edge, ready to storm down on others.

"What's going on?" demands my dad. His poised gaze flickers to Dash and for a second, fear flashes in his eyes that leaves me stunned. My emotions are too frazzled to unmask its meaning.

"Bianca married him without our permission," Mom complains, turning to him. Only to be rendered shocked when he speaks.

"I know." He raises one hand to silence her when she tries to reply. "Dash already told me and they have my blessing. We're going to welcome him into our family."

"But—"

"What's done is done. To celebrate, we'll throw them a reception party next month and invite all our friends and family to properly introduce them as a couple." He stares at Dash for confirmation, who then peers down at me.

"It's your choice, kitten," he whispers for my ears only, and I nod.

I slide my hand into his and face my dad. "We'd like that, Papa."

"Good. Now let's have dinner."

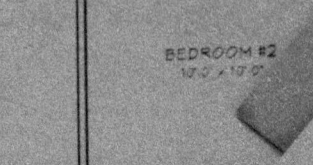

Chapter Forty-three

BIANCA

"**M**otherfucking hell**,**" I mutter to myself as I flush the toilet and amble to my office.
Nothing makes my day turn hellish than when it's the first day of my period, especially when they surprise me while I'm at work. The bane of every woman on the planet's existence.

I dread them almost as much as they're a relief when I tick it off every month. Because the alternate possibility is worse. Actually, they are a pain in the ass either way. I don't care if I sound whiny.

Because hello, mood swings.

Also, I happen to have the worst case of cramps. Or perhaps I have a lower pain threshold. Either way, I have every right to complain.

Tears sting the corners of my eyes as another painful cramp hits my stomach and I take a deep breath. My colleagues are already staring at me weird as I hobble my way to the elevator, not caring I'm leaving in the middle of the day.

I need my bed, comfort food aka burgers, and sleep. Stat.

"Bianca, I needed a favor—"

"Text me," I cut off the new girl who joined today and I wince when my voice comes out rude. "Sorry, I'm not feeling good."

"Oh, no problem. I'll ask someone else."

SIMRAN

I nod with a forced smile and enter the elevator before pressing the button for the parking lot. First day of my cycle is always straight out of a nightmare for me and by the end, I look like someone hit me with a truck and dragged my body through the dirt.

As soon as I get behind the wheel, I throw my purse in the passenger seat and turn on the ignition. Switching on the radio, I pause on the channel playing some current hit song to distract myself from the building ache in my lower belly.

Organizing the engagement party has taken the majority of my time that I completely forgot about my period since I usually take a day off to rest at home.

Liar. Party wasn't the only distraction, my brain taunts.

Fine. So maybe dirty thoughts of Dash has been plaguing and frustrating me. The infuriating man hasn't attempted to fuck me after igniting a fire and thirst that my own hands can't quench since Paris. In his defense, we hardly got a chance.

I'm still mad and horny.

After we'd come back to the apartment from dinner the other day, a deep and an unbidden sexual need had stirred in my pussy. Something about the way he had defended me made the feminine parts of me swoon. The sheer display of his dominance and protectiveness—it turned me on.

I finally understood why women fawned over commanding and domineering men. Since, evidently, I've fallen prey to the same.

Dash's desire was mirroring my own. His expression screaming he was waiting to get me alone, seconds away from ripping my clothes off to finally lay his claim. One step was all we had taken before his phone rang, interrupting us like a cruel twist of fate.

Apparently, there was an emergency at his headquarters which required him to travel immediately. A wave of pining had hit my chest with a force of a thousand bolts because I didn't want to watch him go. I realized with a clarity that I was circling back to my old self and that a simple crush was blossoming into something more. Something scary.

It was at the tip of my tongue to ask him to stay.

But I shoved that urge down.

It was the perfect reality check and maybe distance from him would be good so I could lock my heart again. Though, I kept these thoughts to myself while he packed his bags, glancing at me every so often.

A soft, sensual and drugging kiss was all he had gifted me before he left.

I didn't count on the desperation with which I would miss him. Four days have gone by since he left and every night I come home to an empty apartment, I feel his absence in the quietness. Sleeping alone has become a daunting task without Dash to curl up with and his strong arms holding me protectively.

When I had teased him the other day that he must be enjoying having the bed alone and not having me cuddle into him like a koala since he hated it, he had rendered me stunned by confessing it was growing on him. And that when he comes back, he's spending the whole weekend with me sleeping in bed because he's unable to get any sleep there.

Am I bad for secretly loving the fact that he was missing me too?

SCANDALOUS GAMES

The wait will finally be over tonight. Because I woke up to his text that breathed life into me again.

> **DARLING HUSBAND:** I want you naked on my bed when I come home tonight, wifey.

A rush of arousal had arisen when I saw he had managed to change his name from "Bossy Fiancé" to "Darling Husband" in my phone behind my back. And no, I didn't revert it back to the original name. I physically couldn't.

I assumed his flight was arriving at night but he had surprised me when he told me that it was early in the morning and that he'll be going straight to Kian's office for a meeting with him and his team. I hated it but at the same time, I was relieved he didn't come straight to me because I need to get my bearings.

It was a likely possibility I would have jumped straight into his arms if he had.

The urge is that strong.

I also had the worst case of butterflies in my stomach because even away, he constantly smothered me with his texts, calls, and video calls. Like he was going through the same withdrawal I was. Like he felt as miserable as I did.

He's too perfect at being a fake husband and pretending that what we have is real.

That our bond is more than lust and fatal attraction.

Or maybe it stopped being 'pretend' a while ago... Before I can dare to admit it to myself, I arrive at my apartment building and a few minutes later, take the elevator up to my floor. It's funny how easily I've forgotten my old apartment as my home. When I had gone downstairs one day, it hadn't felt the same or brought the same feelings to rise in my chest.

Until this morning, I was brimming with giddy excitement and actually considered surprising Dash by waiting for him naked. But my stupid period has ruined all my naughty fantasies. Naked and surprise never works in my favor, it seems.

I may sound desperate for his touch, something he easily turns me into with a few filthy words. After all, he has already fucked me. But anal doesn't count. I might be the first woman to let a man fuck her ass instead of her pussy after meeting him after years and enjoying it.

Then again, nothing about him and I is conventional.

The lock clicks and I push the door open before throwing my purse carelessly on the cream-colored sofa. I forget to walk slowly when pain hits my lower stomach as I take hurried steps, desperate to find the bed instead of going to the kitchen.

I'll order from the bedroom.

As soon as I enter it upstairs, tiredness hits me with a force and without bothering to change my clothes, I throw myself on the bed and curl into a comfortable ball. My plan is to always sleep to avoid the worst waves of cramps. Basically, I turn into a live robot, not moving unless absolutely necessary.

Switching on the AC to full blast and turning off the lights, I hike the blanket over my shoulder and will myself to nap. It doesn't take long before I'm halfway asleep with Dash and anticipation for his arrival on my mind.

In my hazy state, I feel I should probably leave him a text but my phone is downstairs.

Never mind, he's always late anyway.

A frenzied and worried voice penetrates through the fog of my peaceful slumber, followed by warm hands pushing my hair back from my face. I push them away when it tickles, not wanting to be disturbed. My whole body aches and if I wake up, it's only going to get worse.

But those grabby hands are insistent and strong, and they actually feel nice.

"You're worrying me, kitten." The soft voice stirs me. *Am I dreaming of Dash?* "Wake up, please."

I blink my eyelids open, trying to recognize my surroundings through the blurriness. My thoughts are all frayed and when Dash's pinched face comes in my line of vision, I jerk awake with a startle.

"Dash." My voice comes out scratchy as I sit up in bed. I swallow the dryness in my throat before asking in a daze, "Is it night already?"

"No. It's the middle of the day."

"Then... why are you here? Shouldn't you be at your meeting?"

"You didn't pick up my calls."

"Huh?"

"I texted and then called you several times but they went ignored," he explains, the angles of his face tight with a mixture of tension and anxiety. His right palm cups my cheek, observing me unnervingly. "Why do you look so pale?"

My stomach chooses the moment to throb in pain and it makes my eyes sting. I hide my gaze, not wanting Dash to notice and give an explanation.

"I'm fine. I left my phone downstairs." I turn sideways, making his hand drop. "You should go to your meeting."

"Stubborn girl. I don't give a fuck about my meeting," he growls, pulling me onto his lap when I move to slide off the bed by using the momentum in his favor. Tilting my eyes back to his, he confesses, "You nearly gave me a heart attack when I couldn't get in touch with you. Do you realize that? Then I find you passed out in bed and looking sick. I'm taking you to a doctor."

"What? No." I push at his chest when he goes to stand. My cheeks flame in slight embarrassment and playing with the top button on his shirt, I say in one long string of words. "Itsmytimeofthemonth."

"You're going to have to speak slowly, kitten."

Kill me now. "I am menstruating, okay? They make me sleepy and achy. I don't need a doctor."

SCANDALOUS GAMES

At first he appears lost and shocked, making my lips twitch. It's plain as day that he's never been around a woman at a time like this. I would find it a whole lot funny if pain wasn't rising with every breath I take.

"What do you need then?" he asks after a long pause, still looking worried.

I can't resist placing a soft kiss on his mouth, shocking him into silence, as I whisper, "Sleep but since you've woken me up, I'm going to take a shower."

I swing my legs to the floor from his lap and he reluctantly lets me go while watching me carefully as though I'll disappear. My heart swoons behind my rib cage that he left his important meeting and came straight for me. No one has ever put me first like he does.

At this rate, he's going to break down the walls I've constructed around my heart.

Or maybe, that's just my hormones talking. Yep, that must be it.

"I swear I'll be fine, Dash. Seriously, go back to your meeting," I call out over my shoulder as I gingerly amble to the bathroom, hoping a shower will provide me much-needed relief.

"Take your shower, kitten." He sighs. Jeez, and he calls me stubborn.

"Oh god!" I mumble, staring in horror at my reflection in the mirror. My hair looks like a bird's nest while mascara is smudged around the corners of my eyes. Don't even ask about my ashen cheeks, the color dull.

And my husband saw me like this. Ugh. So unfair.

Dumping my clothes in the hamper after quickly taking them off, I stand under the shower and sigh in pleasure as the hot water hits my skin. Some of the tension melts from my muscles and I take my time scrubbing my skin. Despite the discomfort, filthy thoughts of Dash's mouth, his cock, run rampant in my mind, igniting a low throb in my core.

Instead of relieving the ache, I end my shower, dry myself, and put on a bathrobe before I pad outside. I find Dash sitting on the edge of the bed, where I left him, and he looks up at the sound of my footsteps.

His piercing eyes darken in lust at my hidden nakedness but his concern for my health wins as he doesn't roam his gaze down the length of my body. I notice he has lost his suit jacket, remaining in a white dress shirt, which is plastered to his muscular physique.

Crossing the distance, he massages the back of my neck. "Feeling better?"

"Mmhmm," I moan, his expert fingers working their magic.

"Have you eaten anything?" My stomach growls in answer and I close my eyes as he chuckles. "Want me to make you a sandwich?"

I make a scrunched-up face at the suggestion. He quirks a brow, his expression soft and adoring.

"Or... I could order you a burger."

His phone rings, interrupting us as it vibrates against my leg from the inside pocket of his pants. I pull back and tell him, "I'll order. Why don't you take the call?"

"Get dressed while I do," he orders, walking toward the balcony with his phone already attached to his ear.

After changing into my comfy shorts and one of Dash's T-shirts I've been sleeping in every night while he was gone, I head downstairs. There's a skip in my step at having Dash back home.

The distance has done the exact opposite of what I had hoped.

My phone is in my purse where I left it so pulling it out, I make myself comfy on the couch. The cramps are a dull throb now but if I don't eat something soon, that'll change. I quickly open the online food app and scan for my favorite restaurant.

Scrolling down, I click Reorder since I always order the same, only to frown when it comes up empty. My already turbulent mood deflates. I search twice but no, the one chicken burger that I loved is gone. Just like the chicken wings and special chutney they took off their menu a few months ago.

To make matters worse, my cramps skyrocket and I clutch my stomach while bending at the waist. It's like I'm triggered and the tears I was holding at bay drip down my cheeks. Deep breaths don't help and I remember I ran out of my pain tablets last month.

Fucking shit.

Dash finds me with my head hanging between my shoulders and I'm pretty sure I'm back to looking like a disgruntled mess. I watch him lower to his knees and rest his palms on my thighs.

"Kitten, what's wrong?"

"Nothing." Hiccups lace my voice.

"Is it the pain? Is it always this bad?"

"Yeah, but I'll be fine," I mumble.

"Then why are you crying?"

"You're going to think it's stupid."

"Look at me," he orders. My blurry gaze meets his and he coaxes, "Tell me."

"They stopped making my favorite burger." God. I sound silly saying it out loud. He's going to think I'm crazy but I'm too upset over the news to care. Those people should've given me a damn warning or a notice or something.

I expect Dash to laugh or tease. Instead, he shrugs. "Then order from another place."

"You don't get it." I shake my head.

"Kitten."

"Go away, Dash." I remove his hand and lie down, facing away from him.

"Eat something before you sleep."

"I'm not hungry," I snap, while knowing I'm being rude. This is why I tend to stay alone on days like these. I don't have the patience to deal with anyone.

Dash intelligently doesn't push, and I hear clothes rustle as he stands to his feet. Then a second later, I hear the front door slam shut.

Great. I've finally succeeded in scaring Dash away.

Chapter Forty-four

DASH

This isn't how I planned to spend my day. Bianca gave me a fright that told me I'm way too deep into her than I imagined. I was ready to kill whoever had hurt her. Ever since my talk with her dad, an irrational fear has settled in my bones that something will happen to her while I'm gone.

It doesn't help that I'm lying to her every day. The longer I don't tell her the truth, the harder she will hate me when she inevitably learns about it. Suddenly, Justin's warning begins to play in my head. I hate to admit that he was right.

She believes I went to my city for a business emergency, when it was the opposite. On my flight back here, I decided to confess to her about that night. Because there's no denying that I crave Bianca with a passion; that it's more than just obsession and I want her to give me—us—a real chance.

And it can only happen once there are no secrets between us.

No shadows of the past haunting us.

Most importantly, her heart is unguarded and willing to love again.

The glimpse I saw beneath her walls when she woke up and smiled at me is forever painted in my soul. It gave a silly hope that she isn't as unaffected by me as she lets on. I just need to prove she can trust me.

I've only gone for an hour, but I miss her with an urgency that's foreign to me.

I drive faster as concern for Bianca overrides every other feeling in my chest. I kept picturing her crying face as I left her on the couch.

It's not long until I'm back and riding up to our apartment. I'm careful as I approach her sleeping form on the couch where I left her. I try not to disturb her but when I move in the open kitchen, she stirs awake.

"Dash."

I carry one of the bags I brought, along with a plate and ketchup, and rest it on the table in front of her. She rubs her eyes before sitting up, and I'm torn when I catch her wincing. I hate that she's in pain and I hate it even more that she has to go through it every month.

Who takes care of her then?

I frown when she fixes her wavy hair, even though they're perfect as always. Primal possessiveness and satisfaction roars in my chest at seeing her looking comfortable and sexy in my clothes. I like that something of mine is touching her skin, a sight of my claim.

I'm turning into a caveman for this woman.

Settling beside her, I unpack the food I brought and push the plates toward her. "Eat," I order.

Her gaze flies from my face to the plates in front of her and she blinks twice at the sight of her favorite cheesy chicken burger that the restaurant no longer serves. Well, they didn't until about an hour ago.

Bianca gasps, "How?"

"Doesn't matter. All you need to know is it's back on the menu." When she makes no move to eat, I pick the plate up and place it on her lap. "Would you like me to feed you, wifey?"

That puts her into action and I smile when she takes a huge bite, moaning happily at the taste. Her adorable nose is pink from all her earlier crying yet she's the most breathtaking woman I've ever seen. The little joys she finds in life both fascinates and inspires me, especially as she enjoys the food.

"Seriously, how did you make it happen?" she mumbles between bites.

"Whatever my wife wants, she gets." It's as simple as that.

I itch to kiss her, even with a drop of tomato sauce on the corner of her mouth while a blush darkens her cheeks and her lashes lower to hide the desire in her soft eyes at my words. It makes the bribe I gave to the restaurant's chef to continue serving her favorite burger worth it just to see the smile on her lips.

And I might have also issued a threat to close down his place if he thought of defying me. Bianca doesn't need to know any of that.

Once she's finished and attempts to stand, I stop her. I grab the plate from her hand and carry it to the kitchen. I saw the exertion on her face as she walked. Returning to her side, she notices the other bags in my hand.

"Don't tell me all those have burgers in them," she jokes.

"I got some other stuff I thought might help."

With a curious expression, she takes the bags from my grip and rummages inside. For the first time, I feel unsure and wonder if I forgot something. Her gaze softens at every item she unpacks. When she looks up, the corners of her eyes tear up again and my chest expands with concern.

"Kitten." Wrapping my arms around her, I sit down with her on my lap and murmur, "Why the tears?"

"I can't believe you went and bought all of this," she whispers, waving her hand at the dessert I bought. Red velvet cake, of course. Chocolates, among some other snacks she loves. Ice cream, too, which I put in the freezer. And lastly, a heating pad for her pain, and medicine, just in case. "I thought I scared you away."

"You think I'll leave while you're in pain?" Silly girl. I tease, "You're not getting rid of me that easily." I breathe easy when she laughs, a sweet and throaty sound. "Let me know if I missed anything."

"Miss? You've bought, like, a care package that a girl could only dream of." In a flash, her gaze narrows playfully and with a bit of jealousy. "I think you lied when you said you've never had a girlfriend. How else would you know what to buy?"

"I might have asked for Rosalie's help," I confess, her eyes turning wide as saucers. Fitting. I couldn't believe I called her too. "Pretty sure I ruined my broody asshole reputation. I'm never going to hear the end of it, am I?"

"Afraid not. But it'll get you brownie points."

"Speaking of brownies, do you want to have your dessert here or in bed?"

"Bed."

Nodding, I stand while cradling her bridal style, making one of her arms wrap around my neck and other clutching the pastry box. She opens her mouth to protest but I cut her off, "You're not walking today."

As I climb the stairs, Bianca is quiet but I feel her gaze burning into my face and making me wish I could read her thoughts. My cock jerks at her close proximity, her soft skin pressed against mine and soft breaths tickling my neck. Never imagined I would feel content just holding a woman. With Bianca, I'm learning new things about myself every day.

If Justin witnessed the way I am with her, he'll think I have a doppelganger he didn't know about.

In the bedroom, I lay her down on the bed, then stuff pillows behind her back so she can lean comfortably, before I switch on the TV. I scroll through the selection of movies and put on some random horror flick with a good rating, knowing she enjoys the genre despite the fact that they make her scared shitless.

I twist around to catch her watching me intensely. I approach and lean over her frame, my hands on each side of her hips. "What are you thinking, kitten?"

"You remembered I love horror movies?"

"Watching you was my favorite pastime." That blush is going to be the death of me.

"I didn't think you actually paid attention when you watched me all those times."

"You mean when you pretended I didn't exist and failed," I tease, making her roll her eyes. Tucking a strand of hair behind her ear, I confess, "I noticed every little thing about you, kitten. I still do."

Our gazes remain locked for the longest second and I don't care if she peers down to the deepest, cracked parts of my soul. Never thought I'd find someone who could mend those pieces, but she has me feeling differently. When she speaks, her voice is a teasing whisper.

"You're suspiciously good at being a pretend husband, Dash. A secret kink, perhaps?"

"I have a *you* kink, Mrs. Stern." Placing a kiss on her pink cheek, I straighten. "Enjoy the movie. I'll take a shower."

Her soft hand captures my wrist, stopping me before I've even taken a step.

"I miss— I'm glad you're back, Dash."

When was the last time another person cared enough to miss me? The answer is never. Bianca doesn't realize what the magnitude of hearing her say that does to my heart. Or maybe she does. My voice comes out gravelly with emotions clogging my throat. "I missed you too."

Minutes later when I come out of the shower, the sight that greets me is funny and I laugh under my breath. Bianca sits with her arms clutching the pillow like a lifeline and peering at the TV screen from behind it. I stifle another laugh when she mutters at the actors, warning them not to go inside where they'll run into the ghost.

"They can't hear you, kitten." A scream rips from her throat and she hurls the pillow in my direction. It lands at my feet and I quirk an eyebrow. "Is that how you're going to defend yourself if a burglar ever attacks?"

"No. I'm going to use you as a human shield and run away."

"A human shield, huh?"

"Don't worry. I'll come back for you." Mischief flickers in her pupils as she mutters, "Eventually."

I cross the distance while she feigns innocence after running her hot gaze over my abs, but she gives it away when she licks her bottom lip. I hate that I have to wait another few days before I can ravage her body.

She scoots to the side, making space for me as I sit with my back against the headboard. Laying down, she snuggles into my side with her head resting on my chest. I play with her silky hair, my attention riveted to her while she focuses on the movie. Every time a scary scene comes, she shudders and scratches my abs with her nails.

My cock involuntarily reacts at being surrounded by her scent, innocent touches, and it's not long before I'm pulsing and rock hard. She can't see because of the fluffy blanket and remains oblivious to my silent torment. At one point, I'm certain I'm going to die.

Death by blue balls—it would make one memorable headline.

I distract myself by focusing on the movie and it's not long before she drifts off to sleep with my fingers still sifting through her tresses. Instead of taking a nap like I should after the long hours of traveling, I stare at Bianca's sleeping form.

I smooth the frown lines that appear on her forehead whenever a cramp hits her while in sleep, hating the sight of her discomfort. Her lips form a small pout that I can't resist but bend to softly kiss until she tightens her arm around my waist.

I'll never get enough of her. She's under my skin.

My obsession.

My wife.

Chapter Forty-five

BIANCA

(SEVEN YEARS AGO)

My boyfriend is nowhere to be found. I circle around the club he brought me to where his friend threw a birthday party. Instead of sticking by my side, Niall has abandoned me to do God knows what while perfectly aware I hardly know anyone.

The music is too loud, sweaty bodies are jammed in every corner, and blinding colorful lights are making me dizzy. Honestly, I don't get the freaking hype of a night out at a club. All night, I've been fighting off grabby hands and slimy flirts with bad breath.

Fuck. I need to get out of here.

I would call a cab and leave if I hadn't stupidly given my phone to him since I decided to forgo my purse, thinking it'll get in the way of dancing. Well, if you consider throwing your arms in the air as a form of dancing, because that's the only move possible on the crowded dance floor.

This is the last time I ever listen to Rosa's advice, since she's the one who made me wear a dress with no pockets. Otherwise, I wouldn't be in this predicament.

When the light flashes bright for a second, I make out a few people from our group on the floor above, peering over the railing. Maybe Niall's upstairs too. I crane my neck and find the staircase in the left corner and push through the mass of bodies to climb.

It's the first time I'm upset at Niall's behavior.

Who runs off leaving their girlfriend all alone?

Ever since my awful and embarrassing run-in with his stepbrother, Niall's mood has taken a turn for the worse. It has mainly to do with the fact that Dash is constantly hovering around since his return, which doesn't allow us to have any alone time.

Our relationship has come to a standstill.

Because Dash has apparently made it his mission that I die with my virginity intact. I can't believe the asshole actually eavesdropped on my private conversation. Then boldly taunted me. I almost punched him in his too smug, handsome face.

Not handsome. Stupid, ugly face.

Liar.

As if that's not bad enough, he does little things to cause a rift between Niall and me. Like roaming around half naked in the house, cornering me without touching, and stalking me with his stormy eyes whenever we're in the same room. One time, I was in the kitchen and he leaned right over my frame to pull something out from the top shelf.

My traitorous body reacted by shivering at his intoxicating scent.

And he does it all while Niall is around, so I have to spend my night calming him down. It's a miracle they haven't come to blows yet. Niall doesn't understand that Dash is doing it on purpose. Except, I can't figure out the reason for it. Or where their toxic rivalry stems from. Somehow, I've become their latest victim.

Tonight was supposed to be mine and Niall's chance to have some fun, like we used to. Now, that's ruined too.

When I reach upstairs, the area is less crowded. Thank goodness.

"Hey, Piya," I shout at the girl, whose name I can remember. "Have you seen Niall?"

"Nope." She turns back to her friend.

"Fuck," I curse, frustrated.

Switching directions, I amble down the hallway at the back near the restrooms. The quiet that greets me is a balm to my building headache. Except it's shattered as soon as I sigh in relief.

"You've got to be kidding me," I mutter, when a garbled moan reaches my ears. Of course, the popular restroom hookup.

Seems like everyone is getting lucky and fucked except me in this universe.

Fuck it, I'll borrow someone's phone and call a cab. Or I'll just march to the nearest bus stop. I turn around with every intention to walk away, when the same arrogant voice I hear in my nightmares reaches my eardrums.

Dash.

The devil of my personal hell.

As I hear his groans, followed by a loud moan, suddenly an enticing idea forms. The man ruined my night and sits eclipsing over my sex life like a black moon, so the least I can do is ruin his. Tit for tat and all that.

Slipping off my heels to avoid making a sound, I tiptoe closer to the door,

SCANDALOUS GAMES

which is slightly ajar.

Only he could not be bothered to lock it.

I peer inside, hiding my body behind the wooden door, and catch the couple mere feet from me. My plan to march inside and interrupt until the girl has to leave evaporates in flames at the sight of them. Dash has the girl kneeling between his feet, her top undone and bunched at her waist. I swallow when he thrusts his hips, sliding his cock deeper into her waiting mouth while she stares up at him.

A strange sensation spreads over my entire body. *Arousal.*

No way. I'm not getting turned on by watching my boyfriend's off-limits stepbrother throat fuck another girl. The one constantly and silently tormenting me these past few weeks.

And yet I am.

My heart is racing faster. Nipples, hardening beneath my dress, and I feel wetness pool between my thighs. His face contorted in lust is visible in the mirror above. Thick muscles in his arms flexing as he holds the girl's hair captive in his fist. The sexy groans as he derives pleasure from the girl forever imprinted on my mind.

It's erotic and filthy.

They are strangers yet their chemistry is more palpable than Niall and mine. Niall has never taken control and suddenly, I wish he would instead of treating me like a porcelain doll. This should be us. Driven with lust and making out in dark corners.

With my attention drawn back to Dash, I take in the sight of his abs clenching while their sounds get louder. My first instinct is to run but then I remember if anyone's at fault for my dull sex life, it's this man himself. And I'll be damned if I don't give him a taste of his own medicine.

Just then, his hooded gaze clashes with mine.

They darken with madness instead of the thawing ice they usually stare at me with. My lips part when he doesn't stop, his pace not even slowing down. When my eyes inevitably fall to his thick shaft, I wrench them back to his face and watch his lips curl into a taunting smirk.

I lost it.

Flashing him a twisted smile, I step farther inside and clutch my chest dramatically before yelling, "You bastard! You're cheating on me again?"

His face falls in absolute shock and so does the girl's, who pushes his dick away and hastily covers her naked breasts. Standing up, she stares at him in horror. "What the fuck?"

I'm not finished, feeling emboldened at catching him off guard. Bet he didn't see that coming. "Didn't you learn your lesson after giving that poor girl and me chlamydia, Dash?"

He tucks his dick away while the girl screeches, "You asshole! You said you didn't have a girlfriend."

"I don't," he calmly replies, not at all perturbed by two hysterical women. Even if one is acting.

"Wow!" I fake-whimper and fan my face as though I'm trying not to cry. "I can't believe this. And to think I wanted to have your babies."

"Liar!" The girl slaps his chest and I stifle my laughter. "You better not have given me an STD."

"We didn't have sex." His tone is dry.

It only makes her angrier. While she hits him again, his gaze meets mine above her head and I wink until his eyes narrow in warning. I'm surprised to see there's amusement in them as well. I quickly mask my features and sniffle when the girl relents and turns to walk out.

She pauses beside me and with an embarrassed hue to her cheeks, whispers, "I'm really sorry. It's always the hot ones, isn't it?" I nod and she pats my shoulders soothingly. "Dump him."

With one last scathing look at Dash, she disappears after slamming the door. I drop my hands and square my shoulders with a satisfied smirk. "Good luck finding another girl in the club."

"Still holding a grudge, are we?" he muses, inching closer.

"We're even now."

Twisting around, I open the door halfway. My spine tingles when Dash snaps it shut with his hand above my head before I've even taken a step. His hot breath shuffles my hair when he leans down to whisper in my ear, "Has my brother fucked you yet?"

"None of your fucking business."

"So no." He hums before mocking, "Poor kitten."

"My name is Bianca," I snap through gritted teeth.

"I know, kitten."

Don't hit him.

I don't dare turn around. Not when his lips brush my cheeks. Not when he traces one single finger down the length of my spine, leaving a tingling sensation in their wake.

"You shouldn't touch me." I hate the tremble in my voice, and the breathlessness. I summon more steel in my tone. "I'm Niall's."

His hand drops but he makes no move to stop crowding me. "Then why isn't he here? I doubt he'll be pleased with you staring at another man's dick."

"Let me go."

"Say my name first," he demands in a gravelly tone.

"Why?"

"I want to hear it."

I shake my head and his fingers grip my waist. It's like he's punishing me for saying Niall's name while branding me with his touch. I'm trapped between him and my only escape. I would give in to his demand if it didn't feel like crossing a line. I'm already crossing a few just by letting him touch me, no matter how innocent it is on my part.

One move and he's sucked all the power I held when I came in.

"Say my name," he coaxes in a soft, seductive whisper. "And you can walk out."

It's just a name. Say it. It doesn't mean anything.

"Let me go... Dash."

SCANDALOUS GAMES

The second his heat vanishes, along with his masculine scent, I run until I land back in the chaos. It seems I'm nowhere safe from the turbulent force that is Dash.

No matter how hard I try, I can't stop the flashbacks of him with that girl out of my mind. It replays as I push through the bodies and continues till I'm outside, struggling to catch my breath. The cool air feels refreshing on my heated skin. The quiet of the night, a welcoming surrounding without the god-awful music damaging my eardrums.

Now I just need to find my way home.

The street is deserted with a few people mingling on the side of the road since it's a little after midnight. I make out the taxi station I saw earlier and decide it's my safest bet. After bending down to slide my heels back on, I amble down the dark street.

Anger rises within my chest at Niall and the asshole stunt he pulled tonight. I bet if he knew Dash was at the club too, he wouldn't have let me out of his sight.

"Stupid asshole men," I curse. "I'll teach them a less—"

A scared yelp slips from my throat when a rough hand yanks on my arm, pulling me into a dark alley. I fight against the grip, only for another person to grab and shove me hard against the brick wall. Pain stings the back of my skull into a thousand pinpricks of needles.

"Look at those tits, man," a drunken voice taunts.

Another man laughs. "Our lucky night."

Oh god, no. Fear like no other flashes through my mind and my fight-or-flight instinct kicks in. I yell while kicking one in the shin with my leg. "Let me go. Help! Hel—"

One of the drunk guys covers my mouth, cutting off my plea. I can barely make out their faces through my blurry eyes as tears form. They appear older and bigger than me, making my terror rise tenfold. This can't be happening.

I bite down on his hand just as his friend gropes my breasts. He drops his hand with a curse.

"Fucking bitch," he slurs before yelling at his friend. "Hold her tight."

They are clumsy due to the alcohol coursing through them and are slow when I kick my leg out again. This time, managing to hit the one holding me captive between his legs until he howls in pain. Without another thought, I run, and their footsteps follow.

The distance is short to the wide road but it feels like a mile. I almost slip when my ankle twists in my high heels but I push through the pain. Sweat dots my forehead and my heart is in my throat. Their ugly laughter sends another trickle of terror down my spine. When a shadow appears in my path, I think it's another dangerous guy until I look up.

"Dash," I cry out.

His concerned face twists into rage and I throw myself into his arms, relieved beyond measure at his presence. He catches me and tears free fall harder while I cling to him.

Pair of footsteps pull to a stop behind me and one of them snickers, "Found your boyfriend, you little cocktease?"

SIMRAN

Dash goes rigid before taking a menacing step, but I clutch him harder. His arms tighten when my body shivers uncontrollably, and I whisper, "Don't."

I feel his rough exhale, every inch of him locked with violence, but I've never been gladder when he puts me first.

"Walk away before I bury you both into the ground," he threatens.

The stupid drunks don't heed his warning. "After feeling those tits, I'll die happily."

In a flash, Dash's warmth disappears before I hear bones crack, followed by a pained wail. I whirl around and gasp as one of my assaulters sits on the ground, clutching his bleeding nose, while Dash pummels the other one with quick, hard punches.

"Dash! Stop," I shout. "Please."

Throwing a painful kick to the gut to both of them, he returns to my side. His eyes are still livid but they soften slightly when they lock on mine. His torn knuckles cup my cheeks gently and he asks, "Tell me you're okay, Bianca."

I'm only capable of nodding.

"I'm taking you home." Taking my hand, he guides me, but stops as soon as he notices me limping, and curses, "Fuck. What did I just ask?"

"I twisted my ankle."

Bending down, he picks me in his arms while I wrap mine around his neck. As he carries me back to the club, he demands in a hard voice, "Where the fuck is Niall?"

"I-I don't know. I lost him inside the club," I reply with a wince.

His features twist into rage again but I know it's for his stepbrother, not me. "Why would you leave the club alone? Where's your phone?"

"He has it. So I couldn't call a cab." My answer doesn't help and he roughly exhales.

"Don't ever put yourself at risk like that again," he demands, meeting my eyes. "Promise me."

The protectiveness in his depths takes me aback. Suddenly, I see him in a new light and it's nothing like the way Niall described him. I hold his gaze as I promise, "I won't."

We reach his car and he buckles me into the passenger seat before coming around to slide behind the wheel. The ride back is silent and the tension doesn't disappear from him until we are at his house. I'm once more back in his embrace as we step inside and when he walks in the direction of the stairs, I stop him.

"No." He stares questioningly. "I don't want to stay alone."

Understanding dawns and he instead lays me down on the couch, arranging the cushion against my head. Straightening, he says, "I'll be back."

I'm still shaken by what happened outside the club, coming close to thinking I'll be assaulted, or worse, raped, if Dash hadn't showed up on time. I don't care if he followed me or was there by chance, I'm just grateful he was there.

Few minutes later, he returns and places a glass of water and painkillers in my hand. "For your ankle."

I thank him for the pill and everything he did tonight. While I drink the water, he covers my naked legs with a soft blanket. After switching on some random movie on the TV, he settles beside me at the end of the couch with one arm stretched along the back.

It's the first time we're civil around each other and it doesn't feel awkward. My eyes keep drifting between him and the screen until I begin to feel sleepy. When the events of tonight catch up on me, I want to forget everything. Still, a burning question that's plaguing me for a long time slips from my mouth.

"Why do you hate Niall?"

Vivid green eyes collide with my brown ones and I'm almost certain he won't answer me but he does and the coldness in them renders me stunned. "He would have to mean something to me for me to hate him."

"Yet you're always riling him up."

"Just because I don't hate him, doesn't mean I like him, kitten."

I roll my eyes and face forward again. There's more he isn't telling but I'm too exhausted to peel his mysterious layers. Eventually, heaviness sinks in and it's not long before my eyelids close. Somewhere in my unconsciousness, I hear Dash whisper, "I never had a reason to hate him... Until you."

Chapter Forty-six

BIANCA

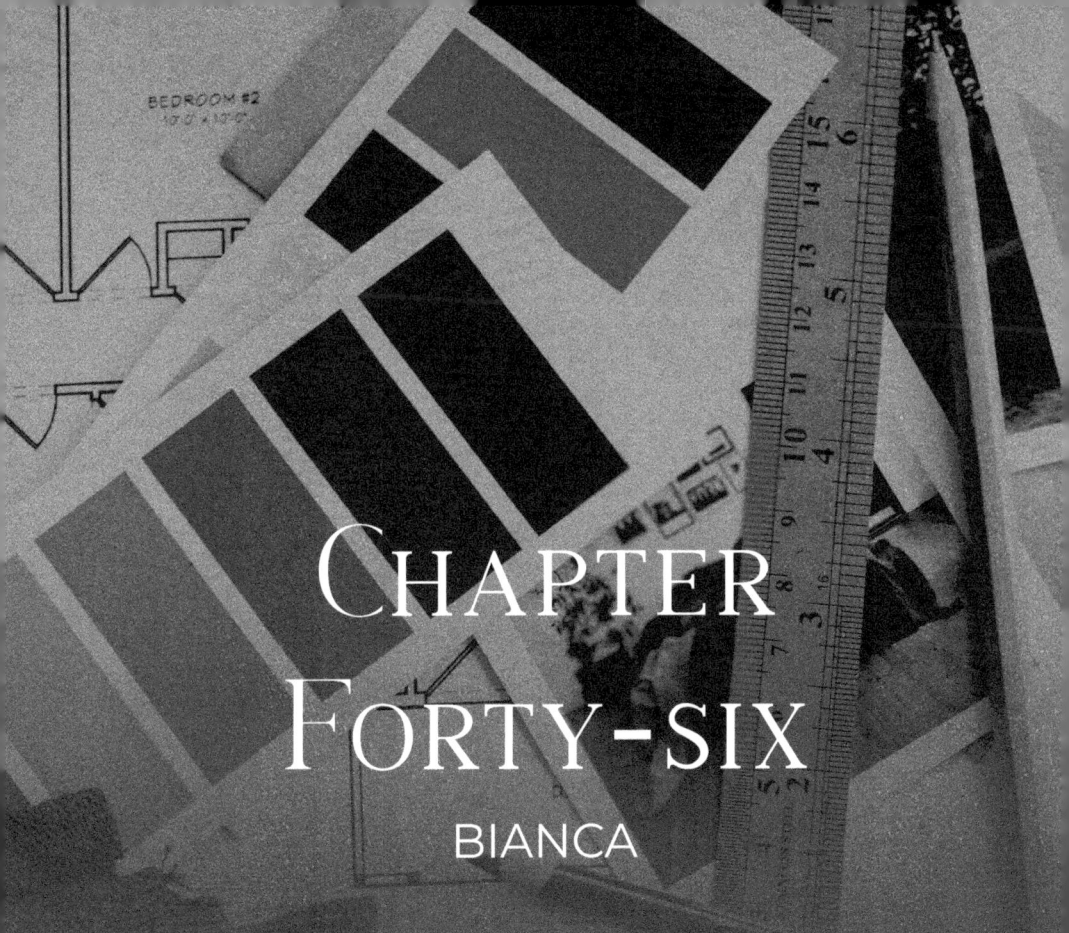

I shake myself off the memory of Dash saving me outside the club. Ever since he took care of me last week, it's like I'm reliving the past with new eyes, one not brainwashed by Niall. My ex, who didn't even ask me the next day about how I got home from the club. Not even apologizing for ghosting me at a party he invited me to.

I am, however, madder at myself that I never confronted him. I was blinded by what I thought was love. It was the first red flag that I shouldn't have ignored. Because things only escalated from then onward.

If I'm being completely honest, things shifted between us after the first night Dash crashed into our lives.

The niggling fear in the back of my mind warns me that Dash crashing into my world has always led to destruction, chaos, and heartbreak.

That this one may not be so different either.

And yet, there's no stopping me from falling headfirst. Even if I wanted to, he won't let me go. Besides, we've come too far to jeopardize everything now. Especially as I listen to Arya tell me about her conversation with our dad the other day.

"I have a feeling he will say yes, Bee," she says in a singsong voice. "As soon as your engagement party is done, I will ask Aryan to talk to him."

SCANDALOUS GAMES

"At least wait a couple of weeks before you ask him to pop the question," I reply, halting her daydreaming. Once Arya gets excited about something, she becomes like an unstoppable bulldozer. "And shouldn't he propose to you first?"

When my sister insisted she wanted to come with me to my dress fitting appointment, I was over the moon. Because with each passing day, I'm getting more and more of my old sister back. The utter joy it brings me is indescribable.

I have invited my best friends, too, but only Iris will be coming since Rosa had to travel for a charity event with her future parents-in-law. Mostly, it's a publicity move to portray an ending to the long rivalry between the two families. The public believes it was a recent decision. Except, they don't know it has been years in the making, since the day Rosa turned fifteen.

"He's old-fashioned, Bee," answers Arya, pulling me from my thoughts. "He would like our dad's blessing first."

The exact opposite of my broody and intimidating husband. Whoa... I'm getting way too comfortable and casual with the word *husband*.

"What about my blessing?" I tease her.

She abruptly stops in the middle of the sidewalk and I would've fallen had our arms not been intertwined. Gazing at me, she nervously questions, "Do you not like him?"

"I was kidding, Ari. He's perfect for you."

Her bright smile returns as we resume walking, only a few minutes away from the store. Warmth spreads through my chest that my opinion matters to her.

"I know I've been a bad sister lately, but I love you, Bee." Her confession has my heart thudding and I give a small smile. "I'm glad you found your soulmate too."

The pressure on my chest returns tenfold. If only she knew how far from the truth she is. Thankfully, our arrival to the wedding dress store saves me from replying to her. The doorman holds the door open and the moment we cross the threshold, a bubbly Iris in a pretty summer dress greets us.

"You're here," she exclaims, wrapping me in a hug. "God! I want to buy everything in here. If only I could afford it."

"Nathan needs to spoil you more," comments Ari in a teasing tone.

Iris chuckles. "He does plenty."

Nathan and Iris are very private about their relationship. It even took a while for her to open up to Rosa and me. It's only when she's drunk that she spills the dirty deets about Nathan, who is very much like his older brother Kian: reserved and tends to keep to himself. His relationship with Iris began with friendship and it shows every time they are together.

The three of us are huddled together chitchatting that we almost forget the reason why we're here. It isn't until one of the assistants clears their throat that we remember with a sheepish grin.

"Please come this way," says the lady. "I have your gown ready in the dressing room for you to try on."

We follow after her and I can't wipe the excited grin off my face. Unlike my friends, I'm a certified shopaholic. In my opinion, there is no such thing as too many clothes. So, even though the engagement is all for show, I couldn't help myself.

SIMRAN

In Paris, I was too overwhelmed and enraptured by Dash that the thought of shopping never crossed my mind. He had already spoiled me enough. Also, had I tried to buy anything, he probably wouldn't have let me pay for it. And I didn't want to be indebted to him more than I already am.

The second we round the corner, both Ari and Iris gasp in awe at my beautiful golden lehnga, glittering as it hangs in the middle of the room. The moment I laid my eyes on it, I fell in love and knew it was *the dress*. The color is so rich that it takes your breath away at first glance.

"Fuck! That is so pretty. You're going to look gorgeous," praises Ari.

"Dash won't be able to take his eyes off you," teases Iris.

"Oh, he's going to be fighting off other men who dare to stare at you."

"He does give off possessive vibes, doesn't he?" says my best friend with amusement lighting her eyes. Iris has let me know on more than one occasion that she wants Dash and me to become a real couple, especially after I poured my heart out over the video call in Paris.

Ignoring their bickering at my expense, I admire my lehenga which is sexy yet elegant. The skirt is big with a short train flaring at the back but it was the side slit reaching to the top of my thigh that sealed the deal for me. The cropped blouse with the sweetheart neckline and slim shoulder straps, on the other hand, complements the skirt perfectly. The back is held by two strings that tie in a knot in the middle.

"Hurry, Bee. I'm dying to see it on you," an eager-looking Iris says while my sister nods from beside her.

They both lounge on the large sofa placed in the middle while I go to the changing room with the assistant following behind me with the dress. She waits while I remove my jeans and top until I'm in my panties and bra to help me into the dress. The fit is perfect in all the right places and the skirt is lightweight and easy to maneuver.

When I return, Ari and Iris are gossiping and laughing over champagne. I clear my throat and as soon as they see me, they go speechless. With a smile, I give them a twirl and hear their intake of breath.

"I have no words," cries Ari.

"I would marry you myself."

"As if Nathan will let you," I tease Iris.

Setting aside her flute, Iris aims her phone toward me and points her finger before ordering, "Come one, show us those curves."

"Shake that ass," hoots Ari, making me laugh.

"This isn't a strip show, you two." They continue to chortle, not at all ashamed, and I think the champagne has gone to their heads. "Hey! Click some pictures on my phone too."

"Why? You wanna send one to your dear husband?"

"Shut up."

"Send some in the sexy lingerie I saw." A mischievous glint appears in Iris's gaze. "Or... there's always the infamous naked selfies. I bet he'll come running."

Yep. She's definitely drunk.

SCANDALOUS GAMES

"Never mind, return my phone."

She shakes her head and orders me like she's my personal stylist and shopper, "But seriously, you must try them. Wait, I'll bring them."

She's gone before I can say a word. Her hands are full with different sets and colors, more each daring than the last, and she dumps them all in my arms. Twisting me around, she pushes me in the direction of the changing room while instructing, "Try and take your time. We'll be here."

"Yes, your highness," I mutter, making her and Ari chuckle.

This is the best day ever. Tons of shopping and hanging out with my favorite people. I only wish Rosa were here too. At least she'll be back for my reception party this Saturday. I can't believe a month went by so fast and all the arrangements are done. I'm just praying there'll be no drama, which always seems to be the case when Dash and my parents are in the same room.

After managing to take off my dress all by myself, I rifle through what Iris chose for me and silently curse under my breath. My sneaky friend has selected the most daring lingeries I've ever seen. They're either completely see-through or barely keeping my goods covered. One even has a slit in the panties for easy access. My cheeks flame.

Although, Dash would probably love them.

Before I know it, I'm putting on the red lace set with the secret slit. I might as well be naked but I won't deny it's super sexy. Oh well. I might as well buy it. I try on a few more pieces. I also like a sheer purple baby doll but it's small and my breasts spill out of the cups. So, when I try to remove it, the zipper in the back gets stuck.

"Damn it." Pulling aside the curtain, I peek outside and shout, "Iris, I need help."

At the sound of footsteps, I leave the curtain halfway open and face the mirror. Bending down, I've just touched my fallen top when a pair of shiny black leather shoes come in my line of sight. With a shocked gasp, I almost tumble forward when they come closer and strong hands grip my waist possessively.

"Need help, kitten?" a husky voice whispers.

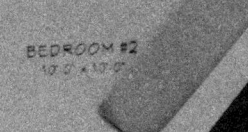

Chapter Forty-seven

BIANCA

My stunned gaze collides with Dash's in the mirror, and I stammer, "Dash."

A predatory expression darkens his green orbs as they hold mine captive. As if he willed my body with a silent command, wetness gathers in my pussy and I clench to soothe the ache. His fingers flex as my arousal permeates the air while I become impossibly turned on by the sight of the over-six-feet-tall, dark, and handsome man.

My husband.

My kryptonite.

The muscles beneath his suit pull taut like he's fighting some inner urge. My mind is frayed, lust too heavy at his mere presence, while he sucks all the oxygen out of the small space. He's impeccably dressed in his posh business suit while I have my tits spilling out of my top and my ass against his slowly hardening cock.

"What are you doing here?" I gasp past the slight hitch in my voice. I move to stand but his fingers don't allow me, tightening painfully in a warning.

"Stay," he growls low.

An electric shiver courses down my spine and my breathing quickens at the domineering command in his dark voice. The difference in our clothing, only heightening my depraved lust.

SCANDALOUS GAMES

Ever so gently and slowly, he traces his fingers up my back and pushes the soft material until cool air caresses my skin. All thoughts about how he ended up here and found me, dissolve into nothingness with his seductive touch. Days' worth of hunger and tension hits my body all at once and I know he's feeling the same.

He continues his agonizing torment until I'm itching to jump his bones. A desperate moan slips out when he thrusts his cock. The sound of my need snaps his tightly laced control. Gathering my hair in his fist, he tugs hard until my back is arched.

"Look in the mirror and take out your tits."

My hard nipples scrape against the lace as I push it down and the friction sends a zap straight to my clit. My breasts shake with every breath. His attention lowers to them and a violent shudder rocks my body as he pinches my nipple without any warning. He circles the other before giving it the same treatment.

"Play with your pussy."

I'm all too happy to oblige as I push my hand underneath the thong and touch my wet folds before rubbing up and down. His rough hands don't stop their assault on my sensitive nipples. He palms and squeezes my breasts before spanking the hard tips.

"Dash!" I cry out, forgetting anyone could hear us. His eyes stay locked on my moving hand as I circle my clit, trying to chase the building orgasm. But it's his fingers I'm aching for.

"Give me your fingers. I want to taste how wet you are for me."

His guttural request sends another surge of arousal and I bite my lip as I bring my wet hand to his lips. I watch in the mirror as he devours and licks my juices with a hungry groan. I almost come undone as his eyes close in satisfaction.

"You like my taste?" I purr.

His eyes flash open before turning wild, and he smirks. "You're my favorite flavor in the world, wifey."

I blush and try not to melt into a puddle. The hand in my hair tightens while the one playing with my sensitive breasts reaches between my thighs and cups my pussy. He grinds the base of his palm against my clit while sliding two fingers in deep. He traces me from my opening to my clit before pinching it roughly.

"Did I tell you to stop touching yourself?" He raises one arrogant eyebrow while continuing to caress and trace my drenched slit. When I hesitate, he yanks my wrist and inserts my finger inside and... *His own.*

Our eyes remain locked as he moves our fingers together in a slow but deep rhythm in my pussy. It feels naughty, illicit, and so goddamn hot that I gush even more. The wetness has his jaw clenching and heat darkening his angular face.

"You feel yourself clenching, kitten? How you're choking our fingers like a greedy girl? Nothing comes close to heaven compared to this," he rasps in a guttural tone that has my walls tightening, and he smiles devilishly before plunging in another finger. "Did you touch yourself while I was gone?"

"No."

"Good girl." Fucking me faster, he thrusts against a secret spot that has me seeing stars. "This tight pussy is mine, kitten. You come when I allow you and never without me. Understand?"

"Yes," I moan.

I pant heavily as his thumb flicks my clit while our fingers are still inside. Dash is a filthy, deviant man and just when I think he can't be more filthy and deviant, he proves me wrong. And I like it. A lot.

The woman in me driven by lust and wantonness.

When I bite down to stop from screaming out my pleasure, he increases the pressure and like a dirty savage, demands, "No. I want to hear the little sounds you make, kitten. You're going to scream my name as I make you come like this. Bent over, tits on display, while I play with your cunt like my dirty whore."

"Oh god!" I whimper when he shoves two of his fingers to the hilt.

Finger fucking me ruthlessly, he barks, "Not God. Your husband."

Three fingers become four until I'm stretched and too full. With every thrust, I rise on my toes, incapable of everything except clenching around his hand. The pleasure, so intense after being deprived of it for weeks that before I know it, my orgasm barrels down on me.

"Yes! Dash!" I sob his name again and again.

I haven't even come down from my high when I find myself turned around and pushed against the mirror. My lips part in awe and exhilaration when he lowers to his knees, rips off the expensive lingerie, and crushes his mouth against my dripping pussy.

"Oh fuck!" I moan.

His broad shoulders hold me spread open, fingers digging into my inner thighs, as he eats me like a starved and possessed man. He's unhinged, messy, and loud as he lashes my slit with his tongue. I shudder violently as he shoves his tongue inside my opening and fucks me like he would do with his cock.

It's maddening. Combusting. Pure ecstasy.

In the reflection in the opposite mirror, I look like a prey captured by a vicious hunter who is ripping me apart with each suck and bite.

As if that's not enough, he cups the back of my knee and throws it over his shoulder so he can tongue fuck me deeper and harder. My fingers pull at his hair and he growls like a beast when I grind and thrust my pussy against his lips.

"Don't stop," I plead when another powerful orgasm builds.

"Scream my name, wife."

I shatter at the possessive claim, splintering into pieces. He sucks my clit while thrusting his fingers so wave after wave of pleasure sends me on a cloud. His hands are the only things holding me up while I clutch his shoulder.

When my moans die down, I peer at him through blurry eyes. The primal satisfaction in his light pupils warms my chest. Kissing my pussy softly, he lowers my leg and rises to his full height. I'm an utter mess while he's still perfectly dressed, except for his mussed-up hair.

We silently bask in each other's warmth before he breaks the silence.

"You're making it a habit of me storming out of my meetings."

"But I didn't call you."

"Then I'm guessing Iris is the one who sent me your picture from your phone?"

SCANDALOUS GAMES

My eyes widen when I remember she and my sister are right outside and I gave them a free porn show. "Oh my god!"

He reads my mind and chuckles. "Don't worry. They're not outside."

"You're a corrupt influence, Dash."

"Who else am I going to corrupt if not my wife, kitten?" he muses before running his thumb over my exposed nipples, desire flashing in his gaze. "Especially when you looked so innocent yet sexy in this lace. Did you wear it while thinking of me?"

I have half a mind to deny it but I find myself unable to. "Yes."

"Buy some more so I can rip it off you later."

I shake my head at his insatiable appetite. Who am I kidding? I'm just as bad.

"As you wish, darling." I wink, loving his reaction at the endearment.

"You're going to be the death of me, woman."

Smiling, I push at his chest. "Get out before we get caught."

He arches one eyebrow with an amused expression. "After last time, you should know your commands don't work on me."

"I still need to get dressed."

"Then by all means." He backs away and leans in the corner. "I'm not waiting outside."

Sighing at his controlling tone even though butterflies are dancing in my belly, I take off the ruined baby doll that I'll have to pay for anyway. His eyes lazily trace every inch of my naked and flushed skin, still glowing from the two mind-blowing climaxes while he rubs his bottom lip with his thumb. The move, so sexy and smooth.

I'm staring at his mouth when he commands huskily, "Give me a kiss."

My heart flip-flops behind my rib cage as I close the small gap between us and lay my palms on his chest before rising to meet his lips. I lick the seam teasingly until his tongue tangles with mine and I suck it softly, deriving a groan from his chest.

He lets me take the lead and the rush is addictive. I grasp the lapels of his jacket and crush my breasts against his abs and kiss him deeply. I taste a combination of me and him on his tongue and a familiar possessiveness flares inside of me.

He greedily palms my ass, tugging my pussy against his pulsing cock. I ache to make him come in my mouth, but he feels content just kissing me and I don't want to break the sensual moment. A gate has opened in our intimacy and I'm scared yet hooked on the feeling.

We're both breathing heavily when we pull apart, my arms circling his neck as he embraces me.

"You're never going shopping without me."

"As long as I get to come on your tongue."

"Anything for my wife."

As soon as I'm dressed in my jeans and top once more, I twist toward Dash. Intertwining our hands—like he always does—he walks us out the dressing room and to the store, where we find my sister and best friend.

They both have guilty yet smug grins on their faces as they approach us.

"Oh, fancy seeing you here, Dash," says Iris innocently.

"He told me about the text, Iris."

"Well then, did you like my surprise?"

I bite my lip but the blush on my face says it all. Dash wisely stays quiet but I can feel the male satisfaction pouring off of him. He is too pleased with the outcome.

Arya takes mercy on me and questions Dash. "Are you also coming with us to grab lunch, Dash?"

"I already had my favorite lunch."

Oh my god. I flush red from head to toe because there's no missing the double meaning behind his words. The grin on Iris's face splits into a naughty smile while Arya isn't doing any better.

Dash is unashamed and turns to me. Kissing me on the lips, he murmurs, "I'll see you at home, wifey."

All throughout the day, I taste him and me on my lips until there's no hiding the truth to myself.

This—us—isn't fake anymore.

But the question is… Am I willing to risk my heart again?

Chapter Forty-eight

DASH

Every day for the past month, I feel like I'm playing a dangerous losing game.

A game of Russian roulette.

Except, there's an invisible gun rounding the shots. Every second I don't confess the shameful truth to Bianca, the guilt sits heavy on my chest while eating me alive.

How do you tell the girl with a broken heart that you're the cause of it? That in my cruel desire to destroy my asshole stepbrother, I ended up shattering her instead. The wreckage of which she bears the scars of to this day.

And that it's not even the worst sin I've committed.

Or the only life I eviscerated.

Ever since I've admitted to myself that I need Bianca like a necessity, that she's slowly making a home in my cold, beating heart, the mere thought of being separated from her terrifies me. An emotion I didn't feel even during the darkest time of my life.

She's the light at the end of the tunnel that men like me search for their entire lives. And if I end up in the pits of darkness because of my mistake, it'll be the end of me.

I let her slip away once, but not again.

Especially after feeling her warmth, her laughter and mischievousness, the sass and cuteness. After watching her lower the walls she's built around her heart. There's a brightness and hope in her eyes that I felt missing the night she stumbled into my life again.

The secrets and the pain she carried has disappeared.

And a deeper part of me knows it's because of me. She's letting me in, and damn if it doesn't fill my chest with pride. She makes me feel whole in a way I've never experienced before. There's nothing I wouldn't do to give her the whole world. Lay the stars and the moon at her feet.

Because Bianca and I are an inevitability.

In a twist of fate, we always find our way back to each other. And if I truly want her to love me like I'm falling for her, I need to bare my soul to her and give us a fair chance.

I just need to get through this long reception party unscathed first. I trust her parents not to pull a stunt as much as I would trust a dentist to operate on my heart. Zero. And it's hard to ghost a function when it's thrown in your honor. Besides, my wife wouldn't let me risk jeopardizing her little sister's future by offending her parents. She thinks it'll twist her parents' view regarding love marriages. Hate to tell her but it was already screwed.

"I heard they've invited the media too," Bianca reveals from beside me while we sit in the back of the limousine heading to the party.

She looks absolutely stunning tonight in her golden dress that complements the color of her soft brown eyes. The moment she came out of the bedroom in all her golden glory, I haven't been able to take my hungry eyes off her. Her luscious tits peek from the top of her blouse and tease my cock with every breath she takes. And so does the bare stomach visible above her skirt.

I'm almost regretting not insisting on a proper marriage ceremony, just so I could watch her walk down the aisle in a red dress and claim her in front of the entire world.

If she wasn't wearing my ring on her finger, a clear message that she belongs to me, I would seriously be worried about murdering any man who dares to look, let alone talk to her. I fear my possessiveness will never fade for this woman, much like my obsession.

I almost miss what she says as I become distracted by her naked leg peeking from the slit in her skirt. It's dangerously high for my liking. The fact that I can easily touch her pussy if I desire appeases me a little.

I really need to fuck her again and this time, her cunt and... *mouth*.

"Do they make you nervous?" I softly ask, concern overriding my lust for her. "You don't have to face them if you don't want to. We'll take the back entrance."

"It's okay. I'm not giving my parents a reason to be pissed tonight."

Fuck that. "We're going through the back, kitten."

"I can handle a few minutes in front of the media." I'm not convinced but she grabs my hand and stares at me under her eyelashes. "Please, Dash."

"Fine. But we're not stopping for pictures."

She smiles, still holding my hand. This woman has me wrapped around her fingers and doesn't even know it.

SCANDALOUS GAMES

It's not long before we arrive at the lavish hotel despite the rush-hour traffic. The driver rounds the hood after idling and opens our door. I step out first and instantly, countless cameras start snapping pictures, the flashes almost blinding, followed by their incessant screaming of our names.

"Mr. Stern! Mr. Stern! Look here!" they yell from my left. "Dash! Bianca!"

I shield Bianca as she carefully steps out of the car with her camera-ready smile poised on her lips. Except, only I can make out the anxiety lurking beneath the confident mask. It makes me want to take her far away from here.

Tilting her chin until those mesmerizing eyes meet mine, I whisper, "Don't look at them. Just hold my hand." I take our joined hands and place them over my heart. "And focus on my heartbeat."

Kissing her softly, I keep her close to my side as I guide down the velvet carpet and the mass of reporters toward the shining lobby. I don't let go of her and neither does she as we reach inside. When she faces me, the smile on her face is genuine and relieved. Her red siren lips begging to be kissed, if only we didn't have an audience.

"You look like a temptress tonight, kitten," I rasp in a raw voice. "Beautiful and breathtaking. I'm not letting you out of my sight."

"I'd seriously be worried about your possessiveness if it wasn't part of our fake arrangement, Dash," she flippantly teases, a strange emotion flickering behind her pupils.

My body goes rigid as my mind becomes stuck on her casual remark. When she finds no traces of amusement in my eyes, nervousness flashes across her face.

"Dash," she murmurs.

"You think this," I point between us, my voice hard, "is an act?"

"Don't tell me you've caught feelings for me."

I never stopped. I take one step and she takes another back until I have her cornered against the wall. Despite her heels, she has to tilt her head back to maintain our eye contact. I put my hands above her head on either side.

"Answer my question, wife. Do you really believe that when I call you mine, take you around the world, lose my mind when I don't hear from you for two seconds, and run to you like some lost puppy, I'm doing it all for show?" A hundred different emotions play behind her soft and wide eyes. Lowering my voice, I demand, "Or how about the little things you do for me when we're alone? Don't think I don't notice you hide my chargers every night just so I don't work late or when you hug me every night because you can't sleep alone. How about the fact that you've never once taken off my ring? Is it all for show too, hmm?"

"No," she whispers so softly that I almost don't hear it. Even if I didn't, the truth is in her expressive eyes that hide nothing.

Pulling her flush against my chest, I lean until our lips are a breath away, so she doesn't mistake my intentions. "This stopped being a *fake arrangement* the moment you kissed me, kitten. In fact, it was never about your sister. It was always about getting closer to you. You were never supposed to be Niall's. You are meant to be mine. It's seven years overdue."

Her mouth opens, but I'm not done talking. "Just know this. I'm going to take you, make you mine in all the ways that exist, and if there isn't one, then I'll forge my own. Until you're mine. My everything."

Footsteps sound behind us before she can say another word and the voices of her friends cut through the air, breaking Bianca out of her trance. I reluctantly give her space when she pushes at my chest while I still hold on to her waist.

"Do you ever keep your hands off of her, lover boy?" mocks Rosa, making Bianca blush harder.

When we face her friends, Iris is biting her lip to stop from laughing while Rosa stands with her hands on her hips. They make a perfect duo: dark and light with one wearing a black gown and another in white.

"I can see you're back, Rosalie," I drawl in a dry tone. "Did the in-laws kick you out of the city?"

"Dash!" hisses Bianca while Iris snickers before instantly shutting up when Rosalie glares at her before aiming it my way.

"How about you worry about *your* in-laws?"

"Stop, you two," admonishes Bianca.

With a haughty expression, Rosa stomps to Bianca's side and steers her toward the well-lit hallway, leading her away from the ballroom where I can see the guests mingling. Some even looking curiously in our direction.

"Where are you taking my wife?"

"You can have her back when it's time for the new couple to walk to the stage," Rosalie throws over their shoulder.

I don't move until they disappear around the corner and like the lover boy she called me, I immediately miss Bianca. Thank God Justin isn't here or he'd be laughing his ass off.

"I get it now," a familiar voice speaks from behind me, startling me.

I twist just in time to see my new business partner, Kian Singhania, step out from the shadows, holding a glass of whiskey in his hand. As usual, his dark eyes hold no single emotion. They almost appear dead like a bottomless pit and calculative as though the world and everyone in it is a code he wants to crack.

No wonder the media calls him merciless and apathetic.

Steeling my spine, I reply to his remark, "What?"

"Why you ran out of the meeting like the hounds of hell were after you." Taking a sip of his drink, his head tilts as he says in a remote voice, "You're crazy about your *wife*."

The way he puts emphasis on 'wife' raises my suspicion immediately. The corner he was standing in is hidden and dark, which means he could have been standing there and listened to the whole conversation between Bianca and I while we remained oblivious. Probably even heard about our little secret.

Just another complication I didn't need.

Pocketing my hands, I narrow my gaze while he remains steadfast and unfeeling. "How long have you been standing here?"

"Long enough."

Fucking hell. It takes all my power to keep my mask in place because if there's one thing I hate, it is having my back against the wall. However, before I can threaten him, he beats me to it.

"Don't worry. Whatever you do outside of our company doesn't interest me." Stepping closer, he advises, "However, you should be more aware of your surroundings because secrets like that could be disastrous and scandalous in the wrong hands."

"I'm well versed with scandals, and I don't intend to have another."

"If only we lived in a world where it was a possibility."

With those ominous and true words, he disappears into the crowd while I'm left wondering if Bianca and I are fooling ourselves that we'll survive this unscathed.

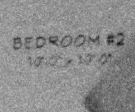

Chapter Forty-nine

BIANCA

"I think I have a crush on Dash," I blurt out, leaving my best friends stunned as soon as we lock ourselves into one of the rooms upstairs. They stare at each other with a look I can't decipher. Pacing back and forth, I push past the rising scary feeling in my throat. "Actually, no. I'm pretty sure I'm *falling* for him."

The second I admit it out loud, I wait for the wave of panic to hit and the impulse to run in the opposite direction, but strangely enough, none of it comes. All I'm left with is an exhilarating rush, a lightness in my chest like I'm about to jump off a cliff with no fear of crashing. Because my heart knows Dash will be there to catch me.

I face Rosa and Iris, who are wearing twin expressions of glee and satisfaction… Not shock, like I expected. What the hell? Why aren't they in hysterics like I am and telling me I wasn't supposed to develop feelings for my fake husband?

"Oh fuck! It's too soon. Too fast. Right?" I yell, which puts them into action.

In a flash, they are by my side and guiding me toward the couch before pushing me down to sit. Rosa tilts my chin and commands, "Deep breaths, Bee. Slow and deep breaths."

"I'm just like those stupid heroines you warned me about, Ro."

"You're not stupid," says Iris, holding my hand. "You're human."

SCANDALOUS GAMES

"I went and fell in love with my fake husband." I shake my head with a soft laugh. "And I didn't realize how much until he made me see it and basically told me it stopped being a pretend relationship for him, too, before you both interrupted us."

"So that's why he looked like I rained on his parade," mutters Rosa.

"Did you tell him you love him?" questions Iris. She and Rosa hold their breaths while waiting for my answer.

"No."

"Why the hell not?" hurls Ro.

Her reaction throws me off because she's always been outspokenly against me catching feelings for Dash, warning me again and again to guard my heart and not cross the lines.

I narrow my eyes suspiciously. "Why the sudden change of heart, Ro?"

"Oh, her heart was always in the same place," Iris rapidly says under her breath.

"What the fuck?" I curse, staring between the two of them. "What aren't you two telling me?"

Rosa shrugs while looking at her nails as she confesses, "So maybe I had a hidden agenda in pushing you toward Dash."

"Explain."

"I pushed you into his arms because for the first time in years, I saw the spark in your eyes as you gazed at him, Bee. Beneath the hate, I saw that you wanted him. In the past, you constantly chatted about him and I bet he was the man who saved you outside the club when you went with Niall. Even when everything fell apart, you ran to him. Dash has always challenged you and I knew he was someone you could never scare away, like you've done to other guys over the years. So yeah, I took a risk."

"So you decided to play Cupid?"

Her face scrunches but she rolls her eyes. "Yes."

"And what if it had backfired and only one of us fell in love? It would've fucked with our plans." Huffing out a breath, I shake my head. "We still don't know if he's in love with me or simply just likes me."

"Oh, please. The man walks around with stars and hearts in his eyes every time he's with you. It's not even funny," quips Rosa. "You should've heard his voice when he called me to ask how to take care of you because you were on your period. You hold on to a man like that."

"Besides, everything worked out perfectly," points out Iris.

"I still wish you had told me, Ro."

"Then you would've never said yes, and I just want you to be happy like you deserve," she softly murmurs before winking. "And lover boy clearly does. Besides, this will make a hell of a story to tell your grandkids."

"Have I woken up in another dimension? You're not Rosa." Iris snorts from beside me.

"Shut up."

The laughter dies down and they curiously ask, "Why didn't you tell him how you truly feel?"

"Because I'm scared," I spill to Iris, and she squeezes my hand soothingly as I continue in a dreamy voice, "I thought I could resist Dash, but he sneaked his way past my walls anyway. His bossy demands used to drive me mad, still do, and yet, I can't get enough of them. Every feeling with him is heightened and uncontainable. He's showing me it's okay to trust; to free fall. He's making me dream of a life I gave up on a long time ago, and it fucking terrifies me."

"Then it's time you took a risk."

"Where have you been, Bianca?"

"Hello to you too, Mom," I greet my beautifully dressed mother as she rushes to my side the moment I enter the hall with my best friends. "I was with Rosa and Iris upstairs."

"*Namaste*, Aunty," they both say to her, and she genuinely smiles before hugging them both.

"How is Nova? I thought you were going to come with him," probes my mom curiously while Rosa gives a strained smile. Although my mother remains oblivious.

"He is traveling, so he couldn't come."

"Really? His mother forgot to mention that when I ran into her earlier."

"I'm sure she didn't know since Nova tends to forget to inform people sometimes. You know how it is, Aunty. Workaholic men," Rosa smoothly lies, making my mom chuckle.

"Well, you girls enjoy." Turning to me, she orders, "Don't wander upstairs again. I'll come find you later."

As soon as she's out of earshot, Iris eyes Rosa suspiciously and arches one eyebrow before demanding, "Is Nova even aware there's a party?"

"Please tell me you didn't lock him in a basement or something?" I'm not kidding because it's a high possibility.

"Jeez. How evil do you guys think I am?" retorts Ro, but the almost serene and saccharine smile on her face gives it away. When she realizes she's not fooling us, she begrudgingly admits, "Fine. I may have hacked into his calendar and changed the date to tomorrow."

Iris and I gape at her. "You hacked into his calendar?"

"Fuck no. I just flirted with his assistant until he did it for me. I was almost tempted to ask he fuck up with his meetings, too, but didn't want the poor guy to lose his job. Obviously, he has nothing going for him if he's working for that arrogant vulture."

I'm intently listening to Rosa that I miss the two hulking frames, Nova and Nathan, stalking in our direction, until Iris slaps my arm and flicks her chin behind Ro, who remains clueless to our diverted attention. She goes on with a smug smile while her fiancé, who wasn't supposed to be here, stops right behind her with a dark glint shadowing his features.

SCANDALOUS GAMES

Iris opens her mouth but after a shake of the head from Nathan, she glares at him but listens.

"Umm, Ro," I whisper.

However, my best friend is unfamiliar with subtle clues and doesn't notice the shift in the air. She doesn't even pause as she continues her not-so-victorious speech.

"Besides, he's more useful to me with his job safe. I mean, the possibilities to fuck with Nova are endless. This ought to teach his sexist ass to not hire a male assistant."

"I thought you didn't want to fuck me, Rosalie?" drawls Nova before leaning down and murmuring in her ear, "Have you changed your mind?"

Rosa freezes, mouth parted mid-sentence, and she blinks rapidly. It lasts only for a second before her expression deflates to someone who got told Santa isn't real. But in true Rosa fashion, she perfects her resting bitch face reserved for her dearest fiancé before turning to him. He towers over her yet she still looks like his equal.

Nathan comes to stand beside Iris and wraps his arm around her waist so she's tucked into his side. I smile inwardly when she melts in his arms trustingly and he gives her a wink. The three of us watch with amusement as Rosa taunts Nova.

"The only fucking happening between us is in your dreams."

The vehemence in her tone is met with a sadistic grin and they look like they're seconds away from turning the ballroom into bloodshed. People openly stare at our little group and Nova seems to sense it, too, because he smoothens his features. As though he's done it a million times, he tugs a still glaring Rosa into his arms, smiling when she growls under her breath.

"Easy, sweetheart. You don't want to cause a scene at your best friend's party, do you?" At his softly spoken warning, the fight leaves Rosa's body and once she has a smile in place, he delivers a threat. "Besides, you'll have plenty of chances to fuck with me as you work for me."

"Work for you?" repeats Rosa sarcastically. "Did you hit your head on the way over here?"

"You're my new assistant since I had to fire my previous one." When she opens her mouth to argue, a curse poised on her lips, he hardens his gaze and speaks in a domineering tone, "Behave, Rose."

Rose. What the fuck?

He says it in the same baritone that I've been on the receiving end of for the past two months, courtesy of Dash. The spine-tingling commanding tone that equal parts turns on and infuriates me.

Do all these men learn it at a secret school or something? Or put something in their water? Maybe it's black magic.

Whatever it is, it shuts Rosa right up, leaving Iris and me gaping with our jaw slack. Even scarier is the blush darkening our moody friend's cheeks.

Yep. Black magic it is.

I blink when Nova aims his charming smile at me and says, "Congratulations on the nuptials, Bianca. I have to admit, I didn't see it coming after the last time."

Suddenly, I recall that he witnessed the scene at the club when I ran into Dash. Not flustering under his intense gaze, I shrug and reply, "The heart wants what it wants."

"Indeed." Still holding our friend captive, he informs us, "I'm going to steal my fiancée, if you don't mind."

"Well, I mind," snaps Rosa.

"Nobody asked."

Nodding at Iris and Nathan, he pulls Rosa after him until she has no choice but to follow. She gives me an apologetic smile over her shoulder. Nathan, who was quiet until now, smiles warmly at me. He looks ravishing in his all-black three-piece suit that does nothing to hide his ample muscles.

"Congratulations, Bianca."

"Thanks, Nathan."

Everyone knows Nathan as the good and perfect son of the Singhania clan, unlike his older brother, Kian, who is the black sheep of the family. He is ever the gentleman, charming and following in his father's footsteps. However, considering he's Nova's best friend, I know he couldn't be as flawless as the media paints him.

Nevertheless, he adores the world of Iris and it's enough reason for me to trust him. Just then, she lightly smacks him on the arm and scolds, "Why didn't you warn me about Nova?"

His lips curve to the side. "Just like you warned me about Rosa?"

"I just found out."

"Mhmm... Dance with me."

"But Bee—"

"Go on, Iris." I wave her away. "I have to meet my parents anyways."

As I glance around the grand room, I'm taken aback by the stunning decorations. The chandeliers hang from the ceiling. The stage, adorned with thousands of flowers to provide a gorgeous backdrop. Elegantly dressed men and women mingling and enjoying themselves around the vast room. Few, including my friend and Nathan, dancing while a live band plays soft acoustic music.

My parents really went all out for this party. Extravagant and over the top. Except I know it's another act to show off their wealth to their friends, our extended family, and business rivals. You know, to make up for the fact that their daughter eloped and had a private court marriage.

They don't realize it'll only feed the gossipmongers.

These are the people I've grown up around, yet I wouldn't trust any of them. Few rush to my side and congratulate me, and I give them a polite smile with a thank you. I'm so glad I didn't choose a heavy dress to wear. Otherwise, I'd be limping like a duck. I honestly just want to survive the next couple of hours without any drama. And if luck isn't on my side, then thank fuck there's alcohol.

Among the throngs of people, I search for Dash, but he's nowhere to be seen. Probably mingling with the guests since he has also invited a few of his colleagues. I think I even glimpsed Kian, which is a surprise since he never comes to these gatherings.

As I gaze at the familiar faces, I hate to think Dash has no family remaining, which makes me wonder if he's still in touch with Niall and his mother. Did he keep in touch with them after the death of his father? The urge and curiosity to ask about them always strikes me, but I hold my tongue. His relationship with them was complicated and tumultuous enough. I don't want to touch any bad nerves, which I unknowingly end up doing.

Maybe he'll tell me on his own.

"Bianca beta." My mom emerges out of nowhere, intent glimmering in her eyes. Grabbing my hand, she pulls me in the direction she came from. "Come on, there's someone I want you to meet."

"Have you seen Dash, Ma?" It's been almost an hour since I left him in the hallway. I especially begin to worry when there's no glimpse of my father either. "Where's Dad?"

"They are both together. Your father is introducing him to his friends."

Before I can interrogate her further, we come to a halt in front of one of her longtime friends. Mr. and Mrs. Patel are our neighbors and they have an export business. They are actually one of the nicest couples I've met and have practically seen me grow up. Beside them, I notice their tall son, whose name I can't recall, but last I checked, he was studying abroad.

"*Namaste*, Aunty." I face Mr. Patel before greeting. "Uncle."

"Oh my god! Look at you, Bianca," Mrs. Patel praises before wrapping me in a warm hug, her bangles clanking softly as she pulls back. "Just as beautiful as I remember."

"Thank you, Aunty. So glad you came."

"Do you remember Dhruv, Bianca?" My mom introduces us with that same sparkle I saw earlier. Twice as bright now. "He just returned from London and is set to work in your father's firm."

Alarm bells start to ring in my head as my mother's voice takes on a high quality, her expression almost sickly and adoring as she gazes at Dhruv. He certainly looks like he's enjoying the attention, or maybe it's simply because she's his future boss's wife.

My intuition, on the other hand, screams something fishy is happening. I would excuse myself if it didn't seem rude. So, masking my annoyance, I play along. "I remember. My dad must think highly of you."

"I'm just honored he took me under his wing," he replies and while he gazes at me, I get a queasy feeling in my chest. It rises to my throat like smoke when my mother speaks.

"I was thinking you could show him around the city, beta. A lot has changed since he lived away for years."

Oh hell no. I sharply look at her and that's when I recognize the earlier spark for what it is. My own mother is trying to set her very married daughter up on a date. No, not a date. A freaking affair. Dhruv suddenly looks hopeful and salivating at the prospect.

Dude. You're literally at my wedding reception party.

"Oh no, she doesn't have to," intervenes Mrs. Patel, albeit reluctantly.

"I wish I could but my work is hectic at the moment," I immediately cut in before my mom could.

Dhruv isn't deterred. "How about a dance then?"

"Don't be rude, Bianca. One dance won't hurt." Then my dearest mother all but thrusts me into his arms before I have a chance to politely decline.

Dhruv doesn't notice my reluctance or simply chooses to ignore it as he boldly rests his hand on my back and guides me to the dance floor. My heart thunders behind my rib cage as I nervously search for Dash.

He isn't going to take kindly to another man dancing with his wife. Especially after his intimate confession that has settled like an intoxicating elixir in my veins.

"I almost didn't come to the party but I'm so glad I did," says Dhruv flirtatiously as he pulls me close and takes my hand to lead the dance. "You're more gorgeous than I remember."

"You do realize I'm a married woman?" I scornfully ask. Politeness be damned. "And this is my wedding reception party, not a season of *Bachelor in Paradise*, right?"

The jerk laughs before revealing, "That's not what your mom said."

"Excuse me?"

"She told me your marriage isn't going to last once you realize Dash is not the perfect partner for you. She would like us to be together, someone close to your age, and a man your father respects with a family, not an orphan like your husband."

Each word is an arrow viciously stabbed in my back.

Everything fades into the background until a searing pain beats in my heart. My mind is so disoriented that I miss the atmosphere in the room shift until a cold chill sucks all the warmth. It raises the hair on the back of my neck and I feel his presence before I hear his granite voice.

"Hands. Off. My. Wife."

Chapter Fifty

BIANCA

Dhruv, who apparently has a death wish, doesn't remove his hands at Dash's threatening command brimming with unleashed violence. Dash's hard chest presses against my naked back and I can feel the tension radiating from his body and seeping into my own.

Without giving a foolish Dhruv a chance, one strong and possessive arm circles my waist. One tug and I'm free of the other man, who finally develops the sixth sense that tells him my husband isn't someone to be messed with. That he made a big fucking mistake.

Panic swells inside my chest when Dash steps forward, going toe to toe with him while holding me flush against him. His size and physical strength, intimidating, especially with the dark expression he's wearing as he stares Dhruv down.

My heart skips a scared beat when a vicious smirk graces his lips. Goosebumps rake on my skin when he speaks in a low and mocking voice, "So you think you're a better man for my wife?"

Oh no. He heard everything. He has to know it means nothing. That I don't believe it.

Dhruv has the decency to look uncomfortable, especially with the guests pausing and watching the whole scene like a train wreck waiting to happen. Even the others have stopped moving on the dance floor.

"We were just dancing, man."

"You dance with lots of married women, then?" Dash sneers until the other man looks close to pissing himself. "Do you see my ring on Bianca's finger?"

"Y-yes," he stutters.

"It means she's mine. My wife. My woman," Dash growls, with so much emotion that it takes my breath away and I can't look away from him. "She will never be yours. Not in this lifetime or any other. Touch my wife again and I'll cut off your hands. Speak to her and I'll take out your tongue. You see where I'm going?"

"Yes. Yes, I understand."

"Run before I change my mind."

Dhruv scurries away like those cartoon characters leaving a cloud of smoke in their wake. Except, nothing about this is funny. The silence and the tension in the room is deafening with every pair of eyes on us. Some even boldly record us, like we're a source of entertainment they can't wait to share stories about. Or probably sell the inside scoop to the media. They observe Dash like he's a caged animal, afraid yet oddly mesmerized.

The one thing I was absolutely worried about happened. My parents have to be watching among the crowd. Yet they are the last people I'm concerned about. My whole being is attuned to my husband, who I feel is fighting an inner battle. His fingers dig into my waist while the other is clenched into a fist. Facing him until he's forced to meet my gaze, I'm not prepared for the tumultuous emotions flashing in his eyes. A pain I've never witnessed in all these weeks with him.

It's not jealousy. Or mere possessiveness, but something far deeper and darker.

"Dash," I take his fist and slowly uncurl his fingers, "talk to me."

The darkness doesn't fade from his features. If anything, it burns brighter and something twists in my gut when he tugs his hand free.

"I need some air."

As brusquely as he came, he walks away. Leaving me bereft, cold, and wondering what the hell just happened. I don't even think before I chase after him. His broad shoulders disappear around the corner at the other end of the room and into the back hallway.

I walk as fast as I can in my skirt while my heels clack on the shiny floor. From my periphery, I catch my mother walking in my direction and shout my name but I ignore her. I will be dealing with her later. She went too far this time.

As soon as I'm in the hallway, I look left and right and curse when I don't see Dash. The lobby is deserted and I know he wouldn't just leave, so I go in the opposite direction of the exit. An instinct guiding me, like some invisible thread connects us.

There is a double door, leading to the garden, and that's where I see his silhouette through the glass wall. His back is facing me when I enter, my heels ruining any attempt of disguising my presence. He still doesn't turn around, not even when I'm within touching distance.

It stuns me because it is so very unlike him.

Ever since we met, not a day has gone by when he isn't holding me one way or the other. Like touching my skin breathes life into him.

SCANDALOUS GAMES

"Look at me, Dash." My voice carries over the chilly air while darkness cloaks us.

"Get back inside, kitten."

Every syllable is underlined with a tangible warning. A sane girl would heed it but nothing about us has been in the spectrum of sane. So, of course, I ignore it.

"No," I growl. "You don't just threaten a man for touching me for a few seconds and then walk away like it never happened."

His shoulders bunch and tighten. "Walk. Away."

"What have I told you about bossing me around?"

He whirls around to face me with a ferocious heat in his eyes and I almost stumble back from the power of it. The green pupils, reminding me of a dark, rainy forest, seconds away from swallowing you whole. Instead of running, I ache to be swept into them.

"And what have I warned you about letting another man touch you?"

"He was nobody." My words don't penetrate past the storm playing havoc in his eyes.

"Why does every man think they can have you? I can't fucking stand it. Especially when you stubbornly refuse to admit we are real." His voice is low, pained, as his head tilts, the light from the nearby lamps playing over his chiseled face. The scruff on his tight jaw, giving him a roguish look. My gaze drops to his lips as he growls darkly, "First it was Niall, and now some random stranger."

"I can't change my past, Dash. You can't be jealous of every man I've dated," I whisper softly. "It'll only drive you mad."

A non-sarcastic laugh spills from his mouth and he takes a step back when I inch closer. His gaze softens tenderly at the hurt on my face when he distances himself. "You don't want me touching you right now, kitten. Because if I do, I'm going to fuck you until you can't walk."

His filthy warning sends a zap straight to my clit. I lick my lips before a plea falls from it, "Dash..."

"What I feel for you isn't something as fickle or simple as jealousy, kitten. It runs far deeper than that in my veins." His gaze turns molten while I burn in those flames. "You, my wife, are an obsession I can't tame. An addiction I can't quit. A dream I can't help but chase."

Ruined.

Utterly and helplessly ruined.

Dash Stern ruins me for all other men with those words. He all but obliterates them into smithereens because no one has ever looked at me like he's gazing at me at this very moment. Those piercing eyes, letting me peer into the depths of his soul as he bares everything—how I make him feel. The truth of it dismantling the walls that I built around my heart.

Our breathing turns ragged while he remains unmoving, not touching me even as my eyes beg. Does he really not see that I crave him just as madly?

That despite my determination to never let him in, he ruthlessly made his own place in my heart like a thief?

And he proves me right when he utters, "I don't care if it scares you and you want to keep your heart caged, but I'm done hiding my feelings. My biggest mistake was letting you walk out of my life seven years ago when I should've made you mine, and it's not happening again."

Stupid, stubborn man.

Closing the distance between us before he has a chance to react, I yank him down by his tie and crush my lips against his. Dash, who's always in control and fierce, is rendered stunned and speechless for the first time. His heart skips a beat before beating as rapidly as mine and I feel the slow rise of his chest against my own.

I fucking smile.

Cupping the back of his neck, I kiss him like I'll die if I don't. Pressing myself harder as though I want to bury myself inside his skin, I lick the seam of his lips. The second my tongue drags across his bottom lip, it snaps him out of his trance. With a deep groan that vibrates directly to my pussy, he takes control and ravages my mouth in a searing and toe-curling kiss.

"Fuck," he curses, wrenching our lips apart. Our hooded eyes clash and he growls roughly, "You never fucking listen."

"You were talking too much," I tease, heat flashing across his face. Our breathing rough and hearts racing, I give in to us. "I'm yours, Dash. And no one is tearing us apart."

Chapter Fifty-one

Dash

"Say it again," I roughly demand. Eyes glazing over with lust, her grip in my hair tightens as her trembling lips rasp against mine, "Yours."

"Again."

"I'm yours, Dash."

Fusing our mouths together in another hard kiss, I shove her against the nearest wall and lock her wrists above her head. Addicted to her taste and the sound of my name on her full lips, I push my tongue inside and suck on hers until she writhes.

Whimpering, moaning, and so utterly pliable underneath my possessive touch.

If more than a hundred people weren't just a few feet from us, I would've torn off her dress the second she said she's mine. When I peer into her face, her eyes convey the same desire. The same potent lust. I had planned to fuck her after we ditched this party so I could take all the time in the world and taste her all over before claiming her with my cock.

My patience snapped once I saw her on the dance floor.

Now, I can't spend another breath without feeling her clenching around my dick.

My need is so dark and feral that my mind chants only one thought.

Take her. Own her. Bind her to me.

SIMRAN

Biting her bottom lip between my teeth, I soothe the sting away before kissing along her jaw, her neck, and stopping my mouth on her pounding pulse. Shivers dance on her smooth skin when I scrape my teeth on her collarbone before biting hard.

"Ahh... Dash!" she screams, head thrown back. The fact that she doesn't care if anyone hears her turns me the fuck on and calls to my depraved side.

And then... there's no holding back.

I untwist her hair from the fancy updo it's in until the waves fall in rivulets down to her waist. Pushing her knees apart with my leg, I run my fingertips up her naked thigh through the slit.

"You wore this thinking of me, kitten?" With every inch I trace, the closer I get to the wet heat that I know will be dripping for me. Leaning back, I stare at her heavy-lidded eyes and roam mine down her delectable curves. "Were you secretly hoping to get fucked by your husband? Knew I wouldn't be able to help myself from pounding this cunt?"

A ghost of a smile appears on her lips and she licks them before whispering, "Maybe."

"You have an insatiable pussy, wife," I taunt, sliding my finger underneath her lace panties. The material, so wet that it sticks to her folds. "Always so fucking soaked."

Dipping one finger between her swollen slit, I glide it from her hidden clit to her entrance and circle it teasingly. Her eyelashes flutter while she breathes heavily, making her dark areolas peek from her dress' neckline. My mouth waters to taste those sweet brown nipples and I hate not being able to rip her blouse.

"Why do you always have to torture me, Dash?" she whimpers, frustrated.

I narrow my gaze and let her arms drop before circling her throat and fill her weeping pussy with two fingers to the hilt. I twist them so hard that my palm slaps on her clit every time I bottom out. "If anyone is in torture, it's me from not being able to wrench your top down so I can suck on those hard nipples. I'm the one in torture for not being able to tear that fuck-me dress into pieces just to gaze at that beautiful body. Give me lip again and you'll be walking naked out of here."

At my dirty threat, she clenches around my still thrusting fingers. She and I both know I'll never allow anyone to stare at her as long as I'm alive but like the naughty vixen, she gets off on the fantasy just the same. My cock becomes as hard as granite with every moan I steal from her.

I stretch her hole for my girth by pushing another finger and hitting her inner bundle of nerves that has her grinding and moving her hips fast. Full to the brim with three digits, yet she's begging for more, her face twisted in pleasurable pain.

"Good girl," I rasp while flicking her clit. "Ride my hand. Just like that."

My eyes lower to her bouncing breasts while she clutches my suit jacket. I press closer and crush my mouth against her, swallowing the desperate moans. I finger fuck her harder and deeper until she tries to rise to her toes to escape my ruthless pace but my grip on her delicate neck doesn't allow her.

"I-I'm going to come," she mumbles against my lips just as her inner muscles clench. When her rhythm falters and the blush on her skin spreads lower, I know she's close. Tilting her jaw so I can see the pleasure swarm her pretty face, I pinch her clit until she shudders violently.

"Scream my name, wife."

"Dash!"

Her pussy spasms and jerks under the force of her climax. Her cries, echoing in the garden for anyone to hear. When I pull out my fingers, they are glistening with her juices. Her eyes flick open when I push them between her parted lips.

My voice is hoarse as I command, "Taste yourself."

My cock throbs painfully and jerks in my pants when she sucks greedily on my fingers. I stare, mesmerized, at her mouth as one of her hands grips my wrist and tongues my digits like she would my cock. Her soft and hooded gaze doesn't stray from mine.

The smug look and the feel of her lips is what sends me over the edge.

Keeping her pinned to the wall, I tug my wrist free and unclasp my belt roughly before unbuttoning my pants. I need to be inside her. Now.

Apparently, she wants the same because one small hand collides with mine and she impatiently lowers my zipper. I would smirk if I wasn't out of my mind with hunger for this woman. Blind to the world but her. I hiss between gritted teeth when she pushes the same hand inside my briefs and wraps her fingers around my girth.

"Take out my cock, kitten."

Because she loves to drive me mad, she strokes instead of obeying and does it just the way I taught her. With a growl, I slap her hand away and take out my aching dick, leaking with precum. Stroking the column of her throat, I lower my hand and squeeze her tit. "Now isn't the time to test my patience. Got it?"

"But I want to—"

"You can play with my cock all you want when we get home." Flicking my chin, I order, "Spread those legs. Wider."

The slit in her skirt rides high as she does. Stepping closer, I grasp the back of her knee and wrap it around my waist. Pushing my hand between her thighs, I grip the edge of her flimsy panties and rip it off with one hard pull. Bianca's face pinches when the material cuts into her skin but when I touch her pussy, I have to swallow a groan to find her juices leaking and dripping down.

"You love my barbaric side, don't you? Fucking you where anyone can walk in?"

Her flush deepens at my smirk and her silence is all the answer I need.

Fisting my length, I rub the crown on her inner thigh, running along her wetness while enjoying the tremor that rocks through her. She sucks in a sharp breath in anticipation and arousal when I inch my dick closer to her waiting pussy.

Like a good girl, she holds the top of her skirt and reveals her bare and shaved pussy for my lustful gaze. Her swollen clit, peeking out from between her pussy lips. Our mutual groan of pleasure fills the air when I slide my cock in and trace her length.

"Fuck. That feels so good," she whispers, her fingers digging into my shoulder.

"Tell me again, kitten."

Our eyes lock and she understands what I'm asking. "I was always yours, Dash.

Make me yours again." *Thrust.*

With a snarl, I shove my whole length inside her to the hilt. The force of my thrust makes her nipples spill from her neckline and I bend down to take one in my mouth. She runs her nails down the back of my neck as I pull out completely before driving into her pussy.

Seven fucking years, I went without this feeling and it's like coming home.

Still tight and heavenly as I remember, she ruins me for all other women.

"More. Please." She begs and I oblige by biting down on the hard nub and pulling until she chokes my shaft.

Her cunt is so wet and slippery that she easily adjusts to my size. I couldn't have stopped even if I tried. I'm as deep as our bodies allow, yet it's not enough. Nothing short of running in her bloodstream will be enough.

Grabbing both her knees, I hold her against the wall and thrust savagely and mercilessly. With each plunge, I replace the touch of any man who thought she was theirs. Who believed they stood a chance with her. Who fucking dared to come near her.

"Mine." The sound rising from deep within. "*My* wife."

"Yes."

"Look at you taking every fucking inch, kitten." I growl against her parted lips. "For such a good girl, you have a greedy pussy."

"I can't believe I have you inside me again, Dash."

"Your pussy was always mine to own." *Thrust.*

"It was only a matter of time before I had it again. Now I'm never letting you go, wife." *Thrust.*

"My cock will be the last you'll ever know." *Thrust.*

"Ahh… Yes. Yes!"

Her pleasured cries urge me on and I slam inside her harder. Deeper. Rougher. Every time I bottom out, her pussy squeezes like she's trying to keep me in. The feel of her maddening and satisfying all at once. Her full tits shaking from the drive of my thrusts, leaving only the obscene slapping sound in the air.

Helpless to resist, I spank her right nipple and pinch before paying the same attention to the other. The rougher I become, the wetter her cunt becomes. She gushes her juices and I feel them drip to my balls as they slap against her.

She's so far gone in her lust that she doesn't realize I'm fucking her bare. It feeds the possessive beast in me. It's a good thing she's on the pill because there's no way I'm fucking her with a condom ever again.

Sliding my hands to her ass, I tilt her hips and grind the base of my cock against her clit. She meets me halfway when I lean down and our mouths meet in a sloppy, wet kiss. When she teasingly sucks on my tongue, my shaft pulses and twitches inside her.

"You're a filthy little cocktease, wife." I grunt, pulling out until only the head of my dick is in before forcing it to the hilt again and again. Savagely and viciously until there's no telling where she begins and I end.

Until another orgasm builds in her cunt.

"Come for me again," I demand, circling and flicking her clit. "Let me feel that

SCANDALOUS GAMES

pussy choke my dick."

Suspended between me and the wall helplessly, I don't ease my punishing rhythm. I whisper filth in her ear and continue my assault on her sensitive nub until I'm the ground she worships on. Few more hard thrusts and she convulses around me with a pleasured yell. I twist her nipple, prolonging her orgasm.

Before she can come down from the high, I pull out and whip her around until she's facing the wall. Bending her by fisting the silky strands of her hair, I drag my dick from her clit to her entrance and plunge my cock deep in her gaping cunt.

"Dash! Oh fuck! Too deep."

"But you take me so well, kitten." Spanking her ass, I gruffly bark, "Stay still while I fill you with my cum."

Her palms slap on the wall, failing to find purchase as I chase my orgasm. My balls, pulling taut while her cries are music to my ears. I harshly grip her around the waist and lose myself in the sensation of her tightening and clenching. Milking my cock for all it's worth.

As if she's consumed in the unhinged way I'm fucking, no holds barred, and it's sends her over the edge again. Like my filthy little whore she is, Bianca shatters again. It triggers my own and I spill my thick cum in spurts inside her.

"Fuck!" I chant like a mindless beast.

When I finish, I curl my arm around her waist and pull her against my heaving chest. Grabbing the front of her throat, I bring her lips to mine and kiss her softly, reverently. When her shiny brown eyes meet mine, my heart squeezes inside my chest.

An urge I never possessed or dreamt to ever feel rises within me. Love. Contentment.

I've fallen for her.

With it comes another scary thought.

Will she forgive me when I confess the brutal truth?

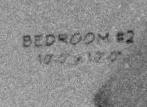

Chapter Fifty-two

BIANCA

The second I pull back from Dash's embrace, I miss his warmth like an addict.

Both of us reek of sex after mating like two animals without a care about their surroundings. My hair is no longer in the elegant bun I spent hours on, my blouse askew, and if that didn't scream I was fucked to within an inch of my life, the flush on my skin betrays our filthy, jealousy-driven romp in the garden.

Meanwhile, Dash isn't bothered in the slightest by his rumpled state. Though he is not as bad as mine. His hair is tousled and falling over his eyelashes, tie lopsided. With controlled movements, he tucks his still half-mast cock and smoothens his jacket.

The sinewy muscles, flexing like a thirst trap.

And damn. My pussy flutters *again*.

Blinking back to reality, I try remembering how long we've been gone. Did someone come searching and saw us fucking shamelessly? While I begin to panic and wonder how I'll ever explain myself to others, Dash is calm as a bird and stares at me in his unnerving and penetrating way. Like I'm a fascinating creature that will disappear if he blinks.

After everything, this small habit of his still gives me butterflies like a silly girl.

His gaze is no longer burning with anger and violence, which gives me a little peace. I hate the shadows that darken his beautiful features when his unhinged and possessive side flares. Next time he becomes that unhinged, I'll just let him work it out by fucking me as he pleases. It seems to work like magic. And ends with my pussy satisfied from countless delirious orgasms.

He arches one eyebrow, as if he can hear my illicit thoughts. "I know that look, kitten. You craving my dick again?"

At the mention of his cock, I jolt when I realize he didn't wear a condom. How can I be so reckless? I flick my gaze to his and the calm expression he's wearing has me stuttering, "Y-you came inside me."

Primal satisfaction flashes across his sharp features. "I did."

"What if I get pregnant? You don't even know if I'm on the pill."

"Don't tempt me with ideas, kitten."

Unbelievable. "You're not giving me a baby until I'm thirty."

My gasp is audible when what I just blurted out in my post-orgasmic haze sinks in. This is even worse than saying I love him, which I might as well have. Because apparently, my inner hussy is very eager to have his babies.

Babies. What the hell?

I cover my mouth when a smile appears on his lips. The brightest I've ever seen, and it softens his rugged angles. He becomes infinitely more dangerous to my heart.

"Don't you dare." I point my finger at his chest. "Pretend you didn't hear that!"

He wisely listens but his silence and that panty-melting smirk is just as smug and delighted as any word he could've said. Ignoring him, I right my blouse while taming my curls as much as I can under the circumstances. My skirt has fallen back into place but every second, I can feel his cum leaking from my pussy. The asshole even ruined my panties, which I find torn and thrown on the ground mere feet from me.

"Give me your handkerchief," I demand, extending my hand. When he doesn't, I look up. "Dash!"

"Why do you need it, kitten?"

My shyness decides to kick in. "You know why."

"No."

"Never mind. I'll just go to the restroom."

Faster than light, Dash grabs my wrist and I collide against the wall. He cages me in while resting his bent elbow on either side above my head. Cupping my chin, he tilts my face so I can't look away and feral eyes connect with mine.

Roughly grazing my bottom lip with the pad of his thumb, he growls, "You will walk just like this into that room. With me on your arm and my cum dripping from your tight pussy. So when they all look at you, they'll know, once and for all, that you're claimed."

My retort dies on my lips when he steals them in a hard, drugging kiss.

Until I forget my own name.

My legs feel like Jell-O and my head dizzy when he pulls back and I sway closer to him. Then intertwining our fingers, he guides us and we enter the room as he promised.

Him on my arm and his cum sliding down my thighs.
Every step, reminding me of the ache he left behind.

"Well don't you look freshly fucked?" says Rosa, appearing on my side like a genie out of its lamp.

"Could you be any louder?" I hiss, glaring at her. I'm already struggling not to run from the way every pair of eyes are watching Dash and I covertly, sneaking glances before whispering behind their palms. I certainly don't need my best friend giving them juicy ammunition to gossip about.

Ignoring me, she smirks at Dash, who is fighting off his own. Rosa casually takes a sip from her drink before commenting, "You made quite a scene, lover boy."

"I tend to live a scandalous life, in case you haven't noticed."

I side-eye the alcohol in her hand suspiciously when she laughs. Yes. My grumpy best friend laughs. "Why are you both suddenly joking around like friends?"

"Don't be jealous, wifey," Dash teases, tapping my scrunched nose playfully. "You know you're the only one who can make me laugh."

"It's true," says Rosa, who has suddenly turned chatty tonight. "I don't think I've ever seen lover boy smile unless he's staring at you."

Meanwhile, I'm trying not to blush harder than I already am. His intense gaze softens ever so slightly and I have to calm my racing heart that wants to melt into a puddle at his feet. I'm so lost in him that I miss a very drunk Iris heading our way until it's too late.

"Oh my god, Bee! You did it. You told Dash you're falling for him."

Ground. Swallow me, please.

First, babies, and now this. I'm continuously making a fool out of myself. From the corner of my eye, I catch Rosa tug a blubbering Iris away and leaving us alone. When I hesitantly meet an extremely quiet and very still Dash, I expect amusement waiting for me.

Instead, tender and yearning green eyes stare back at me.

He looks like a broken boy yet hopeful, like I'm the lifeline he was searching for. There's no other words to describe it. I recognize it because I felt the same way until he came alone.

Until he made me believe in love again.

"Is it true?" he hoarsely whispers.

"Yes."

His chest heaves as though he's struggling to breathe and with that same unbelievable and fascinating look eclipsing his pupils. Doesn't he really not believe he's lovable? Has nobody ever told him they love him?

"You're falling for me, kitten?"

"I am, Dash." I smile, cupping his cheeks. "So are you going to catch me?"

"Always."

SCANDALOUS GAMES

I rise and meet his lips halfway in a kiss that is both a vow and a promise. The kiss, nothing like the ones in the past. It's slow like we have all the time in the world. It's loving when two broken hearts mend. It's everything.

When we pull apart, we're both breathless and delirious. My heart, full and lighter than it's ever been.

I'm about to tell him we should just skip the rest of the stupid party that was another elaborate scheme of my parents to tear us apart. But I frown when Dash suddenly becomes serious and a ghost of an apologetic expression shadows the happiness in his eyes.

"There's something I need to tel—"

"Excuse me, everyone!" My father's smooth voice booms from the stage, cutting off whatever Dash was about to say.

My attention is stolen by my parents and my sister. The low chatter and the music dies down as everyone focuses on my dad, standing tall with his reserved and charming smile he's honed over the years as a host. My mother stands dutifully beside his side. However, only I can tell her smile is strained.

Dash pulls me close as we listen to my father closely, waiting for our cue.

"I would like to thank all of you for taking the time out of your busy schedules and joining my family tonight for such a joyous occasion. As you all know, my lovely older daughter, Bianca," he waves his arm in our direction before continuing his speech, "has finally married the love of her life, Dash Stern, who I'm proud to have joined my family as my son-in-law. I would like to introduce the happy couple, Mr. and Mrs. Stern."

Thunderous claps spread around the ballroom and congratulatory words are whispered as Dash and I walk through the parted crowd and toward the stage. Dash squeezes my palm reassuringly knowing I don't like being the center of attention. Like before, he raises our joined hands to his chest to let me feel his heartbeat and it calms me instantly.

My father envelops me in a hug and kisses my forehead the second I step on the stage, and does the same to Dash, minus the kiss. Except, there's no warmth behind it because it's all an act, a fake display of a united front. I have no right to judge myself despite the happy twist my game took.

My biggest fear was losing myself. Instead, it ended up being my parents. They've shown me a side of them that I cannot unsee as I realize their reputation is everything to them and worth more than my happiness.

When my mother embraces me, I bend and whisper in her ear, "You will no longer have a daughter if you ever pull that stunt again, Mother."

She freezes at the rage in my voice, one I would've never dared to use. When I lean back, the perfect smile poised on her lips cracks ever so slightly. I shake my head disappointedly when she doesn't even attempt to deny my accusation.

My righteous mother holds her head high and hardens her gaze before sneering without losing her mask, "He is no good for you, Bianca. You're too blind to see it now. Mark my words. That man is going to break your heart."

I don't bother with a reply because it's nothing short of banging my head against the wall. It will only hurt me. However, the damage has been done. Because for the

SIMRAN

rest of the night, her warning doesn't stop haunting me like a bad omen.
　I just hope I prove her wrong.

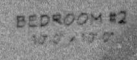

Chapter Fifty-three

BIANCA

What's it called? Fuck bunnies or puck bunnies. I don't know. Well, whatever the hell it's called, the gist is Dash and I spent the whole weekend fucking like bunnies. On every surface. In every room. And our apartment is big. So you can imagine just how many times and ways and positions he made me come.

Does that make me a sex addict?

Apparently, there's a difference between Dash holding back and… Not.

The man's libido is insatiable and ever since I gave him free rein and laid my heart on my sleeve, he has become obsessed and possessed like a madman. And god! I love every second of it. Because I've been just as bad, unable to keep my hands off him.

He claims this is our mini honeymoon before we go on a real one.

But now, Monday is here and we have to burst our little bubble. I was tempted to play hooky and entice my husband, too, but I've already spent all my paid leaves from work while Dash pushed back his meetings. I'm quite shocked I was able to keep him away for so long.

Or maybe it was because I hid all his chargers again.

"I know you said you want babies at thirty," Dash says with that mischievous glint in his eyes. "But how many are we talking, kitten?"

"Oh my god!" I groan, hiding my face, but he tugs my hand free while smiling softly.

When I push at his hard chest, he doesn't budge. Instead, he pushes more of his weight down on my naked body. Both of us should be hurrying to get ready for work but Dash is holding me captive in our bed. Still gloriously naked and distracting me with his eight-pack abs, which I finally got to lick, and his cock teasing the inside of my thigh.

"We are still pretending I didn't blurt that out like a fool."

He's unruffled. "One? Two?"

"Still pretending."

"I bet you've picked their names too."

"You do know what pretending means, right?" I mock before rolling my eyes. "I should've gotten you that damn dictionary."

He laughs. The sound is so carefree and like music to my ears. A mesmerizing sight. The sunlight streaming through the open balcony makes the green in his eyes look unreal. They are such a unique shade that I always get lost in them.

I graze the crinkle around his eyes with my fingertips, loving the sight of them. My grandma always used to say that one can always tell a person has lived a happy and joyous life by their laugh lines. That every line and wrinkle have a story to tell.

It saddens me because Dash has none. His laugh lines got buried underneath a cold mask to protect what little he had. So now, I just want to make him smile and laugh as much as I can. He says he never had a family. I'll show him that he finally does.

Me.

Us.

"I will get you to tell me one day, kitten," he promises with a wink.

My smart-ass retort dies on my tongue when he yanks the blanket to reveal my breasts for his starving gaze. His messy hair teases my collarbone when he bends to lick my nipple lightly, leaving a wet trail as he repeats the sensual motion on my other breast. Restraining my wandering hands, he pushes them into the mattress and plays with my breasts.

Laving. Sucking. *Biting.*

As if he didn't spend the entire weekend painting me with his hickeys and finger-shaped bruises, his teeth dig in with the intent to leave more knowing I'll be wearing them the whole day as a reminder that I belong to him.

"I could feast on these tits for hours, kitten." He grunts, scraping the sensitive tips with his teeth. I whimper and his mouth becomes rougher until I'm grinding against his hard cock. "So perfect."

When his grip loosens around my wrist to cup them and circle the hard nubs, I snake my hand between us and wrap it around his thick shaft. He jerks in my fingers and groans loudly when I stroke from the purple crown to the base.

Our foreheads touch and breaths mingle as I stroke him again. A new wave of wetness pools between my thighs when I take in the sight of him. My fingers barely meet as he swells in my hand. It's a miracle he even fit inside me without bruising my insides. His cock, hitting places I only thought was a myth.

SCANDALOUS GAMES

"Squeeze harder," he growls against my mouth.

I obey and watch pleasure swarm his angular face. I'm unable to look away as I stroke him faster. Precum leaks from the slit on his dick and I rub it over him. His hand palming my breast travels lower and my back bows when he plunges two fingers to the hilt in my core.

"Dash!"

Another sharp and rough thrust. "Keep stroking my dick, you little tease."

His fingers don't slow their punishing pace, making it harder for me to focus when all I want to do is succumb to the drugging sensations he's effortlessly evoking in my body. I slide my hand up and down his length, using his precum as lube.

"Tell me I own this cunt," he demands harshly.

"You do."

"Say the words."

"You." His fingers thrusts. "Own." *Thrust.* "My." *Thrust.* "Cunt."

With every word, he throbs and pulses in my grip, going impossibly hard like they triggered the primal male in him while bringing us both near the edge. He's unabashedly dominating and animalistic in bed. Every time he growls a dirty command, my pussy clenches while electricity runs down every inch of me.

"Good girl."

When he hits that secret spot again, stars dance behind my vision. Desperate to come but not without him, I tighten my fingers around his length and stroke him in tune with his ruthless fingers plunging inside me.

Nipping my bottom lip, he grunts, "Tightest fucking pussy. Needy and begging to be filled."

"Only for you. Give me more. Fill me, Dash."

His hips thrust in my hand while he flicks my clit in slow and teasing circles. Our bodies become sweaty while his masculine scent drugs me. The wet slapping sounds are like an illicit symphony, driving and urging us higher. So close.

"Fuck. Come with me, kitten."

"I ne-need," I stutter. The ache, rising to a painfully high degree but I can't fall over the edge. Sensing my body's need better than my own, Dash slams his fingers against the same spot over and over.

"Give it to me," Dash growls. "Come on my fingers like my *filthy little whore.*"

I scream when he ends his dirty praise with a stinging slap to my pussy. My orgasm barrels down and I feel it on every inch of my shuddering body.

Through my fog of lust and heaven, I hear his own roar of pleasure before I feel his white hot cum splatter on my pussy. His palm makes a wet sound as he jerks his cock, spilling every drop on my skin.

A beast marking his mate.

His body drops on mine and I bask in the weight of him. His rapid heartbeat while our slick bodies come down from the mutual high. His harsh breathing slows down while placing lazy kisses over my collarbone.

I trace his muscular back before traveling up to his hair.

He inches his head up, kissing my mouth.

Running my fingers through his unruly hair that falls over his forehead, I smile and whisper, "I kinda miss your short hair."

His lips quirk, not expecting it. "I thought you didn't pay attention to me."

"I didn't."

"Liar."

"Shut up."

My heart melts when he doesn't hold back a silky laugh. He becomes strikingly handsome when he does it.

"So you did like at least one thing about me."

"Fine. I did. You looked extremely hot. Broody. Intense." He arches one eyebrow playfully, as if to say, 'do I not find him attractive now?' I slap his chest and murmur, "You are all those either way. Happy now, husband?"

His gaze becomes feral at my endearment. I read his sinful intentions and just as his fingers aim for my waist, I slip out from underneath him. I cock my hip while lifting my chin at him. "You're not making me late for work."

Leaning on his forearm while those chiseled abs tighten deliciously, his hooded eyes roam over my naked form as I stand near the bed. I can't hide the way my traitorous nipples harden under his attention and when he licks his bottom lip, I tremble as though he's caressed me.

"Stop that," I grumble.

He innocently says, "Stop what?"

I roll my eyes, barely resisting to fall for his sensual charms and walk toward the bathroom. Without turning around, I warn, "You better be up after I'm done showering."

I'm in the air a second later with his arm spanning my waist and he bites my earlobe before playfully growling, "Are you bossing me, kitten?"

"Yes." He swats my ass and I yelp. "Hey!"

"Here's an order for you, wifey," he says, trailing kisses down my neck before enclosing us in the bathroom. "You're never taking a shower without me."

"Fuck. We're never going to be on time for work, are we?"

"Good thing I'm your boss for the day."

Chapter Fifty-four

BIANCA

Dash's office building is as stunning and intimidating as I remember. In fact, it is the tallest high-rise on the block and befitting for the Stern and Singhania name. In a way, it makes complete sense that both men decided to merge their companies. After all, they're so similar in many ways. Both are self-made billionaires and made their businesses away from their fathers' shadows, choosing to make their own legacy.

"Okay, so ground rules."

"You and your rules, kitten," Dash mutters, helping me out of his car. Towering over me, he inclines his head and raises one eyebrow. "I thought we were done with those."

I smooth my black pencil skirt as I straighten and slide my purse over my shoulder. Mustering my firm voice, I lay the rules while ignoring his scowling face. "You will not give me special treatment in front of your employees. We will behave strictly as professionals. And absolutely not giving me intense flirty eyes. Just treat me like any other employee and pretend I'm not your wife for the day."

His nostrils flare and gaze sharpens as he yanks me flush against him. "You are *always* my wife. There never will be a time-out. Understand?"

"I don't want them to think you hired me because I'm your wife."

"You weren't my wife when I hired you."

"That's worse. They'll say I seduced you for the job."

Instantly, his expression softens at my distress and obvious spiraling. "They will not think that because once they meet you, they'll know I hired you because you're the best. Your passion and dedication shows that with every word. You demand respect the second you walk into any room, kitten. And if you recall, you also put me in my place."

I chuckle at the memory, especially the way he had caged me against the door. His honest and confident praise sends a rush of happiness straight to my heart. It's not that I don't believe in myself or need validation but sometimes, it's nice to be appreciated and seen. Especially when your parents think you're wasting away your career. Mine have always treated my degree as silly and reduced my job to that of a glorified decorator for rich people.

In other words, it's beneath the Chopra name.

Until now, I didn't realize how snobbish my parents are.

"Besides, if anyone dares to insult you, I'll fire them," Dash declares, yanking me from my thoughts. His jaw set and eyes gleaming with intent.

"On second thought, no firing anyone either."

"Sorry. The boss disagrees."

"Dash!"

Stealing my purse to hold it himself, he shuts and locks his car before intertwining our hands. Tugging lightly, he guides us toward the sliding doors and mutters, "For someone who despises being late, you sure do it often, wifey."

"Jerk," I mumble under my breath.

"What was that, kitten?"

"Nothing."

I feel his amused smirk all the way to the entrance of the chic and brightly lit lobby. It's nothing like the last time I was here. For one, there are staff and formally dressed executives milling around. Even the bitchy receptionist from hell is all peachy and smiles. Possibly because she sees me on the arm of the CEO as we pass by her.

Everyone's attention snaps to us immediately. The energy in the air shifts at my husband's commanding aura. The firm set to his chiseled jaw and crisp business suit demanding respect, despite the fact that he's gripping my girly purse. The women stare in awe and with stars in their eyes at his sweet gesture since it is heavy with the folders I'm carrying.

I'd be drooling at him, too, if I wasn't so concerned with the attention on us. I try to tug my hand from Dash's but he keeps his grip firm. He doesn't even spare anyone a glance and continues to walk us down the lobby to his private elevator.

So much for no special treatment.

As soon as we're inside the elevator, I breathe easy and twist to face him. He smirks at my fiery expression with a satisfied gleam in his pupils.

"FYI, you being mad only makes my dick hard, kitten." He growls.

My nipples harden beneath my thin blouse and his attention locks on them like a hungry wolf. He straightens from his perch in the corner and backs me into the opposite one. Toying with the end of my hair between his finger and thumb, my

SCANDALOUS GAMES

breath hitches and I stare, mesmerized, at his lips.

I swallow.

He runs his tongue over his teeth.

Tilting my chin with his hand around my throat, just possessively holding, he bends until our mouths are a breath away and groans, "But when you melt like this for me, I ache to lock you in my heart and never let go."

My heart hits the floor in a puddle.

The elevator stops and he lets go, standing to his full height. My skin feels flushed and hot and all he did was touch me. *Caress me.*

It's scary how a single touch can affect me so vividly.

We step out and he places his palm on my lower back. I'm still daydreaming when I realize we've reached a glass-walled conference room, which is right across from his private office. I don't miss how the blinds to his are open unlike the last time.

"I asked my assistant to set up the room for your meetings," Dash speaks, putting my purse on the long mahogany table. "She'll send each of the executives one by one once you've settled. Let her know if you need anything else."

"Thank you," I say politely before innocently asking, "and will you be watching me all day? Can't take your eyes off me, darling?"

"I have seven years to make up for, kitten."

My stomach flips when he says it so casually. I thought Dash's hate and possessiveness was dangerous but it doesn't hold a light to his romantic and unbidden side. It's more powerful and addictive than any drug could be. Deadlier than any poison could be.

And he doesn't even know he's being romantic.

It's what makes the butterflies take flight in my chest.

Our eyes are still locked when we're interrupted by his assistant, whose name I remember is Lara from when he told me a while back. Giving me one last heated look, Dash heads to his office where he perches behind his king-like desk. I'm staring in his direction when Lara clears her throat and I flick my gaze to her sheepishly.

"Side effect of being newly wed," she says with a laugh and flashes her own wedding band. "My husband and I were the same."

"Sometimes I hardly believe he's mine."

"I'm sure he feels the same." Switching topics, she passes me a document. "I printed the meeting schedule with the executives' names so you know who will be joining you."

I grab and look it over. "Thank you."

"You have time before Mr. Singh arrives. I'll let you be," she informs me. "I'll be right outside if you need anything."

"Cool."

In the midst of the chaos of everything else, I completely got sidetracked from my first solo project. The one my mentor and boss is counting on me to slay. If the rumors are true, it might lead to a promotion. So, I cannot fuck this up because it will depend on the testimonials. For the next one hour, I look over the material I brought in preparation for the interviews and a common questionnaire. My goal for today is to get a sense of their individual style and blend it with a common theme.

"Hey, Bianca, Mr. Singh is here," interrupts Lara, poking her head through the door. "Shall I send him in?"

"Yes, please. I'm all set." I rise from my chair just as he enters the room and I greet him with a small smile. "Good morning, Mr. Singh."

"Please call me Jay."

He shakes my hand with a firm grip and I regard him silently. He appears to be in his fifties with a warmth radiating from him that tells me he must be well liked. Something about him instantly puts me at ease. Once we sit down, him across from me, I begin my first meeting with excitement building in my chest.

"So, Jay, what is your vision for your ideal space?"

Time flies as I talk to Jay, who is absolutely hilarious and jovial as he regales me with stories about work and family. This is one of the perks of being an interior designer. I meet all kinds of people who are unique in their own ways. Almost like you're reading a book where you live a hundred lives. Of course, it does wonders to bring your clients' visions to life, which is its own kind of rush.

All through the meeting, I feel Dash's stare digging into my back and try not to squirm. It's as if we are tethered by an invisible thread. It takes all my power not to succumb to the temptation and do the same. How I am able to focus on listening is a mystery.

After Jay, who invited me and Dash for lunch, I interview two more top executives before Lara pokes her head in again. I look up when she taps on the door and I'm instantly curious by the expression on her pretty face. Nervousness reflects in them.

"About your next meeting," she hesitantly says.

I frown while skimming the doc to familiarize myself with the name. "Is Aditya late or something?"

"No. It's just he's kind of a flirt in the office," she explains before wincing like she's embarrassed. "He's a little cocky but harmless. Still—"

I cut her off after sensing the hidden meaning. "You're worried Dash will be pissed."

"Well. The gossip of the reception may have made rounds."

"Of course," I say with a dry laugh before schooling my features. "It's sweet of you but rest assured, I know how to handle advances of unwanted men. Just send him in."

I have half a mind to ask for the privacy shutters but it will only raise suspicion as I can see from my peripheral vision that Dash hasn't done the same. He types away on his laptop with his infamous concentrated mask. This is the intimidating businessman who ruthlessly runs his company.

"Mrs. Stern."

I stop my ogling at the new voice and stare at none other than Aditya, head of operations. My smile is reserved when I speak to him. "Just Bianca."

"Ahh... No formalities." He grins and I realize he was aptly described. "I like

SCANDALOUS GAMES

that."

In retrospect, I should've stuck to Mrs. Stern because now he's staring back at me as though I gave him an opening. Unlike others, I won't be letting my guard down around him. I blatantly ignore his last remark. But again, he remains unruffled.

"Why don't you have a seat and we'll begin."

I have to hide my shock when he boldly grabs the chair right beside me. Not wanting to be rude since he is technically a client, I sit down and subtly shift so there's an appropriate amount of distance between us. Casually flicking my gaze behind him, I sigh in relief to see Dash is busy on a call.

"I have to say," my companion drawls while resting his arm on the table. "You're as pretty as everyone described."

Is this guy for real? Since when did it become sexy to flirt with a married woman? If it were any other circumstances, I would give him an earful on how to treat women. Seems a lot of men need lessons on chivalry these days.

"How about we focus on making your office attractive instead?" I reply in a firm tone that I reserve for difficult clients. In his case, with no sense of boundaries.

"Of course, Bianca. I trust your beautiful mind to create magic."

Swallowing the nausea at his terrible flirting skills, which I bet only works half the time because of his decent-looking face, I pull open the 3D plan on my tablet and bring us to the agenda of the meeting, which he apparently assumes is a date.

For the first few minutes, I'm able to keep us on track and he answers me genuinely. Of course, not without throwing a few innuendoes here and there. However, tension slams into me when he not so subtly shifts closer to my chair, his leg touching mine. He disguises the move as wanting to peer closer into my tablet when I point at something.

"I would like the portrait to be hung on this wall," he says, leaning into my personal space. I almost jump out of the skin when he subtly grazes my thigh, right above my knee. I'm about to push him away when a loud bang startles us.

My head snaps at the dark sound while Aditya flinches away from me. Dash enters the room with seething calmness. His razor-sharp eyes zooms on me and he doesn't miss the slight trepidation shadowing my features from one of his employee's touch. The restraint and serenity he's portraying is far scarier than threatening.

"Out." One word and he sucks all the oxygen out of the room.

"Boss," Aditya laughs awkwardly.

"You're fired."

So much silence that you can hear a pin drop before a frazzled Aditya finds his voice past the initial shock. Yet again, I'm left stunned and speechless. However, this time Aditya deserves Dash's wrath. There's no way this man doesn't have a single harassment complaint against him. This was no harmless flirting.

"What for? You can't just fire me," blurts out Aditya, his face red with embarrassment and shock. He pretends as though he is a victim. "I deserve the right to three strikes and a valid reason."

"Here's your strikes," Dash says, crossing the distance to him. "You walked into this room. You made my wife uncomfortable. And you dared to lay a finger on her."

"I didn't touch her!"

Dash switches his gaze to me. "Bianca?"

"He did."

"You have two seconds before I call security," Dash warns threateningly.

Aditya points his finger at Dash and growls, "This isn't over. You will hear from my lawyer. I'm going to sue your ass for wrongful termination."

Dash ignores his rambling, completely unbothered by the threat he issues as he storms out. When I glance outside, the whole office is raptly watching the debacle and a fuming Aditya walking out. I begin to panic and second-guess if I made a bigger deal and overreacted. I wouldn't want to jeopardize Dash's position and reputation because of me. He must sense it because a second later, his palm cups my cheek and forces my gaze to his.

"Don't."

"But—"

He shakes his head. "No one touches you unless they're ready to face the consequences. I will deal with him."

"Okay," I whisper. "I still want to continue the rest of the meetings."

He nods just as a nervous Lara enters the room behind him. "Mr. Stern, I'm so sorry. I should've stopped it."

"It wasn't your fault, Lara," I assured her softly.

"Go and inform HR," orders Dash. "And send the next person in."

She scurries to obey after an apologetic smile my way. I arrange the scattered papers and frown when Dash casually drops on the seat that Aditya vacated. His silk shirt stretches across his abs as he sits with his legs crossed.

"What are you doing?" I demand, cocking my hip.

"I'm staying for the rest of the discussions."

The hell. "No, you're not."

"I am."

"You're seriously crashing my meetings?" I grumble at his firm tone. "I don't need a bodyguard. I have survived twenty-five years without you, you know. I'm perfectly capable of handling any situation."

"I never said you weren't." Flicking his chin at my chair, he orders, "Sit down, kitten. I won't be disturbing you."

"Instead, you're going to sit here all intimidating." His lips tilt to the side at my taunt and amusement dances in his green flecks. "Don't you have your own meetings to annoy people?"

"I promise you won't notice I'm here." *Impossible.*

With that, he pulls out his phone and begins tapping on it. With a resigned huff, I plump down on my chair and purposefully shift it far away from his. I don't make it two steps before his long arm reaches out and he tugs me back to his side. He does this without looking up from his phone.

Minutes pass and I keep getting distracted. So, I decide to do something before the next one arrives.

"Well, if you're going to crash my meeting, you might as well do something useful," I mutter and he raises one eyebrow curiously. Sliding the extra pen and pad

SCANDALOUS GAMES

I brought with me to him, I tap it with my finger and sweetly order, "Take notes for me."

Shock flashes across his eyes and I shrug innocently. He actually goes speechless like no one has ordered him before.

"Kitten got your tongue, Mr. Stern?" I smirk.

Before he can retort, the next person waltzes in, his gaze flicking to Dash before they connect with mine. Dash gives me a heated warning at the mischievous intent in mine. It sends a shiver down my spine but I ignore it as I focus on our companion.

"Don't mind Mr. Stern," I tell him. "He has graciously agreed to be my assistant for the day."

Chapter Fifty-five

DASH

I have been reduced to an assistant in my own goddamn company. By none other than my sassy little wife.

And because I'm a fool for her, I write the goddamn notes, when I should be going over the financial reports my CFO sent me for the upcoming shareholders' meeting. My world used to revolve around her but somewhere along the way, she's become *my world*.

Of course, she wouldn't have let me get away with shadowing her meeting. I let her think she's the boss, letting her bask in the power she's wielding over me at the moment. Because every time our gazes clash, there's a sparkle in her chocolaty eyes that makes it worth it.

My employees stare at me through the glass wall like I'm an alien. Or as though I've grown two heads, but one glare from me and they scurry back to their desks.

The one sitting across from us is another story. Bianca has them mesmerized and charmed with every word she speaks. Especially when she entertains their stories with a genuine laugh. They freely share their thoughts with her as though talking to an old pal. I've learned more about the people I closely work with in a few hours than I have in years.

There's not a shadow of a doubt in my mind that Bianca would run her own successful designing company one day.

SCANDALOUS GAMES

My gaze is drawn to her mouth as she speaks, "I think I have everything I need to know. I have so many ideas floating in my head already."

"I'm looking forward to seeing them," replies Vinod, my marketing head. He laughs as he jokes, "Maybe then I'd be excited to come to the office."

"The six-figure salary you get paid isn't enough, Vinod?"

His face falls as though he forgot I was here and becomes flustered while I coldly stare. Nervously straightening his tie, he backtracks, "Oh no, Mr. Stern. I meant that it will be a perk, nothing more. Well, I'll leave. Have a meeting soon."

"You can't resist, can you, Dash?" teases Bianca, once he exits.

"You're the only irresistible thing in my life." I smirk when my favorite blush darkens her cheeks. Sliding the notepad to her, I say, "Your notes."

I wait as she scans the points I scrawled and blinks like she can't believe I actually listened. I have to hide my amused smile at her bewildered expression. Meanwhile, I admire her curves and the cleavage showing as she bends. My cock jerks with the need to plunge into her mouth as she bites the corner of her lip in concentration. Rising to my full height, I discreetly adjust my lengthening shaft.

"Wow. These are actually good," she comments before joking, "so, should I pay you by the hour or…?"

Circling behind her, I lean down and slam the notebook shut. Her slight intake of breath has my lust skyrocketing when I cage her small frame against the desk. Her intoxicating scent, hitting me like a wave from the ocean. An electric shiver courses down her spine the second my lips touch her ear.

"I want you in my office," I command. "Naked. On your knees. Waiting for me."

Kissing behind her ear softly, I straighten. She stands on shaky legs and it takes all my willpower to not just bend her over the desk, flip her skirt, and fuck her right here, right now.

"Leave it," I growl when she tries to pack her stuff. "Go. Now."

My rough command sends her running. I watch the sway of her delectable hips all the way to my office that has the privacy blinds drawn. My assistant knows to do it when I'm not there. I take my time going after Bianca. I want her on edge, eager and writhing for my cock, until pleasing me is her solo desire.

Having her close and not being able to touch her is fucking tortuous and hellish. I want to drive her as mad as she's been doing to me all day.

When I can't take it any longer, I stalk toward my beautiful obsession and enter. All the blood rushes to my stone-hard dick when my hungry gaze lands on her lithe little body. Every inch of her, now bare for my view.

Fuck. She's breathtaking.

Thick, wavy hair falls down her spine, few loose curls framing her sharp cheekbones and the slope of her neck. I cannot decide whether I love her full tits that push against every dress she wears enticingly or her tight waist that fits my hands perfectly. My gaze travels lower to her thighs and her glistening pussy that is as close to heaven as I'll come.

She's utterly and stunningly perfect. The whole package. Like God etched her just for me.

Mine.

Feral lust slams into me seeing her obeying my orders like a good girl.

Her hooded eyes collide with mine and I let her glimpse the pleasure in mine at her beautiful obedience. Hers slowly roam over my clothed body like she can't help herself. Her tongue peeks out to lick her lips when her eyes pay extra attention to my shaft tenting my pants.

I stay right against the door and shrug off my suit jacket before carelessly throwing it on the couch to my left. Unbuttoning my cufflinks, I roll my shirt sleeves over my forearms and don't miss her eyes following the movement. I bite back my groan as she fucking trembles and squeezes her thighs to relieve the ache I ignited.

Her crimson face flashes to mine when I take a step in her direction. Crooking my finger, I give her a silent command to come to me. I watch as she runs her soft hand over her thighs before rising slowly but I halt her, shaking my head.

"Crawl, kitten."

Her lips part on a breathy exhale while her nipples tighten into hard little peaks. Those brown orbs widen for a fraction of a second before they ever so slowly darken with desire and fascination. I keep my gaze pinned on her, memorizing every play of emotion as she fights and fails to resist my filthy demand.

We both know she loves our erotic little games. Her cunt creams with every illicit and dirty command. The little vixen was just waiting to be corrupted. Waiting for a depraved animal like me to coax it out.

"Be my good little whore and crawl to me," I growl.

My lungs seize when she lowers to her hands and knees without breaking our connection. Her perky tits jiggle obscenely as she moves while her hips sway enticingly. I stroke my pulsing cock beneath my pants with each inch she crosses until she stops at my feet.

Peering at me under her eyelashes, she seductively purrs, "I need you in my mouth, Dash."

"You're a little cock slut, aren't you?" I taunt and it's the goddamn truth. I've never met another woman who loves giving head as much as this greedy one does. And fuck, if she doesn't do it like a pro as she takes me to the back of her throat. "Always horny to suck my dick?"

"Yes," she moans, resting her hands on my thigh. "Fuck my mouth, Dash. *Please.*"

Fisting her hair, I roughly unfasten my leather belt. Tilting her head back, I slap the purple crown on her swollen lips and bark, "Open."

I shove between her parted lips. Her hot and slippery mouth, ever so inviting as it envelops half of my shaft as much as my grip allows. The pleasure shooting up my spine is a heady rush and I slam the rest of my thick girth to the hilt. I'm merciless as I pound into her throat, my balls slapping her chin.

"Fuck!" I curse, staring at the ceiling as I try not to bust. "Did you enjoy making me work for you, kitten?"

"Mhmm." Mischief dances in her expression. I thrust and still inside her until she chokes. I let her breathe in a lungful of air before slamming in again.

"Maybe I should let them see what a horny little girl you are behind closed doors." *Thrust.* "Let them see that sassy mouth full of their boss's dick, choking on

SCANDALOUS GAMES

it." *Thrust.* "Sucking and milking my cum like a good girl." *Thrust.*

My jaw clenches when her soft whimpers and moans send vibrations straight to my balls. She's a mess with her lips stretched wide as she swallows my dick, spit and tears mixing on her cheeks. It's her eyes, though, that have me transfixed as they stare passionately. My lips curl to the side when I catch her fingering her pussy, high on lust.

Before she can make us both come, I pull out and she whimpers in protest. Bending down, I pick her up around the waist and in two strides, I have her thrown on her back on my desk. Papers clatter and fall to the floor but I can't seem to care. All I see and care about is her.

Laid out like an offering for me to feast on.

Hair fanned out like a halo while she's staring shyly and pleading at me.

I yank her ass to the edge and circle her delicate throat with one hand. Palming one heavy tit, I flick the hard nipple and pull until she grinds her pussy on thin air, seeking friction. Spanking her bruised nub, I snarl like a wild beast, "My wife needs a reminder of who owns her."

"Oh yes! Show me." She nods, reaching her arms to touch me. "Just fuck me, please. It aches."

"Beg me to redden this pussy first."

A shudder racks her and she begs prettily, "Spank me, Dash. I'm yours to do as you please, darling."

Those words are like gasoline on my twisted and violent lust for her.

A goddamn kryptonite.

"Spread those thighs." My gaze travels to her glistening cunt. Her tiny clit, peeking out through her slit. My mouth waters and because I'm powerless, I dip my head and lick from the puckered hole to her clit. One taste. That's all I allow myself.

Holding her immobile, I bring my palm down to her wet folds in a hard smack that echoes along with her sharp cry. My nostrils smell her arousal as her juices spill down the inside of her thighs.

"Pretend to hate it all you want but you love getting spanked, kitten." I smile smugly and thrust one finger to the knuckle. She clamps down on it like a vise. I suck on my finger to taste her before spanking her again. *Hard.*

"Ahh…"

"Good girl. Let them all hear how good I make this pussy feel." As realization dawns through the lusty fog that we're still at my office during work hours, she bites her lip in a futile attempt. I tsk. "Too late, kitten."

Fiery eyes clash with mine but they fall closed when I redden her pussy like I promised.

Spank.

Spank.

Spank.

I release her throat just as she shatters, crying out my name as she climaxes. She's still in the throes when I position my cock at her dripping entrance and shove myself to the hilt in one savage thrust. It sends another wave of ecstasy through her shaking body as her orgasm prolongs.

"So goddamn tight. Wet. Slippery," I say through gritted teeth. "Can't get enough of this cunt. Never deep enough."

I'm nailing and pounding into her so hard and violently that my desk shakes while my eyes are hooked to her bouncing tits. Wrenching her upright, I suck one brown nipple in my mouth and bite.

"Dash! I feel you everywhere." She moans, clinging to me.

Circling her neck, I keep rutting into her wildly and yank her lips to mine so I can fuck them with my tongue. Her hips lift, meeting each thrust with a thrust while our tongues duel in a sloppy, wet kiss. My cock swells even more when she rips off the top button of my shirt and I hiss when she scratches her nails on my skin.

"Yes. Mark me, kitten." I huskily groan. "I'm just as yours as you're mine."

Nothing is hotter than her need to paint me as hers. My balls pull taut when the little vixen bends and bites my shoulders. The second she sucks and licks the same spot, I'm a fucking goner. With one vicious and deep thrust, I spill inside her wet heat.

"Milk my cock, wife." I grunt as I jerk off inside her. "Let me fill that hungry pussy."

Lewd moans fall off her pretty lips as she whispers, "*Yours*."

Chapter Fifty-six

DASH

Bianca is rearranging my desk when I return from the adjoined bathroom after changing into a new shirt, courtesy of my wife for wrinkling and ruining the previous one. I shake my head with a smile, finding it both hot and cute that I make her go wild with maddening lust.

"You don't have to do that, kitten," I say, startling her. "Lara would've done it."

She whirls around and cocks her hip. "And let her know we fucked on your desk?"

"Your sweet cries have already made certain of that."

"I'm never returning here again," she says dramatically.

"Didn't take you for a quitter."

She sticks her tongue out and goes back to arranging my desk. I'm searching for my phone when I notice her gaze lock on a file that is now splayed wide open. My heart drops when I realize the exact document she saw and watch her curiously pick it up to read. I steel my expression when she softly asks, still reading through it.

"You run a charity for a hospital?"

"Yes," I gruffly answer.

Her eyes connect with mine, bright with intrigue and amazement. Still holding the folder, she questions, "What is it for?"

"It is for the ER departments in all of the hospitals in the city, to serve the poor families who can't afford the bills, and those who don't have insurance. The money raised is used as funding for any shortage they may face."

"Wow, Dash. That's really amazing," she says proudly. "You must have saved so many lives with this initiative."

"I have money. They need it," I reply simply. She stares at me as though I'm a hero when I'm anything but. A hint of sadness pinches her features but she quickly masks it. They soften like she sees good in my soul that is obviously lost to me.

She doesn't realize I'm only good to her and no one else.

Her voice is gentle yet firm, leaving no room for argument. "A lot of people have money, Dash, but not everyone has the heart to help others like you are. So don't downplay the difference you're making in those families' lives."

A pang like no other hits my chest out of nowhere.

Guilt.

It's the single feeling coursing and burning in my veins. I'm still lying to her and every second that passes is a little too late. Like I'm putting nails in my own coffin. In us.

Fuck. I should just tell her but as I gaze at her ruby-colored cheeks and pouty lips from my rough kisses and her collarbone imprinted with my teeth, the words form but don't come out. The fear of losing her again glues me in place. I'm still stuck in a war between my heart and mind when she flips to the next page and stills.

"This says you're hosting a gala next week."

With measured steps, I cross the distance until she peers at me. "It's a boring annual gala. Few hours of schmoozing the guests. It's the only part I hate."

"So how long will you be gone?"

I read the unspoken question burning in her pupils. That little hope sparkling as she waits for me to ask her to come with me. However, it douses into ashes when I take the folder from her hands and drop it on the desk. I hated myself a little more just then.

There are too many skeletons buried back in my city. The wretchedness of which I don't want to taint her with.

Tucking one wayward curl behind her ear, I softly murmur, "My flight is this weekend and I'll be back after four days."

"Oh, okay."

"I didn't think you'd want to come with me, kitten, after everything that happened. So I didn't ask."

"Yeah. It's fine." She waves her hand, giving a sad smile. "I'm just going to miss you."

Just like that, my resolve crumbles. The disappointment shadowing her features— which were brimming with happiness a breath ago—becomes my undoing.

"Come with me."

"What?" She gasps, lips curling to one side.

"It's time you make new memories. Happy ones with no regrets." I grab the back of her neck and pull her mouth closer. "And I want to give them to you. Will you

SCANDALOUS GAMES

let me, kitten?"

"Yes," she cries out before kissing me on the lips. I deepen it and sink my tongue past the seam of her lips and lick every crevice until it's her taste I'm drunk on. Our breathing is harsh like we ran a marathon when we part, her hands clutching my shirt like a lifeline.

With a tender smile dancing behind her pretty eyelashes, she confesses, "I lied, Dash. You were never a mistake."

"I know, kitten." I kiss her forehead. "The moment I caught you in my bedroom, I knew you'd be mine. No matter how long it took."

"Even if I'd been a crazy stalker?"

"Especially then."

She laughs and my lips lift of their own accord. But as I bundle her in my arms tightly and gaze at the skyline before me, the conflicting feelings rise again. I bury the havoc they're wreaking inside my chest. I ignore the voice screaming in my head, saying I'm making a mistake taking her back home.

Nevertheless, the past never escapes us, no matter how fast we run from it. It's always faster. Suffocating us like chains. Venomous.

The only way it loses its power and hold over us is to face it head-on.

It's time I face mine. Because it's the only path with which Bianca and I can stand a chance. I'll tell her the whole truth and show her that I'm not the man I once was.

Vindictive.

Reckless.

Heartless.

And maybe, just maybe... I'll right my wrongs and seek redemption for my sins.

***

Bianca traces her fingers on my abs as we lie on our bed in the middle of the night. The smell of sex and her fruity scent, permeating the air. After I fucked her twice more, once in the kitchen and then on the balcony, we collapsed on the bed in a sweaty mess.

Neither of us are too tired to sleep, so we talk. More like, I *listen* while she delights me with stories of her childhood. They all revolve around her late grandparents and Rosa, who she has known since kindergarten. The reverence with which she speaks about them makes me obsessed with her even more. Every tiny detail, feeding my obsession for her.

She's lying halfway over my chest with her soft breasts pressing against my skin. I play with her long hair. The strands are so soft, they almost slip through my fingers. I swear caressing her is my favorite pastime.

Locking her fingers on my abs, she rests her chin on the top and stares up at me shyly. I memorize the shape of her pert nose, the curve of her eyes, and the miniscule birthmark on the corner of her bottom lip.

"You're the prettiest woman I've ever seen, kitten," I rasp softly and push a curl behind her ear. "It physically pains me when I have to take my eyes off you for even a second."

Her eyelashes flutter shyly and she leans into my palm, my thumb caressing her cheek. I still when she kisses the inside and speaks so softly that I almost don't hear what she says. It's the intensity and sadness behind her words that smacks me in the chest first.

"I stopped believing in love for a long time, Dash," she murmurs.

The pain reflected in her eyes has me wanting to take it away and burn it to the ground. I don't spook her as a faraway look darkens her eyes, lost to the memories.

"I thought it only existed in fairy tales. And when Niall broke my teenage heart, it felt like he pierced it with a knife and gouged the little daydreaming girl inside me into pieces."

"Kitten," I whisper, my voice raw. Bringing her closer, I tuck her underneath my body while I lean on my elbow.

She smiles brokenly and continues, "I grew up seeing superficial love. The kind that could be bought with money while I ached for the unconditional kind. The one that my grandparents had. For the longest time, I thought I didn't deserve it. Until I stopped chasing the happily ever after I always yearned. I hate that I allowed Niall the power to make me give up on love, but mostly myself for doing so easily."

Bianca bares the deepest and darkest parts of her heartbreak. The sorrow she lived through all these years. It's like a vicious knot tying around my throat because all this time, I thought she had moved on. That she was happy. Instead, she had been hurting and drifting.

Just like I was.

"You're right, kitten. You don't just deserve to be loved because you're the kind of woman who becomes a man's entire world. The kind where his existence begins and ends with you. The kind where he lays the stars and moon beneath your feet just to glimpse your smile."

"Isn't that obsession, Dash?"

"Maybe love and obsession are the same," I whisper. "Because with you, my wife, I feel both."

"Until you, it would've scared me but you've made me brave to fall in love again, Dash. I believe it with every fiber of my being and I'm not scared to wear my heart on my sleeve," she confesses with tears shining in her eyes. "Because of you, Dash."

My fingers tighten and I lean until our foreheads touch. Until I can gaze to the depths of her soul. I kiss her lips through the tears and groan, "You make me believe I deserve it too, Bianca. I feel it every second, every breath I take when I'm with you. Because until you, I thought I would die alone and I didn't care if I did. Now, I want to spend the rest of my life with you."

"I wish I had met you first, Dash."

"Me too, kitten." My voice is gruff. "Me too."

Laying on my back with her soft body cocooning and clinging to my hard one, I watch her fall asleep. However, sleep eludes me and I stay awake the whole night, staring at the woman fate dropped in my path. My entire universe. The love of my

SCANDALOUS GAMES

life.

I never thought I could feel anything for anyone but goddamnit, I have fallen for her.

I love her.

Yet the weight of my past sits like a log on my chest, like we're heading for a downfall.

An unstoppable collision.

And I don't know how to stop it.

Chapter Fifty-seven

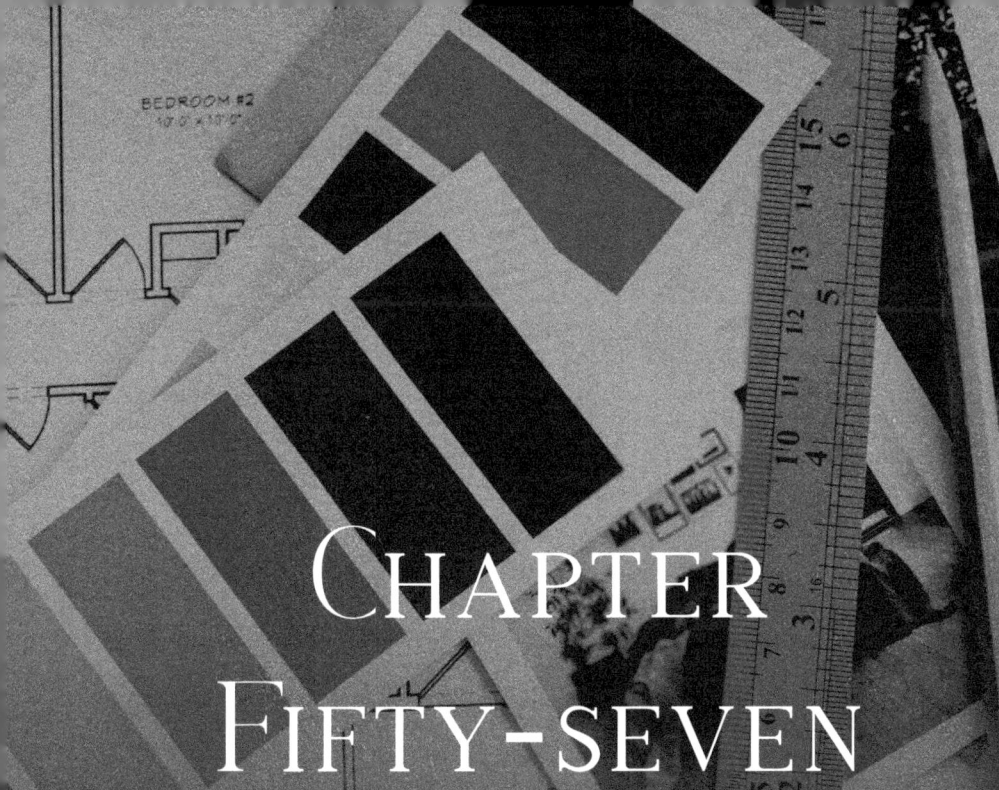

BIANCA

Nerves tickle my belly with both fright and excitement as Dash and I drive down the familiar streets of his hometown and my heartbreak. The city feels like it hasn't changed at all. Except, I'm not that naïve eighteen-year-old girl anymore.

Déjà vu slams into my psyche as the car passes through the same street where Rosa and I shared an apartment. The sun rises, blinking at me from above as I gaze out the window. Never in a million years had I thought I'd be returning to this place with bittersweet memories. In fact, I had vowed to myself I would never come back.

But if I truly want to let go of the hold of my past, I need to face my fears. With Dash and his comforting presence beside me, I am confident I will. It's like he said… Time to turn those awful memories into pleasant ones.

"Do you still own your house?" I ask Dash, who has my hand on his lap.

The fear of running into Niall is a constant and crushing weight on my chest. Once I left, I never found the courage to confront him and neither did he try to win me back or apologize. Of course, the urge to call him arose when the intimate memories became too much, but Rosa was always there to talk me out of it.

Dash continues to rub circles with his thumb as he meets my gaze and answers, "No. I sold it. Even if I had, I would have never taken you back there."

SCANDALOUS GAMES

His thoughtfulness brings a smile to my lips and a swarm of butterflies. "Where are we staying then?"

"My apartment. We're almost there."

"I know we haven't discussed this but what will happen between us when you have to move back?" I ask, trying to feign nonchalance. Even though I'm desperate and holding my breath to hear his answer. The funny thing is my biggest fear has been getting cheated on and yet, I've never once doubted Dash's devotion. Despite his playboy reputation. Strangely enough, he's always made me feel as though I'm the only girl in the world. "Your whole life is here and mine is back home."

"I go where you go, kitten."

My heart soars and beats faster as though he hung the moon. "But what about your company here?"

"I've already talked to Kian and we'll be promoting someone to run the branch here while I relocate to the new branch."

"When?" I gasp, shocked.

"The day we got married."

"That was presumptuous," I tease. However, my blushing cheeks betray my true feelings. "You didn't even know if I liked you."

"We're inevitable, kitten. I would've waited as long as it took."

"Does this mean we won't divorce like we planned once Arya is married?"

I squeal when in a flash, he yanks me until I'm straddling his lap. His rough and large hands grab my ass and he spanks me once, right where the driver can see through the rearview mirror.

"Dash!" I whisper-hiss, turning crimson red.

"Say anything about leaving me again and I'll do more than spank your ass," he growls. One hand travels up my spine and tangles in my hair. I bite my lip to swallow the moan elicited by his raw display of dominance. "You sealed your fate to mine once you signed those papers. Whatever our future holds, we'll make it work. I'm never spending another second, let alone a minute, without you again, wifey."

Using his grip, he crushes my mouth against his and kisses me roughly. I forget about our audience and moan against his lips, seeking friction against my aching clit as I grind my hips against the fly of his jeans.

I swear he wore casual clothes today on purpose. I just know he wants to drive me crazy and feel aroused throughout our whole flight. When I saw him dressed in a dark green tee with denim jeans, I was brought back to the past. His knowing smirk told me he knew where my mind went.

I'm in a daze when he rips his mouth away and I chase his lips, wanton for his taste. He's fighting the same battle and it takes me a second to realize we've arrived at his place. The driver is no longer in the front seat and groaning, I hide my face in Dash's shaking chest.

"I'll have to add 'new driver' to my list now." He growls in my hair.

"What? No. Stop firing people on my behalf."

"He knows the sound of your moans, kitten. If I see him again, finding a new job will be the least of his worries."

I freeze at the possessiveness in his tone and notice something dark reflecting in his eyes. Shaking my head, I lightly tease him to dissolve the savage look he's wearing. "Or maybe next time, don't spank me."

"We'll take the limos instead."

My jaw drops at his idea and before I can sass him, he slides out of the car and takes me with him. Gently dropping my feet to the ground, he takes my hand and guides us toward the tall building. It is way more stunning than the one we live in back home.

The doorman greets Dash formally before giving me a small smile. As we walk down the lobby toward the elevator, I casually ask, "Which floor is yours?"

"All of them."

I almost stumble at his smooth answer and whip my head to his. "All?"

"I only reside in this building and own it completely."

He's not joking. "What do you need the whole damn building for?"

"My cars."

I'm afraid to ask how many he has and shut my mouth as we climb up the stairs to the penthouse. I understand now why he bought my building, too, but I'm unable to comprehend why he gave up this gorgeous one to live in mine. Even the inside of the elevator is high tech and luxurious. I can't imagine what the rest of the floors look like.

"I'll give you a tour later," he softly informs me and I smile.

The elevator opens straight into the hallway, lit with bright lights and white tiles. The walls have abstract paintings adorning on each side. A myriad of dark and intricate colors that match the personality of the man who owns it.

Dash is quiet but I can sense his intense gaze observing me as I glance around his home—his sanctuary. It is sleek and modern. The walls in the living room are painted off-white and furnished beautifully. The rich black rug, a stark contrast. Like it was pulled out of a magazine.

Yet for all its lavishness and grand architecture, it still lacks the homely feel. The one that blossoms into your chest when you enter. The feeling of belonging.

"You have a beautiful place, Dash," I compliment, turning to him.

He stands, leaning against the island in the open kitchen with his arms crossed. His lips tilt to the side in amusement and he says, "You hate the place, kitten. I can read you like a book."

I glance away sheepishly and he chuckles.

"I'm not offended. Money can buy everything, but not a family." His tone is dry and emotionless. "My home is proof of that."

Crossing the distance, I rest my hands on his broad shoulders while his circle around my waist. "You have me."

As my words linger between us, his gaze softens and I feel his heartbeat race against my chest. He looks at me like I gave him the world while the sharp angles of his handsome face almost become boyish. Without wasting a second, he lifts me into his arms and carries me toward another hallway.

Ripping the front of my summer dress, he grunts, "I'm going to fuck you on every surface of this place until it's your scent I'm breathing in, in every room I walk into."

Chapter Fifty-eight

BIANCA

There's an ache in my pussy when I wake up the next morning.

Thankfully, being clouded by Dash and surrendering under his dirty words, filthy demands, and rough touch chased away all my bad thoughts. I was almost disappointed when I found his side of the bed empty. That disappointment all but disappears when I notice that he had left a note on the bedside table saying he needed to leave early to oversee the preparation for tonight's gala.

Except, he sneakily hadn't mentioned that there was a surprise waiting for me just after breakfast. It arrived in a flourish with a zealous and vivacious bunch of three women, who were sent to spoil, pamper, and dress me for the function.

I was treated like the queen of the castle the whole day.

I'm so busy gawking at my reflection in the full-length mirror, that I don't recognize the woman staring back at me. My long curly hair, which no amount of spray could tame, is straight and flowing down my naked spine. The evening gown I'm wearing is a light purple, sheer corset dress. The intricate lace and silk hug my curves like a second skin, while the bottom flares into an A-line skirt with a high slit.

It took the three of them to get me into it without tearing it with one hard pull. But so, so worth it. I can't wait for Dash's reaction when he sees the deep V of the neckline. My breasts, held by two thin straps.

"That dress is perfect for the belle of the ball," sighs one of the girls, Ria, dreamily.

"You belong on a red carpet, sweetie," says Pia.

Mia, who is fussing with my hair, also chimes in, "Man, I wish you were a lesbian."

Yep. They all have rhyming names. The comical expression on my face had them chortling. I grin at Mia's remark, who flirted with me nonstop, because her comments were kinda flattering. She's such a cutie and if I had a friend who was into girls, I would totally set them up.

"Stop, you guys. It's all because of your magic hands," I say genuinely.

"Just imagine what else I can do with those hands," winks Mia while wiggling her fingers.

"You're incorrigible."

"Your loss, honey."

"Not denying it."

"Your husband is one lucky man."

"Tonight, he will be." I smirk and they howl in laughter. "Thank you, guys. This was the best day ever. I wish you all lived in my city. My friends would've loved you."

"We do travel for clients, actually."

"Really? My best friend is getting married soon. Would you be interested?"

"Hell yeah!"

"Perfect."

The pinging of my phone startles us and I grab it to see a text from Dash.

> DARLING HUSBAND: Are you ready, kitten?

Biting my lip, I turn to the mirror, snap a quick selfie in the mirror with a seductive smirk and send it to him. His reply is instant.

> DARLING HUSBAND: Fuck.

> DARLING HUSBAND: Do you want me to kill everyone at the party tonight?

> ME: So I guess I shouldn't tell you I'm not wearing any panties.

> DARLING HUSBAND: Are you trying to kill ME, wifey?

SCANDALOUS GAMES

> ME: You always fuck me at parties. So I'm making it easy, darling.

> DARLING HUSBAND: Keep dirty talking to me and we won't make it to the party on time. And when we do get there, I'll make you walk with my cum in your cunt and a vibrating plug in your ass.

My pussy quivers at his salacious threat and I clench my thighs to relieve the ache. I berate myself for stupidly playing with fire. His filthy mouth always leaves me soaked and speechless. All I can think about now is his cock piercing my pussy and ruthlessly pounding into me. The need to touch myself skyrockets my lust.

> DARLING HUSBAND: Dare to touch your pussy and I'll make your ass red.

Damn him. How did he know? Just then another text pings.

> DARLING HUSBAND: I'll be there in an hour.

I tell the girls about Dash's expected arrival and they spend the next hour doing last-minute touches before they leave with a hug and goodbye and a promise to see each other again. I'm alone for less than two minutes when I hear the chime of the elevator and determined footsteps walking down the hallway.

My pulse pounds in my throat and with his threat still running through my veins, my pussy clenches in desperation. My skin feels like it's on flames and my heart stops when he rounds the corner. His black tux molds to his muscular physique perfectly and his chiseled face that God carved from stone is dark and stormy with carnal intent.

Tongue tied, no sound comes out as he slowly takes a step. His piercing eyes send shivers down my spine as they possessively run all over me. I don't even finish admiring him before I'm inching back as he stalks closer. He continues the predatory dance until I'm pinned between the wall and his towering frame.

"Oh god!" I cry out when he thrusts one finger in my pussy without any warning.

"Fucking drenched." He slides another in while his thumb rubs circles on my clit. "Is this what you wanted, wife? Needed this eager little hole filled?"

"Yes. Don't stop."

"Never."

I clutch his shoulder as a tremor racks my body and the ache heightens to a familiar peak before I fall toward ecstasy. Moaning and panting, I ride his fingers desperately. My pussy, seeking a friction only his fingers can give.

"I'm fucking your ass tonight for giving me a hard-on in front of my staff." Thrusting faster and harder, he commands, "Now come on my fingers."

Two savage thrusts, a pinch to my sensitive clit, and I shatter on a silent scream. The climax is so powerful that I shudder again. Dash bends and his teeth latch onto where my neck and collarbone meet, and he bites. *Hard.*

Marking me.

Possessing me.

Owning me.

My body feels lightweight as he slowly pulls out his fingers. He traces my folds once more before bringing his fingers to his mouth and licking off my juices. The act is so hot and erotic, especially when his eyes become hooded and primal with lust.

"Keep staring at me like that, kitten, and your dress will be a torn heap on the floor."

"We're not ditching the gala," I defiantly say, and his lips curve to the side. "Besides, Justin would hate me if I kept his best friend away."

His eyes flash with jealousy at the mention of his best friend's name. "I'm afraid his best friend title is up for debate."

"Why?"

"He tried to steal you from me."

I roll my eyes. "He did not."

"He flirted with you."

"Pretended."

Dash's broad shoulders roll in a shrug. "Pretend or not, no one but me gets to touch you. So if he knows what's good for him, he'll keep his distance from you."

"Look at it this way. If he hadn't, you'd still be keeping me at arm's length. So maybe forgive him this time."

"I would've said yes."

"You do know you're stubborn, right?" I taunt playfully.

"So are you, kitten. You wouldn't have given up until I said yes."

"True."

Shaking his head in amusement, he wraps my hand in his and growls, "We are late again because of you, wifey."

He chuckles when I smack his chest and call him a lying jerk. It was entirely his fault.

As promised, a shiny black limousine is waiting for us. The driver nods and we slide into the back seat. The ride begins and as I gaze out the window while watching the streets fly by, the weight of my past lifts off my shoulders. All I feel is bone-deep happiness. With each new memory I create with Dash, the old sad ones disintegrate.

I glance at my husband and notice that he's deep in thought. He's staring out the window on his own side while his thumb caresses his jaw absentmindedly. Our thighs touch as he leaves no space between us. Pressing even closer, I rest my head

SCANDALOUS GAMES

on his shoulder and when he kisses my forehead, I thank the angels for sending him to me again.

Maybe, it takes being heartbroken once to meet the one we truly deserve.

Just like weathering a storm before we reach the peaceful high.

If only I knew that a storm is yet to come.

When we arrive at the seven-star hotel hosting the charity function, Dash orders the driver to take the back entrance so we don't have to go through the sea of flashing cameras. My protest that I can handle it goes unheard and shushed with a hard kiss.

Inside, though, I'm grateful.

Spotlights are not my thing and never will be.

The party is in full swing as we enter the ballroom and instantly, we are swarmed by people wanting to meet and converse with Dash. Some congratulating us on our recent nuptials making the headlines while few discuss business. Dash is polite as he makes small talk and I love when he pulls me into the conversation, genuinely interested in what I have to say.

The names and faces all blur as time passes. I thought I'd be bored but hearing everyone praise Dash for his efforts and the difference he's made over the years in so many lives fills me with pride.

"Hey, beautiful," a familiar flirty voice drawls. "Long time no see."

"She's my wife, you dickhead," growls Dash. "Go find someone else to call beautiful."

"Dash," I scold.

"Shame you couldn't teach him manners, Bianca."

"You aren't so innocent either."

Justin's smile falls while Dash smirks and hides his chuckle in my shoulder.

"Hey! I'm the reason you're both together," Justin says. "Don't hate on the Cupid."

"Seriously. People need to stop taking credit for us being together."

"Who else said it, kitten?"

"Rosa."

Both men freeze in shock. Their eyes widening in disbelief at her name, and it is hilarious. They look at each other before Justin asks, "Are you sure you're not confusing her with Iris?"

"Rosa can be soft, okay."

"Whatever you say, kitten," Dash drawls but I know they don't believe me.

Before I can fire back with a response, someone interrupts our private circle. The man looks at Dash and informs, "The organizer wants you in the back, sir. Please come with me."

Instead of answering, he faces me. "Will you be okay?"

"Of course. I have Justin to keep me company."

"I'll be back soon." Kissing me once, he follows the guy and disappears down the hall.

"Want to have a drink, beautiful?" asks Justin.

"Yes, please."

He offers his arm like a gentleman and I rest my hand in the crook as he guides me to the bar and teases, "So, you two, huh? When did that happen?"

"What can I say? I'm irresistible." I smirk. "And he's a catch."

He laughs boisterously and the sound draws the attention of a group of girls who trail their gazes over him in admiration. Justin winks when he notices and they giggle. I sit on the high stool while he orders our drinks. I'm impressed when he remembers my choice.

"Resisting you was never the issue, beautiful. You and him were a long time coming."

Dash had mentioned something similar and it makes me pause. "Did you know he liked me back then?"

"Like?" he scoffs. "The man was obsessed with you, Bianca. I'm surprised he didn't just steal you away."

Justin says it so casually as he takes a sip from his drink, that it escapes his notice how I freeze at the tidbit he shared. The word *obsession* rings in my ear and a strange feeling courses through my brain. The more I think, the more little snippets come to the forefront.

I've been in love with Bianca for as long as I can remember.

Though it took her a while to finally see me and confess she feels the same.

You may never give your heart to me but I won't let anyone else have it either.

Could it be that Dash behaved that way on purpose? Antagonize us so that he could ruin my relationship with Niall?

No. It can't be. I'm being absurd. It's probably just my old habits resurfacing, sabotaging every good thing that's happening in my life. The same old fears and wounds, holding me back from being happy and trusting.

"Bianca?"

"Yeah?" I blink back to reality at Justin's pinched voice.

"You all right?"

I push the ludicrous thoughts away and grin at him. "Of course. I just thought Dash had a small crush on me."

"It was always more. I don't think he realized until you left." Turning serious, he genuinely confesses, "He has spent his whole life believing he can't be loved. So, I'm happy he found you."

A man interrupts us before I can reply and notice that it's Justin's colleague. The air feels suffocating all of a sudden and I don't understand it. So while they talk, I make an excuse. "I'm going to the ladies' room."

Then I ran.

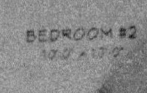

Chapter Fifty-nine

BIANCA

There's always a moment in your life—an intuition. An inkling. A premonition—when we realize our worst fear is winning. It's the same feeling running through me right now.

It's drowning me.

Clutching me.

Crushing me.

And we know what they say... Intuition is like a guardian angel. Yet mine feels like the devil perched on my shoulder. Justin's words have left an unsettling sentiment in my chest. I'm unable to shake it off, overthinking every memory. Every interaction. *Everything*.

Dash always had an air of darkness about him. The intensity and ruthlessness, screaming he didn't let anything stand in his way if he desired something. *Someone*. When he had confessed the same that day in Paris, I thought it was a harmless crush. Attraction. Lust at first sight.

But it was more. Deeper. *Darker*.

The one moment that sticks out the most as I replay that night is the lack of surprise on his face when I knocked on his bedroom door. He didn't look shocked to see me.

Almost like he was waiting.

Or is my mind playing tricks on me? I'm concocting a manipulative tale for no reason. I shake my head. I think being in this city again is fucking with my head. Since yesterday, Dash and I were inseparable and when it's just us, I forget the world around us.

Gazing at my reflection in the mirror, I force myself to let go of the incessant doubts. I'm letting Niall's hatred for his stepbrother cloud my judgment of the man who has been nothing but my protector—my possessive and mischievous beast of a husband.

I'm not going to let my fears win. Not again.

Giving myself a once-over, I wash my hands and walk out the bathroom in search of Dash. Hopefully, he's free by now and even if he isn't, I'd rather stay by his side.

Justin is nowhere near the bar where I left him when I enter the ballroom. Fuck. I was going to ask him because I don't even remember which direction Dash went. Pulling out my phone from the small bling clutch I'm carrying, I decide to call Dash. It goes straight to voicemail, so I decide to text him.

I'm typing away without watching where I'm going when a sweet voice calls my name, one I haven't heard in ages but still remember like it was yesterday.

"Bianca."

Whirling around, I collide with none other than Niall's mom. I'm beyond shocked to see her here even though I shouldn't be. After all, she is Dash's stepmother, but I didn't think he was in touch with her or that she was invited.

"Seema Aunty?" My voice is small when I speak.

Seems like the years that's gone by haven't been kind to her because she appears older than her age, even though her beauty hasn't vanished. Seema Singh has always been a stunning woman, especially in the beautiful sari she's wearing tonight. However, there is sadness and a vivid pain in her eyes that pinches my heart. She glares at me, the warmth she once held for me now missing.

"So you do remember me," she sneers, and I'm taken aback by the cutting tone filled with hostility and hatred.

Is she mad at me for breaking up with her son? It's the only explanation I can come up with. I bet he never told her he cheated on me. Glancing around nervously, I wait for Niall to pop up out of thin air with that cocky smile of his.

"Of course, Aunty," I say politely. I'm honestly quite surprised that I had enough strength to maintain my composure. "It's been years. How have you been?"

"You really have some nerve to return here, little girl."

"Excuse me?"

Ignoring me, she continues in the same tone while staring daggers at my wedding ring. "I had to see for myself if you did marry that bastard who thinks throwing money will rid him of his sins."

I take a threatening step forward and warn, "I suggest you watch your tone when you talk about my husband, Aunty."

"Husband?" She just laughs manically. "He finally made you his, like he always wanted. Actually, you two belong together. You never deserved my son anyways."

"I'm undeserving?" I shake my head sadly and years' worth of anger, pain, and

SCANDALOUS GAMES

betrayal comes boiling out, tipping me over the edge. "Do you even know what he did? I loved him and he cheated on me. And he didn't even have the decency to apologize."

Eyes widening in disbelief for a second, she stumbles back and whispers ominously. "You don't know?"

Her voice is so low I almost don't hear it.

"Know what?"

My confused question snaps her out of the temporary haze and her features harden. When she speaks, her eyes tear up while her voice is a mixture of raw agony and malice. "Your husband killed my son."

A silent deafening roar echoes in my ears at the revelation.

Killed my son.

Killed Niall.

Dash killed Niall.

"Niall? Wha... No."

The room disappears as if the earth was yanked beneath me. It's like someone pushed me into a pitch-black well with no way to climb out. My breath freezes in my throat as panic and shock cuts off the oxygen to my lungs. Niall's mom cruelly continues, ripping me open until I'm sinking in her pain.

A loss I can't even imagine.

A death she blames me for.

Just like that, all the resentment and anger I carried for Niall vanishes until I'm left with a hollowness in my heart. Until one single truth remains.

I gave my soul to a liar. A traitor. Maybe this is what I deserve. My karma for deceiving my family. I thought I was fooling the entire world but the biggest player turned out to be Dash.

"You're no better than your husband because you were the reason he was even out that night, chasing after you. You say you loved my Niall yet not once did you bother to reach out to him over the years. Shame on you for accusing him of cheating. That boy loved you more than anything."

Tears stream down my face while she raises her voice, drawing hundreds of eyes on us.

"I'm s-so sorry," I apologize brokenly. Nevermind the fact that I remember with clarity what I saw. She's right. I should've called. Checked. Been stronger.

And Dash.

His betrayal kills me the most. He fucking knew all this time and god, I let him into my life. My body. *My heart.*

Oh, how he played me for a fool. Everything falls into place. The fact that he never discusses his past, especially what happened to Niall. How could he hide that? A heartbreaking sob breaks past my lips and I swallow the broken whimper.

"Your husband kills everyone he touches. First his mom and then my son." I look through blurry eyes while listening to her deliver blow after blow. It hits me like a thunderstorm that she doesn't even utter Dash's name. "He didn't even spare his father. Now you already know he's a killer and a liar, save yourself before he kills you too.."

Shoving my shoulder, she walks past me. Someone clicks my picture from my right and I run with my dignity on the floor and my heart shattered once more. Not shattered.

Killed.

Stabbed.

Left to bleed.

But I'm not running away like a coward. Mustering what little strength I possess, I go search for him. I find the event planner in the hallway and stalk toward her.

"Where is Mr. Stern?"

She startles at my rough voice, her gaze nervous when they see my tear-stained face. "Ma'am. No one is allowed back here."

"I said. Where. Is. Dash?"

She flinches and stammers, pointing to her left. "He's upstairs. In Room 101."

My anger rises with every step and during the elevator ride. It's a welcoming emotion compared to the searing pain of heartbreak and betrayal. I can't allow myself to break and crumble right now. He doesn't deserve my tears.

He never deserved *my love.*

Loud, angry voices greet me when I land on the right floor and I follow the sound, recognizing one of them as Justin's. Each inch closer is like I'm marching to my own doom. My gait falters at the fact that I not only got played by one but two men. Justin lied to my face too, acting like a friend when he's just as guilty.

"Why the fuck haven't you told her the truth?" I halt right outside at Justin's sharp tone. "She deserves to know."

"You don't think I know that? That I haven't tried to confess?" Dash sounds pained, but not enough to douse the fire in my veins. He's an actor. A manipulator. A fucking liar.

"Oh, come on, Dash. You bloody live with her, so don't bullshit me." Lowering his voice, he solemnly says, "She is in love with you and you're betraying her, man."

"I didn't think she ever would." Dash huffs a humorless laugh. The sound, like a brick to my chest. "I thought I could get her out of my system, sate my obsession and walk away. I should've known she'll bury herself deeper."

My vision blurs just as a sob rises to my throat. I slap my palm on my mouth to cover the sound.

"Then tell her the truth."

"I will."

"If you truly care for her, then you'll tell her Niall is gone and that you broke them up by setting him up so she would catch him cheating."

No. No. No. I stumble, clutching the wall as another wave of anguish unfurls in my stomach. He wouldn't do that. Dash can't be that vicious and cruel. But his rough shout digs the knife harder and deeper into my back. I bleed until I'm numb.

"I can't lose her. She won't forgive me."

I rub the tears away and straighten.

"No, I won't."

The men freeze as I stagger into the room. Dash's terrified and guilty eyes collide with mine. When he sees the haunted look on my face and tears of betrayal,

SCANDALOUS GAMES

twisted agony darkens his sharp angles. Somehow, he realizes I heard everything and he takes a step forward, his arm reaching for me. "Kitten."

"What did you do?"

"Please, kitten. I was going to tell you."

"What did you do!?" I yell.

Chapter Sixty

DASH

(SEVEN YEARS AGO)

Love really turns people blind.
The prime example of that notion sits in front of me when I come downstairs and I'm met with the sight of the clinging couple. Niall and Bianca. Still together.

My hand balls into a fist as she sits on his lap with her melodic laugh spilling in the room while he kisses and nips all over her delicate neck. Since I'm a glutton for punishment, I stare at the reverence in her pupils as she runs her finger over his jaw with a shy smile. I also watch him. The way he possessively gazes at and holds her. The arrogance on his face as he knows he has everything he could ever want. Perfect family. Perfect friends. Perfect girlfriend.

I'm not the least bit surprised by Bianca, not after I watched her pretend like nothing ever happened. The fact that she almost got raped outside the club because her boyfriend forgot about her. No, like a goddamn lovesick fool with a warped sense of loyalty, she had invited him back into her arms the next morning.

Why the fuck do I care if she still wants him?

And how many times do I have to remind myself that it's none of my business? She must really be desperate for love if she's continuing to date my scumbag of a stepbrother. She will soon learn that having the biggest heart is the worst weakness,

SCANDALOUS GAMES

and soon... her biggest mistake.

I got distracted by her soft beauty and was caught in her web for a second. But it's time I snatch what Niall values the most—Bianca.

My stepbrother only cares about two things: his reputation and his possessions. If anyone threatens either, he lashes out. And I plan to use the same weakness against him. Over the weeks, I've slowly and passively planted the seed that I desire Bianca. It helps that she always fucking blushes in my presence and despite how hard she tries, her eyes always stray to mine when I'm in the same room.

Especially after I saved her the other night.

In his jealousy-induced brain, Niall mistakes it for a crush on her side when it is anything but. He's so stupid he doesn't realize she is devoted to him.

He doesn't notice my presence but her dark brown gaze collides with mine and she sucks in a sharp breath, freezing on his lap. They begin to move down my naked chest but snap back up when she realizes the involuntary action.

Our eyes lock as though an invisible thread tethers us.

I just know she's thinking of the scene in the club when she watched me deep throat a random girl. I almost smile when I recall what she did after.

Our connection breaks when there's a loud slamming of the door and my best friend, Justin, rounds the corner. Niall's head snaps in his direction and his eyes turn into slits. He hates his guts just as much as he hates mine. Solely on the fact that we are close.

Justin ignores his glare and meets me in the kitchen, making Niall's head turn and notice my presence. His eyes narrow in comical rage at my half-naked state in front of his girlfriend, who looks anywhere but at me. Just to fuck with him, I run my gaze over her languidly, purposely spending a little too long on her tits.

I smirk before listening to Justin.

"When the fuck is he going to remove the stick up his ass?"

"When the sun stops shining."

"So... never."

I pull out a mug from the top shelf and pour myself a cup of coffee before offering one to Justin. The lovey-dovey couple stays bickering on the couch. As I lean against the counter facing them, I sip the black liquid while my attention drifts to her.

Like a moth to a flame.

Except, she will be the one getting burned.

"Shit. You want her."

I go still for a moment but casually deny it. "No. I don't."

"So you wouldn't mind if I have a go at her?"

"Breathe in her direction and I'll snap your neck."

I curse inwardly when the bastard laughs and slaps me on the shoulder. "Stop drooling over your brother's girl. It won't end well."

"She won't be his for long."

His brows draw together in suspicion. "Whatever it is. Don't fucking do it, Stern."

Mood sour, I throw the rest of my coffee in the sink and ignore his warning.

My mind is already made up. I'll probably be doing her a favor. "Is the party still on?"

"Obviously."

"Invite Niall."

"The fuck. Why?" His lips pull in disgust as he flicks his gaze to Niall.

"Just do it."

"Whatever. The asshole probably won't even come."

Oh, he will, and he'll show up with Bianca to flaunt her in my face. It'd be the last time he ever does, though.

An hour after the party is in full swing, they arrive and I smirk. Bianca looks nervous and apprehensive like she'd rather be anywhere else. The tight-as-fuck purple dress she's wearing molds to her ample curves enticingly. I run my tongue between my teeth as I realize it barely reaches the tops of her thighs and slides up even higher as she walks.

The urge to shove Niall's arm from her ass rises to the forefront of my vision and turns it black with red-hot jealousy. I gulp the rest of my whiskey down and slam the glass on the bartop. If I let my desire for the siren of a woman cloud my judgment, I won't be able to go through with tonight.

I never claimed to be a good man. And I won't start now.

Maybe once it's all over and she's no longer in love with Niall, I'll make her mine.

I already know what she likes, her favorite food and movies. I also know she's clumsy, loves to talk, funny, and she intrigues me like no other. Because of her, I spend my weekends at home just to catch a glimpse of her rather than traveling, which I love. Because of her, I don't hate the city as much as I used to.

So maybe I'm doing it more for selfish reasons.

The corner I'm standing in gives me a full view of the room, the mass of sweaty bodies on the dance floor, some playing pool in the corner. Niall runs into his friends, slapping their backs and laughing with them while oblivious that Bianca is uncomfortable, even as she smiles.

Seriously, what does she see in him?

"So, is that the guy you want me to fuck?" hums Justin's friend, Teresa, sizing Niall up and down with a heated gleam in her eyes.

"Seduce. Not fuck," I clarify. "Long enough until the girl with him sees you two together."

Teresa is always looking for a good time, especially if it'll ruin someone else's night. I met her through Justin, who she hooks up with when he wants to blow off some steam while she does it in the hopes of dating him. The whole town knows he's the heir to the Merchant legacy and the next CEO of his family's real estate company.

SCANDALOUS GAMES

So it didn't take much convincing after I told Teresa that Niall is a trust fund kid and will have his own company—my father's—to run one day. After she heard this, she was all game.

"You're an evil man, Dash," she muses seductively while running one finger down my chest. "Breaking that poor girl's heart. You want to steal her from him?"

I push her hand away from my chest and dryly reply, "How about you stick to your business?"

"Fine."

"Take him in one of the rooms upstairs once he's away from her."

She flicks her hair back and retorts, "I know the drill."

Shaking my head, I watch her strut her way to Niall and his friend's little group and introduce herself. My stepbrother secretly leers at her ass before roaming to her face. I curse his stupidity for ignoring the beautiful girl he's lucky to have and chasing after another pussy. In this room, Bianca outshines everyone. No other woman holds a candle to her innocence.

If she were mine, she would become my entire world. Until her, I didn't realize how much I craved to have just that.

The night goes on and it isn't long before Niall ghosts Bianca. Yet again.

Instead of moving from my spot, I observe her. She's standing in the crowd, small eyes scanning the dark room while worrying her bottom lip. A tempting and innocent little bait if there ever was one.

My phone vibrates in my pocket, so I pull it out and read the text.

> TERESA: Show time.

> ME: You have 15 fifteen minutes.

> TERESA: Only need five. *wink emoji* Looks like we'll be doing that girl a favor after all. Because guess who invited me to the room. Hint... Not me.

Fuck. Does this mean he's cheated on Bianca more than once? A flicker of guilt inserts into my psyche but I shove it down. Pocketing my phone, I focus on my obsession just as another guy approaches her. Jaw clenching, I push through the crowd and stop right behind her. She shivers while tilting her head to the side, sensing my presence.

"Scram," I growl at the little shit.

He scatters away after one look at my face. Bianca twirls around and lifts her chin defiantly. Crossing her arms that push her full tits together, she taunts, "Stalking much?"

I fight the urge to smile and stay quiet.

"Why can't you leave me alone?" she grumbles in annoyance.

"That seems more of your boyfriend's thing, kitten."

"He went to get me a drink."

"You're a terrible liar."

Her face goes beet red and my dick hardens, imaging the same color while she chokes on my shaft.

"He—he'll be back," she stammers.

I lean down as she swallows and hover my mouth against her ear, inhaling her scent. When she sharply inhales, I ache to bite into her skin. Instead, I taunt, "Or maybe he likes to sneak away too."

She shoves me back at my insinuation and angrily growls, "He would never."

"Why? Has he finally fucked you, kitten?"

Doubt creeps in just as an embarrassed flush appears, giving me my answer. With a smirk, I turn around and walk away. And when I look back, she's already halfway up the stairs.

Come morning, my stepbrother will finally learn life is neither fair nor perfect.

And Bianca... she will remember me as her savior when I've always been the villain.

Ten minutes later, when I slide behind the wheel ready to leave, there's a text on my phone. Attached to it is a photo of a hurt Bianca standing in the doorway. I throw my phone, unable to stare at her crying face.

The sense of victory I expected never comes and I drive away.

It's almost after an hour that there's a knock on my bedroom door and I jerk it open, coming to a halt.

"Bianca."

Chapter Sixty-one

BIANCA

My heart thumps in my throat every time I open a room in the hallway upstairs and they come empty or already occupied. Dash's parting taunt replays in my head and I hate letting him get to me.

Niall would never cheat. Just last week, he said he loved me and apologized for being a shitty boyfriend. We went on a date and spent the whole week at my apartment since Rosa went home. It was perfect.

It has to be another one of Dash's sick games. I saw the disappointment on his face when he found Niall and me together after the night of the club. This is his way of getting back at me.

Damn it. What am I doing?

I pause my hand on the last door open and intend on going back downstairs. I wouldn't insult Niall for a single moment of doubt. Lowering my fingers, I back away and turn.

"Fuck yeah. Spread those legs, baby."

I freeze in the dark hallway. It's none other than Niall's rough groan. For a second, I believe I'm hallucinating when he grunts again. I would recognize that voice anywhere. Everything happens in slow motion.

With shaking fingers, I shove the door and it makes a creaking noise, just like in horror movies. The sight that greets me is much worse. Nightmarish.

They don't notice my presence. Or the sound of my heart breaking into pieces. Their moans as Niall fucks some random girl from behind are like cries of a witch; scratching and bleeding me.

Tears sting my eyes and I can't hold them back. When the initial shock wears off, I slam the door against the wall and yell, "You asshole."

My boyfriend's—*ex-boyfriend*—head snaps at the loud bang and his eyes widen into saucers when they clash with mine. The girl moans about why he stopped while he blinks rapidly, expecting me to disappear.

"Bianca… baby," he softly says, still inside her. She finally turns and makes no attempt to shove him off. She isn't even regretting it and shrugs. I flick my gaze back to him and point in his direction.

"We're over."

I run and the tears I was holding back by a thread fall until I'm numb. Someone calls my name when I push through the bodies downstairs but I keep running, desperate to get away from here. Anywhere.

As if God recognizes my pain, electricity cackles in the sky and it begins to rain. And it's not soft and slow. It's lashing like a thunderstorm.

In an instant, I'm drenched. My hands shake around my phone as I book a cab. I don't remember how long I stand shivering and soaking outside in the cold night until it arrives and I'm sliding into the back seat. I can't remember telling the cab driver my address or how I ended up at Dash's place, until I'm knocking at his bedroom door.

"Bianca."

My blurry gaze collides with his handsome face as his lock on my tear-stained face. They stopped falling sometime during the ride. My eyelids close for a second as the image of Niall and the girl fills my vision and I know it will forever haunt me.

Suddenly, my anger returns full force. I gave him everything and he threw it all in my face. If he thinks I'm going to forgive him and cry, he's dead wrong.

"Bianca."

Awareness sinks in that I'm standing in a wet dress outside the room of my ex-boyfriend's mortal enemy. He's half naked and his black sweatpants hang low on his hips with that infamous V on display. His stormy eyes don't soften, but grow darker and intense. That granite jaw of his clenches the longer I stay mute and my heart palpitates.

I really look at him, absorbing every single little detail, and give my body free rein to admire the expanse of his chest and eight-pack abs. Dash is all man with the broodiness and violence. All sharp angles and chiseled features. And I hate it even as shivers race down my skin, not from cold but him.

The bane of my existence.

His goddamn words came true.

And I just want to erase everything that's happened tonight. I want to feel desired. Wanted. Loved. Even if it's just for a night and by a man I should despise but can't.

"Why are you here?" he literally growls.

He goes absolutely still when I press myself against his hard body. Apart from

SCANDALOUS GAMES

the thundering of our hearts and the rain pelting outside, the air is silent. His abs tighten when I softly graze the muscles with my fingertips and rise on my toes to kiss his neck. The silence stretches as seconds pass and he doesn't react. He doesn't even touch me.

Am I that undesirable?

Is there something wrong with me?

The tears return and I push off him, backing away. An involuntary sob spills off my lips and I whisper, "I-I'm s-sorry."

I turn, only to be pulled back into a pair of strong arms. One hand wraps me in an embrace while the other tucks my head against a steady heartbeat. Ugly sobs keep coming as I cry and he doesn't say a word, only holds me through it all, even as my tears soak him.

When the pain turns to a low throb, I meet his powerful gaze watching me tenderly. But I also need his hate, his angst that he reserves for me.

"Do you want me?" I demand, my voice low.

His fingers in my hair tighten and he grits, "Bianca."

"Because I want you to be my first."

"Bianca," he sighs, letting me go, and runs his fingers through his hair. "I don't deserve it. Don't deserve you."

"No, you don't. But I'm giving it to you anyway."

His chest heaves like he's fighting for the control he's losing. But when his resolve doesn't crumble and he shakes his head, rejection stings me once again. "Go away."

I flinch and stark pain flashes across his face. With a curse, he yanks me into his arms once more. I wrap my legs around his waist as he picks me up and slams my back against the wall. "You don't know what you're asking for, kitten. Because I'll want everything. Every first."

Nothing left to lose, I sell my soul to the sinful devil.

"Make love to me," I rasp, resting my forehead on his. "*Please.*"

My plea has his eyes dropping to my lips and when he leans forward, I turn my head away. "No kissing."

He freezes but then I feel his fingers push my hair away from my face and turn my cheek to him. He whispers softly, "Okay."

Lowering me to my feet and without breaking our connection, his hand finds the zipper on the side of my dress. My chest caves when he slowly lowers it and even though he's already seen me almost naked, this moment feels different. Once my dress and heels are gone and I stand bare before him, his gaze drops like he can't resist.

They caress the tops of my breasts, my nipples that harden more under his attention, and stop between my thighs on my soaked panties. The urge to hide myself ignites but with one shake of his head, I clench my fingers on my sides.

"You're too beautiful." His voice is guttural while his features turn primal. "Every inch of you."

Picking me up, he carries me toward his bed before laying me on my back. Every thought evaporates as I lean on my elbows and watch him push his sweatpants down until there's nothing separating us.

My eyelashes flutter when he kneels and I gasp, feeling his palms graze my legs and trace upward. The simple touch makes me delirious and I hate how right it feels. It confuses me. I bite my lip when his fingers reach my waist and curl into my panties, pulling them until I'm completely naked.

My pussy was now on display for the forbidden man. I close my eyes, unable to handle the hunger in his eyes as they stare at me.

"No. You don't get to hide, kitten." He growls darkly. "Look at me."

I shake my head, tightening my eyelids. My back arches when I feel his lips lay a soft kiss on my inner thigh and repeat the same gesture to the other side. He leaves no part of me untasted, soft kisses marking me until his breath flutters on my folds.

I hate how wet I am for him.

"Hide all you want, Bianca," he rasps before promising, "but my name will be the only and last thought in your head long after I've claimed you."

Without warning, he runs his tongue through my slit, parting my lips so he can lick between them. Deeper. Hungrier. My eyes fly open on a pleasurable moan.

Rough hands push and hold my hips down when I try to get away from the arousing sensations. He tastes me gently and reverently, like he has all the time in the world. Flicking my clit, he wraps his lips on my rosebud and sucks softly.

"Ahh..." I gasp as he slides one thick finger to the knuckle.

He stops pushing when he feels my barrier and plays with my clit to distract me from the slight discomfort. Minutes pass as he works me until a low throb begins in my lower belly. The ache intensifies, and I clench around him. Two fingers become three, stretching me.

"Good girl," he praises. "Come for me. Ride my hand."

His dirty command sends me over the edge. It's more powerful than any orgasm I've ever had. Gentle hands cup my cheeks and push strands of hair away. When I blink my eyes open, Dash is leaning over me, his hard body enveloping mine in his warmth.

"Last chance, kitten."

"Don't stop," I whisper while he waits. He looks at me the exact way I've desperately ached for Niall to do. It pains me that another man is giving me the things I yearned for.

His arm reaches into the side drawer and he sheathes himself in a condom. I grab the nape of his neck while he spreads my legs by cupping the back of my knee. My lips part when the crown of his cock rubs against my clit. His jaw hardens when he feels me become slick even more. Sliding his hand between our bodies, he runs his cockhead over my folds. Once. Twice. *Thrice.*

My nipples scrape against his chest as I dig my nails into his skin and scratch his back, silently begging him to end the agony. An empty ache builds in my core and I need him inside me.

"Please."

"Say my name."

I shake my head and he circles my entrance teasingly. "I hate you."

"Say. My. Name, Bianca," he demands in a deep voice.

SCANDALOUS GAMES

A tear slips as I whisper, "Dash."

He pushes inside and immediately, my body resists but he's patient and plays with my clit until I relax. Slowly, he enters me and the feeling is strange and exhilarating at once. The slight burn only intensifying the feel of having him inside.

When he hits against the barrier, I murmur, "Dash."

"You feel so good, kitten." His voice strained.

His cock throbbing inside my walls and I can't help but clench.

Pulling out until only the tip is inside, he thrusts inside but doesn't stop until he pierces through my virginity in one deep thrust. I scream, feeling like I'm being ripped apart. It hurts so much. Soft kisses over my face pull me out of the haze of pain and I realize Dash has stilled inside, letting me adjust to his size.

"Breathe for me, kitten."

"Dash."

"Good girl," he rasps. "The worst is over. Tell me when to move."

His head dips as he tastes and peppers kisses over my skin that's raised with goosebumps. His mouth, such a contrast to the slowly ebbing pain. I arch my back when his tongue flicks my nipple and I grab his hair, pressing his lips harder against me.

But he's having none of it.

He sucks and pulls on my nub with his lips softly and teasingly. Tingles spread all over my body when his greedy fingers explore my curves possessively.

"Please move, Dash. I need... more."

Wild eyes clash with mine and I feel his dick lengthen even more. I clench and he groans and rolls his hips so his groin leaves a delicious friction against my clit. He pulls out gently while watching my every reaction on my face. If I wince, he pauses and kisses my neck, the tops of my breasts until I sigh in pleasure. Then he enters me slowly.

"Ahh... yes."

"So goddam tight." He punctuates his words with another deep and slow thrust.

Love. He's making love to me, claiming and erasing the bad memories until his name is all I can think of. Just like he promised.

"Let me kiss you, kitten," he begs, his eyes latching on to my lips.

"No."

His arm reaches above my head to grab the headboard and he gives another tortuously slow plunge. The corded muscles of his arm tightening like he's fighting for control. I moan in pleasure, an ache rising in my belly and he does it again. My toes curl as I raise my hips to meet his with every downward thrust.

"Scream my name, Bianca."

"Dash!"

"Who's inside your wet cunt?"

"Dash."

Letting go of the headboard, his weight presses against mine and I wrap my legs around his waist, pulling him deeper. His thrusts become gentle and circling my neck, he demands, "Who's making love to you?"

"*You.*"

SIMRAN

Our breathing turns harsher and when he thumbs my clit without mercy, I shatter around him and he follows shortly after with a loud groan. His muscles flex when I try to push him off and his head rises from the crook of my neck.

"What are you doing, kitten?"

"Leaving."

"It's raining heavily."

"I don't care. I'll find another cab," I growl. "Move."

In a flash, he wrenches my arms above my head, locking my wrists in one of his, and declares, "You're not going anywhere."

"Unless you're planning to fuck me again, I'm not fucking staying."

Darkness swarms his features and my belly flips. The Dash I know all too well returns with a vengeance. Smirking, he taunts, "I don't fuck the same pussy twice. So you have two choices. You listen like a good girl and stay, or I fuck your virgin ass."

He holds my defiant stare arrogantly, expecting me to choose the first. I call his bluff.

"Do it." His smirk falters for a fraction of a second. "Fuck my ass, Dash. You had my virginity. Might as well steal another."

I smile in victory when he lets my arm go and slides off the bed to stand at the edge. I only get to bask in my satisfaction before he flips me onto my stomach and slaps my ass. A stark contrast. As if he's still expecting me to back down. When I don't, he growls.

"As you wish, kitten."

Shivers dance down my spine while my sore pussy becomes drenched at the anticipation of feeling him in my ass. Because damn him, I want it. I crave him. And he knows it.

A gasp spills from my lips when he yanks me to the edge and tilts my hips up. The move has my breasts pressing against the sheet and my ass and pussy on display. I don't turn to peer at him, afraid he'll witness the lust in my eyes.

"Last chance," he repeats again.

"Fuck me, Dash."

His breath teases my folds, wet with my juices and proof of my lost virginity.

He's not going to...

My thought goes incomplete before it is answered in one long lick. I buck against Dash's mouth as he eats my pussy, groaning like an animal tasting the proof of his ownership. My fingers fist the sheet below me as I grind against his tongue and fall apart.

And then I let him own me wholly.

Hours later, when I'm sated and spent, Dash murmurs in ear, "Stay here, kitten."

The second his footsteps disappear and the bathroom door slams shut, I leave everything behind without a goodbye.

I lock his memory in a dark corner of my heart.

Never to be touched again.

Chapter Sixty-two

DASH

I already know I'm going to find her gone when I return from the bathroom but it hurts nonetheless. Yet I don't understand why.

She can't mean so much to me in such a short time. Especially not in a few stolen moments.

The empty bed stares at me and I drop the cloth I brought to clean and take care of her. For a moment, I think of going after her but I stop the insane urge. Tonight has been hell for her and even though I should feel guilty for stealing her virginity after playing a part in her breakup, I'm unable to. Especially knowing Niall hasn't done this the first time.

He doesn't deserve her.

He never did.

So, I let her run away just this once. But one day, I'll make her mine. No matter the price.

The rain has turned into a light drizzle which eases some of the tension in my mind that Bianca will safely reach her apartment. I scan the lonely room that smells like her and lock eyes on her silk panties, which fell near the bed. Closing the gap, I bend and pick it up.

I would keep it as a souvenir but it's a reminder I claimed her under false pretenses. A better and stronger man would've resisted the magnetic draw of her innocence. But when she stood at my doorstep with her wet dress that hid nothing, no amount of power on this earth could've stopped me.

However, it was the sound of her broken sob and the hurt of rejection that made my black heart crack into pieces. The consuming need to take her pain away erased any protest on my part, along with the line between right and wrong.

With a sigh, I decide to throw her panties, when there's a loud crash downstairs. My head whips toward my door when it's followed by angry footsteps climbing the stairs.

Niall.

Took him long enough.

The first thing I notice when he appears in my doorway are his bloodshot eyes and the fact that his shirt is inside out. Probably left in a rush to chase after Bianca. He looks haggard and the worst I've ever seen. Maybe he did love her. Just not enough to respect and not cheat on her.

"Where is she?" he shouts.

Frantic eyes search my room and as he stumbles inside, he races over to shove open my bathroom door, as if he'll find her there. Disgust fills me when I realize he reeks of alcohol.

"Where. Is. She?"

"You just missed her, little brother," I drawl, lifting her discarded panties with my finger.

He zooms in on the little material and goes ramrod straight. His hands ball into fists while his entire face goes red with rage, and I smirk.

"No. She wouldn't betray me," he mumbles.

"She did. Twice."

I dodge his punch when he runs with his fist raised but the alcohol he consumed has made him slow and tipsy. When he tries another futile and juvenile attempt, I throw his back against the wall and punch his nose for good measure.

"I know you set the whole thing up, you prick," he growls, wiping the blood off his face.

"I'm not the one who put your dick inside another girl."

Infuriated by my answer, he points his finger at me. "I will win her back. Once I tell her the truth, we will be together again."

Is he fucking delusional? I almost pity the guy before curling my lip. "If she even believes you."

"I know why you did it," he snarls. "You always had your eye on her. Do you think removing me gives you a chance? Do you think you'll swoop in and be her hero? News flash, brother, she will never be yours 'cause you're the reason for her heartbreak. Once she learns you're no better than me and slept with her after knowingly sending her into that room, she won't talk to you, let alone see your face."

I flinch, because every word is the truth, but I still maintain my composure. "Then maybe you should've held on to the best thing that ever happened to you."

"You might have had her body, but her heart will always belong to me." Laughing maniacally, he taunts, "You'll only ever be the second option, Dash."

SCANDALOUS GAMES

I punch the wall when he's long gone.

The high I felt being inside Bianca has now been replaced with the low that comes later. As I'm sulking over Niall's words in the dark while gazing out the window, the ringing of my phone yanks me out of my musings.

Who the fuck is calling me in the middle of the night?

The second I read the name on the phone, an ominous voice screams inside my head that my life is about to fall into bloody shards.

"Seema Aunty," I greet Niall's mom, and I freeze, hearing a hiccup on the other side.

"Niall's been in an ac-accident, beta." She sobs before rapidly talking, "He's near your house. P-please go. Your father and I are on our way."

The phone call yanks the earth from beneath my feet and everything is a blur after that.

The bloody scene that greets me will be forever imprinted in my soul. Sirens and loud voices yelling at each other. However, my eyes are stuck on the unmoving figure laying on the ground and for the first time, I feel something other than hate and anger towards Niall.

Shame and remorse bring me to my knees.

Hands pull me back as I try to get closer and past the ringing in my head, I can't hear my own voice. I shout that he's my brother and somehow shove through the bodies.

"He's got a pulse," someone says.

Our parents arrive and a fresh wave of agony sets me on fire when I watch the one woman who treated me as her son cry when she sees Niall bleeding on the ground. His body is twisted unnaturally. And I just know, he was on his way to Bianca.

Fuck. What have I done?

When they carry him away in the ambulance, my father approaches me and asks in a lethal voice, "What did you do, boy?"

Kill everything I touch.

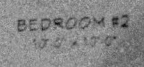

Chapter Sixty-three

BIANCA

(PRESENT)

Silence darkens the whole room.
Every detail about that awful night as I relive it through the eyes of the truth kills me bit by bit. A page of my life that got stuck but was unfurled today. Lives were set to be ruined seven years ago. All because of rivalry.

Hatred and envy.

Damaged souls.

Because of me.

Dash had betrayed me. Not once but *twice*. And I fell for his devious charm, his twisted manipulation each time. Suddenly, my mom's warning replays in my mind, taunting me. Despite it all, my heart still aches for him.

Just how sad is it?

"Niall is really dead?" I stammer over the beating of my heart. "So his mom wasn't lying?"

His eyebrows furrow in cold fear. "When did you meet her?"

"What does it matter?" I shout. "How could you hid this from me?"

"Because Niall isn't dead. He's in a coma," he says, and for the first time, I hear the pain in his voice. The guilt. The agony. The shocking revelation hits me like a ton of bricks. "The accident caused irreversible damage to his spinal cord. He hasn't

SCANDALOUS GAMES

woken up ever since."

"Oh god!" I cry, walking backward.

He comes closer, but one look from me and he stills. Tears glisten in his eyes as he watches me pull away from him. The sight of him twists and crushes my insides harder. "I'm so sorry, kitten. I didn't want you to find out like this. I swear I was going to tell you after tonight. You have to believe me."

"Believe you?" I laugh brokenly. He flinches at my sharp tone and when my tears escape, his arm reaches for me again. "God! You must have been laughing at me the whole time. I willingly let you in my life, my body, and worst of all, I gave you my heart. No wonder you fooled my parents and acted like the perfect husband."

"Don't. Everything was real, kitten."

"How could you? You could've just told me he was cheating on me. Why did you cruelly send me upstairs and let me see them together? Seven years, Dash. I spent seven fucking years with a broken heart, thinking I wasn't good enough to be loved, to be cared for. I stopped trusting people. Do you even know how lonely that feels? I bared my deepest fears to you."

"I know, kitten. I'm sorry."

Crossing the distance like he can't bear to stay away, he pulls me into his arms. I shake my head and hit his chest. Again and again. Sob after gut-wrenching sob. He takes every punch until I grow tired.

"You fucking broke me, Dash." I shove but his arms tighten. "Let. Me. Go."

"I can't." His tone broken. "Please forgive me, Bianca."

His arms drop when I shove hard and distance myself from him. "I never should've trusted you. I'll never forgive you for this, Dash. Never."

"Don't say that, kitten. Please. You're my world. I can't survive without you."

The words I longed to hear from him burn like a flaming rod against my chest. His pained eyes stare into mine lovingly, letting me feel the truth, but then again, he's always been a great actor.

"You don't hurt the ones you love, Dash," I angrily say. "You betrayed me, used and lied to me. I was never a person to you. Just a toy you wanted to snatch from your brother. You deserve to be alone."

He stills at my harsh words yet the longing in his light pupils doesn't diminish. They beg me to stay and when a tear slips down his cheek, something inside me shatters.

The wound in my heart is like a live wire.

"You love me, Bianca. Don't do this to us."

"I warned you, Dash," I whisper, repeating my words. "I'm incapable of loving anyone. Least of all you. How can I, when you're the one who made me stop believing in it?"

He staggers like I physically hit him and the raw guilt shadows his features. It slowly twisted into horror like his worst nightmare and fears came true. Wiping my tears, I leave him standing and run.

He shouts my name but I don't stop.

Why did I think coming to this city would be different this time? It will always be the place of my heartbreak. My scars. My ruination.

In my haste to get away, I didn't realize I ran toward the front exit where the media and the camera crew were waiting. I flinch when the first shutter goes off and I cover my eyes when thousands of flashes hit my tear-stained face.

Oh god.

Panic swells inside my chest and my breathing turns choppy as I try to evade them. It's like they are surrounding me from every direction. My heels break but before I can fall down the stairs at the entrance, two strong arms appear and yank me inside the threshold.

"Kick them all out. Now!" Dash barks. He tilts my face and demands in a raw voice, "Are you okay, kitten? Look at me, please."

"Don't touch me."

I slap his hands away, burning at the touch. He's the last person I want around me.

"Please let me get you out of here."

"No. Let me go."

"Never. You're still my wife, Bianca."

The photographers are still going strong. My mind warns me to stay quiet but when I hear him call me his wife, I lose my calm, and hurt and rage combine. How dare he still call me his?

"I'm your *fake* wife. The marriage was a sham, remember?" I shout. "None of it was real."

His fingers tighten when I hurl the words, and the same heartbreak I felt years ago mirrors in his eyes. We remain in a silent battle and it takes me a second to notice the crowd of partygoers have gathered around us. Their faces, shocked and horrified. I realize what I blurted out in a fit of anger and panic.

No. No. No. My head feels dizzy as my surroundings blur around me. My lungs cave, like they can't get enough air. Justin appears in my periphery and says in a low voice to Dash, "Let her go, Stern. I'll take her home."

"No," he growls, like he knows it's the last time he'll ever hold me.

"Look at her, she's seconds away from having a panic attack."

When he notices how I'm leaning my weight on him, my strength gone, worry shadows his features. I hear the reluctance and anxiety in his voice. "Okay. I'll be right behind you guys. Take her in my car. It's waiting in the back."

Justin nods and I'm shifted into the other man's arms as he soothingly whispers, "I've got you, beautiful."

I bury my face in his chest as he hugs me to his body, but I know the damage is already done. Now, everyone will know my shame. The treachery I did against my own family.

The fear is nothing compared to the pain in my heart.

The second we are alone in the back hallway, my breathing returns to normal—albeit slowly. The driver is waiting with the car. He opens the door and Justin helps me inside before sliding in himself. Numbness spreads in my bones and I just want to disappear. I can't stay here.

"I need to call someone," I whisper to Justin.

"Okay, beautiful."

SCANDALOUS GAMES

He passes his phone and I type Rosa's number. She picks up on the first ring.

"Hello?" her voice is rough and confused from sleep.

"It's Bee." I hiccup.

"Bee? Is everything okay? Whose number is this?"

"I need you, Ro."

"What happened? Are you hurt?" she rapidly fires. "Wait... why do you sound like you're crying?"

"I-I... It hurts, Ro."

"Talk to me. You're scaring me, Bee."

"Dash."

My voice trails off but she understands. "Pack your bags and text me the address. I'm coming to get you." In the background, I hear her shout at someone to fuel the jet her family owns. "Stay strong until I get there, Bee."

"Okay."

"I love you."

When I hang up the phone, Justin makes an attempt to speak, "Bianca—"

"Just take me to the airport," I cut him off. "I'll wait there."

With a sigh, he orders the driver to turn the car around and I gaze out the window. Loyal to his selfish best friend, he defends him and tries to explain.

"Whatever anger you feel at him right now, it is nothing compared to what he feels for himself to this day or the guilt he carries. He blames himself for not stopping a drunk Niall after he left his house, but tragedy waits for no one."

"I don't blame him for the accident. It was nobody's fault and I know if it was in his power, he would've done anything to save him," I murmur. "All he had to do was tell me the truth, Justin, and I would've forgiven him."

"Dash grew up in a dysfunctional home with a father who kept his emotions to himself and neglected him. When you've lived like that and someone comes along to fill the empty hole for the first time, you just want to hold on to that ray of light. You're that ray to him, Bianca." He pauses and I feel his eyes on me, but I don't look while crying silently. "You've both suffered enough. So don't sacrifice your future for the sins and mistakes of the past."

It's too late now.

It's over.

Chapter Sixty-four

BIANCA

During the flight, Rosa holds me in her arms in my tattered dress and ruined makeup while I spill everything to her. About the past. Tonight. Running into Niall's mom.

The news of his coma.

Dash's betrayal.

She cries along with me while murmuring apologies and assurances that everything will be all right. I tell her it isn't her fault but guilt is a heavy emotion. Once it latches itself on to you, it's hard to let go. Except, she has nothing to be sorry for. Because unlike Dash, her intentions were good and pure.

"I should have never let you marry him, Bee," she whispers. "I'm so sorry."

"I don't want to think about him."

"Okay."

Before the plane lands, I change into the clothes Rosa packed for me and I feel marginally better after throwing the dress Dash bought me into the garbage. It's petty but I don't care. The ride to Rosa's apartment is quiet and when we arrive, a haggard and worried Iris meets us in the lobby.

As soon as she sees us, she runs and wraps me in her warm embrace. The tears fall, as if I'll never run out of them. Getting my heart broken by Dash is worse than any pain I could've ever imagined.

SCANDALOUS GAMES

"Everything will be okay, Bee. I promise," Iris soothingly murmurs. "Come on, let's get you upstairs."

The elevator opens directly into the hallway of Rosa's penthouse and they take me straight to the bedroom.

"I'm going to take a shower."

"Okay, love," Iris says. "We'll be right here."

"We love you, Bee."

Under the spray of the shower in the bathroom, I let the cold water beat down on me until my skin is as cold as the iciness in my heart. But no matter how hard I scrub, I can't wash away the memories wreaking havoc on me. I don't even remember sliding down to the floor until my best friends find and somehow help me into clothes and lay me down on the bed.

I curl into a ball while they both lie on either side of me and hug me tight until I fall asleep.

The next morning is much worse. A hellish nightmare.

After waking and freshening up, I enter the kitchen and find Iris and Rosa sitting on the island, quietly arguing. They stop when they notice me and one look at them, I know something is terribly wrong.

"What happened?" I ask, trepidation in my voice.

"Bee. I don't think it's a good idea," says Ro, like talking to a caged animal.

"Just tell me."

They share a look before Iris takes a deep breath and sadly utters, "There's a video of you calling your marriage a sham and arguing with Dash all over the news. Everybody believes it because Dash never denied it. The same person who saw you at the restaurant is now claiming he heard you two discussing it."

"Let me see it."

Rosa stands up abruptly. "No. You're not. It's not worth it, Bee."

"I want to see it." I cross the distance and hold my hand out, waiting.

They try to give a united front but when I don't budge, Iris gives Rosa's tablet with a sigh. A voice inside my head screams to not relive it again. Ignoring it, I tap *Play* and watch. It's like a slow motion version of watching a train wreck happen. The media shows no mercy as they jump over each other to snap our pictures. However, my eyes are stuck on Dash.

The way he appears behind me. His veneer of calm and confidence, blown to pieces.

He looks torn. Broken. Lost.

It's swallowed by rage upon landing on the photographers. Then as soon as I scream and pull the curtain over our dirty secret, he's back to looking hopeless. When Justin takes me from his arms, he stares at my back knowing we'll never be the same.

Every bone in my body screams to run back to him.

I slam the tablet on the island at the foolish urge. Rosa rests her palm on mine and consoles, "It'll blow over before you know it."

"It was always going to end this way." My voice is devoid of emotion. "It was only a matter of time. Scandalous games like ours never stay in the dark."

I push away and turn when Iris asks, "Where are you going?"

"I need to see my parents."

"We're coming with you," they say at the same time, but I'm already shaking my head.

"I have to do this alone."

"We'll stay in the car." Rosa shushes me when I open my mouth to protest. "It's the only compromise I'm giving you. And until this mess blows over, you're staying with me."

Iris comes over to join us and pulls me into a hug, whispering, "Just because you have to do something alone, doesn't mean you need to."

"Okay."

The three of us are ready and out the door in Rosa's car as she drives to my parents' house. The paparazzi is camped outside when we arrive and I'm grateful for the tinted glass so they don't see my face. I couldn't bear to look at myself in the mirror. But as we wait a few seconds for the security gates open, they shout and hurl insulting and demeaning questions. It's enough to make my empty stomach wretch.

"I swear to God, I'll get all their names and send my dog after their asses," Rosa growls, glaring at them from the front.

If it were any other circumstance, I might laugh at her antics but I've never felt more lifeless.

"You sure you don't want us to come with you?" questions Iris.

"I'll be fine," I reply and drag myself out of the car before walking to the front gates.

One of the maids opens them up and her expression says it all. With a swallow, she informs me, "They are waiting in your father's office."

I nod and make my way upstairs. The wooden door looms in my face, feeling like I'm walking to a lion's den. And even before I knock and open it, I know affection and sympathy for my broken heart will not be waiting for me.

My father sits behind his large desk while my mom stands on his side. When his gaze drags to mine, he is livid. The man, who in all my twenty-five years, has never let emotions get the best of him and always stayed calm through the storm, is now glaring at me.

Shame makes me lower my eyes, knowing I'm the cause of it.

"Is it true?" he quietly asks.

"Yes."

"Why?"

One word and I flinch as though he struck me. One word and it encompasses all his emotions. Anger. Disappointment. Disgust.

"A sham marriage, Bianca? Really?" cries my mother. "I knew that whole

SCANDALOUS GAMES

whirlwind romance story was too good to be true."

I muster my inner strength and lift my chin as I confess, "I did it for Arya."

"How does your sister fit into this, Bianca?"

"You left me no choice, Papa." A tremor races to the tips of my toes as I give a sad smile and tell him the truth. Hoping against hope he'll understand that I never wanted to disrespect them. "You both were so fixated on my marriage that you completely neglected the one daughter who actually longed for it. Because of me, you wouldn't even consider her wedding. Your traditional values didn't let you see the hurt it was causing her. We knew you'd say no. So, I decided to marry in name to please you both, hoping you'll finally notice Arya."

"So you sullied our name instead of talking to us."

"When have you both listened to what I have to say?" My voice rises and a sad sound spills from my lips. "It's always been about what you want, how you're feeling, or how I'm such a big disappointment and never good enough. And, Mom," I look at her sharply and accuse, "when was the last time you asked how I was doing? If I'm happy or sad, huh? It's always who's getting married to whom. Sometimes I wonder if you both even love me or if I'm just a commodity you want to pawn off to another."

"Enough!" shouts my dad, nose flared and eyes narrowed into slits, as he slams his fist on the table. "Our legacy is built on the traditions and values you're insulting, Bianca. Your generation has become selfish and reckless, forgetting that these rituals are important and keeps this society going. If I let Arya marry first instead of my older daughter, your reputation will be tarnished. It was for your own sake. We wanted to find a good man for you to settle down with."

"Even if you know that I'm not ready and will never be happy?"

"Don't be so dramatic, Bianca." My mom huffs. "In time, you would've come to love and respect your husband."

"Now that your farce of a marriage is over and that man is out of your life for good, you will marry the man of our choice," announces my dad. "I'll fix the damage from last night."

"No."

They freeze at my answer and a chill spreads all over the room.

"If you want to be a part of this family, you will do as I say." My dad threatens.

"Then it's a good thing I never was to begin with."

I walk away, leaving them stunned. I'm so done with everyone bulldozing into my life and expecting me to follow their rules. I'm done being used as a pawn for everyone's agenda. I'm just done.

In the hallway, I collide into Arya, who looks just as worse as me.

"Oh my god, Bee. I was looking for you," she cries, thick tears streaming down her beautiful face and sadness in her eyes. She's the only family I have left. "Why? Why did you do it? I told you I was gonna be fine."

"You're my little sister, Ari." I rub her tears away and cup her cheeks. "Of course, I would sacrifice anything for your happily ever after."

"Not at the expense of you."

"It doesn't matter. Just know, you'll finally get your dream wedding."

"What do you mean?" she whispers at my sad tone, holding my hand tightly. "Say something, Bee."

I wrap my arms around her small frame and hug her tightly. "I'm always here if you ever need me. I love you."

She calls my name but I have nothing left to say.

Rosa and Iris rush to my side when I step outside and one of them asks, "What did they say?"

"Nothing that surprised me." I shrug.

"I'm sorry, Bee," Iris consoles.

"Fuck them," growls Rosa. "You have us."

I give a shaky smile, grateful for the world's best girlfriends. We slide into the car and I tell Rosa, "I want to get my stuff from the apartment."

"Are you sure? I can ask someone to bring it," she suggests.

"It's okay. He won't be there."

"Okay."

Chapter Sixty-five

BIANCA

Memories of Dash and I walking countless times through the lobby of our building flash like a colorful and bright kaleidoscope before my eyes. My heart would burst, giddy with excitement and a rush of desire, knowing he was waiting upstairs. He would surprise me by coming home early and cooking for us. How fickle are human emotions. You can look at the same memory and either feel happy or sad. It's the last emotion running in my veins.

Memories are the absolute worst.

One moment, they make you feel like you're at the top of the world.

And the next moment, they taunt you with a reality of what will never be. Will never last. Was never meant to be.

"Bianca."

A hand shaking my arm yanks me to the present. I look up to see my friends watching me with concern. The elevator has stopped at my floor.

"We can do this tomorrow, Bee."

"No." I tuck my hair away and walk toward the end of the hall. "I want to do this before he returns. *If* he returns."

They follow quietly, having my back no matter their protests. With shivering fingers, I insert the key, only for the door to be yanked open from the inside. Startled, I almost stumbled backwards from the force of it. My heart slams against my ribs when my eyes connect with Dash's.

A broken and lost version of him.

I drag my gaze down and realize he's still wearing last night's clothes while dark circles mar his dull eyes—he looks like hell. Like me. His appearance screams he went to the ends of the earth for a glimpse of me.

When they finally land on mine, his chest expands as he roughly exhales and runs his gaze all over me.

"Kitten?" He rasps, "Where did you run off to? I couldn't find you."

Words get lodged in my throat and I stagger at the stark pain in his voice. The anxiety. He looks like he hasn't slept. I'm hauled backward when he tries to touch me and a fuming Rosa comes in his path. His sad eyes don't stray from mine and I look away.

"Please, kitten. Give me a chance to explain."

"You had your chance, Stern," growls Rosa. "Leave her the hell alone."

"This doesn't concern you, Rosalie." Looking over her head at me, he begs, "I'm not going anywhere unless you talk to me, kitten."

"Will you leave after?" I ask, knowing he'll never leave me alone unless I listen to him. Besides, he at least owes me an explanation.

Torment darkens his features as he wars with himself over the choice. Ultimately, he only has one. His shoulders hang as he replies, "Okay."

"You don't owe him anything, Bee."

"It's all right, Iris."

Rosa reluctantly steps aside and I slide past her. The door closes, leaving us alone. Both of us soak each other in, as if we spent a lifetime apart even though it's only been one night. But the distance in our broken hearts might as well be oceans wide.

A wayward tear falls down my cheek and in a flash, he crosses the distance.

"I'm sorry." His thumb swipes another tear that manages to escape my eyes. "For everything."

"I hate you."

"I hate me too."

"You wanted to talk. So talk." I push him back and he watches me, like I took away his lifeline. "Why did you lie, Dash?"

"Because I never thought you'd mean so much to me, Bianca. At first, I stupidly thought I could sate my obsession for you and walk away once our arrangement ended. I didn't realize I was fooling myself until it was too late and by then, you sunk deeper into my skin, my veins, and my *heart*, than I thought possible. Every day I didn't tell the truth, it killed me." He roughly exhales before running his hand through his already messy hair. Tortured eyes connect with mine and he shakes his head with a broken smile. "All my life, I just drifted and swayed without an anchor. I never had anything permanent. I'm always searching for one place to call my own. To call my home. Because I never had one. But then you came along and I realized I was searching for the wrong thing. My home wasn't a place. It was you, kitten. Your heart is my home."

My heart cracks into tiny pieces at his broken confession. My arms ache to reach

SCANDALOUS GAMES

and hold him without letting go, but the sting of his betrayal and lies outweighs it. The second the same realization grips him, the flicker of hope dies into ashes right in front of me. When I speak, it disappears completely.

"It's too late, Dash." My tone is sad. "They're nothing but empty words now."

I go still when he's suddenly surrounding me again with his arms caging my body against the door. Our breaths mingle when he rests his head on mine.

"I vowed to kill myself before I ever hurt you again but I failed. Terribly. I should've told you the truth from the beginning but I was afraid to lose you. Only, I forgot you don't lose what you never had." Tilting my chin with the tip of his finger, he roughly confesses, "I know I've lied to you, but never about how I felt for you, kitten. Every moment, every word, every touch, every feeling… all of it was real and I'm not just talking about the past couple months. I was yours long before I knew what belonging to someone meant."

"Stop," I whimper, his confession bringing a raw pain to my chest. I turn my head, letting his grip fall, and push him away. His scent, which was beginning to feel like home, now felt like gasoline on my open wounds. The ones he inflicted. "Let me go."

"Let me hold you a little longer if it's the last time, kitten," he begs me, and I taste his tears on my lips. "Please."

I let him because I'm not strong. This isn't how I imagined us to end.

One of my hands winds into his shirt as I hold him one last time, memorizing the feel of him, just like I did seven years ago. I stare down in confusion when he presses something small and cold into my palm.

A heart-shaped key.

"I saw you watching the couple in Paris, kitten. When I heard about the love lock tradition, I thought it was silly but seeing you sitting there pretty and the smile you gave me when I caught you staring, I finally understood the desire. I knew I couldn't leave without doing it. So I went back, bought one, and locked it for us. Except I couldn't throw away the key."

Oh my god.

Suddenly, I remember him making an excuse and running to the restaurant. He went for this.

"Why didn't you throw it?" I whisper, making him look at me with a smile.

"Because my heart belongs to you. The only lock where I want all my love to be safeguarded for eternity is in your hands. The key belongs to you, kitten. If I'm not with you, then I want you to have a piece of me. I might've stolen your body seven years ago but you've stolen my soul."

"I love you." His lips ghost over mine. "Goodbye, Bianca."

The door opens and closes after he leaves. I stand in the same spot with my fingers wrapped around the key. Just like that, he's gone.

Like he promised.

The same day, I sent him signed divorce papers to his office and the engagement ring.

The next day…

They return signed and sealed.

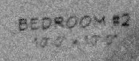

Chapter Sixty-six

BIANCA

(SIX MONTHS LATER)

All my life, I've lived by other people's expectations.
My parents'.
My boyfriend's.
Then my sister's.
    I tried to find happiness between trying to live up to their demands, convincing myself along the way it was what I desired as well. I'm always putting their needs before mine. When you're conditioned in such a way and the little glass house finally splinters, it feels like the end of the world. A dark abyss pulls me deeper.
    Until I was left with two choices.
    Either hide until the scars become permanent and fear poisons me slowly or… I could pick myself up. I had already chosen and lived through the first. I wasn't going to waste another seven years of my life without really living and just drifting wherever the wind took me.
    I also knew it wouldn't magically make my heartbreak disappear.
    But I had to try.
    For myself.
    I needed a fresh start to heal, away from the city I grew up in, away from the shadows of my family, and away from the harrowing and bittersweet memories.

SCANDALOUS GAMES

Especially from the ghosts of my past. Once I knew I couldn't stay there any longer, I did what I always dreamt of.

Moving to another city and starting my own interior designing company.

The hardest part was telling my best friends about my decision and living without them by my side, but they understood. The second was quitting my dream job with my mentor. The one I worked so hard to achieve. However, if someone was going to understand my choice better than anyone, it was her.

After all, she had once been in the same place that I was today. Young and brokenhearted. And she has chosen to put all her pain into focusing on her second love. Her last words of wisdom that stuck is to not let work become my whole life. She said it happens slowly and before you know it, it sneaks up on you and you realize it's all you're left with. She also mentioned that it comes with a heavy price.

The price of closing our hearts forever.

She said one must learn to live through the pain and to let it make them stronger because nothing is worse than living with regrets. It was the most she had said to me in the years I worked for her. A softer side of her that I didn't know existed.

The city of Vellington, where I moved, is a beautiful and wholesome place. The weather, the people, and the food—everything is quaint, sweet, and *homey*. It wasn't long before I fell in love.

They say nothing breaks like a heart but someone also said everything happens for a reason. It is true but that doesn't mean it doesn't hurt any less. Even in a whole new city, little things remind me of Dash. Just saying his name brings an ache to my chest. A longing to feel his skin against mine. His heartbeat in my ears.

In another lifetime, maybe he and I would have stayed together.

Except, our fate came with an ending written in stone.

Or timing was never right.

The urge to cyberstalk him to see what he's doing in his journey to take over the world always comes in the middle of the night when I'm lying alone in an empty bed. But then I remember how I'm still not over him completely. How difficult it is to just breathe without my heart hurting.

Summoning what little strength I have, I shut down the stupid urge. Obsessing over him would have been taking a step backward. So the first month when I shifted my mindset, I went on a mission to find an apartment in a safe society, and once I settled, I began to focus on building my business. Working as a freelance interior designer is tough when you're starting out, even if you have experience.

Luckily, Zara helped me land my first client, Sitara Singh, who prefers to work with freelancers who will devote their time and energy solely on hers. I was told if I impressed her, her testimony alone will go a long way since she's a rich society wife and has tons of connections.

I was apprehensive to meet her at first since I grew up around women like her, but I was pleasantly surprised when we met and talked. She was down to earth, kind, and welcoming. After our first meeting itself, she hired me. It was my first big win in a long time and it gave me the sense of confidence I was searching for.

It wasn't long before I submerged my heartbreak into building my client base with her glowing recommendation and before I knew it, I had to search for an office to rent out since I could no longer work from my small apartment.

As I look back, I realize how far I've come. I was a one-woman show until today, doing everything on my own, like scheduling, meeting with vendors, laborers, and it began to take a toll on my health. So, I decided to hire an assistant to help manage my schedule and enable me to focus on my favorite part of the job—designing. Bringing my clients' visions to life.

Arriving at the building where I rent my two-room office, I park my car. In an hour, people will be showing up for the job interviews I'm conducting today.

"Hello, Miss Chopra."

I meet my elderly security guard's warm eyes and pretend to scold him, "How many times have I told you to call me Bianca, Shammi?"

"I will do no such thing during working hours," he declares.

I shake my head because the man is stubborn. He's really fit for someone of the age of seventy and I was surprised to learn that he's been working here for twenty-something years. Everyone loves his charming smile and mischievous eyes. If he did ever try to quit, no one would let him leave. I, myself, consider him one of my friends in the city.

"Here. I brought you lunch."

When I pass him the tiffin box, his gaze narrows and he suspiciously asks, "Cooked extra by mistake again, miss?"

"Oh yes," I say because otherwise he won't accept it, but we both know I'm lying. It's the least I could do for all the times he stays behind when I'm working late and walks me to my car at night. With a wave, I walk inside and call out over my shoulder.

"Have a good day, Shammi."

The next hour flies by, with me sorting and arranging my office properly. If the interviewees saw the clutter and just how disorganized I am, a few might just turn tail while the rest would demand a raise from the first day. Raj, my first interviewee, will be arriving any minute now. I check my watch when there's a knock at my door. I open it to find him here and welcome him with a warm smile.

"Um. Hi, I'm Raj," he says, slightly nervous. "Are you Bianca?"

"Yes. I was just waiting for you," I tell him, before inviting him in. "If you're ready, we can start. And don't be nervous."

He laughs low and some of the tension eases once we sit at my desk. As I observe him, I get a feeling that he's still in college and probably looking for a summer job. I interview him with an open mind because even though he might not have a lot of experience, he may have the skills I need. Besides, one has to start from somewhere.

After Raj, the next person is already waiting for me and she looks confident. Over the next couple of hours, I run through interviews, and man, it is as tiresome as it is fun. By the time the last interviewee leaves, my shoulders slump because only one out of the eight caught my eye but she can't start for another two weeks. And I need one right now. Or I might not have a business by the time she returns.

My second-best option is Raj, but I will have to train him. A lot. That will be another headache. However, I don't see any other choice. It's almost evening and I decide to at least get some work done before I leave.

SCANDALOUS GAMES

Shammi is always scolding me about how I'm a workaholic—the one quality I despise—since I always work late hours until I'm bone-deep tired. If only he knew the truth. That the thought of returning to my empty apartment is a painful reminder that I'm alone.

That the nights are the hardest.

That working late until I'm ready to pass out is the only way I can hold on to my sanity. The only way I don't dream of him. The only way I don't miss being cocooned in his arms.

No matter how hard I try, he's still as deep in my heart as ever.

Shoving those dark thoughts down, I turn from the unlocked door to walk to my desk.

"Any chance you're accepting a walk-in?"

I go still when the deep and smoky voice registers in my brain. The one that haunts my soul day and night. My hands freeze in midair as I blink, believing my mind is playing a cruel joke.

He's not here, Bianca.

Even in my head, it sounds like a futile lie because the next second, his rich scent envelops all the oxygen in the room. I feel his dark presence to the tip of my toes and a shiver crawls up my spine. My traitorous body, betraying me by singing and tingling at the rich timbre of his voice.

I couldn't possibly have conjured him up, right?

Yet I know it will be him when I turn around.

Time slows down or so it feels, when I slowly turn around with my heart in my throat. A sharp jolt racks my body when I see his handsome face.

He's here.

Dash is here.

In my city.

Thick emotions get lodged in my throat because he looks like my Dash, but one detail has a visceral reaction pulled out of me. He cut his hair. Closely cropped hair frames his impenetrable green eyes, still piercing and magnificent as ever, with sharp cheekbones that could cut glass and a chiseled jawline hidden beneath his trimmed beard.

His powerful suit is replaced with worn denim jeans and a black button-down with the sleeves rolled. The bare skin of his arms running with veins and a sprinkle of dark hair that make his forearms look sexy. I don't think I'll ever get rid of the effect his broad and muscular body has on me.

He looks like the Dash I ran into the first time in his bedroom.

Except, there's no coldness and darkness radiating from him. The invisible thread that binds us stretches to its limit, ready to snap at any second. While my starving eyes are soaking him in, so are his with such an intensity it steals my breath away.

"Yo-you're here," I dumbly whisper, waiting for him to vanish so that I'll think he was just a figment of my imagination.

"Kitten."

I jolt again and blink. The shock of seeing him standing a mere foot from me wears off, his earlier question hitting me like a ton of bricks. Does he think he can just waltz back into my life and demand, what? A job?

Hmm, he's still as arrogant and dominating as ever...

How the fuck does he even know I'm here? Rosa and Iris are the only two people who know and they would never tell him. I guard my expression, summoning all the anger and hurt I felt after he betrayed me, and glare at him.

"What are you doing here?"

"What does it look like, kitten?" he says, stepping further into my space. "I heard you're hiring and, well... I'm looking for a job."

"I'm not your kitten." He fucking *smiles*. And god, I want to throttle him. "And don't you have your own company to run? Or did you suddenly run it into the ground?"

"I sold my shares to Kian and stepped down as the CEO."

The information renders me speechless. His company was his blood, sweat, and tears. Afraid of the answer, I still ask, "When?"

"The day you left." He speaks calmly as though he's talking about the weather. His perceptive gaze scans my office, memorizing every detail. When it returns to mine, it softens around the edges. Hands in his pockets, he bounces on his feet once and drawls, "So, are you going to be interviewing me or what?"

"I'm not giving you a job."

"Why? Is the position already filled?"

"I find it hard to believe that you're poor all of a sudden, Dash. I'm sure you can survive without a job." He doesn't miss when I purposely don't answer his question. "Or did you spend all your billions already?"

"Are those questions part of the interview?"

I forgot how relentless and cunning he can be. I'm not playing into one of his games. Especially when I don't know the rules. I meant what I said. He and I are over. Being together has never fared well. Besides, you know what they say.

Fool me once, shame on you.

Fool me twice, shame on me.

Fool me thrice... Well, I'm not giving him another chance.

"Why are you really here, Dash?"

His friendly mask cracks, letting me peer into the man who walked out of my life after wrecking me in the aftermath of his storm.

"I told you, kitten. I go where you go."

Chapter Sixty-seven

DASH

Bianca was put on this earth to be mine. To breathe life into my cold, dead heart.

Only this time, I'm not letting her go without a fight. I might have walked out on her that day but I never intended to be gone forever. And if I have to spend an eternity begging her to take me back and give me one last chance to prove we belong together, I'll do it with a smile on my face.

Our past may have been built on lies and secrecy but our future will not be tainted by their ghosts. She knows all my deepest sins, my ugliest scars, and darkest fears, so, if she still hasn't kicked me out yet despite knowing it all, it gives me hope that maybe I stand a chance.

It might be small but when you've survived through a dark never ending tunnel, it might as well be as bright as the sun. I'm going to grab and hold on to whatever she'll give me.

Because living without her isn't a possibility.

I thought I knew what the darkest times for me would be like, but I truly understood its meaning in these past six months that I had to spend alone. Without her. My world. My kitten. *My wife.*

A goddamn paper isn't going to decide our fate. In my heart, she became mine the moment she propositioned me to be her fake husband.

"I'm not letting you back in my life again," she spits out angrily and crosses her arms. "Certainly not for a job you don't need. I'm going to give it to someone who actually deserves it."

I can't keep the smile from my face because her anger is better than the shell of a girl I turned her into when I left. It would have killed me if I was the reason who made her lose her fire. But I'm glad that's not the case, because the defiance always perched on her cute nose.

Of course, I'm not surprised because she may doubt herself but she is the strongest woman I know. The most beautiful.

The moment I had found out she moved to another city and all her stuff was gone from our apartment and hers, it was like a permanent dark cloud had appeared over my head, locking me in darkness. All I knew was she was gone and I didn't know where she went.

The knowledge of not being able to see her, possibly forever, was too hard to bear and I had slipped into a hellish phase. My nights were spent in a drunken stupor because it was the only way I could sleep without waking up in a nightmare.

I survived living with a lonely family.

I survived reliving Niall's accident.

Through the guilt.

But the mere idea of losing the one good thing that ever happened to me and knowing I sabotaged it because of my mistake was too much and it pushed me over the edge. Had Justin not found me and been there to talk some sense into me, I don't know what I would have done. It took me a month to get my life in order.

I had so much to repent for and a lot of healing before I could be the man Bianca deserved.

A few days after Niall's accident, I had confessed everything to his mom. Because after all the efforts she made to include me in the family, I couldn't lie to her. I told her about his breakup minus the cheating part, our fight and that I sabotaged his relationship by sleeping with her which led to him chasing after her that night. She had kicked me out and told to never return in her life.

Over the years after my career took off, I secretly helped by taking care of Niall's medical finances and bringing the best doctors to help him. However, none could fix his condition. The damage was too severe and it was highly unlikely he would ever wake up.

This truth was the hardest one to accept.

Some nights, I still blame myself and probably always will.

I should've known my stepmother will put two and two together with my involvement in the charity. I regret not keeping my part anonymous but my name alone helped bring others to give to the charity. It was easy enough to find she had sneaked into the gala by saying she was my stepmother after she found Bianca was going to there through media.

She wanted to ruin me like I ruined Niall's life.

And she succeeded by taking the only person who ever loved me unconditionally. Except this time, I wasn't going to wallow in self-pity. It took months but eventually, I was able to let go of the guilt enough to realize you can't control everything in

SCANDALOUS GAMES

your life.

I knew it was time to win Bianca back, even if it meant going to the ends of the earth.

I wasn't losing her again.

Her best friends were the only two people who knew where she moved but they hated my guts and it was understandable. I deserved it. They were loyal to a fault and wouldn't help me. But I wasn't going to let her go just like that. So I went to her office, hoping they might have a clue, but it was a dead end until I ran into her boss, Zara.

She came in like a godsend and I don't know what she saw but the woman told me where my Bianca had gone. And on the next flight, I was here. Except, finding the city she lived in was only the first obstacle. Her boss had made sure the work was cut out for me. It took another few months of searching through every interior designing company in the city, and that was full of dead ends. Until it hit me one night that I was doing it all wrong.

There's only one reason why Bianca would leave her dream job: to make her dream a reality. The same day, I found my sweet kitten.

She didn't see me when I came here the very next day, but when I first laid my eyes on her after all these months, I finally breathed air into my lungs. I swear, time had stood still like it does in those silly rom-com movies as I soaked up every inch of her. Just catching a glimpse of her is like a dying man's last wish come true.

Her hair was longer, skimming the top of her ass, which swayed enticingly with every step as she skipped to her building on the sidewalk. However, the first thing I noticed was the weight she had lost and that her cheeks looked sunken as though the weight of the world was on her shoulders. It broke my heart.

The guilt swam back with a vengeance. I couldn't ignore the fact that I was the reason she had to start over in a new city. After all, this was the second time I made her run from the ones she loved.

I vowed it would be the last time and that I would fix everything if it's the last thing I do.

So here I am, shooting my shot. Her anger is a sweet balm, letting me know her spirit is as strong as ever. I would've never forgiven myself if I had broken it.

"The door is behind you. Leave," she orders, forcing my attention to fixate on her. "And don't ever come back."

The rejection stings but I don't dare to move. I'll take every punch with a smile because the more she does it, the more alive I feel. Like she resurrected me back to life.

"I was told the boss is pretty sweet," I quip teasingly before wincing, "Didn't know you'd be biased and kick a man when he's already down."

Her eyes flare with the same fire she aimed at me the first time we met. One hand falling to her hip, she retorts, "You deserve it."

"I do."

"Then leave."

"I'm only here for an interview." I try another tactic. "If you think I'm not qualified, I'll go."

SIMRAN

Nose twitching adorably in annoyance, she taunts, "Liar."

"I will leave." Then come back tomorrow. But she doesn't need to know that.

We both stand in a silent stare-off where I notice the slight blush forming on her cheeks. There's a slight hitch in her breath, and when her lips part, I can no longer resist letting my hungry eyes trail lower. As if she can feel the energy between us twisting into hotter degrees, she huffs out, "Fine. Let's get this over with." Turning around to go behind her desk, she mumbles under her breath, "Like his bossy ass can handle working for someone else."

I hide my chuckle and sit across from her. The memory of fucking her on a similar desk has my cock hardening behind the zipper of my jeans. Fuck. It's going to be painful not being able to touch her. The job, whether she gives it to me or not, is just an excuse to be close to her.

A message to let her know I'm never leaving her side.

I clear my throat when her gaze drifts to my abs and lock there. Cheeks turning pink, she flicks those eyes to mine and pretends I didn't notice. Switching her expression to indifference, which she fails, she asks her first question, "Why do you want this job?"

"I'm in love with the boss." I tell her the truth. Her hand flies to her chest, where a thin chain peeks through her top. She drops her hand when I stare a little too long. "I want to be in her life any way she'll have me."

"I'm not your boss yet," she murmurs. The slight hitch in her voice betrays how I still make her pulse race. Stubbornly lifting her chin, she taunts, "Can you take orders?"

Keeping my face straight is a hardship. Somehow, I manage and calmly answer. "Yes."

She gives me a look saying I'm full of shit. If only she knew I would happily obey every order she throws at me, if it means she'll take me back. I would crawl, drop to my knees, and plead if she told me to.

"Have you been an assistant before?"

"Yes."

It shocks her. "Really?"

"My first two internships were as an assistant at high school and my first year of college. I hated asking my father for money so once I was old enough and people were willing to hire me, I began working odd jobs. So yeah, I have experience."

The careful and aloof mask she placed crumbles and a swirl of sorrow and longing bleeds through. For a fraction of a second, the woman who fell in love with my black soul stares back at me. Then the shutter comes down again and I hate it.

"I have all the information I need," she declares, standing abruptly.

I slowly rise even though every bone in my body protests. My fingers twitch by my side, aching to yank her flush against me. "Is that all you want to ask me, kitten?"

"What else is there to ask?"

"Whether I thought about you every second for the past six months?" My tone is desperate and laced with pain. "Because I have. That the worst fear I ever felt was finding you gone and that every day since, I've spent searching for you. I miss you,

SCANDALOUS GAMES

kitten."

"No. No." She shakes her head. An empty laugh spills from her lips and her voice comes out sharp. "No words are ever going to make me forgive you. You don't get to walk back into my life and disrupt it again. We are over."

"You and I are the endgame, kitten," I remind her, and vow, "we will never be over. And if I have to spend the rest of my life reminding you until you believe it, I will. I'll do anything for you except let you go. I already did it twice, and I won't survive it again."

"Then I'll prove you wrong."

Her defiance brings a smile to my lips and I wink. "Okay. But just know, I'm as stubborn as you are and I always win. You chased me last time; now it's my turn."

Leaving her stunned and fuming, I walk out.

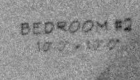

Chapter Sixty-eight

BIANCA

I hired him.
    The second he left after all but promising he won't leave me alone and daring me at the same time, I sent him a text, aware I was giving away my new number. Maybe it was his plan all along. But I have an agenda.
    I'm going to show his arrogant ass that I don't want him anymore. So maybe I'll have to torture myself by working closely with him and drown in his rich and intoxicating scent that still drives me wild. In the end when I prove him wrong, it'll be worth it.
    My concentration disturbed, I grab my purse and walk out of my office after locking the door. I'm a bundle of mixed emotions, each fighting to rise to the top as I take the elevator. When I exit through the lobby, Shammi's head snaps up and his gaze widens in bewilderment.
    Am I dreaming or are you leaving early, Bianca?"
    I laugh at his teasing joke and smirk. "Yes. I like to keep you on your toes, old man."
    "That you do."
    "Good night, Shammi."
    "I'll see you tomorrow, Miss Chopra."
    I shake my head. It seems I only attract stubborn men in my life. My eyes scan

SCANDALOUS GAMES

the still crowded parking lot for signs of Dash and hate when disappointment flares.

Don't fall into old habits, Bianca, I remind myself.

The drive back to my apartment is spent second-guessing my decision of hiring him. I'm even more shocked he accepted it. I might be the first woman in the world who has a billionaire working as her assistant.

Suddenly, many ideas pop inside my head with ways in which I can make his life hell. Fetching coffee and food, running errands like my laundry, and, the best, photocopying using the printer in my office, which is absolute shit. I have lost count of how many times I've kicked it in frustration and gave up on it.

Yeah. That's going to be his first task tomorrow.

Half an hour later, I'm riding up the elevator to my floor and when I jump out, I frown at seeing the empty apartment opposite mine with the door left open and surrounded by boxes. Excitement builds at having a neighbor. There are a total of four apartments on my floor and two are occupied by an old couple and another girl, who I hardly see. Maybe the new one will be different. I could cook and welcome them with brownies. I might buy them, since cooking only leads to a hurricane in the kitchen.

I decide to say hi and hurry down the hallway. My feet skid to a halt when two muscular arms appear to pick up one of the large boxes and I catch a glimpse of the closely cropped head of hair before it disappears.

Stomping down the rest of the way, I round the corner and peer at my ex-husband and heartbreaker moving across from me, looking right at home. My traitorous gaze draws to the naked back muscles—which look like a work of art, meant to be sketched on a canvas—flexing deliciously. They disappear into the waistband of his denim jeans he wore earlier.

"Have you changed your profession to a stalker now?"

As though he was waiting for me—of course he was—he takes his sweet-ass time turning around. I bite my lip, drooling at the sight of his triceps as he pushes the big box easily onto the long kitchen island. A sheen of sweat glistens on his chest and those damn abs clench, making my neglected pussy perk at being in the same vicinity as him.

"Is that how you welcome your new neighbor?" he teases.

"Not unless they're a stalker."

"A stalker you hired as your assistant."

Smart-ass. "Move out."

"Already signed the lease." He shrugs.

I pray for patience while cursing at myself for still being attracted to this infuriating man. "You know what, I'll complain to my landlord that I don't want you as my neighbor."

I'm actually good friends with him so I know it could work. He has a crush on me, so maybe I could work that in my favor. I'm going to play dirty if Dash is too. I smugly stare at him but it falters when he crosses the distance until he's towering over me. Goosebumps prick my skin and his gaze caresses them like a wind.

"Okay," he murmurs, not the least bit worried at my threat. "In fact, we can discuss it now. Save you the trouble of writing an application."

"What?" I ask, confused, but when he arches one perfect eyebrow and waits, my jaw drops. "You did not just buy another apartment complex..."

His lips tug into a boyish grin at my reaction. Is he insane?

"You can't keep buying every damn building I live in, Dash."

"I like to invest in real estate." Giving a flirtatious smile that makes my insides sing, he says, "So want a tour, kitten?"

"Never, stalker." I whirl around and walk up to my door.

"Don't tell me you're afraid of being alone with me, kitten?"

My hand dropping halfway to my lock, I sharply twist to face him and answer, "I am."

He freezes and all traces of amusement vanish from his face.

"I'm scared that every word out of your mouth is another lie. I'm scared you'll destroy me again if I spend so much as a second alone with you. I'm scared to trust you. But what I'm most afraid of is that I still can't hate you as much as I wish to. That I can't erase you from my memory."

I don't wait around for his reaction and enter my apartment, knowing my nightmare that I kept at bay now awaits me. That all these months of progress and the bubble I created where he didn't exist just went up in flames.

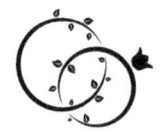

The next morning, he's waiting for me at my door, dressed in another pair of fitted denims and a dark green button-down that complements his beautiful eyes.

"Morning, kitten," he greets me, before taking in my purple summer dress that I paired with sandals. I'm flushed by the time his eyes return to my face, burning with a heat that makes my toes curl. I'm almost disappointed when he doesn't whisper something filthy or pull me close. As if he can read my naughty thoughts, his mouth twitches.

"Drive with me?"

"No, thank you." I saunter toward the elevator. He follows closely.

"We could save gas."

"Since when do you care about the environment?"

"Any reason that gives me a chance to be with you is important to me."

So he hasn't lost his smooth talking skills. Good for him. I ignore his remark when he reaches the elevator and we step inside. Our fingers touch when we go for the button at the same time and a zap goes straight to my clit.

Electricity cackles between us and I finally find one thing I hate about my building. The elevator is too compact and it only constricts when people enter from the next floor, pushing my back against his hard chest.

My eyelids fall close at the contact and when I try to move forward, both his arms lock around my waist and trap me between his thighs. I can feel his thick and *hard* cock digging into my lower back.

Deprived of any sexual touch, especially his, since I left him, every nerve ending

SCANDALOUS GAMES

in my body lights up and I all but forget I'm supposed to be resisting him. The feel of him turned on because of one small touch has me grinding my ass against his dick. We're in the corner in the back, with no one paying attention to us, which makes me feel bold.

I slow grind once and before a moan can slip out, one of his hands travels lightning fast and covers my mouth, swallowing the sound.

His breath teases my ear as he bends and growls, "Behave."

The one domineering word throws a bucket of cold water all over my arousal. Once I'm aware of my momentary lapse in judgment, I go still. Thankfully, the elevator stops and people step out. My panic recedes.

Damn it. I fucked up by hiring him.

"Don't," he warns, caging me in and staring down at me. "Don't fight us. Hate me, curse at me, fight with me, but don't ever pull away from me, kitten." His voice turns thick with emotion when he says the last part. The desperation and fear creeping in his tone makes me pause.

I don't owe him anything but the vulnerability has me whispering, "Okay."

His eyes drop close as he exhales roughly. When they open, some of the anxiety eases. "I know I broke your trust and I don't expect you to forgive me so easily or anytime soon. So put me through hell, make me beg, and take all the time you need, but please come back to me. I've been lost, only drifting aimlessly since you left. I don't want to feel lost again."

"What if I can never forgive you?"

"The day we married, you became mine for seven lifetimes, kitten," he murmurs, running his knuckle down my cheek. "So I have all the time in the world."

The conviction and promise in his tone causes the first crack in the walls around my heart. Now, I'm not sure who will prove the other wrong but one thing is certain… he's a step ahead.

Chapter Sixty-nine

BIANCA

He fixed the damn copier. Apparently, his touch is like fairy dust. Everything turns pretty and functioning.

All my devious plans to make his life just a bit hellish in the last two weeks have been met with sinful defeat. I can't even fire him because he is actually pretty good at being my assistant. Okay, I'm lying. He's better than good. He's perfect.

Just having him take most of my day-to-day burdens has made my life a whole lot smoother. The first week itself, he organized all my files, set up my website that I had almost given up on, and sorted out my calendar so I don't over exert myself. If I thought he would find this position beneath him, he proved me wrong.

I hate how easily he has made himself at home in my life again.

Everywhere I turn, he is there.

Ever since his return, I've not worked even a minute late, which hasn't gone unnoticed by Shammi. And let me tell you, he hasn't missed *anything*.

Like how Dash and I arrive at the office together, even if in separate cars.

That I stare and drool over him when he isn't looking.

Or the way Dash is constantly and protectively by my side like my personal shadow.

Questions swirl in Shammi's perceptive eyes and I know he's waiting for the

SCANDALOUS GAMES

perfect moment to bombard me with them. And that's tonight at dinner at our favorite restaurant. I can't cancel because he will know something is up. I also desperately need someone to talk to because I'm losing my mind.

My head and heart are at war.

Ever since my last talk with Dash, he has been patient like a saint—a quality I didn't expect from him. He's still possessive and protective in the little things he does as he takes care of me. Like nothing has changed between us at all. But I notice small changes that are bringing my guard down around him.

When I was married to him, there was a mysterious air cloaking him. An invisible wall buried deep beneath his other layers. A burden he seemed to carry. However, they don't exist anymore.

There's a lightness around him.

Each night, he asks me out for dinner or tempts me with a horror movie night at his place just to have me spend time with him after work. But I say no every time. My rejection, never crushing his determination to try again.

I had convinced myself I had cut him out of my heart but the truth is, he never left. Not for one lingering second. Whenever I stare at him too long, a tiny voice inside me murmurs...

Can I trust him?

My heart says yes, while my mind screams no. A tug-of-war is ensuing and I don't know which voice to listen to.

A high-pitched laugh pulls me from my musings and I scowl because I know that sound. It's my super-flirty and very married client, Neeta. When her annoyingly screeching laugh that she believes to be sexy bleeds into my ears again, I rise from my desk and peer through the window in my office.

Red-hot jealousy flares.

She stands in a skimpy dress that barely holds her breasts, which she is currently thrusting into Dash's face—or at least trying to—while resting her greedy paws on his arm. Seriously? Why is she here? I already finished designing her guest house a couple of days back.

And Dash—why isn't he taking her hand off him?

Who cares? We're not together. He can flirt with whoever he wants. With that thought, I push back from the window. My resolve only lasts for a second before I'm turning back and yanking open my door. At the loud thump, the woman startles and drops her hand before reluctantly looking at me. Annoyance creeps into her plastic face at the interruption.

I give a saccharine smile. "Neeta, I didn't know we had an appointment."

"Oh no. We don't," she replies, flicking her wrist like she's the goddamn queen or standing at a beauty contest. "I was just in the neighborhood, so I thought of coming by to say hi."

"How nice. How is Mr. Seth?"

Her smile falls when I blatantly ask about her husband. I feel Dash's amused attention on me, which I ignore. I'm not jealous. Just wouldn't want him to make a mistake by sleeping with a married woman.

All lies, Bianca, my mind taunts.

She clears her throat. "He is good. Actually, I'm getting late. It was good to see you, Bianca." Her lecherous gaze drools over Dash desperately and she drops her voice to a purr. "Dash. Hope to see you soon."

The second her suffocating perfume vanishes, Dash's laser focus lands on me and they narrow in warning when I try to sulk back to my office.

"What was that, kitten?"

"What?" I nonchalantly reply. "I just came to say hi."

"So you weren't jealous a second ago?"

I huff a laugh and roll my eyes. "Of course not. I have no reason to be."

"Really?" he taunts.

"Yes," I snap. "You can fuck whoever you want. Just leave my clients alone."

"It's a good thing I only have eyes on the boss."

His seductive and dark voice turns my nipples into hard peaks, making his attention zoom in on them. Can he tell that his proximity leaves me so turned on, that each night I have to overwork my vibrator just to fall asleep? That only thoughts of him, the memory of him growling filthy orders in my ear and the way his cock would stretch my pussy, can make me orgasm?

"Stop looking at me like that because I can only be patient for so long, kitten." His low and threatening growl pushes through the cloud of lust.

"I am not," I deny, and the mocking look he gives has me blurting, "and besides, I have a date tonight."

His nostrils flare, pupils turning dark with possessive intensity, sending chills up my spine.

Fuck. I think I just poked the bear.

Still, I hold his stare defiantly.

"You're lying."

"No. Did you think I was going to sit around with a broken heart again?"

"Is this a test, kitten?" He's on me before I can run. Firm fingers tilt my chin and his lips ghost over mine. I tremble. "Because I will fail. Did you forget what happened the last time?"

"I'm single now, Dash. I can go on a date if I damn well please."

His fingers squeeze my chin, making my lips part and my pussy wet. I need his lips on mine. Including his drugging kiss. Yet he doesn't bridge the tiny distance between us.

"Tell me one thing and I won't stop you from going on your little date."

"What?"

"Tell me you don't love me anymore."

My heart stammers against my rib cage while he waits. "I haven't forgiven you."

"That's not what I asked," he says, undeterred. And asks again, "Do you love me or not, kitten?"

"What difference does it make?"

"Yes or no?"

My hands ball into fists, unable to push him again. Because being in his arms is like coming home. I hesitate because, damn it, I'm unable to say no because it physically hurts me knowing it'd be the biggest lie I'll ever tell. I realize a little too

SCANDALOUS GAMES

late that I'm clutching the pendant hidden beneath my top when his attention lands on it like a hunter.

I instantly drop my hand while my heart races.

"Why are you always wearing it, kitten?" he demands, voice low.

"It's nothing."

"Show me."

"No." Panic swells in my chest while my pulse pounds rapidly.

His other hand lashes out, wrapping his fingers around the chain. I fight him off but he's stronger and he tugs it from my neckline in one swift move. My body goes absolutely still and I close my eyes.

I hear his rough exhale before he whispers hauntingly, "You kept it."

I shut my eyelids tighter and shake my head slowly. His fingers, which were curled around my jaw, move to cup my cheek and his thumb traces it softly. "Look at me."

He saw it. How could I be so reckless?

"Please, kitten."

Trapped under him, I reluctantly obey his low command but don't dare meet his stormy eyes. He clutches the small heart-shaped key in his palm that I couldn't throw away. Instead, I wore it around my neck daily, holding on to a piece of him like a lovesick fool.

Suddenly, his fingers disappear as he steps back and a smile graces his lips, turning his face lethally handsome. Like he found his answer.

"Don't let me catch you on a date, kitten," he warns before he leaves.

Technically, I'm not going on a date. Just going on a simple dinner with my only friend.

But maybe I should've alluded to that fact. Or maybe I'm secretly craving to be chased. To break the control he's suddenly practicing like a preacher.

Maybe I'm just testing to see if there's any power behind his warning.

What I can't decide is the reason why I'm pushing him tonight. Is it because I want him back or to use his actions as an excuse to kick him out of my life, which has suddenly become colorful ever since he came back in it?

His domineering command just called out to my defiant side and I decided I was going to let him simmer in jealousy. It's not like he can find me, since he doesn't know where I'm going or with whom.

I don't know what my non-answer told him nor do I crave to know.

When I arrive at the family-owned restaurant, Shammi is already waiting for me at our usual table in the back and gives a wave upon seeing me. I plump down across from him and just as I was afraid, he bombards me with an interrogation.

"What does that boy mean to you, kid?"

I go for acting innocent. "What boy?"

"You trying to fool me?"

"He's my ex-husband. I mean, ex-fake husband." Shammi quirks one wrinkled eyebrow in equal parts curiosity and amusement. I sigh loudly. "It's complicated and a long story that ends with my heart being broken."

"He's here to win you back."

"He says he'll wait as long as he has to," I share, and then nervously ask, "he doesn't mean it, right? Nobody waits for long and everyone eventually moves on."

Shammi's expression softens before he quietly probes, "Tell me everything first."

Even though it's painful, I tell Shammi the whole story from the very beginning and once I begin, the words and all the emotions I held inside come pouring out like a river. All the while, he quietly listens without interrupting, no expression giving away his inner thoughts. When I finish, he's quiet for a long time and when he speaks, it's not what I expect to hear.

"Did I ever tell you how I met my wife?"

I frown and sit back. I only know they were married for a short time and she passed away a few years ago. "No. You haven't."

"The first time I met her was before my very first tour in the army. She studied in an all-girls college across from my training base and both of us had sneaked out one night with our respective friends. Our groups collided at a bonfire party and it was love at first sight. I know you kids these days don't believe in it but it happens and it exists for a few lucky ones. Sometimes, two people's souls click and they are bound forever. My wife was that person for me and it was the same for her. We spent that whole night talking and laughing and learning everything about each other." His voice drips with something more powerful than love. The soulmate kind of love. I listen attentively as he continues.

"When morning came, I had to return to my base, but I knew I needed to see her again and that she was the one. But cellphones didn't exist like they do now and I couldn't just ask for her number. Letters were our only mode of communication. We promised we were going to make it work and for months, we did until it was time for my first tour. We were too young to get married and I didn't have any money in my name back then. So, of course, I couldn't ask her parents for her hand in marriage. I promised I would do it once I returned.

"In the beginning, we exchanged letters, the one thing that kept me going through the toughest times, but one day, they went unanswered. I was devastated and when I came back, I found out she had died and that her parents had moved."

"What?" I ask, aghast.

He gives a shaky smile, tears stinging in his eyes, but he pushes through. "She wasn't, of course, but that's what her family wanted me to believe and they had told her vice versa. They didn't want her marrying a poor man, so they lied. But when two people are meant to be, they find their way back to each other, and we did, twenty-five years later at a crowded restaurant. It was her voice and soulful eyes that I recognized her by. The moment our gazes clashed, I knew she hadn't forgotten me either. At first, I thought I had died and was dreaming as we stood still. I never cried, not even when I found out I lost her, but that day, I wept. It was

SCANDALOUS GAMES

such a surreal moment. When we talked, it was like no time had passed but the trauma we went through ran deep. I had never married while she was divorced with a son. Since then, we have been inseparable. She confronted her family, who still didn't accept us, but I wasn't letting her go again and I married her the next day."

My cheeks are soaked with tears as I hear his heartbreaking story. I can't imagine the agony he's been through. What if he never met her again?

The mere thought of Dash being ripped away, gone forever from my life, has my throat closing and darkness swarming my vision. The ache in my chest is so terrifying and vivid that I feel like I'll pass out.

I suddenly understand why Shammi told me this as I meet his own glistening eyes. Giving me a small smile, he grabs my hand with his wrinkled and warm ones.

"Life is too short to live in the past, sweet Bianca," he says. "Everyone makes mistakes and, yes, that boy made the worst by lying to you, even if he did so because in his broken way he loved you. It is inexcusable. But you have to ask yourself, is it worth punishing him for it for the rest of your life when you could be spending it happily living together? Because that boy will spend his whole life for another chance, taking every punishment you give him. You are his soulmate and I know this because he looks at you like I did at my wife."

"I'm scared." My voice is small.

He caresses my hand and squeezes. "That's love, kid. It is scary, exhilarating, and magical once you fall. It's also the greatest gift. Yours is waiting with his arms wide open. Be brave to take the jump."

Shammi lets my hand go just as I feel *him* behind me.

Chapter Seventy

DASH

The stubborn little minx really went on a fucking date.
    And I know why. It's because I saw the necklace with the key I gave her.
    She kept it.
    Wears it.
    Right against her heart.
    If that doesn't scream, her heart beats for me, nothing else will. So her going on this date is another attempt to draw the line, to balance the power in her favor, but it's too late. She should know better than to let another man think he stands a chance.
    She thought I wouldn't find her but she forgot that I maintain her calendar now, where she puts everything. Even her weekend plans. It simply said… Dinner with S. The second I read it, my already thin patience snapped. I'm done with these games.
    It's time to make her mine once and for all. She wants to punish me a little more, she can do so from my goddamn side while sleeping in our bed and living in our house.
    Tonight, I'm going to win back my wife.
    I slam the door to my car when I arrive at the restaurant and stalk inside. It's a small place, buzzing with laughs, the clattering of spoons, and the staff rushing

SCANDALOUS GAMES

between tables when I enter. Since my body and soul are connected to hers, I find her in a second, sitting in the corner in the back. All my laser focus is on my kitten, so when I get closer and catch her swiping away tears, her beautiful face red, my vision blurs.

That S better not be the reason behind those tears.

I twist between tables and cross the distance to theirs before coming to a standstill when I see the old man sitting across from her. Wait, where have I seen him?

And did he make her cry?

"Kitten."

She jumps at the sound of my voice and her head snaps toward mine. Shock renders her mute for the first few seconds while the old man smiles knowingly. He is awfully happy for someone who has my woman crying across from him. It pisses me off but my priority is her.

"How did you find me?" she blurts out, a hiccup lacing her voice.

I rush to her side and bend to cup her face, worried she's hurt somewhere. I turn to the man and growl, "Did he hurt you?"

"Shammi? No."

The name rings a bell and I remember him as our security guard. Her dinner plan was with him. It makes sense. Another fact hits. My fiery Bianca bluffed me into believing she was going on a date. Twice now, I've been fooled by her.

Still, my worry doesn't vanish at her answer. "Then why are you crying?"

"Take her home, boy," the old man orders me, and I instantly recognize from his posture and the air around him that he was in the army. It's all in the subtle way he holds himself and the unwavering glare. However, his eyes swim with a warmth my father never possessed.

"Kitten, you wanna go home?"

"Yes."

I take her hand as I help her up. As she grabs her purse, a look passes between them that I can't decipher but I let it go. For now. I hate the sadness shadowing her brown eyes. When I keep holding her hand, she doesn't attempt to pull away and the small gesture fills my heart with so much hope and happiness, I could burst.

I dare to hope she is letting me in.

"Please tell me you're okay, kitten?" I softly ask, grazing her wet cheek with my knuckle once we sit in my car.

"I am," she whispers before gracing me with a tentative smile. "It's time we have a talk, Dash."

"I'm not leaving you," I declare. I'll give her anything but that.

"Okay."

Again that flicker of hope lights up inside me and with a deep breath, I focus on driving back to the apartment. We arrive twenty minutes later and no words are spoken as the elevator climbs to our floor. I'm still cupping her hand, running my thumb back and forth across the back of it when the elevator pings. The feel of her skin, soothing me while my heart is racing like a damn roller coaster.

"Do you want to come to my apartment?" she offers as we reach her door.

I nod.

My lungs fill with her ocean and divine scent the second I walk inside her apartment for the first time. However, I don't notice anything else because my eyes are pinned on her. The soft light she left on is playing shadows across her stunning face framed with thick eyelashes. They flutter hypnotically, her eyes fixated on me.

My gaze becomes greedy in the silence as it travels down her body to her tits falling and rising with every breath. The thin purple top, not concealing our chemistry that hasn't lessened as it burns brighter than ever.

"You're killing me, kitten," I roughly mutter, inching closer. "Say something."

"You really hurt me, Dash."

"I know."

I bridge the gap between us with another step, and another, when she doesn't stop me. This goes on for a while until we are only a lingering breath away. Because I'm insatiable and she doesn't push me away, I grab the back of her neck and her waist, pulling her flush against me.

I just hold her.

Until our heartbeats become one.

"I thought I knew what love was but in reality, I didn't truly know. It wasn't until I fell for you that I truly realized its true meaning. Just how encompassing it is that my world began and ended with you. Just how devastating it was when you shattered it, and yet I couldn't get you out of my head or stop loving you for even one second. I missed you with every fiber in my being, Dash."

My heart and willpower breaks all over again. A better man would walk away but I need her too much. There may be a better man for her but no one will love her like I do.

She's my muse.

My obsession.

My world.

"I can't take back the things I've done, kitten. So let me spend the rest of our lives showing you how sorry I am. I love you so much. You're my home, kitten. Let me in."

Her fingers wind their way around my neck and she pulls me down before whispering, "Promise me you'll never break my heart again."

My chest expands at the vulnerability in her pupils. "Never again."

"Promise me I'll never have to live without you again."

"You will never get rid of me even when we turn old and gray. You give me another chance and you're stuck with me for eternity."

"Promise."

"I promise." My lips touch hers. "Does this mean you've forgiven me? I need to hear you say it, kitten."

"I forgive you."

Three words and they free the black cloud over my head. The weight of the guilt in my soul, lessening almost immediately. I have a lot to make up for before it goes away completely.

Bianca frowns when I separate from her but her eyes widen when I drop to my

SCANDALOUS GAMES

knees and pull out the ring she left behind. I always carry it with me, waiting for the moment when I make her mine again. Her eyes sheen with more tears as her hand flies to her mouth before her lips split into a loving smile.

Only this woman could make me a ball of nerves.

Emotions clog my throat but I push through.

"Marry me and be my wife one last time, Bianca. No more lies. No more secrets. Just you and me and the babies we'll have when you're thirty." The sweetest sound slips from her lips and I ask her to be mine for forever this time. "Will you be my home, kitten?"

"Yes. I'm yours, Dash," she cries out, and I slide my ring onto her finger.

I catch her when she throws herself into my arms and I crush my lips against hers, tasting her tears of love and happiness. I devour her mouth while drowning myself in her.

"Say it again."

"I'm yours."

"I need you, kitten." I groan against her mouth and she moans, nodding desperately.

"Fuck me, Dash."

"Not fuck." I tuck her hair away and tell her, "I'm going to make love to my fiancée."

Bending down, I carry her bridal style to the couch nearby. I'm so strung up and dying to sink into her pussy that I can't wait a second longer. I will love and fuck her on every surface until morning comes. Until our names are the only sound on our lips.

"Just so you know, you're still going to be my assistant for the foreseeable future."

I chuckle. "I'm yours to command, kitten."

My kitten is just as desperate because her hands tear at my clothes, unbuttoning my jeans before she lowers the zipper and wraps me in her fist. I groan when she squeezes and strokes once.

"So greedy, kitten."

"I need your cock inside me," she pants, biting her lip and making me come undone. The word *cock* spilling from her innocent mouth has me thrusting in her hand.

With a growl, I shove her skirt above her waist and push my hand between her thighs. I slide her soaked panties to the side and she rubs the head of my dick along her wet slit.

"Put my cock in that tight hole," I command.

The moment she aims my cock against her entrance, I thrust inch by slow inch until she writhes and shudders. Grabbing her hands, I raise them above her head and intertwine our fingers, holding her immobile beneath me.

"More. Don't stop."

"Never."

"Yes."

"Eyes on me, kitten."

SIMRAN

When they lock with mine, I kiss her, and once she falls apart, shouting my name, I spill in her clenching walls and claim her as mine.

This time, forever.

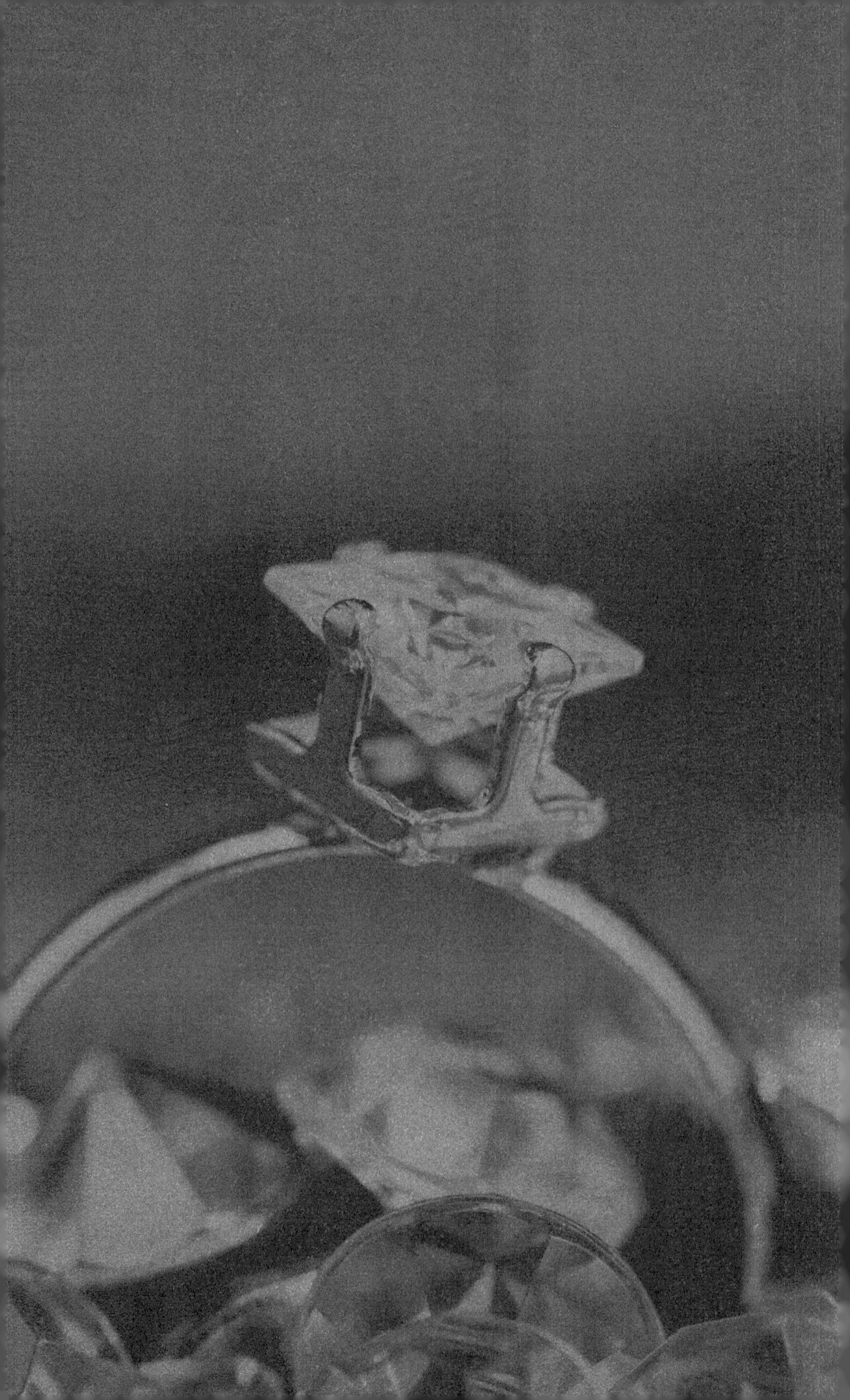

ACKNOWLEDGEMENT

As always, I firstly want to thank my lovely and super amazing readers for choosing to read my books and showering them with love. I live to read your reviews, edits and messages. They make all the countless sleepless nights, hardships, anxiety worth it. I really hope you enjoyed Dash and Bianca's epic romance and all the swoony gestures he does for her. Don't worry, this isn't a goodbye to these two. You will meet them very soon since I have more couples to write in this series.

Next, I want to say the biggest thank you to my superbly talented and wonderful editor, Rumi. She's a gem I've found in this book community. This book honestly wouldn't have been possible without her had she not been patient and waited for me to get the book to her. I'm so lucky to have you in my corner.

Another wonderful person I want to thank is my sweet and amazing proof reader, Lily. Her attention for detail and turning my manuscript perfect is a gift. I live to read her comments and constructive feedback that always leaves a smile on my face and encourages me to keep improving. I'm so grateful to have you on my team.

My amazing street team, you are my biggest cheerleader for recommending and sharing my books. Some of you have been me with since my journey as an author began and some I met along the way—thank you so much for giving my books so much love.

My ARC team, thank you so much for taking the time to read my books and leave such wonderful reviews. They make my day and I'm always looking forward to them.

Lastly, I want to thank my family for continuously supporting me on this writing journey and encouraging me to keep going even when it gets tough and I doubt myself. I wouldn't be where I am today with your unconditional love and guidance. Thank you for believing in my dreams and showing me every day that I can do this. I love you all to the moon and back.

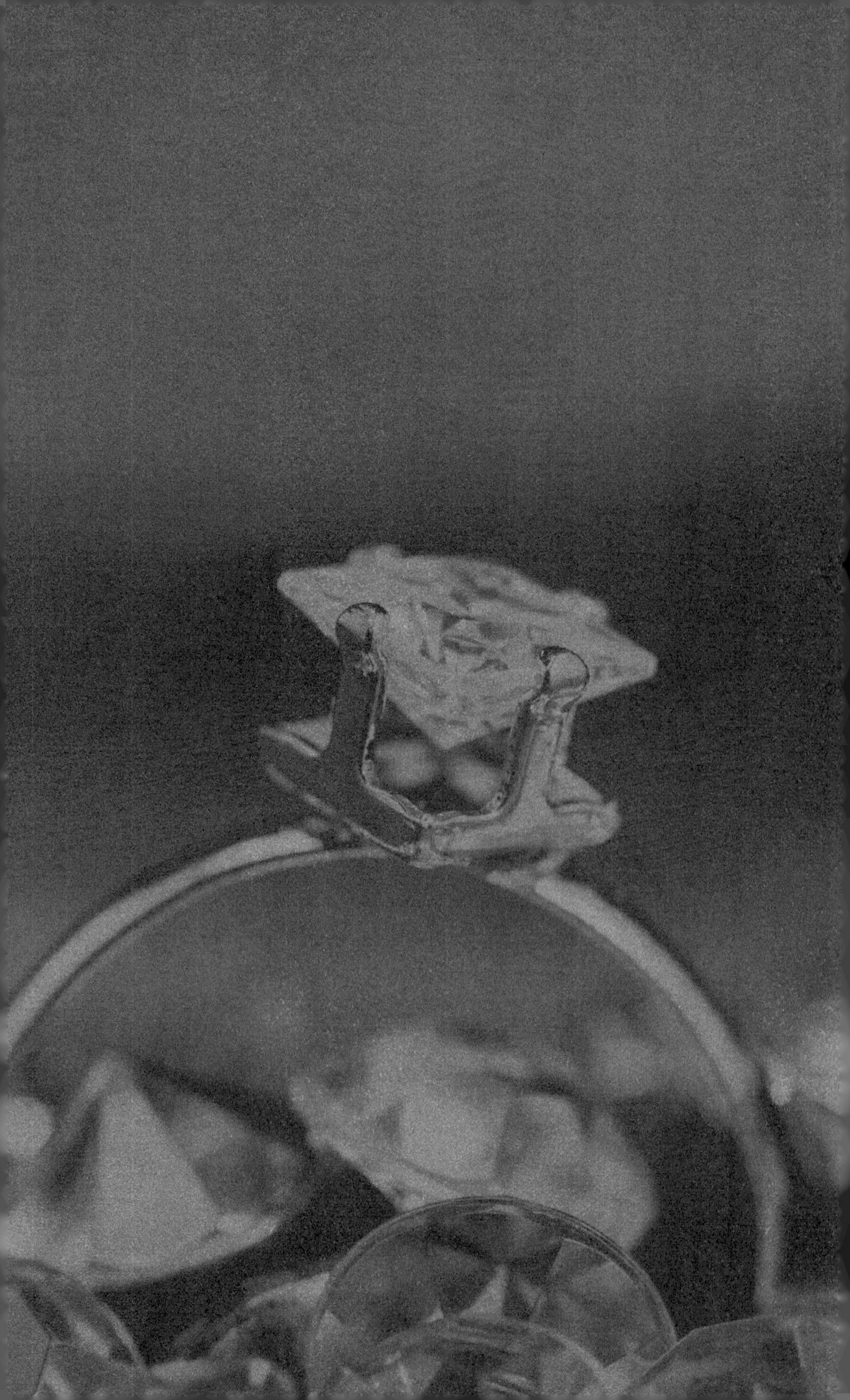

MY BOOKS

If you guys don't already know, I also write dark and taboo romance. If you enjoyed my writing and want more, check out my below books.

TABOO AND DARK ROMANCE DUET
Will he ever be mine (Meant to be duet #1)
She will always be mine (Meant to be duet #2)

STANDALONES
Wicked Fate – A Dark Enemies to Lovers Romance.
Mayhem on the hills (Valley of the Gods #0.5) – Dark New Adult Romance

All my books are available on Amazon and free to read in Kindle unlimited.

ABOUT THE AUTHOR

My name is Simran and I'm twenty-five years old. I'm from a small city in India with big dreams. I have always been into reading romance novels and somewhere along the way, I had an urge to write my own book one day and it finally happened.

It still feels unbelievable and gives me the greatest joy in the world. Other than reading, I also enjoy binge-watching Netflix and listening to music which also plays a huge role in my writing.

I'm very active on social media and would love if you guys wantto connect with me there and you can also sign up for my newsletter for all my latest updates.